There were armed guards standing at several busy intersections, and small groups of them patrolled the corridors like cops on a beat. The humans we saw watched the patrolling Qesh with expressions ranging from boredom to terror; no one tried to talk with the invaders, and for their part, the invaders didn't seem predisposed to interfere with the human crowd.

About ten minutes passed before we started getting signal breakup, and then the image dissolved into pixels and winked out. The transmission, shifting around randomly across tens of thousands of frequencies each second, probably couldn't be monitored by the Qesh, but it *could* be blocked, by tens of meters of solid rock if nothing else. What we received before that happened, though, had been useful.

And disturbing. If the humans were cooperating with the Qesh, had they already given the invaders access to their computer records?

Had the Qesh already learned the location of Earth?

And how could we find out if they had?

By Ian Douglas

Star Corpsman
BLOODSTAR

Star Carrier
EARTH STRIKE
CENTER OF GRAVITY
SINGULARITY

The Galactic Marines Saga

The Heritage Trilogy
SEMPER MARS
LUNA MARINE
EUROPA STRIKE

The Legacy Trilogy
STAR CORPS
BATTLESPACE
STAR MARINES

The Inheritance Trilogy
STAR STRIKE
GALACTIC CORPS
SEMPER HUMAN

STAR CORPSMAN
BOOK ONE

BLOODSTAR

IAN DOUGLAS

HARPER Voyager
An Imprint of HarperCollins Publishers

HARPER Voyager
An Imprint of HarperCollins*Publishers*
10 East 53rd Street
New York, New York 10022-5299

Copyright © 2012 by William H. Keith, Jr.
Cover art by Fred Gambino
ISBN 978-0-06-189476-3
www.harpervoyagerbooks.com

First Harper Voyager mass market printing: September 2012

Harper Voyager and ⟩ is a trademark of HCP LLC.

Printed in the U.S.A.

10 9 8 7 6 5 4 3 2 1

As always, now and forever,
Brea

BLOODSTAR

Chapter One

I'M JUST GLAD I'M NOT AFRAID OF HEIGHTS.

Well, at least not much.

Our Cutlass hit atmosphere at something like 8 kilometers per second, bleeding off velocity in a blaze of heat and ionization, the sharp deceleration clamping down on my chest like a boa constrictor with a really bad attitude. I hadn't been able to see much at that point, and most of my attention was focused simply on breathing.

But then the twelve-pack cut loose, and my insert pod went into free fall. I was thirty kilometers up, high enough that I could see the curve of the planet on my optical feed: a sharp-edged slice of gold-ocher at the horizon, with a deep, seemingly bottomless purple void directly below. We were skimming in toward the dawn with all of the aerodynamic efficiency of falling bricks. The Cutlass scratched a ruler-straight contrail through the black above our heads, scattering chaff to help conceal our drop from enemy radar and lidar assets on the ground.

The problem with a covert insertion is that the covert part is really, *really* hard to pull off. The bad guys can see you coming from the gods know how far away, and you tend to make a lot of noise, figuratively speaking, when you hit atmosphere.

But that's what the U.S. Marines—and specifically Bravo Company, 1st Battalion, the Black Wizards—do best.

"Deploying airfoil," a woman's voice, a very *sexy* woman's voice, whispered in my head, "in three . . . two . . . one . . ."

Why do they make our AIs sound like walking wet dreams?

My insertion pod had been a blunt, dead-black bullet shape until now, three meters long and just barely wide enough to accommodate my combat-armored body. The shell began unfolding now, growing a set of sharply back angled delta wings. The air outside was still achingly thin, but the airfoil grabbed hold with a shock akin to slamming into a brick wall. Deceleration clamped down on me once more—that damned boa constrictor looking for breakfast again—this time with a shuddering jolt that felt like my pod was shredding itself to bits.

The external sensor feeds didn't show anything wrong, nor did my in-head readout. I was dropping through twenty-two kilometers now, and everything was going strictly according to . . . what the hell is *that*?

Red-gold ruggedness seemed to pop up directly ahead of me, looming, night-shrouded, below—and *huge*, and I stifled a shrieking instant of sheer panic. It was the crest of Olympus Mons, the very highest, most easterly slopes catching the rays of the Martian dawn long before sunrise reaches the huge mountain's base. That twenty-two kilometers, I realized with a shudder, was measured from the areodetic datum, the point that would mark sea level on Mars if the planet actually had seas.

Olympus Mons, the biggest volcano in the solar system, rises twenty-*one* kilometers from the datum, three times the elevation of Everest, on Earth, and fully twice the height of the volcano Mauna Kea as measured from the ocean floor. I was skimming across the six nested calderas at the summit now, the rocky crater floor a scant couple of kilometers beneath my fast-falling pod. The calderas' interior deeps were still lost in midnight shadow, but the eastern escarpment, seemingly suspended in a mass of wispy white clouds, caught the light of the shrunken rising sun, and from my vantage point it looked like those vertical rock cliffs were about to scrape the nanomatrix from my pod's belly. In another moment, however, the escarpment was past, the 80-kilometer-wide caldera dropping behind with startling speed.

The plan, I'd known all along, was to skim just above the volcanic summit, a simple means of foxing enemy radar, but I'd not been ready for the visual reality of that near miss. My pod was totally under AI control, of course, the sentient software flexing my delta wings in rapid shifts far too fast for a mere human brain to follow. The pilot was taking me lower still, until the escarpments behind loomed *above*, rather than below.

Olympus Mons is *huge*, covering an area about the size of the state of Arizona, and that means it's also flat, despite the summit's dizzying altitude. The average slope is only about five degrees, and you can be standing halfway up the side of the mountain and not even be aware of it.

The slope was enough, though, that it put the bulk of Mount Olympus behind us, helping to shield us from enemy sensors ahead as we glided into the final phase of our descent. The active nano coating on the hulls of our pods drank radar, visible light—everything up through hard X-rays—giving us what amounted to invisibility. But no defense is perfect. If the enemy had known what he was doing, he'd have had whole sensory array farms across the mountain's broad summit—not to mention point-defense lasers and antiship CPB batteries.

Hell, maybe they did and we were already dead in their crosshairs. My sensors weren't picking up any hostile interest, though. I wished I could talk to the others, compare technical notes, but Captain Reichert would have burned me out of the sky himself for breaking comm silence.

Follow the download. Ride your pod down. Leave the thinking to the AIs. They know a hell of a lot more about it than you do.

Two hundred kilometers farther, and the base escarpment of Olympus Mons, a sheer five-kilometer cliff, slipped past in the darkness. Across the Tharsis bulge now, still descending, beginning a shuddering weave through the predawn sky to bleed off my remaining speed. The three-in-a-row volcanoes of the Tharsis Montes complex slid past. Then the Tharsis highlands gave way to the broken and chaotic terrain of the Noctis Labyrinthus, a twelve-hundred-kilometer stretch of badlands where we did *not* want to touch down under any stretch of the imagination. I swept into the local dawn, the sun coming up directly ahead with the abruptness of a thermonuclear blast, but in total silence.

"Landing deployment in twenty seconds," the sexy voice told me.

"Great. Any sign of bad guys picking us up?"

"Negative on hostile activity. Military frequency signals from objective appear to be normal traffic."

"That," I told her, "is the sweetest news I've heard all morning."

Download
Mission Profile: Ocher Sands
Operation Damascus Steel/
OPPLAN#5735/15NOV2245

[extract]
    . . . while Second Platoon will deploy by squad via Cutlass TAV/AIP to LZ Damascus Blue, location 12° 26′ S, 87° 55′ W, in the Sinai Planum. Upon landing, squads will form up individually and move on assigned objectives utilizing jumpjets. Units will be under Level-3 communications silence, and will if possible avoid enemy surveillance.

    Second Platoon Objective is Base Schiaparelli, located on the Ius Chasma, coordinates 7° 19′ 30.66″, 87° 50′ 46.40″ W. . . .

The Black Wizards' LZ was on the Sinai Planum, south of Ius Chasma, some 3,500 kilometers southeast of the summit of Olympus Mons. This was the scary part, the part where everything could go pear-shaped in a *big* hurry if the bastard god Murphy decided to favor me with His omnipotent and manifold blessings. "Double-check me," I told her as I ran through the final checklist.

I saw green across the board projected in my mind.

"All CA systems appear functional," the voice told me. She hesitated, then added, "Good luck, Petty Officer Carlyle."

And what, I wondered, did an AI know about *luck*? "Thanks, girlfriend," I muttered out loud. "Whatcha doing after the war, anyway?"

"I do not understand your question."

"Ah, it would never work anyway, you and me," I told her, and I waited for her to dump me.

Half a kilometer above the red-ocher desert floor, my AIP-81 insertion pod peeled open beneath and around me as if at the tug of a giant zipper, and abruptly I was in the open air and falling toward the Martian surface.

But not far. The delta-winged pod continued to open somewhere above me, unfolding into an improbably large triangular airfoil attached by buckyweave rigging and harness to my combat armor. The jolt when the wing deployed fully felt like it was going to yank me back into orbit. The ground was rushing past, and up, at a sickening pace, and I resisted the urge to crawl up the rigging to escape the blur of rock and sand.

Then the autorelease fired and the harness evaporated. My backpack jets kicked in, the blast shrill and almost inaudible in the thin atmosphere, kicking up a swirl of pale dust beneath my boots as they dropped to meet their up-rushing shadows.

I hit as I'd been trained, letting the armor take the jolt, relaxing my knees, letting myself crumple with the impact.

And I was down.

Down and *safe*, at least for the moment. My suit showed full airtight integrity, I couldn't feel any pain, no broken bones or sprains or strains from an awkward landing. I stood up, just a little shaky on my feet, and took in the broad expanse of the Martian landscape, brown and rust-ocher sand and gravel beneath a vast and deep mid-morning sky, ultramarine above, pink toward the horizon.

I was alone. Even my girlfriend was gone, the circuitry that had maintained her abbreviated personality nano-D'ed into microscopic dust.

Well, not entirely alone. Somewhere out there in all that emptiness were forty-seven men and women, the rest of my Marine insertion platoon.

First things first. Navy Hospital Corpsmen are the combat medics of the Marine Corps, but our technical training makes us the sci-techs of Marine advance ops as well. Planetology, local biology and ecosphere dynamics, atmosphere chemistry—I was responsible for *all* of it on this mission, at least so far as Squad Bravo was concerned.

I knew what the answers would be. This was *Mars*, after all, and humans had been living here for a couple of centuries, now. But I drew a test sample into my ES-80 sniffer and ran the numbers anyway. *Do it by the download.*

Carbon dioxide, 95 percent, with 2.7 percent nitrogen, 1.6 percent argon, and a smattering of other molecular components, all at 600 pascals, which is less than one percent of the surface atmospheric pressure on Earth. Temperature a brisk minus 60 degrees Celsius. Exotic parabiochemistries powered by the unfiltered UV from the distant sun. Thirty parts per billion of methane and 130 ppb of formaldehyde— that was from the microscopic native critters living at the lower permafrost boundaries underground, the reason we'd abandoned plans to terraform the place. Gotta keep Mars safe and pristine for the alien wee beasties, after all.

I recorded the data, exactly as if we had no idea *what* was on Mars, and uploaded it to the squadnet. I also needed to—

"Corpsman, front!" The voice of Corporal Lewis came over my com link. "Marine down!"

Shit! "Moving," I said, my voice sounding uncomfortably

loud within the confines of my helmet. I called up the tacsit display on my in-head, getting my bearings. There were ten green dots—the one at dead center was me—and one off to the side flashing red. I turned, getting a bearing. Private Colby was *that* way, 2 kilometers away. Corporal Lewis was with him.

"I've got you on my display," I told Colby. Under a Level-3 comm silence, we were using secure channels—tightly beamed IR laser-com signals relayed both line of sight and through our constellation of micro comsats in orbit. The setup allowed short-range communications with little chance of the enemy tapping in unless he was directly in the path of one of our beams, but we were still supposed to keep long-range chatter to an absolute minimum.

I took a short and lumbering run, kicked in my jets, and flew.

Service Manual Download
Standard-Issue Military Equipment
MMCA Combat Armor, Mk. 10

[extract]
. . . including alternating ultra-light layers of carbon buckyweave fiber and titanium-ceramic composite with an active-nano surface programmable by the wearer for either high or low visibility, or for albedo adjustments for thermal control. Power is provided by high-density lutetium-polonium batteries, allowing approximately 300 hours service with normal usage depending upon local incident thermal radiation.

Internally accessible stores carry up to three days' rations of air, water, and food, which can be extended using onboard extractors and nanassemblers. Service stores of cryogenic hydrogen and oxygen [crH_2/crO_2] can be carried to further extend extraction/assembled expendables.

Combat armor mass averages 20–25 kg, though with

full expendables load-out this may increase to as much
as 50 kilos. . . .

Flight Mode

Mk. 10 units are capable of short periods of flight depending on local gravity, or of jet-assisted maneuvers in
a microgravity environment. The M287 dorsal-mounted
jumpjet unit uses metastable N-He$_{64}$, commonly called
meta, as propellant, stored in crogenically inert high-
pressure backpack tanks.

Proper maintenance of meta HP fuel tanks is vital
for safe storage, transport, and operation of jumpjet
units. . . .

Marine combat armor isn't really designed for flight, especially in-atmosphere, but the Martian air is thin enough
that it's close to hard vacuum, and my "flight" was more a
series of long, low bounds across the rocky, dark red-brown
terrain, aided by the low gravity—about .38 of Earth normal.
That meant I got more boost for my buck, and just a few
quick thruster bursts brought me down in the boulder-strewn
field where Private Colby was curled up on the sand, his arms
wrapped around his left shin, with Corporal Lewis at his side.

I'd checked his readouts during my flight, of course—at
least when I wasn't watching my landings to avoid doing
what I suspected Colby had just done to himself—landing
like shit and breaking something. Just because you weigh
less than half what you do on Earth here doesn't mean you
don't still have your normal *mass*, plus the mass of your
combat armor. Bones can only take so much stress, and
a misstep can snap one. Colby's data feed showed he was
conscious and in pain, respiration and heart rate high, suit
intact. Thank the gods for that much, anyway. A breach in
the suit brings with it its own list of headaches.

"He hit a rock, Doc!" Lewis said, looking up as I slid to a
halt in loose sand. "He hit a rock coming down!"

"So I see. How you doing, Colby?"

"How do you fucking goddamn think I'm fucking feeling goddamned stupid-ass bullshit questions—"

I had already popped the cover on Colby's armor control panel, located high on his left shoulder, and was punching in my code. Before I hit the SEND key, though, I hit the transparency control for his visor, then rolled him enough that I could peer through his visor and into his eyes. "Look at me, Colby!" I called. "Open your eyes!"

His eyes opened, and I looked at his pupils, comparing one with the other. They were the same size. "Your head hurt at all?" I asked.

"Goddamn it's my fucking leg not my head Doc will you fucking do something fer chrissakes—"

Good enough. I hit the SEND key, and Colby's suit auto-injected a jolt of anodynic recep blockers into his carotid artery. Nananodyne can screw you up royally if you have a head injury, which was why I'd checked his pupils and questioned him first.

"Can we get him up on his feet, Doc?" Lewis asked.

"Don't know yet" I said. "Gimme a sec, okay?"

I jacked into Colby's armor and instituted a full scan. Infrared sensors woven into his skinsuit picked up areas of heat at various wavelengths and zipped a picture of his body into my head. The data confirmed no pressure leaks—those would have shown up as cold—but there was plenty of bright yellow inflammation around his left shin. No sign of bleeding; that would have appeared as a hot spot, spreading out and cooling to blue inside the greave. Colby was relaxing moment by moment. Those nanonarcs target the thalamus and the insular cortex of the brain, switching off the doloric receptors and blocking incoming pain messages.

Heart rate 140 and thready, BP 130 over 80, respiration 28 and shallow, and elevating adrenaline and noradrenaline, which meant an onset of the Cushing reflex. His body temp was cooling at the extremities which meant he was on the verge of going shocky as blood started pooling in his core. I told his suit to manage that—boosting the heat a bit and gently relaxing the constriction in the arteries leading to the head to keep his brain fed.

That would hold him until I could take a close-up look at his leg.

In the old days, there wouldn't have been much I could have done except locking his combat armor, turning his left greave into an emergency splint. If the patient wasn't wearing full armor, you used whatever was available, from a ready-made medical wrap that hardens into a splint when you run an electric current through it, to simply tying the bad leg to the good, immobilizing it. By keying a command into Colby's mobility circuits, the armor itself would clamp down and hold the broken bones in place, but there was one more thing I could try in order to get him up and mobile.

I reached into my M-7 kit and removed a small hypo filled with 1 cc of dark gray liquid. The tip fit neatly into a valve located beside his left knee, opening it while maintaining the suit's internal pressure, and when I touched the button, a burst of high-pressure nitrogen gas fired the concoction through both his inner suit and his skin. Nanobots entered his bloodstream at the popliteal artery, activating with Colby's body heat and transmitting a flood of data over my suit channels. I thoughtclicked several internal icons, deactivating all of the 'bots that were either going the wrong way or were adhering to Colby's skinsuit or his skin, and focused on the several thousand that were flowing now through the anterior and posterior tibial arteries toward the injury.

I wanted to go inside . . . but that would have given me a bit *too* intimate of a view, too close and too narrow to do me any good. What I needed to see was the entire internal structure of the lower leg—tibia and fibula; the gastrocnemius, soleus, and tibialis anterior muscles; the tibialis anterior and posterior tibial arteries; and the epifascial venous system. I sent Program 1 to the active 'bots, and they began diffusing through capillaries and tissue, adhering to the two bones, the larger tibia and the more slender fibula off to the side, plating out throughout the soft tissue, and transmitting

a 3-D graphic to my in-head that showed me exactly what I
was dealing with.

I rotated the graphic in my mind, checking it from all
angles. We were in luck. I was looking at a greenstick fracture of the tibia—the major bone that runs down the front
of the shin, knee to ankle. The bone had partially broken,
but was still intact on the dorsal surface, literally like a stick
half broken and bent back. The jagged edges had caused
some internal bleeding, but no major arteries had been torn
and the ends weren't poking through the skin. The fibula,
the smaller bone running down the outside of the lower leg,
appeared to be intact. The periosteum, the thin sheath of
blood vessel- and nerve-rich tissue covering the bone, had
been torn around the break of course, which was why Colby
had been hurting so much.

"How's he doing, Doc?"

The voice startled me. Gunny Hancock had come up out
of nowhere and was looking over my shoulder. I'd had no
idea that he was there.

"Greenstick fracture of the left tibia, Gunny," I told him.
"Shinbone. I have him on pain blockers."

"Can he walk?"

"Not yet. He should be medevaced. But I can *get* him
walking if you want."

"I want. The LT wants to finish the mission."

"Okay. Ten minutes."

"Shit, Gunny," Colby said. "You heard Doc. I need a
medevac!"

"You'll have one. Later."

"Yeah, but—"

"*Later*, Marine! Now seal your nip-sucker and do what
Doc tells ya!"

"Aye, aye, Gunnery Sergeant."

I ignored the byplay, focusing on my in-head and a sequence of thoughtclicks routing a new set of orders to the
'bots in Colby's leg. Program 5 ought to do the trick.

"How you feeling, Colby?" I asked.

"The pain's gone," he said. "The leg feels a bit weak, though." He flexed it.

"Don't move," I told him. "I'm going to do some manipulation. It'll feel funny."

"Okay . . ." He didn't sound too sure of things.

Guided by the new program download, some hundreds of thousands of 'bots, each one about a micron long—a fifth the size of a red blood cell—began migrating through soft tissue and capillaries, closing in around the broken bone until it was completely coated above and below the break. In my in-head, the muscles and blood vessels disappeared, leaving only the central portion of the tibia itself visible. I punched in a code on Colby's armor alphanumeric, telling it to begin feeding a low-voltage current through the left greave.

Something smaller than a red blood cell can't exert much in the way of traction unless it's magnetically locked in with a few hundred thousand of its brothers, and they're all pulling together. In the open window in my head, I could see the section of bone slowly bending back into a straight line, the jagged edges nesting into place. The movement would cause a little more periosteal damage—there was no way to avoid that—but the break closed up neatly.

"Doc," Colby said, "that feels weird as hell."

"Be glad I doped you up," I told him. "If I had to set your leg without the anodyne, you'd be calling me all sorts of nasty things right now."

I locked the nano sleeve down, holding the break rigid. I sent some loose nanobots through the surrounding tissue, turning it ghostly visible on the screen just to double-check. There was a little low-level internal bleeding—Colby would have a hell of a bruise on his shin later—but nothing serious. I diverted some anodynes to the tibial and common fibular nerves at the level of his knee with a backup at the lumbosacral plexus, shutting down the pain receptors only.

"Right," I told him. "Let me know if this hurts." Gingerly, I switched off the receptor blocks in his brain.

"Okay?"

"Yeah," he said. "It just got . . . sore, a little. Not too bad."

"I put a pain block at your knee, but your brain is functioning again. At least as well as it did before I doped you."

"You're a real comedian, Doc."

I told his armor to lock down around his calf and shin, providing an external splint to back up the one inside. I wished I could check the field medicine database, but the chance of the enemy picking up the transmission was too great. I just had to hope I'd remembered everything important, and let the rest slide until we could get Colby back to sick bay.

"Okay, Gunny," I said. "He's good to go."

I know it seemed callous, but a tibia greenstick is no big deal. If it had been his femur, now, the big bone running from hip to knee, I might have had to call for an immediate medevac. The muscles pulling the two ends of the femur together are so strong that the nano I had on hand might not have been enough. I would have had to completely immobilize the whole leg and keep him off of it, or risk doing some really serious damage if things let go.

The truth of the matter is that they pay us corpsmen for two jobs, really. We're here to take care of our Marines, the equivalent of medics in the Army, but in the field our first priority is the mission. They hammer that into us in training from day one: provide emergency medical aid to the Marines *so that they can complete their mission.*

"How about it, Colby. Can you get up?"

The Marine stood—with an assist from Lewis and the Gunny. "Feels pretty good," he said, stamping the foot experimentally.

"Don't do that," I told him. "We'll still need to get you to sick bay, where they can do a proper osteofuse."

"Good job, Doc," Gunny told me. "Now pack up your shit and let's hump it."

I closed up my M-7 and dropped both the hypo and the sterile plastic shell it had come in into a receptacle on my thigh. They'd drilled it into us in FMF training: *never* leave anything behind that will give the enemy a clue that you've been there.

While I'd been working on Colby, the rest of the recon squad had joined up about a kilometer to the north and started marching. Gunny, Lewis, Colby, and I were playing catch-up now, moving across that cold and rock-strewn desert at double-time.

According to our tacsit displays, we were 362 kilometers and a bit directly south of our objective, a collection of pressurized Mars huts called Schiaparelli Base. If we hiked it on foot, it would take us the better part of ten days to make it all the way.

Not good. Our combat armor could manufacture a lot of our logistical needs from our surroundings, at least to a certain extent. It's called living off the air, but certain elements—hydrogen and oxygen, especially—are in *very* short supply on Mars. Oxygen runs to about 0.13 percent in that near-vacuum excuse for an atmosphere, and free molecular hydrogen is worse—about fifteen parts per billion. You can actually get more by breaking down the hints of formaldehyde and methane released by the Martian subsurface biota, but it's still too little to live on. The extractors and assemblers in your combat armor have to run for days just to get you one drink of water. The units recycle wastes, of course; with trace additives, a Marine can live on shit and piss if he has to, but the process yields diminishing returns and you can't keep it up for more than a few days.

So Lewis and I doubled up with Colby. There was a risk of him coming down hard and screwing the leg repairs, but with me on his right arm and Lewis on his left, we could reduce the stress of landing on each bound. We taclinked our armor so that the jets would fire in perfect unison, and put ourselves into a long, flat trajectory skimming across the desert. Gunny paced us, keeping a 360-eye out for the enemy, but we still seemed to have the desert to ourselves.

And four hours later we reached the Calydon Fossa, a straight-line ditch eroded through the desert, half a kilometer deep and six wide. It took another hour to get across that—the canyon was too wide for us to jet-jump it, and the chasma slopes were loose and crumbling. But we slogged down and we slogged up and eight kilometers more brought us to the Ius Chasma.

It's not the deepest or the most spectacular of the interlaced canyons making up the Valles Marineris, but it'll do: Five and a half kilometers deep and almost sixty kilometers across at that point, it's deep enough to take in Earth's Grand Canyon as a minor tributary. The whole Valles Marineris is almost as long as the continental United States is wide back home—two hundred kilometers wide and ten kilometers deep at its deepest—where the Grand Canyon runs a paltry 1,600 meters deep.

The view from the south rim was spectacular.

But we weren't there for sightseeing. We rendezvoused with First Squad and made the final approach to Schiaparelli Base. I stayed back with Colby while the others made the assault, but everything went down smooth as hyperlube. The whole sequence would have been a lot more exciting if this had been a real op, but the bad guys were U.S. Aerospace Force security troops, and Ocher Sands is the annual service-wide training exercise designed to work out the bugs and accustom our combat troops to operating in hostile environments against a high-tech enemy.

I can't speak for the USAF bluesuits, but *we* had a good day. Despite Colby's injury and a bad case of the scatters coming down—*someone* was going to get chewed a new one for that little SNAFU—all eight squads pulled it together, deployed without being spotted, and took down their assigned objectives, on sched and by the download. An hour later we had a Hog vectoring in for medevac.

I rode back up to orbit with Colby.

And it was just about then that the fecal matter intercepted the rotational arc of the high-speed turbine blades.

Chapter Two

FOR A CENTURY NOW WE HUMANS HAVE BEEN LURKERS ON THE GA-lactic Internet, listening and learning but not saying a word. We're terrified, you see, that *they* might find us.

The EG-Net, as near as we can tell, embraces a fair portion of the entire Galaxy, a flat, hundred-thousand-light-year spiral made of four hundred billion suns and an estimated couple of trillion planets. The Net uses modulated gamma-ray lasers, which means, thanks to the snail's-pace crawl of light, that all of the news is out of date to one degree or another by the time we get it. Fortunately, most of what's on there doesn't have an expiration date. The Starlord Empire has been collapsing for the past twenty thousand years, and the chances are good that it'll *still* be collapsing twenty thousand years from now.

The Galaxy is a big place. Events big enough to tear it apart take a long time to unfold.

The closest EG transmission beam to Sol passes through the EG Relay at Sirius, where we discovered it during our first expedition to that system 128 years ago. The Sirius Orbital Complex was constructed just to eavesdrop on the Galactics—there's nothing *else* worthwhile in the system—and most of what we know about Deep Galactic history comes from there. We call it the EG, the Encyclopedia Galactica, because it appears to be a data repository. Nested within the transmission beams crisscrossing the Galaxy like the web of a drunken spider are data describing hundreds of millions of cultures across at least six billion years, since long before Sol was born or the Earth was even a gleam in an interstellar nebula's eye. It took us twenty years just to crack the outer codes to learn how to read what we were seeing. And what we've learned since represents, we think, something less than 0.01 percent of all of the information available.

But even that microscopic drop within the cosmic ocean is enough to prove just how tiny, how utterly insignificant, we humans are in the cosmic scheme of things.

The revelation shook humankind to its metaphorical core, an earthquake bigger than Copernicus and Galileo, deeper than Darwin, more far-reaching than Hubbell, more astonishing than Randall, Sundrum, and Witten.

And the revelation damn near destroyed us.

"Hey, e-Car!" HM3 Michael C. Dubois held up a lab flask and swirled the pale orange liquid within. "Wanna hit?"

I was just finishing a cup of coffee as I wandered into the squad bay, and still had my mug in hand. I sucked down the dregs and raised the empty cup. "What the hell are you pedaling this time, Doob?" I asked him.

"Nothing but the best for the Black Wizard heroes!"

"Paint stripper," Corporal Calli Lewis told me, and she made a bitter face. I noticed that she took another swig from her mug, however, before adding, "The bastard's trying to poison us."

Doobie Dubois laughed. "Uh-uh. It's *methanol* that'll kill you . . . or maybe make you blind, paralyzed, or impotent. Wood alcohol, CH_3OH. This here is guaranteed gen-u-wine *ethanol*, C_2H_5OH, straight out of the lab assemblers and mixed with orange juice I shagged from a buddy in the galley. It'll put hair on your chest."

"Not necessarily a good thing, at least where Calli's concerned," I said as he poured me half a mug.

"Yeah?" he said, and gave Calli a wink. "How do you know? Might be an improvement!"

"Fuck you, squid," she replied.

"Any time you want, jarhead."

I took a sip of the stuff and winced. "Good galloping *gods*, that's awful!"

"Doc can't hold his 'shine," Sergeant Tomacek said, and the others laughed. A half dozen Marines were hanging out in the squad bay, and it looked like Doob had shared his talent for applied nanufactory chemistry with all of them. *Highly* contra-regs, of course. The *Clymer*, like all U.S. starships, is strictly dry. I suspected that Captain Reichert knew but chose not to know officially, so long as we kept the party to a dull roar and no one showed up drunk on duty.

The viewall was set to show an optical feed from outside, a deck-to-overhead window looking out over Mars, 9,300 kilometers below. The planet showed a vast red-orange disk with darker mottling; I could see the pimples of the Tharsis bulge volcanoes easily, with the east-to-west slash of the Valles Marineris just to the east. Phobos hung in the lower-right foreground, a lumpy and dark-gray potato, vaguely spherical but pocked and pitted with celestial acne. The big crater on one end—Stickney—and the Mars Orbital Research Station, rising from the crater floor, were hidden behind the moonlet's mass, on the side facing the planet. The image, I decided, was being relayed from the non-rotating portion of the *George Clymer*. The *Clymer*'s habitation module was a fifty-meter rotating ring amidships, spinning six and a half times per minute to provide a modest four tenths of a gravity, the same as we'd experienced down on Mars.

"So what's the celebration?" I asked Dubois. He always had a reason for breaking out the lab-nanufactured drinkables.

"The end of FMF training, of course! What'd you think?"

I took another cautious sip. It actually wasn't too bad. Maybe that first swig had killed off the nerve endings.

"You're one-eighty off course, Doob," I told him. "We still have Europa, remember?"

FMF—the Fleet Marine Force—was arguably the most coveted billet in the entire U.S. Navy Hospital Corps. To win that silver insignia for your collar, you needed to go through three months of Marine training at Lejeune or Pendleton, then serve with the Marines for one year, pass their physical, demonstrate a daunting list of Marine combat and navigation skills, and pass a battery of tests, both written and in front of a senior enlisted board.

I'd been in FMF training since I'd made Third Class a year ago; our assignment on board the *Clymer* was the final phase of our training, culminating in the Ocher Sands fun and games that had us performing a live insertion and taking part in a Marine planetary assault. After this, we were supposed to deploy to Europa for three weeks of practical xenosophontology, swimming with the Medusae. After that, those of us still with the program would take our boards, and if we were lucky, only then would we get to append the letters *FMF* after our name and rank.

"Not the way I heard it, e-Car," he said. He took a swig of his product straight from the flask. "Scuttlebutt has it we're deploying I-S."

I ignored use of the disliked handle. My name, Elliot Carlyle, had somehow been twisted into "e-Car." Apparently there was a law of the Corps that said everyone had to have a nickname. Doob. Lewis was "Louie." I'd spent the past year trying to get myself accepted as "Hawkeye," a nod both to James Fenimore Cooper and to a twentieth-century entertainment series about military medical personnel in the field from which I'd downloaded a few low-res 2-D episodes years ago.

"Interstellar?" I said. "You're full of shit. This stuff's rotting your gray cells."

"Don't be so sure about your diagnosis, Doc," Lewis told me. "I heard the same thing from a buddy in Personnel."

"You're both full of it," I said. "Why would they send *us*?"

"Our dashing good looks and high intelligence?"

"In your case, Doob, it probably has to do with a punishment detail. You on the Old Man's shit list?"

"Not so far as I know."

"So what's supposed to be going down?"

Dubois grew serious, which was damned unusual for him. "The Qesh," he said.

Download
Encyclopedia Galactica/Xenospecies Profile
Entry: Sentient Galactic Species 23931
"Qesh"

Qesh, Qesh'a, Imperial Qesh, Los Imperiales, "Jackers," "Imps"

Civilization Type: 1.165 G

TL 20: FTL, Genetic Prostheses, Quantum Taps, Relativistic Kinetic Conversion

Societal Code: JKRS

Dominant: clan/hunter/warrior/survival

Cultural library: 5.45×10^{16} bits

Data Storage/Transmission DS/T: 2.91×10^{11}s

Biological Code: 786.985.965

Genome: 4.2×10^9 bits; Coding/non-coding: 0.019.

Biology: C, N, O, S, S_8, Ca, Cu, Se, H_2O, PO_4

TNA

Diferrous hemerythrin proteins in $C_{17}H_{29}COOH$ circulatory fluid.

Mobile heterotrophs, carnivores, O_2 respiration.

Septopedal, quad- or sextopedal locomotion.

Mildly gregarious, polygeneric [2 genera, 5 species]; trisexual.

Communication: modulated sound at 5 to 2000 Hz and changing color patterns.

Neural connection equivalence NCE = 1.2×10^{14}

T = ~300° to 470° K; M = 4.3×10^5 g; L: ~5.5×10^9s

Vision: ~5 micrometers to 520 nanometers, **Hearing**: 2 to 6000 Hz

Member: Galactic Polylogue
   Receipt galactic nested code: 1.61×10^{12} s ago
Member: R'agch'lgh Collective
   Locally initiated contact 1.58×10^{12} s ago
   Star F1V; Planet: Sixth
   $a = 2.4 \times 10^{11}$m; $M = 2.9 \times 10^{19}$g; $R = 2.1 \times 10^{7}$m; $p = 2.7 \times 10^{6}$s
   $P_d = 3.2 \times 10^{7}$s, $G = 25.81$ m/s^2
Atm: O_2 26.4, N_2 69.2, CO_2 2.5, CO 2.1, SO_2 0.7, at 2.5×10^{5} Pa
Librarian's note: First direct human contact occurred in 2188 C.E. at Gamma Ophiuchi. Primary culture now appears to be nomadic predarian, and is extremely dangerous. Threat level = 1.

We'd all downloaded the data on the Qesh, of course, as part of our Marine training. *Know your enemy* and all of that. Humans had first run into them fifty-nine years ago, when the *Zeng He*, a Chinese exploration vessel, encountered them while investigating a star system ninety-some light years from Sol. The *Zeng He*'s AI managed to get off a microburst transmission an instant before the ship was reduced to its component atoms. The signal was picked up a few years later by a Commonwealth vessel in the area and taken back to Earth, where it was studied by the Encyclopedian Library at the Mare Crisium facility on the moon. The *Zeng He*'s microburst had contained enough data to let us find the Qesh in the ocean of information within the Encylopedia Galactica and learn a bit about them.

We knew they were part of the R'agch'lgh Collective, the Galactic Empire, as the news media insisted on calling it. We knew they were from a high-gravity world, that they were big, fast, and mean.

And with the ongoing collapse of the Collective, we knew they'd become predarians.

The net media had come up with that word, a blending of the words *predators* and *barbarians*. That was unfortunate, since in our culture *barbarian* implies a relatively low technology; you expect them to be wearing shaggy skins, horned helmets, and carrying whopping big swords in their primary manipulators, looking for someone to pillage.

As near as we could tell, they *were* predators, both genetically and by psychological inclination. Their societal code, JKRS—which is where "Jackers," one of their popular nicknames, had come from—suggested that their dominant culture was organized along clan/family lines, that they'd evolved from carnivorous hunters, that they considered themselves to be warriors and possessed what might be called a warrior ethos, and, perhaps the most chilling, that they possessed an essentially Darwinian worldview—survival of the fittest, the strong deserve to live. The fact that their technological level allowed them to accelerate asteroid-sized rocks to near-c and slam them into a planet was a complementary extra.

These guys had planet-killers.

The Crisium librarians thought—*guessed* would be the more accurate term—that the Qesh constituted some sort of military elite within the R'agch'lgh Collective, a kind of palace guard or special assault unit used to take out worlds or entire species that the Collective found to be obstreperous or inconvenient. But with the fall of the Collective, the Qesh were thought to have gone freelance, wandering the Galaxy in large war fleets taking what they wanted and generally trying to prove that they were the best, the strongest, the fittest—something like a really sadistic playground bully without adult supervision.

That change of status must have been fairly recent—within the last couple of thousand years or so. According to the EG, they were still working for the Collective.

And for all we knew maybe some of them were, way off, deep in toward the Galactic Core, where the R'agch'lgh might still be calling the shots. Our local branch of the EG Library hadn't been updated for five thousand years, however, and evidently a lot had happened in the meantime.

The Galaxy was going through a period of cataclysmic change, but from our limited perspective, it was all taking place in super-slow motion.

"What," I said. "The Qesh are coming *here*?"

"My friend in Personnel," Lewis said, "told me there'd been a call for help from one of our colonies. The colony is supposed to be pre-Protocol, so . . ." She shrugged. "Send in the Marines."

It made sense, in a horrific kind of way. Commonwealth Contact Protocol had been developed in 2194, and it laid out *very* strict rules and regs governing contact with new species. Partially, that was to protect the new species, of course. Human history has a long and bloody tradition of one culture stumbling into a new and eradicating it, through disease, through greed, through conquest, through sheer, bloody-minded stupidity.

But even more it was to protect *us*. We were just at the very beginning of our explorations into the Galaxy, and there were Things out there we didn't understand and which didn't understand us—or they didn't care, or they simply saw us as a convenient source of raw materials. Over the course of the past fifty years, we'd taken special steps to screen our civilization's background noise, and the AI navigators in our starships were designed to purge all data that might give a clue to the existence and location of Earth or Earth's colonies if they encountered an alien ship or world.

A Qesh relativistic impactor, it was believed, could turn Earth's entire crust molten. We did *not* want to have them or their Imperial buddies showing up on our doorstep in a bad mood.

The problem was, the barn door had been open for a bunch of years, and the horses had long since gotten loose. Radio and television signals were expanding into interstellar space at the rate of one light year per year, in a bubble now something like six hundred light years across. Technology researchers liked to insist that the useful information/noise ratio drops off to damned near zero only a couple of light years out; anyone out there listening for a juicy young pre-spaceflight civilization probably wouldn't be able to pick our twentieth-century transmissions out of the interstellar white noise—but the kicker was the word *probably*. We just don't know what's possible; the EG mentions galactic civilizations out there that are on the order of 5×10^{16} seconds old—that's longer than Earth has been around as a planet. I don't think it's possible for us to say what such a civilization could or could not do.

But things get uglier when it comes to our pre-Protocol colonies. There are a lot of them out there, scattered across the sky from Sagittarius to Orion. The earliest was Chiron, of course, at Alpha Centauri A IV, founded in 2109. They're all close enough to Earth to have signed the Protocol shortly after it was written, but there are plenty of colonies out there that for one reason or another have nothing to do with Earth or the Commonwealth. Many of them we don't even have listed, and if we don't know they exist, we can't police them.

But if they were established before the year 2194, they probably still have navigational coordinates for Earth somewhere in their computer network. And someone with the technology to figure out how our computers work, sooner or later, would break the code and they might come hunting for us.

Our only recourse in that case was to go looking for them. If we could contact them and get them to agree to abide by the Protocol, great.

But if they didn't . . . well, as Lewis had so eloquently put it, *Send in the Marines*.

"Now hear this, now hear this," a voice said from the squad bay's intercom speaker. "All hands prepare for one gravity acceleration in ten minutes, repeat, ten minutes. Secure all loose gear and reconfigure hab module spaces. That is all."

"That was fast," Dubois said.

"Yeah, but where the hell are we going?" I wanted to know. I looked at Lewis. "Your friend have any word on that?"

"Actually," she said, "from what he said, hell is a pretty good description."

In fact, though, our destination turned out to be Earth.

Most of the hab space on board an attack transport like the *Clymer* is dedicated to living space. She carries 1,300 Marines besides her normal complement of 210 officers and crew, and all of that humanity is packed into the rotating ring around her central spine, along with the galleys and mess halls, sick bay, lab spaces, rec and VR bays, life-support nanufactories, and gear lockers.

They didn't tell us, of course. After doing a quick check to make sure anything loose was tied down or put away—Doobie's hooch went into a refrigerated storage tank in an equipment locker forward—we strapped ourselves standing against the acceleration couches growing out of the aft bulkhead. Ten minutes later, we felt the hab wheel spinning down, and for a few moments we were in microgravity. I could hear a Marine down the line being noisily sick—there's *always* at least one—but I stayed put until the *Clymer* lit her main torch.

There was an odd moment of disorientation, because where "down" *had* been along the curving outer floor of the hab wheel, now it was toward the aft bulkhead. The bulkhead had become the deck, and instead of standing up against our acceleration couches, now we were lying in them flat. The viewall was reprogrammed to show on what had been the deck. Under Plottel Drive, we were accelerating at a steady one gravity, but "down" was now *aft*, not out toward the rim of the wheel.

They let us get up, then, and we spent the next hour learning to walk again. We'd been at .38 Gs for two weeks.

I was half expecting Alcubierre Drive to kick in at any time, but hour followed hour and we continued our steady acceleration. Thirty-four hours later we were ordered to the couches once more, and again there was a brief period of microgravity as the *Clymer* ponderously turned end for end.

That gave us an idea of where we were headed, though. There'd still been a good chance that we were headed for Europa, as originally planned. At the moment, however, Jupiter and its moons were a good six astronomical units from Mars—call it 900 million kilometers. Accelerate at one gravity halfway from Mars to Europa, and we'd have reached the turnover point in something over forty-two hours. A thirty-four-hour turnover—I ran the numbers through my Cerebral Data Feed in-head processors a second time to be sure—meant we'd covered half the current distance to Earth.

Which meant we were on our way home, to Starport One. Once we were backing down, thirty hours out from Earth, though, we received a download over the shipnet on a planet none of us had ever heard of.

Download
Commonwealth Planetary Ephemeris
Entry: Gliese 581 IV
"Bloodstar"

Star: Gliese 581, Bloodstar, Hell's Star
   Type M3V
M = .31 Sol; **R** = 0.29 Sol; **L** = .013 Sol; **T** = 3480°K
Coordinates: RA 15_h 19_m 26_s; Dec -07° 43' 20"; D = 20.3 ly
Planet: Gliese 581 IV
Name: Gliese 581 IV, Gliese 581 g, Bloodworld, Salvation, Midgard
Type: Terrestrial/rocky; "superearth"
Mean orbital radius: 0.14601 AU; **Orbital period:** 36_d 13_h 29_m 17_s
Inclination: 0.0°; **Rotational period:** 36_d 13.56_h (tidelocked with primary)
Mass: 2.488 x 10^{28} g = 4.17 Earth; **Equatorial Diameter:** 28,444 km = 2.3 Earth

Mean planetary density: 5.372 g/cc = .973 Earth

Surface Gravity: 1.85 G

Surface temperature range: ~ -60°C [Nightside] to 50°C [Dayside]

Surface atmospheric pressure: ~152 x 10^3 kPa [1.52 Earth average]

Percentage atmospheric composition: O_2 19.6, N_2 75.5, Ne 1.15, Ar 0.58, CO 1.42; CO_2 1.01, SO_2 0.69; others <500 ppm

Age: 8.3 billion years

Biology: C, N, H, Na, S_8, O, Br, H_2O; mobile photolithoautotrophs in oxygenating atmosphere symbiotic with sessile chemoorganoheterotrophs and chemosynthetic lithovores in librational twilight zones.

Human Presence: The Salvation of Man colony established in 2181 in the west planetary librational zone. Salvation was founded by a Rejectionist offshoot of the Neoessene Messianist Temple as a literal purgatory for the cleansing of human sin. There has been no contact with the colony since its founding.

"Jesus Christ!" Lance Corporal Ron Kukowicz said, shaking his head as he got up out of his download couch. "Another bunch of fucking God-shouters."

"Shit. You have something against God, Kook?" Sergeant Joy Leighton said, sneering.

"Not with God," Kukowicz replied. "Just with God's more fervent followers."

"The download said they're Rejectionists," I pointed out. "Probably a bunch of aging neo-Luddites. No artificial lights. No AI. No nanufactories. No weapons. That's about as harmless as you can get."

"Don't count on that harmless thing, Doc," Staff Sergeant Larrold Thomason said. "If they're living *there* they've got technology. And they know how to use it."

"Yeah," Private Gutierrez said. "You can tell 'cause they're still alive!"

Thomason had a point. The planet variously called Salvation and Hell was a thoroughly nasty place, hot as blazes and with air that would poison you if you went outside without a mask.

We'd been lying inside our rack-tubes as we took the download feed—"racked out" as military slang puts it. That allowed for full immersion; the virtual reality feed that had come with the ephemeris data suggested that the numbers didn't begin to do justice to the place. The recordings had been made by the colonizing expedition sixty-four years ago, so the only surface structures we'd seen had been some temporary habitat domes raised on a parched and rocky plateau. Bloodstar, the local sun, was a red hemisphere peeking above the horizon, swollen and red, with an apparent diameter over three times that of Sol seen from Earth. Everything was tinged with red—the sky, the clouds, and an oily-looking sea surging at the base of the plateau cliffs.

And the native life.

With the download complete, we were up and moving around the squad bay again. My legs and back were sore from yesterday, but I no longer felt like I was carrying an adult plus a large child on my back. Private Gerald Colby, at my orders, was wearing an exo-frame; they'd fused his broken tibia in sick bay an hour after his return from the Martian surface, but Dr. Francis had wanted him to go easy on the leg for a week or so to make sure the fix was good. That meant he wore the frame, a mobile exoskeleton of slender, jointed carbon-weave titaniplas rods strapped to the backs of his legs and up his spine—basically a stripped-down version of the heavier walker units we use for excursions on the surfaces of high-gravity worlds.

The rest of us had been working out in the bay's small gym space, getting our full-gravity legs back, and taking g-shift converters, nanobots programmed to maintain bone calcium in low-G, and blood pressure in high-G. Marines on board an attack transport like the *Clymer* had a rigidly fixed daily routine which included a *lot* of exercise time on the Universals.

I shared the daily routine to a certain extent—they had me billeted with Second Platoon—but today I had the duty running sick call. It was nearly 0800, time for me to get my ass up there.

I rode the hab-ring car around the circumference to the *Clymer*'s med unit and checked in with Dr. Francis.

Clymer sported a ten-bed hospital and a fairly well appointed sick bay. In an emergency, we could grow new beds, of course, but the hospital only had one patient at the moment, a Navy rating from the *Clymer*'s engineering department with thermal burns from a blown plasma-fusion unit.

"Morning, Carlyle," Dr. Francis said as I walked in. "You ready for Earthside liberty?"

"Sure am, sir. If we're there long enough."

"What do you mean?"

I shrugged. "Scuttlebutt says we're headed out-system. And they just gave us a download on a colony world out in Libra."

He laughed. "You know better than to believe scuttlebutt."

"Yes, sir." But why had they given us the feed on Blood-world?

The doctor vanished into a back compartment, and I began seeing patients. Sick call was the time-honored practice where people on board ship lined up outside of sick bay to tell us their ills: colds and flu, sprains and strains, occasional hangovers and STDs. Once in a long while there was something interesting, but the Marines were by definition an insufferably healthy lot, and the real challenge of holding sick call was separating the rare genuine ailments from the smattering of crocs and malingerers.

My very first patient gave me pause, though. Roger Howell was a private from 3rd Platoon. His staff sergeant had sent him up. Symptoms were general listlessness, headache, mild nausea, low-grade fever of 38.2, lack of appetite, and a cough with nasal congestion.

It sounded like a cold. When I pinched the skin on his arm, the fold didn't pop back, which suggested dehydration. "You been vomiting?" I asked. "Diarrhea?"

"No, Doc," he replied. "But my head is really killing me."

"You been hitting the hooch?" Those symptoms might also point to a hangover.

He managed a weak grin. "I wish!"

When I shined a light in his eyes, trying to look at his pupils, he flinched away. "What's the matter?"

"Light hurts my head, Doc."

I didn't press it. Photophobia with a headache isn't unusual. "You get migraines?"

"What's that?"

"Really, really bad headaches. Maybe on just one side of your head, behind the eye. You might see flashes of light, and the pain can make you sick to your stomach."

"Nah. Nothing like that. Look, I just thought you'd shoot me up with some nanomeds, y'know?"

I had a choice. I could call it a mild cold and have him force fluids to take care of the dehydration, or I could look deeper. There was a long list of more serious ailments that could cause those kinds of low-grade symptoms.

I pulled a hematocrit on him and got a 54. That's right on the high edge of normal for males—again, consistent with mild dehydration. I took a throat swab for a culture, checked his blood pressure and heart rate—both normal—and decided on option one.

"You might be coming down with something," I told him. I reached up on the shelf behind me and took down a bottle with eight small, white pills. "Take these for your head. Two every four hours, as needed."

"Yeah? What are they?"

"APCs," I told him. "Aspirin."

"Shit. What about nanomeds?"

"Try these first. If you're still hurting tomorrow, come to

sick call again and maybe we can give you something stronger. In the meantime, I want you to drink a lot of water. Not coffee. Not soda. Water."

"Shit, Doc! *Aspirin?*"

Yeah, aspirin. Corpsmen have been handing out APCs since the early twentieth century, when we didn't even know why it worked; the stuff inhibits the body's production of prostaglandins, among other things, which means it helps block pain transmission to the hypothalamus and switches off inflammation.

And the "something stronger" would be a concoction of acetaminophen, chlorpheniramine maleate, dextromethorphan, and phenylephrine hydrochloride—a pain reliever, an antihistamine, a cough suppressant, and a decongestant. Nanomedications can do a lot, but in the case of the old-fashioned common cold, the old-fashioned symptom-treating remedies do just as well and maybe better. We don't automatically hand out the cold pills, though, because there are just too many creative things bored sailors and Marines can do to turn them into recreational drugs. You can't get high on aspirin.

Howell looked disappointed, but he took the bottle and wandered out.

Next up was a Marine who was having trouble sleeping, even with VR sleep-feeds in his rack-tube.

Four hours later, I was getting ready to go to chow when a call came over the intercom. "Duty Corpsman to B Deck, eleven two. Duty Corpsman to B deck, eleven two. Emergency."

I grabbed my kit and hightailed it. And I knew I had big trouble as soon as I walked into the berthing compartment.

It was Private Howell, screaming and in convulsions.

Chapter Three

DAMN IT! WHAT THE HELL HAD I MISSED?

Howell was on the deck in front of his rack-tube; the convulsions were hitting him in waves, and each time his muscles contracted he let loose a bellow that rang off the bulkheads. His face was bright red and sweating, his eyes wide open but apparently staring at nothing. A dozen Marines were gathered around him, trying to hold him down, trying to keep him from slamming his head against the deck. Someone had thought fast and jammed a rag into his mouth to keep him from biting through his own tongue.

I knelt beside him and felt for a pulse. Faster than two a second, and pounding.

The fastest way to derail convulsions is a shot of nano programmed to hit the brain's limbic system and decouple the spasmodic neuronic output, a nanoneural suppression, or NNS. That's the way we treat epileptic seizures. The trouble was, this wasn't necessarily epilepsy, and messing with the brain, outside of relatively straightforward pain control, is not business as usual for a Corpsman.

I opened an in-head CDF channel. "Dr. Francis? I need you up here. B Deck, berthing compartment eleven two."

"Already on my way, Carlyle. What do we have?"

"Twenty-year-old male in convulsions. Elevated heart and BP." I hesitated. "He was at sick call this morning with symptoms of the flu."

"Go ahead and initiate an NNS."

"Aye, aye, sir."

I pulled a spray injector from my kit and clicked in a plastic capsule of gray liquid, held the tip against Howell's carotid, and fired it into his bloodstream. Elsewhere in my kit was an N-prog, a handheld device that used magnetic induction to program nanobots after they were inside the body. I switched it on and glanced at the screen.

What the hell? The device was picking up easily twice the dosage of 'bots, and they were already running a program. Not only that, they were recruiting the new 'bots, passing on their programming as the new 'bots flooded into Howell's brain. On-screen, I could see a graphic representation of the nanotech war going on inside his brain—a haze of red dots and gray dots, with more and more of the gray switching to red as I watched.

And the seizures became more violent, horrifically so. Howell's back arched so sharply, his hips thrust forward, I was afraid his spine was going to snap. With each thrust, he gave another bellow. The muscles were standing out on his neck like steel bars, his mouth wide open, and blood was streaming from his nose. This was *not* good. If I didn't get the convulsions under control soon, he would have a massive stroke or a heart attack on the spot.

I punched in my code, then entered Program 9, holding the N-prog close to the side of his head. The remaining gray dots turned green and, slowly, *slowly*, the red dots began switching to green as well.

"C'mon! C'mon!" I breathed, watching the slow change in colors. Green 'bots meant they'd accepted the new program, which would guide them through the brain tissues to the limbic system and to the motor-control areas and the cerebellum, where they should start damping out the neural storm that was wracking Howell's brain.

Damn it. I wanted to call it epilepsy, but it wasn't, though it showed some of the same signs and symptoms. It looked as though Howell's limbic system had just started firing off high-energy signals. The red nano was behind it, I suspected. Somehow, they appeared to be programmed to enter the limbic system and stimulate the neuron firings that had resulted in Howell's bizarre seizure. I could see that the red 'bots were clustered in several particular spots deep within Howell's brain—a region called the ventral tegemental area, or VTA, and another called the *substantia nigra*. I didn't know what that meant; Corpsmen are given basic familiarization in brain anatomy, of course, but detailed brain chemistry is definitely a subject for specialists and expert AIs.

I needed to know what was going on in there chemically. I tapped out a new program code, setting it to affect just ten percent of the nanobots I'd just put into Howell's brain.

Interstitial fluid—the liquid that fills the spaces between the body's cells—is a witches' brew of water filled with salts, amino acids and peptides, sugars, fatty acids, coenzymes, hormones, neurotransmitters, and waste products dumped by the cells. It's not the same as blood or blood plasma; red cells, platelets, and plasma proteins can't pass through the capillary walls, though certain kinds of white blood cells can squeeze through to fight infection. The exact composition depends on where in the body you're measuring, but with nerve cells the interstitial fluid is where the chemical exchange takes place across a synapse, the gap between one nerve cell and another. I was telling the 'bots to begin directly sampling the mix of complex molecules floating among Howell's neurons.

The answer came back as a long scrolling list of substances, but one formula by far outweighed all of the others: $C_8H_{11}NO_2$. I had to look it up in my in-head reference library, and when I saw what it was I could have kicked myself.

Dopamine.

About then is when Dr. Francis arrived. "Make a hole!" one of the Marines barked, and the cluster of people around me and Howell scattered apart. I handed him my N-prog with the formula still showing on the screen.

"Shit," was all he said when he read it.

Using my N-prog, he took over the programming of the

nanobots, checking the progress of Program 9 first. There were definitely fewer of the red specks now, and a lot more of the green. In addition, some had switched over to orange, the 'bots engaged in sampling Howell's cranial interstitial fluid.

The nanoneural suppression routine appeared to be working, once the green 'bots got a substantial upper hand over the red 'bots in numbers. Howell's back was still arched, the muscular contractions were continuing, but they were decidedly weaker now, and expressing themselves as a long, steady quiver rather than the violent thrusting motions of a moment ago.

Dr. Francis was tapping in a new program code. "Neuroleptic intervention at the D2 receptors," he told me. "It blocks dopamine."

The 'bots clustered in Howell's VTA were almost all green now, and the effect was spreading out through the motor region of his cerebral cortex and his cerebellum as well. The motor cortex is what plans and controls voluntary motor functions of the body—muscular movements, in other words. The cerebellum is the part of the brain at the very back and bottom of the organ that regulates the body's muscular movements. It doesn't initiate them, but it does help control them to fine-tune motor activity, timing, and coordination. Those parts of Howell's brain had been completely out of control, causing all of his muscles to lock up in an involuntary, spasmodic seizure. As the motor-control regions relaxed, Howell's body relaxed. His face sagged out of its rigid, openmouthed grimace, his fists unclenched, his spine eased into a more normal posture. Howell was panting now, but his eyes blinked, and he seemed to be aware of us now.

His eyes looked unusually dark.

"What happened, Private?" I asked him.

"I . . . dunno, Doc. I was just relaxing in my bunk, and wham! I don't know what hit me."

"How long have you been doing onan?" Dr. Francis asked, his voice level and matter-of-fact.

"Onan? I . . . ah . . . don't know what you mean, sir."

"Sure you do, son," Francis replied. "You have enough dopamine in your system to trigger a hundred sexual orgasms. You were onanning and o-looping. Feels better than the real thing, eh?"

Of course, when the doctor said that it was all obvious. "Shit!" I said. "He's addicted?"

"That's one word for it," Francis replied, studying the N-prog's screen. "Ah. The dopamine levels are coming down. I think we've broken the monkey's back."

I only half heard him. I was in-head, opening up my personal library and downloading the entry on onan. I'd known this stuff, once, but it wasn't the sort of thing you worked with every day, and I never thought about it.

Download, Ship's Medical Library
"Onan," "onanning"

From "O-nano," a contraction for "orgasmic nano."

Slang term referring to the use of programmed medical nano to affect the pleasure center of the brain directly in order to generate sexual orgasm. Nanobot programs can be directed to effect the release of massive amounts of dopamine in the brain, or to trigger spasmodic muscle contractions, or, more usually, both.

The term "onan" is a play on Onan, the name of a minor character in the Book of Genesis (q.v.).

Cute. I remembered it now. In the Jewish-Christian Bible, there's the story of Onan, who dumped his semen on the floor rather than impregnate his dead brother's wife, which apparently pissed Yahweh off so badly he struck Onan dead on the spot. For years, *onanism* was a synonym for masturbation, and carried with it the idea that God was going to throw a lightning bolt at you if you jacked or jilled off. What generation upon generation of relaxed but guilt-ridden teenagers afterward managed to miss was that the sin of Onan lay in his disobeying God—according to Jewish law he was *supposed* to father a son by his sister-in-law to preserve his brother's bloodline. It had nothing to do with masturbation.

Today, of course, the so-called sin of Onan is long forgotten, but orgasmic nanotechnics are very much with us. You can program one-micron nanobots, you see, to go into the brain's limbic system and trigger the neurochemical processes that result in sexual orgasm. Sometimes we do this deliberately, as a treatment for certain types of sexual dysfunction, but there's also a thriving underground business in providing doses of sex-programmed nanobots that can go into the brain and stimulate an orgasm, and then do it *again*, and *again*, and *again*. . . .

That part, programming the 'bots to give you one orgasm after another every second or two is known as o-looping, and it can be addictive—very highly so.

Not to mention dangerous.

It turns out that drugs like cocaine and amphetamines either trigger or mimic the release of dopamine, and they affect the same areas of the limbic system that light up during an orgasm—the VTA and the brain's mesolimbic reward pathway. In fact, a brain scan taken during an orgasm shows a process ninety-five percent identical to a heroin rush. Drugs and orgasms hit the same part of the brain, and that's what makes cocaine and other such drugs addictive.

That doesn't mean sex is bad, of course. It's natural, normal, and healthy. But deliberately and artificially overstimulating dopamine production can lead to an addiction requiring higher and higher dopamine levels to get the same kick as the dopamine receptors begin closing down. And the program Howell had been running, evidently, had involved overstimulation of the parts of the brain responsible for muscular contraction as well. It was a way to boost the orgasmic feeling, yeah, but it could have killed him too.

The curious thing is that dopamine doesn't give you the feel-good kick itself. Dopamine is the hormone that makes you *want*—it's the *craving*.

But it's the flood of dopamine that makes a heroin addict want another hit.

And it drives our orgasmic cravings as well.

"I take it," Dr. Francis said quietly, "that you didn't check him for dope levels at sick call this morning."

"No, sir."

"Why not?"

"I didn't see any need. It looked like a cold or maybe flu."

"Did you look at his eyes?"

I glanced down at Howell's face. In the harsh light from the overhead, his pupils were so widely dilated that his eyes looked unusually dark.

"No, sir. He was complaining that the light hurt his eyes."

"Uh-huh. Addicts will do that, to hide their pupils. They'll look everywhere *except* right at you. Did you notice that he happened to have a monster hard-on?"

"No, sir." The long bulge at the crotch of Howell's skin-suit was fading, but still hard to miss. Marines shipboard tend to wear nano-grown skinsuits like work utilities, since they're disposable and Marines wear them under combat armor anyway. The things are pretty revealing, which doesn't matter since the old American nudity taboos have pretty much gone the way of the dinosaur, and service men and women sleep and shower communally anyway.

His erection was painfully evident, even now. But, no, I hadn't noticed. There'd been other things on my mind at the time besides Howell's crotch.

"Get a stretcher team and get him down to sick bay," Francis told me. "He should be okay, but we'll need to follow up the neuroleptics, and he'll need a complete scan to check for internal injury, electrolyte balance, and lactic-acid buildup. Once things are back in balance, we'll do a flush on the 'bots, get them out of there." He pinched Howell's arm as I had earlier. "Dehydrated. When you get him to sick bay, put him on IV fluids. Think you can manage that?"

"Yes, sir."

"Hey, Doc?" Howell said. His voice was weak, and it trembled a bit. "Am I in trouble?"

"You're on report," Dr. Francis told him, "if that's what you mean. Misuse of nanomedical technology is damned dangerous. I imagine Captain Reichert is going to have words with you about damaging government property."

"*What* government property?"

"You. Your body."

I'd already used my in-head com link to call for a stretcher team. In the meantime, I helped Howell get up and into his bunk. The other Marines began dispersing, a little reluctantly. It had been quite a show.

And by the time we had him in sick bay, with an IV dripping Ringer's lactate into his arm, we were sliding into Earth orbit, the tugs on their way out to haul us in and dock us with the Supra-Cayambe Starport Facility.

Later that afternoon, Lieutenant Commander Francis called me into his office. "Have a seat, Carlyle."

"Yes, sir."

"You missed some important shit with Howell, son." He didn't sound angry. He sounded *disappointed*, which was worse.

"I know that, sir."

"Why?"

"I . . . no excuse, sir."

"On board ship, our patients tend to be young and very, very healthy. Oh, you'll get the occasional case of appendicitis or a sprained ankle or even a cold, but when one comes to you with vague symptoms like that, you need to consider the possibility that he did something to himself.

"Because our patients on board ship also tend to be very bored. They tend to be good at figuring out ways to subvert the system and apply technology to alleviate that boredom."

I thought about Doobie and his lab-brewed hooch. "Yes, sir."

"That's *especially* true if he comes to you asking for a dose of nanomeds. *Every* technology can be misused in one way or another. It's ridiculously easy for these kids to go on liberty and buy a handheld unit that can program 'bots to do damned near anything, just about. Onans are probably the most common. But they have them for programming a heroin rush, which is pretty much the same thing. Or cocaine. Or even, believe it or not, the feeling of contentment after a good meal."

"Is *that* addictive, Doctor?"

"Can be. I saw one young enlisted woman a few years ago who was anorexic. She used an N-prog to feel full, like she'd just had a good meal, and stopped eating. We almost didn't save her."

"That's just nuts, sir."

"No, it's just *human*. Humans do stupid things, or humans get screwed up in the head and that makes them to do stupid things."

"Yes, sir." I hesitated. "But—"

"But what?"

"I'm curious about Howell, sir. If he programmed the 'bots in his system to stimulate dopamine production . . . that's just the craving, isn't it? How did that cause the muscle spasms? And why did he go into convulsions? I didn't give him any nanomeds this morning. Just aspirin."

"Hm." For a moment, he got a faraway look in his eyes, as though he were listening to something. "Do you know the term *synaptic plasticity*?"

"No, sir. I know what a synapse is."

"The gap between one nerve cell and the next, yes. Synaptic plasticity is the tendency of the connection across the synapses to change in strength, either with use or with disuse. Among other things, it means the ability to change the quantity of neurotransmitters released into a synapse, and how well the next neuron in the chain responds to them. It's an important factor in learning."

"Okay . . ."

"Aspirin can affect synaptic plasticity. One of aspirin's metabolic by-products, salicylate, acts on the NMDA receptors in cells, and that affects the flow of calcium ions across a neural synapse."

At this point, Dr. Francis was way over my head. I had absolutely no idea what an NMDA receptor might be.

He must have sensed my confusion. "Don't worry about it. My guess is Howell had a resident population of nanobots in his brain, programmed to give him an orgasm anytime he wanted, okay?"

I nodded.

"Dopamine is a neurotransmitter. One of the characteristics of neurotransmitters is you get a weakening effect each time you fire them." He waved his hand in a descending series of peaks to illustrate. "You get this much of a jolt, then a little less, and a little less, like this. In an addiction, you need to boost the dosage of your drug of choice to get the same bang for your buck, right?"

"Yes, sir." This was more familiar territory.

"Well, the same thing happens with dopamine. He might even have been going into withdrawal. Dopamine affects the same parts of the limbic system that heroin and cocaine hits."

"Yeah. Headache. Runny nose. General aches and pains."

"Symptoms like the flu," Francis said. "Exactly. So he came to you to get you to prescribe a shot of nano, with the idea that more is better. He could reprogram what you gave him . . . or it looks like the nanobots he already had were set to reprogram anything new. You gave him aspirin instead. Maybe he took them back to the berthing compartment and downed them all, just hoping something would happen. The full chem workup we pulled on him this afternoon showed elevated salicylate levels.

"He might have boosted the programming on his nanobots, too. Upped the power, and maybe set them to deliberately give him an hour of multiple orgasms. We'll know that if we find his N-prog in his locker. One way or another, though, the aspirin increased the efficiency of neurotransmitter uptake—specifically of dopamine. It also might have increased the triggering receptivity of his muscles. Aspirin is a decent muscle relaxant."

The realization of what he was saying had just hit me, bam. "You're saying I . . . I poisoned Howell, sir. I gave him that aspirin, and that's what triggered the convulsions."

"Not at all. I'm saying that when you're working with these people, you need to be suspicious. Paranoid, even. What are they trying to put over on you?" He scowled. "It's ridiculous. Most of them have fuck buddies in the squad bay, for God's sake. Virtual reality feeds from the ship's library let them have sex in their heads with all the hottest erotic stars on the Net. And *still* they screw with illegal nano programmers, trying to get a bigger kick, or they o-loop them to get a whole lot of them in a row.

"What happened wasn't your fault. You didn't know he was doing an onan, or that he was o-looping. But, damn it, be suspicious! If they're showing fuzzy symptoms, or symptoms that don't really make sense, do a scan and check for resident nano! If Howell had access to the stuff, it's a sure bet that a dozen others on the *Clymer* are using, too. I'm going to need to take this to the skipper."

"Yes, sir. Uh . . ."

"What?"

"What about me, sir? Am I on report?"

"Why would you be on report?"

"I screwed up. I missed the nano, I didn't think of addiction when I saw him at sick call this morning, and I gave him enough aspirin to trigger those convulsions."

Francis sighed. He raised his hand and began ticking points off on his fingers. "One, you didn't 'screw up.' You could have been a little more persistent, a little more observant. But his symptoms looked like a clear call. The flu.

"Two. You're not a doctor, nor do you have training in neurophysiology. At sick call, you screen the patients so that I don't have to see all of them, and sort out the malingerers from the ones who are really sick. You're trained to handle routine stuff. Colds and STDs and stubbed toes. Nanogenic dopamine addictive response is *not* routine.

"Three. One of the most complicated and difficult aspects

of medicine is understanding how drugs or nano programs can interact or interfere with one another. It's *amazing* how complicated things can get, with different drugs either reinforcing one another, or cancelling each other out—and with illegal nano, *all* bets are off!

"Four. Aspirin has been around since the late nineteenth century, unless you count shamans prescribing willow bark for pain, which is where the stuff came from. We've understood in general how it works since the late twentieth. But, believe me, even something that's been around as long as aspirin can still surprise you. People have unusual sensitivities, or allergies, or they're on drugs or nano treatments, or they're shooting themselves full of crap that could kill them.

"*And no one can keep up with all of the possibilities.* That's why we have expert systems, AIs with medical databases that let them guide us through the jungle of drug interactions. When in doubt, use them."

I sagged a bit inside. "I do, when there's a question," I said. "But I didn't have a question this time. I really thought Howell had a cold."

"It happens to all of us, Carlyle. We make mistakes, we're not perfect. Things could have turned out a *lot* worse for Private Howell, believe me. They didn't. So . . . you made a mistake. Learn from it. Okay?"

"Yes, sir."

"Good. Questions?"

"Just . . . is this going to affect my FMF training?"

"Hell, no. You're a good Corpsman, and I want you on my team. So as far as I'm concerned, you're in."

"Thank you, sir."

"You want liberty tonight?"

I thought about it. Right then, I really wanted to get off the ship. There was this bar in Supra-Cayambe I really liked: the Earthview.

"Yes, sir. If that's okay . . ."

"Absolutely. Give me your hand."

I extended my left hand, and he passed a wand over it. All

military personnel have a programmable chip implanted in their left wrist and another in the back of their head. They serve as ID—what the military used to call dog tags—and can also carry orders and authorizations. My CDF in-head hardware—my Cerebral Data Feed implants—could also carry orders, of course, but the Navy takes a dim view of enlisted personnel writing or rewriting their own.

What Dr. Francis had just done was give me an authorization, signed by him, my department head, to leave the ship for twelve hours, what both the Navy and the Marine Corps refer to as liberty.

I was free for the evening, unless, of course, we had an emergency recall.

"Have you heard anything about when we're shipping out again, sir?" I asked.

"Not a word. I wouldn't worry about it. If they're putting together an out-system expeditionary force, it's going to take them a while to assemble all the ships. So enjoy your time ashore."

"Thank you, sir."

"Dismissed."

"Aye, aye, sir."

As an ass-chewing, Dr. Francis's lecture wasn't bad at all. In fact, I think he was trying to encourage me. But the talk hadn't made me feel better. If anything, I felt *worse*.

"Hey, e-Car! You going ashore?"

It was Dubois. I'd just walked into the squad bay, on my way to my compartment to change into civvies.

"I guess so," I told him. "I need a drink, or ten."

"Yeah. Francis chewed you a new one, huh?"

"It wasn't that bad."

"It's all over the ship, you know, that he had you on the carpet for dropping the ball with Howell."

"Great," I told him. "*Exactly* what I needed to hear."

I was *really* looking forward to that drink.

Chapter Four

THE EARTHVIEW LOUNGE IS LOCATED AT THE TOP OF THE CAYAMBE Space Elevator, and the place is well named. The view from up there is spectacular.

The Space Elevator went into operation in 2095, a 71,000-kilometer-high woven buckycarb tether stretching from Earthport, atop the third-highest mountain in Ecuador, all the way up to Starport. The other two elevators, at Mount Kenya and Pulau Lingga/Singapore, came on-line later, but Cayambe was the first. A cartel of banking and space-industry businesses built the elevator, and it was run as an international megacorporation until the Commonwealth officially took it over in 2115.

Halfway up, just below the 36,000-kilometer level, is the Geosynch Center, which is a major node of communications and industrial facilities clustered around the elevator, both in free orbit and attached to the cable. It's also the location of the big solar reflector arrays. Starport, however, is all the way up at the top, built into and around the surface of the five-kilometer asteroid used to anchor the elevator and keep it stretched out taut—a stone tied to the end of a whirling string. Ships launching from Starport picked up a small but free boost from the centrifugal force of the elevator's once-per-day rotation.

I went ashore with Doob and HM3 Charlie "Machine"

McKean, flashing our electronic passes at the AI of the watch and riding the transparent docking tube from *Clymer*'s quarterdeck up to the planetoid in a transport capsule.

It was quite a view. The *George Clymer* was nestled into the space dock facility on the planetoid's far side, the location of Starport's Commonwealth naval base. A dozen other ships were there as well, including the assault carrier *Lewis B. Puller*, three times the *Clymer*'s length, ten times her mass, and carrying four squadrons of A/S-60 and A/S-104 Marine planetary assault fighters, plus numerous reconnaissance and support spacecraft. There were civilian ships as well, including a couple of deep interstellar research vessels, the *Stephen Hawking* and the *Edward Witten*.

Most of the Starport planetoid is in microgravity. The rock itself doesn't have enough mass for more than a whisper of gravity of its own, and this far out from Earth, the centrifugal force created by its rotation amounts to about 0.0017 of a G.

That means that if you drop a wineglass, after the first second it's fallen one and a half centimeters—a smitch more than half an inch—and there's *plenty* of time to catch it before it hits the deck.

But, of course, you don't want to be drinking out of a wineglass in the first place. Things still have their normal mass in microgravity, if not their weight, and once the wine gets to swirling in the glass it will keep moving up and out and all over you and the deck in shimmying slow-motion spheres.

Which was why we were headed for the Starport Nearside Complex, the small space city constructed on the Earth-facing side of the planetoid, better known as the Wheel. It's a kilometer-wide wheel encircling the up-tether from Earth, and rotating once a minute to create an out-is-down spin gravity of about half a G.

We caught the thru-tube that whisked us from the Starport Terminal through the core of the planetoid and deposited us at the hub of Wheel City. From there, we floated our way into the rotating entryway and rose through one of the spokes, the sensation of gravity steadily increasing as we rose farther out from the hub.

The Wheel holds the heart of the Commonwealth Starport Naval Base, including the headquarters and communications center, support facilities, and a Marine training module, but over half of the huge structure is civilian territory, a free port administered directly by the Commonwealth. The Earth-view was a bar-restaurant combo located in one of the Wheel segments, and it came by its name honestly.

The entryway checked our passes as we walked in. One entire wall, from floor to ceiling, was a viewall looking down-tether at Earth.

The disk appeared about thirty times larger than a full moon from Earth, a dazzlingly brilliant swirl of azure seas and intensely white clouds and polar caps. The planet was in half-phase at the moment, with the sunset terminator passing through Ecuador and down the South American spine of the Andes Mountains. It was late summer in the northern hemisphere, so the terminator ran almost straight north up the Atlantic seaboard. South, the bulge of Brazil was picked out by the massed city lights of the megapolis stretching from Montevideo to Belém.

North, of course, the New Ice Age still held northern New England and much of Canada in a midwinter's death's grip, despite all the efforts of the mirror array at Geosynch. The Canadian ice sheets, especially, were blinding in the afternoon sunlight.

At the moment, the viewall image was coming through an external camera somewhere on the planetoid; the Earth and the starfield behind it weren't rotating with the Wheel's stately spin. I could see one of the elevator capsules on its way up-tether, gleaming bright silver in the sunlight.

"You been here before, e-Car?" Machine asked.

"Oh, yeah," I admitted. "I like the view."

Doob cackled a nasty laugh. "View is right! The girls here are *spectacular!*"

Which wasn't what I meant, of course, but, hey, when the man's right, he's right. The Earthview was actually divided into halves, separated by a soundproof bulkhead. The side reserved for civilians was rather genteel, I'd heard—fine dining at exorbitant prices, the food delivered by robotic waitstaff indistinguishable from FAB (flesh and blood). They even served real beef there, shipped up-tether for the financial equivalent of two arms, a leg, and the promised delivery of your firstborn.

The Earthview Lounge next door, however, was a bit . . . livelier. Naked FAB waitresses, live sex shows on the black, fur-padded central stage, and throbbing, full-sensory music fed directly through the patrons' implants and going straight to those parts of the brain responsible for hearing and feeling. And the girls *were* gorgeous, ranging from exotic genies to BTL sexbots to winsome girl-next-door types. The joint wasn't reserved for the military, not officially, anyway, but I doubt that most civilians were all that comfortable there. The fleet was in, and enlisted personnel tended to get a bit territorial with their liberty hot spots.

Doob and Machine and I let the door deduct the cover charge from our eccounts and we wandered in, looking for good seats. An enthusiastic ménage-à-quatre was writhing away on the stage, backlit by the half-full Earth, and the place was flooded with blue-silver earthlight. A hostess wearing a plastic smile and some luminous animated tattoos showed us to a table close to the entertainment and took our drink orders. The mood music, a piece I half recognized by Apokyleptos, literally felt like hands running over my body; the audible part was too damned loud, but I dialed my reception down a bit and it was okay after that.

A waitress brought us our drinks and one of those smiles, and we leaned back in the chairs to enjoy the show. I'd ordered a hyperbolic trajectory—vodka, white rum, metafuel, and blue incandescence. I tossed it back, shuddered through the burn, and after that I didn't care quite so much about screwing up with Howell. After my second glass, I didn't care at all about Howell, and after the third I didn't care much about *anything*.

"So I hear you didn't get booted from the program," Machine said. "Lucky."

"I guess," I said, but without much enthusiasm. "I've been having second thoughts, y'know?"

"What, about going FMF?" Doob asked. "Shit, *every* Corpsman wants to go FMF! Best of the best, right?"

"S'okay," I said, shrugging, "*if* you like jarheads." My lips felt numb and I was having some trouble shaping the words.

"Don't you?" McKean asked.

"Sure, when the bastards aren't trying to put something over on you." I was still feeling burned by Howell's attempt to get another shot of nano.

"So why did you volunteer for FMF in the first place?" Dubois asked. "You coulda put in your four and gotten out."

Four years was the minimum enlistment period for the Navy. To get FMF, I'd had to "ship for six," as we say, extending my enlistment to ten years, total.

I shrugged. "I wanted to get rich, of course."

NO ONE JOINS THE NAVY TO GET RICH, OF COURSE. YOU GET ROOM and board and some great opportunities to travel, sure, but base pay is about a twelfth what a good systems programmer gets on the outside, and maybe a quarter of the take-home pay of a 'bot director at an e-car manufactory. No one, unless you take the long view, and have a father who's senior vice president of research and development for General Nanodynamics.

Lots of medical doctors get their start in the Hospital Corps. It offers a good, basic education in general medicine and applied nano, and universities with medical programs smile on ex-corpsmen looking for grants or scholarships. But the economic rewards can be even bigger when what you bring home is a cool and useful bit of xenotech.

That's because, anymore, Navy Corpsmen aren't just the

enlisted medics for the Marines and Navy. Because of their technical training, and the fact that in the field and they're already lugging around a fair amount of specialized gear, they're also the science technicians for any military field op. Sampling the local atmosphere, studying the biosphere and reporting on what might bite, and even establishing first contact with the locals all fall into a Corpsman's MOS, his military occupational specialty—his job description, if you like.

And that means that Corpsmen are perfectly placed to pick up alien technologies when they make first contact, or to bring home innovative ways of utilizing human nanotech. They even get to keep the military-issued CDF hardware that allows in-head linking, and that can provide a hell of a competitive advantage in the civilian world.

So when I finished the series on my basic education downloads, my father, Spencer Carlyle, suggested that I might want to join the Navy—specifically the Hospital Corps—in order to learn skills that would benefit both me and the family.

My grandfather went to work for General Nanodynamics sixty-three years ago when it was a data-mining startup, wading through the Encyclopedia Galactica's hundreds of millions of hours of data, finding the codes that would unlock its secrets and release untold alien secrets of science, technology, and art that we could apply here on Earth. Better, though, is to go straight to the source, to actually learn new methods of materials manufacturing or chemistry or medicine directly from a living xenoculture. It's one thing to pull off the EG's stats on the X'ghr and learn that they're *very* good at biochemistry. It's something quite else to visit the aliens in person and pick their brains.

In 2212, my father led the General Nanodynamics team that developed cybertelomeric engineering from the data brought back from direct contact with the X'ghr eight years earlier.

Telomeres are the end-caps that keep chromosomes from unraveling, but they grow shorter with each division of the cell. When the telomeres wear away after forty or fifty divisions, the cell dies and aging sets in. Cybertelomerics refers to various means of controlling or guiding telomere replication inside cells without generating the out-of-control cell growth and immortality known as a cancer. As a result, humans alive today can expect to live two or three hundred years or more, rejuve treatments can have an eighty-year-old looking like forty, and clinical immortality might be just around the corner. Whether or not human immortality is a *good* thing is beside the point; the biochemical data brought back from the X'ghr homeworld by the crew of the *Hippocrates* promises to utterly transform what it means to be human.

That one bit of xenotech *should* have made my family quite wealthy.

It didn't. That was because the government stepped in and declared telomere therapy a national asset, with patents owned and controlled by the Commonwealth Institute of Health. Dad got a pat on the back and a nice bonus, but do you have any idea how much rich old people would pay for treatments that would keep them going for another couple of centuries? Or keep them looking and performing like VR sex stars?

But the government wants to maintain control of who gets rejuve treatments, at least for now. They say it's to prevent runaway overpopulation; Dad was convinced that we're going to have a lot of very young-looking senators, presidents, and wealthy campaign contributors over the next few centuries.

Cynical? Sure. And he managed to infect me with his bitterness as well. Government of the rich, by the rich, and for the rich: it's a system that's been around for an obscenely long time, and one that's *very* hard to fight. So Dad set out not to fight the system so much as to work with it. If we could nail down another big advance in medicine, materials processing, or chemistry from an untapped xenotech source, we might be able to exploit it off-world—at one of the free-market colonies, maybe—and do it in such a way that the Commonwealth couldn't touch it.

That was the plan, at any rate. Nanotechnics is highly competitive, and new developments and techniques are coming along every day. The field is dominated by three or four big megacorporations and a dozen smaller ones, and the company that doesn't keep up is going to find itself sidelined and forgotten in very short order. General Nanodynamics is about nine or ten in the hierarchy, but it's well-placed to go multi-world and even give IBN and Raytheon-Mitsubishi a run for their e-creds.

My dad got into the field the old-fashioned way, going the route of AI development, but he thought having a Corpsman in the family might increase the chances of landing something big . . . a new technology, a new means of controlling or programming nanobots, a new approach to an old problem, like what the X'ghr did for telomere research.

And I was pretty excited about the idea myself. It wasn't like I was letting my Dad do my thinking for me. I'd wanted to join the Navy anyway, the Hospital Corps in particular, because I had my eye on going to a school like Johns Hopkins or Bethesda University, one with a good medical download program, with an eye to becoming a doctor. I'd never been much interested in following in my father's footsteps . . . or the footsteps of my grandfather and great grandfather. A century of Carlyles in General Nanodynamics, I thought, was *quite* enough.

Besides, to make money, *real* money, we needed to break free of the pack. As an employee of General Nanodynamics, with all of his ideas becoming the intellectual property of the corporation, my dad could manage a living that was comfortable enough, sure, but there is well-off rich, and there is filthy rich with a private Earth-to-orbit shuttle, your own synchorbital private mansion, and maybe a shot at some telomeric genengineering.

If I found myself in a position to bring back some exploitable xenotech, something Dad and his contacts could turn into a few hundred billion creds and a high-living lifestyle . . . hey, why not? I was *in*.

But I needed to go Fleet Marine Force to make it Out There, to give myself even a chance of being on a first contact team or encountering a new technic species not described in the EG.

And after my encounter with Private Howell that morning, I thought that my chances of that were becoming somewhat bleak. If I got dropped from FMF, I was looking at six more years of routine duty—working on the wards of a naval hospital somewhere, or serving as staff at a research station in Outer God-knows-where.

I was wondering if I'd just managed to deep-six my entire future.

"YOU JOINED THE FUCKING NAVY TO GET *RICH*?" MACHINE SAID, laughing. "My God, man, what planet are *you* from?"

"My man," Doob added, "we need to run an EG xenospecies profile on you, *stat*! Lessee . . . 'e-Car: civilization type zero-point-zero-weird. Biological code: *really* weird.'"

"Weird squared," Machine suggested.

The plan to score on xenotech was something I never talked about with anyone, of course. I shrugged off the teasing. "Hey, I'm tracking to become a med doctor, okay? Doctors can bring in the creds same as nanoware specialists."

"Sure, and they work their asses off getting there," Doob said.

Machine tossed off the rest of his drink—something called a "weightless slam," and nodded. "Shit, you know how much ghost-mass doctors carry with them all the time? Ghost in the machine, dude. Ghost in the machine."

Most doctors are connected on a semi-permanent basis to expert AI systems running on the local Net, often with ten or twelve load-links going at a time. That's because no one person can possibly keep *all* of the data necessary in his memory—even in their plug-in cerebral RAM—to maintain a smoothly working knowledge of the pharmacology,

anatomy, pathology, biochemistry, nanotechnic programming, holistics, cybernetics, and psychology needed to treat
patients, and that's just to name just a few. Doctors aren't
necessarily running all of those channels all the time, but
it is, I'd been told, like having ten other people with you all
the time, whispering, guiding, making suggestions, *kibitz-
ing*, whether you are performing surgery or simply sitting
down to dinner.

Some, like Dr. Francis, seemed to handle it pretty well.
Sometimes, he would get a faraway look in his eyes, like
he was listening to someone else while he's talking to you,
but usually you knew it was *him* behind that fresh-out-of-
med-school face. In some cases, though, it became a kind of
high-tech multiple-personality syndrome, where your original self tended to fade into the background as one or another
of your resident AIs took over for you. I was thinking of Dr.
Burchalter, on board the *Puller*, who often didn't seem to be
there when you talked to him. You *knew* you were taking
orders from an expert AI who was running the show.

Ghost in the machine indeed. The term was invented
a few centuries ago by a British philosopher named Gil-
bert Ryle to describe conceptual problems with Descarte's
ideas of mind as distinct from body. Later, it described the
neuro-evolutionary idea that human brains are grown atop
mammalian brains grown atop reptilian brains, and that destructive impulses like hate, anger, or fear arise from those
deeper, more primitive systems we still carry with us.

Nowadays, however, it means losing yourself in a
multiple-AI system, and your "ghost-mass" refers to the
number of active AIs you have resident on your in-head CDF
hardware at any given time.

"I know, I know," I told him. "But I can handle it. I don't
think . . ."

I broke off what I was going to say. Machine was getting
into the music.

It was deeper now, more insistent, more sex-heavy sensu-
ous. The touch-sensie sidebands were creating the feeling

of a naked woman giving me a lap dance—I could feel her weight, feel her squirming against my thighs, feel her hands stroking my chest and face, all in time to the throb of the music. I had the vid bands turned way down, so the dancer's image overlying my vision was ghosted to nearly nothing, a barely sensed shadow, but with three trajectories still burning in my gut it was getting a little hard to focus on the conversation *and* the lap-dancing distraction as well.

It looked like Machine had blissed out completely to the entertainment channel. His head was back, with a silly half smile on his face, and his hands were in front of his chest, running up and down across something we couldn't see.

I glanced at Doob. "I think we just lost Machine," I told him.

"Yeah, looks like he's got a ghost in *his* machine!"

"You look like you're getting into it, too." He had the same silly grin as McKean, and his eyes were starting to go glassy.

"Oh, *yeah*, baby!" At that point, I couldn't tell if Doob was talking to me or to the ViR-gal invisibly grinding on his lap.

I brought the vid up on my implant for a look. She was a virtual-reality genie—the image of a genetically enhanced young woman with impossibly long, silky white hair and an overdeveloped upper chassis. I didn't care much for that phenotype myself; they always looked so damned top-heavy that I kept thinking they were going to fall over. This one was well done, though. The program had her looking deep into my eyes and not blankly staring off into space somewhere. Her eyes were too large for an unmodified human, revealing her look's descent from the conventions of an old Japanese artform called anime, but she seemed to be focused totally on me. I could even smell her perfume.

Of course, if I wanted things to get even more personal, I would have to let them deduct ten creds from my eccount. I was kind of hoping for a real-world encounter with a woman tonight, though, and, after a moment or two, I thoughtclicked a refusal to the offer.

But what the music was giving me was just crotch-teasing, and I found the sensation annoying. So I switched off the vid and the genie's eyes and other oversized assets vanished. I switched off the tactile and olfactory sensations as well, and was left with the music coming over my audio channels alone. Funny. The music seemed a lot flatter and less interesting without the accompaniment of those other rhythmic, layered sensations.

Machine gave a strangled groan, and his hips started to jerk suggestively on the chair, his arms held tightly around the emptiness in front of him. It looked like he'd decided to pay the extra ten creds.

The sight bothered me, somehow. How, I wondered, was what he was doing any different from Private Howell's o-looping? I mean, obviously Howell had been risking serious physical injury with his stunt, and he'd taken things to the point of cataleptic rigidity. He'd lost control on several levels, in fact. The compulsion that led him to risk medical intervention, court martial, and an end to his military career—to say nothing of death from a stroke or a heart attack—suggested that he was addicted.

But addicted to what, exactly? The dopamine and the feel-good endorphins associated with sex, obviously, but the technologies being used to generate those feelings were different in Howell than in Dubois and McKean. Howell had used nanobots programmed to manipulate dopamine levels directly in order to trigger a succession of closely looped orgasms. My two companions were letting music sidebands feed their in-head hardware with the virtual reality illusion of a gene-altered woman having sex with them.

Howell's experience had been more intense, sure, and thanks to the aspirin he'd managed to get his switch stuck in the on position, but in terms of the outcome it was damned hard to see the line between one set of behaviors and the other.

"Hey, sailor," a sultry voice said behind me. "You switched off your sensies. Don't you like the music?"

I turned to face one of the Earthview's waitresses. She was short and cute and her upper chassis didn't look like it was going to pull her over. She wore a sweet smile and a wispy nimbus of blue-white light that didn't do a whole lot to cover what was underneath. The ID projected by her personal circuitry said "Masha," but there wasn't any other information in the broadcast.

"It's okay," I told her. "I was kind of hoping for some *real* action, maybe later."

She laughed, an entrancing sound, and moved just a little closer. "You seen anything around here that you like?"

I gave her a stereotypically lecherous up and down. "Absolutely. What time do you get off?"

She leaned even closer. "Me getting off kind of depends on *you*, doesn't it?"

"I'm Elliot," I told her. I thoughtclicked my personal ID, which broadcast my name, where I was from, the fact that I was U.S. Navy, all the basic, introductory stuff.

"Hi, Elliot. I'm Masha."

She didn't transmit anything from her ID except her name. "Masha" suggested that she likely was from Russia, Ukraine, or the Yakutsk Republic. Her English was perfect, though, so for all I knew she could have been North American, maybe from a Russian immigrant family. It was hard to know these days, with basic language downloads as good as they were.

So why didn't I ask her? Hell, I don't know. Maybe the fact that she hadn't sent more of her own personal data was putting me off. It suggested that she was keeping this on a strictly waitress-customer basis, and I felt as though asking her where she was from would come across as a really lame attempt to chat her up. I was feeling awkward and embarrassed and somewhat torn. Part of me *wanted* to talk her into bed, but as we bantered more, a larger part of me became convinced that she was more interested in my e-cred balance than in *me*.

And what was so wrong with that? The flesh-and-blood waitstaff in places like the Earthview aren't paid all that

well, even when you add in their tips, and the cost of work-
ers' quarters at Starport can eat up your e-cred balance *real*
fast. What they do with their off hours is their business, so
why not?

I was tempted, I really was. Masha looked like fun, and
I certainly wasn't in the market for a long-term relationship.
After Paula? *Hell*, no. I was *through* with long-term hearts-
and-flowers, long romantic interludes, and deeply intimate
relationships.

But the more I thought about it, the more I was convinced
that what I wanted was something more than the clinical
workings of a commercial transaction.

We talked a few more moments, and then she left to get
me another drink—a zero-G floater this time. The trajectory had blasted me pretty heavily; was *that* why I suddenly
wasn't interested in sex? Anyway, I was pretty sure another
trajectory was going to set me hard on my ass. The floater
was milder, would be easier on my system, with a lower percentage of C_2H_6O and less of a kick.

I looked across at Doob and Machine. They both were totally off planet—approaching the inevitable climax of their
links in perfect time with the ménage up on the furry stage.

Masha returned with my drink a moment later, then wandered off to check on her other customers. I looked past the
writhing ménage on stage at the image of Earth suspended
against the stars. Maybe a part of my inability to join in
had to do with how unsettled I was feeling just then. Until
recently, I'd thought I'd known exactly what I was and where
I was going. If I didn't make FMF, though, all of that was
called into question.

Oh, the next seven years would be spent in the Navy,
there was no question about that; I couldn't shout "I changed
my mind!" and take back my signature on my re-up agreement. But holding sick call for service personnel and their
dependents at some naval base Earthside, or *maybe* getting
to work at an outpost off planet somewhere, holding sick
call, running lab tests, performing medscans.

The alert went off inside my skull.

It started as a long, piercing, two-pitch whistle, like the old-fashioned boatswain's whistles of the old-time surface Navy.

"Attention, *Clymer* personnel," a voice said in my head after the whistle died away. "Attention *Clymer* personnel. Now recall, recall, recall. All hands report back aboard ship immediately. This is an embarkation order. Repeat . . ."

I gulped down the remaining half of my floater, hesitated, then put an extra-big tip on the table account for Masha. Across the table, Doob and Machine were blinking their eyes, looking around in a somewhat dazed manner. Recall alerts came through whether your channels were switched off, like mine, or even if they were fully engaged in other activities. I was suddenly delighted that I'd decided not to take the music's genie up on her offer to take things further.

Talk about rude interruptions!

Somehow, they managed to pay their tabs, and we made our way out of the Earthview.

A lot of other men and women were doing the same thing.

Chapter Five

WE EMBARKED FROM STARPORT A FEW HOURS AFTER OUR RETURN to the *Clymer.*

All three of us hit the sober-up in sick bay, a heavy dose of nanobots programmed to break down the ethanol and release oxygen into the blood. The effect is kind of like going from pleasant free-fall sensations to slamming face-first into the deck, but you're thinking more clearly when the shock wears off, and there's no hangover.

Much of the conversation in the squad bay was centered on our precipitous recall. "Damn," Doob said, shaking his head. "I was just about to make it with that genie, too!"

"You *do* know it was all in your head, right?" I asked him.

"What's your point? You make it with FAB, that's all in your head too."

I shrugged. He had a point. Sex was sex, whether you got it on with a virtual reality program downloaded into your brain's sensory centers, or had an orgasm with flesh and blood. In fact, brain scans had pointed out three centuries ago that when it came to a cerebral download of a recorded event, to a remembered event, or to an actual event taking place in physical reality, *the brain can't tell the difference.*

The *Clymer*, with twelve hundred Marines of MRF-7 embarked on board, accelerated under Plottel Drive out-system at 1 full gravity, seeking the flat metric required by the astrogation department, where local space carried only a minimum curvature from gravity. Flat gravitometrics allowed us to switch on the Alcubierre Drive, which would let us cruise out-system faster than light, and in the case of Sol, could be found about ten astronomical units out, a little farther than the orbit of Saturn. We were accompanied by the Marine assault carrier *Lewis B. Puller*, the heavy cruiser *Ticonderoga*, and two destroyers, the *Fife* and the *Decatur*.

They say that the one form of FTL even faster than Alcubierre Drive is shipboard scuttlebutt. We all were wondering what had happened up in officers' country. They'd sent down the briefing on Bloodworld before we'd reached Earth, granted us liberty, and only *then* suddenly called us back. There's a technical term for that—"situation normal, all fucked up," popularly shortened to SNAFU. Global comments, cerebral implants, direct-data downloads, AI intelligences a thousand times more powerful than human brains, and *still* the left hand doesn't know what the right hand is doing.

At 0930 hours the next morning after our departure, an announcement came through for all hands not on duty to rack out. That meant another full-immersion briefing, one with all of us lying down as the command constellation piped in the data. I wasn't scheduled for the sick bay watch until 1600 hours, so I found a free recliner in the squad bay rather than going back to my berthing compartment and my tube, and strapped myself in. I closed my eyes, opened the main channel, and a moment later I was standing once again on Bloodworld.

I say "once again" in a purely virtual sense, of course, since I'd never been there physically. In the previous briefing, the download had let me virtually stand on the tortured planet's surface as the basic ephemeris data scrolled through my skull, and the downloaded simulation unfolded a 360-degree world around me, one that I could, within fairly free limits, explore. This time, though, I was a bit more restricted in what I could look at, and the briefing officer was there as well.

"Good morning, Marines," he said. "I'm Lieutenant Carter. We have some updated intelligence on the Bloodstar situation."

Carter was our company S2, the unit intelligence officer and the guy in charge of operational security. He was short, freckled, and red haired, with a boyish look about him that didn't inspire all that much confidence.

But he generally seemed to know what he was talking about.

"Yesterday," he said, "we briefed you on our destination, Bloodworld. We had received an alert by way of a message drone from naval assets at Gliese 581 telling us that ships believed to be operated by the Qesh had entered the system.

"Since that time, a second message drone has arrived from Salvation. Colonel Corcoran felt it important to fill you in on the latest."

We stood on a plain of black, rugged basalt at the edge of a cliff above a seething ocean. The city of Salvation, the Neoessenist capital, seemed to grow from the rocks a kilometer in the distance, a collection of white domes and truncated pyramids emerging from a cliff face beyond the sprawl of a small spaceport. The red dwarf sun hung low in a deep green sky, partially obscured by the scudding purple cloud wrack. Even at this distance from the star—just twenty-two million kilometers—you could look straight into its ruddy face without discomfort and count the mottled black-on-red splotches of its starspots. Sky color depended on the angle of the incoming sunlight, and on this world it could be anything from sunset red to a deeply contrasting green.

A furious wind was blowing, so powerful that had I been there physically, it would have been difficult to stand. I was aware of it in sim because the viewpoint camera was trembling slightly as spray from the ocean whipped past, and the vegetation nearby—short, scrubby growths with feathery black leaves and rubbery stalks—was whipping back and forth, and, during the strongest gusts, lay flat against the ground.

Bloodworld, you see, is tidally locked with its primary, always turning the same side to face the sun, one hemisphere forever in daylight, the other in darkness. The colony had been established here in the so-called twilight band between day and night; as it circled its star, Bloodworld rocked back and forth, a nodding movement called libration, which resulted in the sun appearing to rise above the horizon for a few days, then setting, the landscape eternally balanced between fire and ice. The planet's atmosphere—one and half times denser than that at Earth's surface—expanded rapidly in the middle of the dayside, creating powerful winds blowing from day to night, winds that served to even out the planet's temperature extremes and keep all of the water and carbon dioxide from freezing out permanently over the nightside.

The image we were watching this time appeared to be from a handheld recorder, unsteady and with a slightly grainy resolution. Possibly it was from a suitcam, or it could have been an upload from someone's CDF RAM if they were equipped with the appropriate imaging hardware. There were data overlays at the upper right, green alphanumerics giving range and positional data, speed, temperature, and other information. Unlike three-sixty sims created by VR AIs, you could only look in the direction the camera was aimed, and the view wobbled and bounced as though the person carrying the camera was jogging over uneven ground toward the city, clearly pausing to lean into the wind with the strongest gusts.

"This vid," Carter said, "was taken by a Marine Specter probe inserted near the Salvation colony. It subsequently uploaded to an RS-90 off world, which in turn sent a message drone back to Earth. We only received the transmission last night. When the Command Constellation saw it, they ordered the recall."

The RS-90 Nightwraith was the Marine Corps' premiere

reconnaissance platform, stealthy, fast, and capable. It would have gone in carrying a number of Specters, robotic recon probes, designed to carry out extensive ground surveillance and transmit data back from the planet's surface. That explained the data overlays, which weren't usually a part of civilian vid feeds. They were giving a weather report at the moment—forty-five Celsius—a bit on the warm side—with a wind speed of ninety-two kilometers per hour.

And then the camera panned to the left, looking out across the seething ocean, then angled up, aiming into the sky, and all I could see was the incoming alien ships.

There were three of them, polished silver reflecting the bloody light, essentially flattened disks with a central bulge and a bite taken out of the trailing edge. The sides curved downward, like small wings or auxiliary stabilizers. I could only guess at the size, but they looked *big* for atmospheric vessels—maybe 100 meters or more across. They were using plasma thrusters to lower themselves gently toward the ground, as clouds of tiny glittering craft spilled from vents or ports along their undersides; I could see the swirling clouds of dust being raised by their jet wash as they settled down one after another on the spaceport in the distance. Human figures were running in confusion among the buildings, looking slow and clumsy in heavy environmental suits. The buildings of the colony began exploding one after another, with sharp flashes and fast-expanding pressure waves clearly defined by the thick, wet air. Each blast geysered a cloud of smoke and debris hurtling into the red sky, clouds that then tattered away with the wind.

The camera jerked and spun; the landscape blurred for an instant with the movement. In another direction, more of the disk vessels were settling to the ground.

An armored figure appeared: gleaming overlapping segments covering a body several meters long. It might have been as big as an extinct Terran rhinoceros, but with a longer body and six legs. The upper body, like the forequarters of the mythical centaur, weaved back and forth, displaying a single centrally positioned arm. The grippers at the end were holding a weapon of some sort.

What sort we couldn't tell. An instant after seeing it, the scene dissolved into white static.

"The earlier reports," Captain Carter said, "have been confirmed with this transmission."

The static gave way to a VR simulation of the colony, fully interactive, the city domes and towers gleaming undamaged beneath the red sun.

"The armored figure you just saw was a Qesh warrior," Carter went on, "and the ships appear identical to the vessels designated as 'Rocs' encountered during our first contact with that species fifty-nine years ago. Clearly, the Qesh have entered the Gliese 581 system and landed a raiding party, at the very least . . . and possibly they have arrived with a full invasion force.

"Commonwealth Military Command is taking this *very* seriously. Our first contact with Qesh raiders took place at a star system ninety-four light years from Earth. Gliese 581, however, is just twenty light years from Sol, a near neighbor as interstellar distances go. Only eighty-eight other stars are closer. CMC is concerned that the human colony on Bloodworld, a network of cities and bases established pre-Protocol, might have navigational data that could lead the Qesh to Earth.

"Marine Deep Recon Force 7 is being deployed to Bloodworld for covert insertion and detailed surveillance in advance of a joint Navy-Marine operation to stabilize the situation."

An invasion, then. *Stabilize*, in mil-speak, would in this instance mean throwing the Qesh off of Bloodworld, or at the very least making certain they didn't pick up any clues to Earth's location.

"Questions?" Carter demanded. "Yes. Abrams."

From my vantage point, it looked like just me and Lieutenant Carter were standing on that rugged, basaltic plain, but his audience included all twelve hundred Marines and naval personnel on board the *Clymer*.

"Sir," the voice of Staff Sergeant Abrams said. "Are the locals white hats? Or black?"

"At this point, Staff Sergeant," Carter replied, "we have no idea. In fact, that's probably the main reason MRF-7 is going in first. Any planetary invasion force will have to know if we can count on the local population for logistical support and intelligence."

It seemed like kind of a dumb question at first. Blood-world was a human colony; that colony had been attacked by Imperial aliens, so of *course* they were on our side, "white hats," in Marine parlance. Right?

But as I thought about it, well, no question is truly dumb, and this one was smarter than most. Those colonists were members of a small and closely knit religious sect, and that fact alone threw the usual rules right out the airlock.

History is filled with examples of small religious groups that went against the mainstream, and which were willing to die for the privilege. Hell, Christianity started off as a Jewish splinter group with some strange ideas about the expected Messiah. The Essene community—after which the Neoessenes had patterned themselves—we *think* was another Jewish schismatic group that had moved out to the desert to live in communes rather than follow the dictates of the Jewish Temple priesthood.

And more recently you have the messianic cults of Jim Jones and David Koresh, the jihadists of the more extrem- ist versions of Islam, and the Aum Shinrikyo, the crazies in Japan who tried to usher in global Armageddon with a home-brewed nerve gas attack on five Tokyo subway trains. A century and a half later you have the neo-Luddie White Seraphim incident on Chiron. Human beings appear to be hardwired for an us-against-them religious mentality, which can be expressed as a fanaticism as destructive as any politi- cal movement.

I suddenly realized that the Commonwealth government must be having convulsions right now about whether those colonists *could* be trusted. Religious fanaticism by definition is irrational. If some of them thought God had told them to hand Earth's galactic coordinates over to the Qesh, what would they do?

Marine Recon 7 would be going in at least partly to determine whose side the locals were on. A secondary aspect to the op would be to try to convince them that their best bet lay in helping us if they seemed undecided.

A hearts-and-minds mission, then. Just freaking great.

"Training sims will begin tomorrow at 0900," Carter said.

The landscape receded suddenly, the surface of the planet dropping away to merge with a planetary graphic, a computer-generated map of Bloodworld showing terrain features crossed by lines of longitude and latitude. I was looking down on the planet's nightside, at a vast splash of glaciers radiating from the midnight area, amid ocean, bare rock, and ice-sheathed mountains.

"At this point in the planning process," Carter continued, as a green, curving line arced down across the glacier, approaching the planet's surface close to the horizon, "we are assuming a landing by D-Mist on the planet's nightside, with a combat skimmer approach to the twilight band."

The planet graphic rotated to show the narrow band circling the world from pole to pole, the narrow strip of approximately temperate surface between the heat of the daytime desert and the frozen ice of the night. Several cities were located there, balanced between light and the darkness.

"Enemy numbers and compositions are as yet unknown," Carter added. "The training sims will cover a variety of possible mission encounters and circumstances. Expect the sessions to continue until we're on our final approach. Other questions? Good. Carry on."

So that was it, then. My first combat insertion, and none of us had a clue as to what we would be up against. The Qesh would be bad enough; not knowing the human reaction to our arrival made the whole situation just a bit unnerving.

The Misty was a smaller cousin of the Cutlass TAV, a

trans-atmospheric lander designed to carry combat-ready troops from orbit to ground quickly and, so far as it was possible, invisibly. The name came from the craft's designation, D/MST-22, which stood for *deployment/maneuver skimmer transport*. Judging from what little we actually knew about the locals' technology, we should be able to slip through their detector net easily enough.

It was the Qesh we'd have to worry about during the approach.

The briefing feed released its hold on my brain, and I blinked, stretched, and sat up. Marines around me were sitting up as well. Sergeant Tomacek looked around and growled, "Where the fuck's Doc Doobie and his hooch?"

"Fuckin' A," Corporal Gregory agreed. "If the aye-ayes're gonna curdle my brain for the next twelve days, I want some anesthetic, know what I mean?"

"How about it, Doc?" a private named Kilgore asked, looking at me. "Where's your buddy?"

I checked my in-head tracker. Doob and the other Corpsmen on board the *Clymer* were all listed there, and a mental glance showed me the current location of each. Shit. The blip representing Dubois was inside his rack-tube in 3/19, snuggled up *very* close alongside the blip representing HM3 Carla Harper, the cute little pearl diver from *Clymer*'s lab.

Looked like he'd scored after all, and with a FAB, this time, honest-to-God flesh-and-blood, instead of a ViRsim lover.

"He's . . . busy," I told the Marines. "But I'm sure he'll be glad to break out the good stuff a little later."

Seeing those two green blips together bordered on TMI—too much information. I wasn't jealous . . . exactly. Carla was a cute little armful who definitely knew her Bac-T and cell chemistries, fun to talk to, easy on the optical nerves, and I imagine she'd be a bunch of fun to cuddle with in the rack. But I'd never tried to find out for myself, I suppose because I was still getting over Paula.

Damn, damn, damn. Here I was accelerating out beyond

the orbit of Mars, headed for the interstellar abyss and a deployment twenty light years from home, and I was still dragging *that* around.

GOD, HAD IT REALLY BEEN A WHOLE YEAR AGO THAT I LOST HER?

I'd joined the Navy early in 2241. Three months of Navy basic in San Diego, followed by six months of near-constant downloading at Corps School in San Antonio. I'd met Paula one afternoon shortly after starting Corps School. She was an AI programmer, a civilian G-7 working on-base with a love of history and an enchanting sense of fun. I was on liberty in downtown San Antonio—at the Alamo, in fact, the site of a famous last stand four centuries ago—when I bumped into her, literally, in the snack shop, and started discussing Davy Crockett and last stands and the park's ViR download recreations of the battle. We'd ended up in bed at a little park'n'fuck outside of SAMMC's main gate for what I'd thought at the time was just going to be a one-night stand.

Three years later—three *fantastic* years that had me thinking I was head-over-heels in love—she was dead.

I'd long since graduated from Corps School by then, but I was still stationed at SAMMC—the San Antonio Military Medical Center, located at Fort Sam Houston on the northeast edge of the city. I'd gone straight from Hospital Corps "A" school to hospital duty at the Navy Orbital Medical Facility in low Earth orbit for microgravity training, then back to SAMMC for Advanced Medical Technology School. Both NOM duty and AMT were "C" schools, and absolutely necessary if I was going to go FMF, and my download schedule was insane.

Busy? My God, I was taking so many training downloads and ViRsim feeds I didn't know who I was half the time. I was getting, I thought, just a taste of what physicians experience when they're running a half dozen live-in expert AIs. But Paula Barton was still with me despite the hours and the week-long stretch while I was in orbit. We were even talking about getting married, though marriage was considered to be a bit on the old-fashioned side, something for love-struck fluffies with big red hearts in their eyes.

I don't know about the hearts, but I was certainly love struck. My *caudate nuclei* were so saturated with dopamine my brain sloshed when I walked, and I had all the signs and symptoms that dreaded mental illness commonly called Being In Love.

So in the spring of '44 I was working at the SAMMC base dispensary, still assimilating those gigabytes of AMT data and waiting for my orders for Camp Lejeune. I had a weekend free and we decided to run up to Glacier's Edge on the Maine coast.

We caught the sub-O out of San Antonio for the twenty-minute flight to Boston. I had an electric eccount, of course, so I checked out the free e-car at the oport for the last leg of the trip up to Acadia. We oohed and ahhed at the 100-meter ice cliffs, of course, and did all the usual touristy things. Sunday morning, we drove out to the dometown of New Bar Harbor and rented a sailboat for a close-in run along the glacier coming down off Schooner Head and Mount Champlain.

She was a four-meter day sailor, sloop-rigged, and with a level-two AI smart enough to take over the sail-handling if the human passengers didn't know what they were doing. I'd had some sailing experience already, so the AI was on standby and we were catching a gentle, cold breeze off the ice, making our way south along the ice-cloaked Mount Desert coast.

And Paula dropped her sandwich.

She had a puzzled look on her face. "I can't feel my right hand," she said, and when she tried to pick her sandwich up off the deck, her fingers refused to cooperate.

It took me a moment, though, to catch on that something was really *wrong* . . . but when she slumped over on the seat next to me, a shock ran through me that I will never, ever forget.

Oh, God, no! No! No! . . .

I dropped the tiller and scooped her up in my arms. Her eyes were glassy, and the right pupil was enormous, the left one small, giving her face an oddly lopsided look. Then I realized that half of her face was drooping, that she was trying to say something out of the left side of her mouth while the right side hung dead and useless.

I couldn't understand the words, but I finally caught on to what was happening.

"AI!" I screamed. "Connect with Emergency Services!"

"I'm taking control of sails and helm, Mr. Carlyle," the boat told me.

"Damn it, I need a link to Emergency Services!"

My in-head circuitry had various radio channels, including communication. It even gave me a navigational fix off of the space elevator, but I was out of range for voice communications.

"What course would you like me to set?" the oat asked me.

"Emergency! Voice! Channel!"

"Do you wish a voice channel with New Bar Harbor?"

"Yes! Yes!"

"Who would you like to speak with?"

"Emergency Medical, damn it!"

"Connecting with Emergency Medical Services."

At last!

"This is Emergency Medical Services, Portsmouth," a voice said in my head at last. "What is the nature of your emergency?"

"I've got a twenty-five-year-old female!" I screamed. "She's having a stroke!"

It took almost twelve minutes for a med-rescue lifter out of Portland Medical to home in on us. During that time, I'd pawed through the on-board medikit—which turned out to be stocked with preprogrammed nano set to close wounds, stop bleeding, and treat sunburn, frostbite, and headaches.

I didn't even have a CAPTR. I had nothing, could do nothing. The feeling of helplessness was overwhelming, terrifying, and savage.

The med-rescue lifter homed in on our sailboat, coming in 10 meters above the chop. Under the lifter's control, the boat's AI retracted the sail and lowered the mast so that the lifter could glide in and hover directly overhead. A grapple frame came down, closed in around and under the sailboat, and hauled us aboard right out of the water.

But by the time they had Paula hooked up to life support, there was no life left *to* support.

And they didn't have a CAPTR either. Not too surprising, I suppose; that technology is still pretty new, and the frontier along the edge of the ice sheet can be decades out of date. But I was left grasping for a reason, *any* reason for what happened, like a fish trying to breath air.

For a long time, I blamed the North Hemisphere Reclamation Project.

I know, I know, it's all perfectly safe. But there've been stories around for centuries about how HFMR—high-frequency microwave radiation—can harm people, causing everything from cancer, Alzheimer's, heart attacks, learning disabilities, and high blood pressure to, well, TIAs and massive cerebral hemorrhage—*strokes*, in other words. The earliest studies go back to the early twenty-first century, maybe earlier, when technologies like cell phone towers were first coming on-line. In four centuries, there's never been a solid, proven link, but there was a lot of controversy on the topic when they started beaming both optical and microwave wavelengths down from the Geosynch solar reflector arrays.

For a century, now, we've slowly been winning the global climate battle against the New Ice Age, partly by warming the waters of the North Atlantic, and partly by focusing heat on the edge of the ice sheets, from Vancouver to Maine. Paula and I both were picking up some microwaves as we toured the edge of the ice cliffs, of course. That second sun in the southern sky, forty or so degrees above the horizon, marked the reflector array at Geosynch halfway up the space elevator, but any harmful microwave component was supposed to be so diffuse it shouldn't have caused a problem.

The nasty high-energy stuff is all focused farther north, and we should have been getting only a little of the halo fringe off the Mount Desert ice sheet.

And maybe it wasn't microwaves at all. Maybe it *just happened* . . . which somehow was far more terrifying. If the dearest person in your life is going to die in your arms, you want there to be a *reason*.

I came real close to dropping out of FMF after that.

Hell, I came pretty close to dying myself.

Chapter Six

I'D BEEN LIVING WITH PAULA'S MEANINGLESS DEATH FOR THE NEXT year, which I suppose was better than the alternative, which was *not* living with her death. There was a time, there, after I got back to SAMMC, when I was thinking seriously of checking myself out. It's simple enough to disable the safeguards in an N-prog, and custom-tailor a few billion nanobots to take you down into coma-level sleep before quietly shutting down all your CNS and cardiac functions. No pain, no awareness, *nothing*. You just go to sleep and never wake up. After about five minutes with no blood flow, your brain starts dying, degrading to the point where you can't even capture the cerebral pattern any longer.

God, I wanted to die.

The problem was that I was afraid I would wake up.

I'd never been very religious. My parents were Reformed Gardnerians, which meant they believed in reincarnation, among other things. I'd never thought that much about it one way or another. So far as I was concerned, I'd live the usual three or four hundred years, then die, and then I'd find out what happened next, assuming that new medical advances hadn't extended the expected human life span even further. No problem either way.

But I *did* start thinking about it after I lost Paula, thinking about it a lot, usually when I was alone in my rack-tube back at SAMMC, lying there in the claustrophobic dark thinking through, step by step, how I could reprogram my N-prog to let me kill myself. What if my folks were *right*? I'd slip off into a coma, the 'bots would shut me down . . . only that wouldn't be the end. I'd wake up on the Other Side, realizing that whatever lessons I'd been supposed to face in *this* life were still there waiting for me. Shit, I might have to go through the whole thing all over again. You know what they say about reincarnation. It's the belief that you keep coming back again and again and again until you get it *right*.

Worse than that, though: What if the pain didn't go away?

The fact that Paula might be waiting for me on the Other Side did occur to me, of course, and for a while, there, it made the nanobot option damned attractive, let me tell you. I got as far as actually working out the program algorithms for my N-prog and assembling the hardware I would need.

But I didn't do it. I couldn't. I was afraid of the pain that went on and on, but I was afraid of the idea of dying, too. I didn't want to live without her, but I didn't want to die, either.

It didn't help that I knew exactly where those feelings of loss and emptiness were coming from physically. We've known for several centuries now about the role played by the caudate nuclei—there are two of them, in either half of the brain—in the messy addiction we commonly refer to as being in love. Dopamine—that same neurotransmitter that Howell used to o-loop himself into convulsions—is emitted by the VTA and other areas of the brain and floods the caudal regions, which are tied in with the VTA circuit. Under the dopamine's influence, we're filled with an intense energy, exhilaration, focused attention, and the motivation to win awards in the form of attention and approval from our love interest. We're able to stay up all night, to be bolder than usual, even to run insane risks when we're showing off . . . all for the sake of love. Being in love, it turns out, actually *is* closely related to being addicted to drugs—and the withdrawal when the love interest drops you or dies can be as painful and drawn out as going cold turkey on a physical addiction.

The first week, I was numb. They gave me ten days' compassionate leave. The funeral was there in San Antonio; after that, I went home to Ohio. I don't remember a whole lot about that time, to tell the truth.

By the time I got back, my orders for North Carolina were in. Still feeling numb, but no longer thinking of ways to turn off the pain, I hopped the sub-O for Wilmington, and a billet with FMF Training Command.

And after that, I was way too busy to think that much about what had happened in Maine.

But one thing stayed with me, and continued to gnaw at me throughout the course. I'd come up short when Paula got hit with the stroke. Yeah, there'd been technical difficulties with a poorly programmed AI on the boat, and, yeah, there's not a lot I could have done, even if we'd been shoreside in a hospital. But Gods, that feeling of abject helplessness . . .

It had me wondering if I was cut out at all for FMF.

SIX DAYS AFTER LEAVING STARPORT, WE WERE TEN ASTRONOMICAL units out from the sun, beyond the orbit of Saturn and traveling at better than 5,000 kilometers per second. The VR sim downloads were relentless and demanding, one possible scenario following the next as the training AIs hammered us with tactics while at the same time probing for weakness.

I think I did okay on the general stuff, treating Marines for a variety of wounds or other injuries while going on simulated patrols across simulated landscapes and encountering simulated ambushes. We must have approached the city of Salvation in fifty different situations—with the inhabitants welcoming us, with the inhabitants opening fire as we drew near, with the Qesh already in possession of the city and the sky patrolled by armored Qesh fliers. In fact, most of the ViRsims had the Qesh already in the city and waiting for us. By the time we made the transition to Alcubierre warp, after all, they'd already been on the planet for a couple of weeks.

One and a half billion kilometers from Sol, the local metric of space was flat enough that the *Clymer* could gather her figurative skirts up around her and slip into her own private universe. Nothing in the universe, neither material nor energy, can travel faster than light, but there's nothing in the universal rules and regs that prevents *space* from doing so. In fact, we know that the fabric of space expanded far faster than *c* during the fraction of a second of universal inflation immediately after the big bang. The Alcubierre Drive, named for the Mexican physicist who first outlined the concept late in the twentieth century, enveloped the starship in tightly folded space. The ship is not moving at all relative to the space within which it's resting; the bubble around it, however, slides through normal space at high multiples of the speed of light, and just happens to carry the motionless starship with it.

The idea is so weirdly counter-intuitive it makes my brain hurt. Fortunately, I just had to worry about field medicine, first aid, and the occasional dopamine cascade, not advanced gravitational topology or torsion-field manipulation.

On the sixth day, we folded into our Alcubierre bubble; on the seventh, we arrived at Bloodstar, 20.3 light years away.

IT LOOKS," PRIVATE HUTCHISON SAID, "LIKE A BIG RED EYE. *STARING* at us."

We were in the squad bay, looking at the image projected on the viewall bulkhead. Gliese 581, the Bloodstar, hung there in the middle of emptiness, a black-mottled orb the exact hue of arterial blood. The corona was easily visible as a pale haze surrounding the disk, as were the jets and loops of prominences extending above the rim. The surface of the disk appeared grainy, like it was made up of low-res pixels, and the starspots covered perhaps 10 percent of its face. A particularly large starspot grouping close to the center gave the impression of the jet-black pupil of a titanic, bloody eye.

And it *was* watching us, or so it seemed.

"This is the magnified view from the bridge, Hutch,"

Gunnery Sergeant Hancock told him. "We're still a long way out—over three AUs. Our naked eyes would see it from here as just a bright red speck."

Gliese 581 only possessed about three tenths of Sol's mass, so the flat metric the astrogators were always looking for went all the way in almost to the three-AU mark—3.1 to be exact—or about 464 million kilometers. The small Navy-Marine task force had emerged back into normal space hours ago, the ships shedding their excess velocity with the dissipation of the spacial torsion field. They retained a velocity of some hundreds of kilometers per second, however, as they hurtled in toward the red dwarf star. Falling tail first, they switched on their Plottel space drives and decelerated, backing down the descending slope at a steady 1 G.

Gunny Hancock thoughtclicked a display icon, and the looming image of the red dwarf dwindled into a graphic of the Gliese 581 system, the planetary orbits marked by red circles with the star at the center. Bloodstar has six planets, all of them tucked in next to their primary so tightly that the fifth planet out has an orbit closer to its sun than Mercury's is from Earth's, and even Niffelheim, the frigid outermost planet, is as far from Gliese 581 as Venus is from Sol.

Even from three AUs out, it was clear that the Qesh were in the Gliese 581 system in force. I could see a swarm of white points around the fourth planet out, each tagged by alphanumerics giving the object's mass, vector, and probable identification.

I looked at the faces of the Marines around me. Most of Bravo Company was there, I thought.

The compartment was crowded. Living space on board an interstellar transport like the *Clymer* is pretty cramped— witness the rank upon rank of rack-tubes in the berthing compartments—but the squad bays are a lot more spacious. Well, we still *call* them squad bays, for tradition's sake, but each is actually an open recreational compartment big enough to accommodate physically an entire Marine rifle company, and that's fifty or sixty men and women. The

deck can grow that many chairs for flesh-and-blood briefings, when we need them, and the viewall can project the
skipper's face for inspiring speeches, or show the tactical
situation, as now, as we dropped into the Bloodstar's inner
system.

Some of those faces showed fear, some curiosity, a few a
kind of smirking disdain. Most, though, had that matter-of-
fact aura of professionalism I'd come to associate with the
Marine Corps during the past year.

But *damn*, there were a lot of Qesh super-ships gathered
around Salvation.

"Just how good *are* the Jackers, anyway?" Corporal Masserotti asked. He was one of the smirking ones.

"Good enough," Hancock replied. "The EG puts them at
type 1.165 G, with an estimated tech level twenty, and that
data is from a long time ago."

Humankind was thought to be a type 1.012 C on the Encyclopedia Galactica's version of the Kardashev scale, with
a TL of around eighteen. In other words, we had FTL and
quantum power taps too, but theirs were quite a bit ahead
of ours, the equivalent, possibly, of a couple of centuries.
Estimating the relative technological capabilities of two
mutually alien civilizations was always more guesswork
than not. Differences in culture, language, and even biology could either mask or exaggerate differences. Take the
T-Cets, who evolved just a few light years from Earth within
the deep abyss of their world ocean. No fire, and apparently
no nuts-and-bolts engineering, but they're so far ahead of us
in chemistry and biological technology that we still don't
understand more than ten percent of what we see in the
Encyclopedia Galactica, and attempts to communicate with
them directly have consistently failed.

In warfare, a difference of only one on the tech level scale
can mean a *lot*; think about what would happen if the atmospheric fighters from the mid-twentieth century tangled with
the wood-and-fabric biplanes of just thirty years earlier.

We knew damned little about the Qesh or the nature of

their technology. Their warships, though, were *big*, sleek, smooth-surfaced, flattened cigars comprised of domes, flutings, sponsons, and blisters that could be as much as five kilometers in length. Even the smallest were longer and more massive than the *Clymer*, and our intelligence people believed that all of their warships were built around powerful mass drivers that could slam twelve-ton masses into their targets with a kinetic yield equivalent to a small nuclear warhead. We didn't know what the Qesh called their own starships. Our intel people had given them designations taken from human mythology, names like Behemoth and Leviathan, to classify them roughly by their sizes.

The graphic was totaling up the types of ships present around Bloodworld—fourteen Leviathans, eight Behemoths, twenty-one Titans, and even one Jotun.

It was a full-strength predarian warfleet.

They appeared to be dismantling the planet's moons.

"Hawking Raiders," Lance Corporal Benjamin Andrews said. There was just the slightest tremor behind his words. "How are we supposed to face *them*?"

More than two hundred years ago, no less an authority than Stephen Hawking, one of the most brilliant physicists ever to delve into cosmology, had suggested that humans might not want to make themselves known to the universe at large. According to him, an alien interstellar civilization might very well care nothing for other sapient species, but travel from star to star stripping worlds of their resources, perhaps preying on less-advanced beings. More primitive races would be unable to stand up to a sufficiently advanced technology, would be unable to stop them from extinguishing all life on the target planet.

Hawking's warning had largely been ignored. After all, a sufficiently advanced species ought to be advanced *ethically* as well as technologically, right? But then we learned how to read the EG, and we started encountering some of the myriad races scattered across our part of the galaxy. We learned that each species out there was ethical within its own framework, and that those frameworks might not have room for other civilizations, or for competition. There were, we learned, entire cultures Out There that roamed the Galaxy in monster fleets, taking apart worlds for whatever they needed. *Predarians*, we called them. Predator barbarians.

And the name, along with "Hawking Raiders," stuck.

"We're not going to face them," Hancock replied. "At least, not right away. And not *directly*."

"That's right," Staff Sergeant Thomason added. "This is MDR. We go in quiet. We go in lethal."

"Recon rules the night!" several voices chorused.

"*Ooh-rah!*" chorused some others.

I wondered how "rule the night" would apply to the Bloodworld's twilight zone. I didn't say anything, though. The Marines were cruising just then on pure, raw emotion.

From the look of those animated graphics on the squad bay viewall, we were hurtling tail first into a nest of hornets. The situation wasn't quite as bad as it seemed, though, because the chances were good that they couldn't see us. Under Plottel Drive, we were warping our own little patch of space to kill our velocity, but the effect couldn't be detected—at least, we were pretty sure it couldn't be detected—across more than a few tens of thousands of kilometers. Our ships had deployed their stealth screens as soon as they entered normal space. Stealth screens didn't render a ship optically invisible, but they did drink up radar, microwave, and even long infrared. As for optical wavelengths, it's amazing how *tiny* a starship is, even a ship as large as the *Clymer*, within a given volume of interplanetary space. The outer hull is a deep, light-drinking black, and you practically have to be on top of the ship to see her. Unless she closed to within a very few kilometers of an enemy vessel, or by very bad luck the enemy happened to notice when she occulted a star, the *Clymer* was damned near invisible to begin with.

So how were we able to see all of those Qesh vessels? Well, they weren't trying to be inconspicuous, for one thing.

Each one was cheerfully emitting a cacophony of micro-wave and infrared wavelengths, pinging one another with radar and lidar, and generally doing just about everything short of hanging out the "Welcome Earth Commonwealth" signs and setting off fireworks. Our AIs could take that data from long-range sensor scans, work out the enemy vessels' sizes and masses, and display the distillate on the graphic projection.

In fact, I had the distinct impression that they were deliberately showing off.

"So how come the bad guys aren't playing it safe and putting out their stealth screens?" Corporal Latimer asked. She shook her head, as if exasperated. "I mean, it doesn't make sense. Why show us their numbers like that?"

"Yeah," Sergeant Gibbs added. "It's pretty freakin' stupid if you ask me."

"Nobody asked you, asshole," Tomacek told him.

"It's a fair question," Hancock said. "And we might have a fair answer if we knew more about the bastards. Best guess is, the Jackers are supposed to be a warrior culture. Think seventeenth-century Samurai in Japan, or maybe ancient Visigoths or Huns. Hiding, sneaking around, that's for cowards. Their culture demands that they show themselves to the enemy."

"The art of intimidation," I suggested.

"It's *still* freakin' stupid!"

"Uh-huh," Hancock agreed. "But there's something else to consider, too."

"What's that, Gunny?"

"What makes you think we're seeing *all* of them right now?"

We all grew a bit more quiet at that as we studied the graphic.

Maybe that massive fleet we could see orbiting Gliese 581 IV was the bait.

"So," Andrews said, "we're outnumbered *and* outteched."

"Maybe so," Hancock said. "But we do have one important advantage."

"Yeah, Gunny? What's that?"

"We're *Marines*."

"That's ay-ffirmative." Thomason laughed. "The poor bastards'll never know what hit 'em."

Sometimes the sheer arrogance of the Marines amazes me.

On the other hand, maybe it's not arrogance when it's true.

Since Captain Samuel Nicholas recruited the first Continental Marines at Philadelphia's Tun Tavern in 1775, the Corps has been America's first and best line of defense. Are American interests at risk? Are American citizens threatened? Does the Army need a beachhead? *Send in the Marines* has been the confident response across the past five hundred years. Now that the United States has become a part of the Terran Commonwealth, there've been frequent calls for the Corps to join with the marine forces of other nations and reorganize as the Commonwealth Marines.

You'll notice that despite the ebb and flow of politics over the years, they are still the United States Marine Corps.

Unyielding, uncompromising, never swayed by fad or fashion, utterly and sincerely certain of themselves, of their esprit, of their essential nature and reason for being, the U.S. Marines remain what is perhaps *the* preeminent elite fighting force of Humankind.

After training with them, after serving with them, I love them. Every last damned one of them.

Even the assholes.

"Enough lollygagging," Hancock growled at us. "If you ladies and gentlemen will remember, we have a training schedule to keep. So all of you amphibious green rabbits pop back into your holes and jack in!"

An hour later, I was packed into a D/MST-22 Manta Ray TMV with forty-seven battle-armored Marines . . . or so it seemed, as the *Clymer*'s training AI fed images, sensations, and BTL impressions into my quivering gray matter.

I say "BTL," meaning "better than life," in the popular lexicon, but "better," here, is a subjective term wide open to debate.

It certainly looked and felt like the real thing.

The Cutlass I'd ridden down to the surface of Mars the week before was a TAV, a trans-atmospheric vehicle, meaning it could travel from the surface of a planet to orbit and back, passing through the planet's atmosphere to do so. A D/MST-22 TMV was a bit more sophisticated, a trans-*media* vehicle, capable of operating in any of several environments—in vacuum, in atmosphere, or under water. Shaped vaguely like its extinct namesake, the Manta Ray had a flattened body and large, triangular wings curving downward at the tips. It carried one full Marine platoon packed into its payload deck—forty-eight men and women with armor, exos, and weapons. Somewhere out there in the watery darkness around us were three more Mantas, carrying the rest of Bravo Company—First and Third Platoons, plus the HQ element.

It wasn't like the Black Wizards were traveling in comfort.

We'd inserted on Bloodworld's nightside, 2,000 kilometers from the twilight zone. Using the laser cutters on the Mantas' bows, we'd melted down through a thin patch of the ice covering Bloodworld's ocean, and were traveling now 100 meters beneath the ice, through a realm of absolute and frigid darkness. According to my in-head, almost ten hours had passed.

I was wondering how much time had *really* passed.

You see, a virtual reality simulation will override your own timekeepers. Sitting there in my armor, wedged in shoulder to shoulder between Sergeant Leighton and Private Marshall, I could remember climbing into the Misty in orbit, remember the meteoric descent across the planet's nightside, remember the ice-melting op and the descent, remember every damned, cramped, claustrophobic minute of the ten-hour passage through the dark.

In fact, the chances were good that the AI program had simply slipped in every couple of simulated hours or so and updated our memories. We *remembered* all of that time having passed, but memories are as easy to create as are the illusions of reality. Easier, even. It's possible to use 'bots to manufacture the appropriate neuropeptides, possible to implant long memory sequences, even to include remembered conversations and cognition.

This is especially true if the memories happen to be of a time when nothing much is happening. It's amazing how hours of thumb-twiddling boredom collapse into a few discrete image sequences. Think about it. A typical period of dreaming lasts a few seconds, and yet when we wake up, we remember, or *think* we remember, long and complicated sequences of dream imagery.

The brain sucks when it comes to keeping accurate track of time.

What all of this meant was that my back and legs ached from being wedged into one position for too long, and I could look back in my mind to what seemed like an eternity of just sitting there. I could remember playing some in-head games, pulling a couple of articles on nanomedicine from my RAM, and engaging in a long conversation with Sergeant Leighton on our private channels, wandering from philosophy to combat to emotional trauma to Marine training and back to philosophy again.

"Hang on, back there," a voice called in my head, interrupting the memories. "We're going up on the roof."

The deck tilted beneath our feet, and I could feel the surge of acceleration. It didn't feel like they were stopping to melt a hole through the ice sheet, so they must have found a patch of ice-free ocean or a polinya, and were heading up to grab atmosphere.

I clicked in to the Misty-D's bow camera for a look outside. We had that option, of course, when the tactical situation permitted it, but for the past ten hours there'd been nothing to see but blackness.

Now, though, I could see a wavering patch of blood-red light up ahead. It expanded rapidly . . . and then light exploded around me as the Manta broke through the surface and emerged into the open air.

The light wasn't all that was exploding. The Qesh were waiting for us.

Freaking great, I thought. *A doomsday scenario.*

They threw those at us in training every once in a while, simulating a battle or a situation that was impossible to survive. They called it a *Kobayashi Maru*, though the origin of that term was lost—probably in the pre-computer confusion of World War II. The theory behind it was simple enough; if we'd already struggled through the worst possible scenario, anything else would be tame by comparison when we faced it for real.

We emerged from the ocean close to a black, rocky beach. We were well into the twilight zone here. The bloody sun was hanging just above the horizon directly ahead, and deep purple clouds boiled across an emerald sky. A quintet of immense, bronze-colored Daitya weapons platforms hovered above the higher ground to the east, spread out to embrace that ragged patch of beach.

The Manta carrying First Platoon was hit almost the instant it clawed into the air, the fireball smearing across the sky in a spray of white-hot fragments. The Mantas carrying Third Platoon and our HQ were hit two seconds later, almost simultaneously.

Then we were hit, but not badly enough to knock us down. Our AI pilot kept us airborne long enough for us to reach the beach, though we covered the last fifty meters in a couple of skips across the dark water.

The Manta's hull rippled open while we were still ten meters in the air. We dropped a couple of meters before our jets kicked in and gave us a semblance of a soft landing, scattered along that beach. I landed in ankle-deep water just short of the shoreline, dropping to my hands and knees as a pressure wave thundered through thick atmosphere. Our

Manta had just exploded almost directly above and ahead of us.

Second Platoon Marines were all around me, struggling to get to their feet after their unceremonious ejection and drop. Fire swept across the beach; someone was shrieking in agony, the scream going on and on and on.

"Corpsman!" someone yelled, and I slogged forward out of the water, already reaching for my M-7 kit. "Corpsman front!"

A lot of Marines were down already. I couldn't see the energy bolts from those hovering weapons platforms, of course, but arcs of molten rock and vitrified sand criss-crossed the beach already. A Marine thrashed and scrabbled ten meters ahead . . . correction, it was *half* of a Marine. His legs were gone, burned away at the hips.

I moved toward him, hunching over as if I were pushing ahead into a savage wind. The surface gravity was almost twice Earth-standard. My exoskeleton compensated, but I could still feel the drag of the extra weight on my torso and head. I felt sluggish.

I could see Qesh infantry ahead, like giant caterpillars in segmented armor, rippling across the beach toward my position.

White flame engulfed me. . . .

Chapter Seven

I WOKE UP WITHIN THE NARROW, CYLINDRICAL CONFINES OF MY TUBE-rack, heart pounding, palms sweaty, and scared out of my mind. I took a long moment to get my breathing under control, and bring down that shrieking flight-or-fight urgency that was permeating my brain, throat, and gut.

It was all a dream. . . .

"Jesus Freaking Christ!"

When my heart rate was under control again, I dilated my tube open and hauled myself out. I fumbled for a suitpatch in my locker, slapped it against my bare chest, and let the Marine utilities flow into place over my body. I then made my way a bit unsteadily out to the squad bay.

The viewall was displaying Bloodstar, still shrunken, smaller, more distant than what I'd seen in the sim. Several Marines were there already, the ones designated as KIA in the disastrous landing scenario. As each man was "killed," he awoke in his tube and, eventually, wandered out here.

"Hey, Doc!" Tomacek called. "Don't you know it's against regs for the Corpsman to get himself killed?"

"Someone forgot to tell the Qesh," I replied.

"ViRsim Qesh don't count," Masserotti said.

"Fuck," Andrews said, laughing. "Sims're BTL, right? Better than the real thing!"

"S'right!" Gibbs added. "You're in big trouble now, Doc!"

Dubois wandered into the squad bay, looking as rattled as I felt. "Someone get the number of that Daitya," he said.

"How'd they nail you, Doob?" I asked.

"We were hit just coming in over the beach. The Misty spilled us, and exploded a moment later. I was still in the water when a bunch of Qesh infantry came storming in."

Oh, right. I should have realized. Dubois was the Corpsman for First Platoon, I was in Second. His experience had been exactly the same as mine, because the AI running that little horror show was doing some clever editing to conserve bandwidth. I'd seen the other three Mantas get scratched, then experienced having mine shot out from under me. But First and Third Platoons, plus the HQ element, all had experienced the same point of view, the same tailor-made nightmare. Everyone in four mantas had felt what it was like to be on board the last surviving Manta, to emerge from the sea in a firestorm of high-energy weaponry, to face armored Qesh warriors descending onto the beach beneath that bloody, blotch-faced sun.

"Shit, I got zapped before I could get to my first patient!" Dubois complained.

"Same here," I said. "Damn it, it wasn't *fair*."

I knew how stupid that sounded as soon as the words were out. Chief Garner was sitting in a recliner in front of the viewall display, and he turned at that.

"Jesus, Carlyle! You think it's supposed to be *fair*?"

Each platoon had one Corpsman assigned to it. Chief Garner was our senior Corpsman, assigned to the company's headquarters platoon.

"No, Chief. I've learned a *few* things since I was sworn in."

"That particular skull-fuck is a worst-case *Kobayashi Maru*," Garner told me. "They want to know how well our Marines can get on without us."

"And we're supposed to learn something from that?" I asked.

"You're supposed to learn that in combat *nothing* ever

goes down like it's supposed to. It's all blood and noise and terror, and you have to slog ahead and do the best you can, no matter what."

"But they *killed* me five seconds after I hit the beach!"

"So maybe it's not about you for a change."

I suppose it made sense. Corpsmen have been the medics for the Marines for centuries now, at least since World War I. Marines do receive training in basic first aid, though, for those times when a Corpsman's not available.

"So . . . hey! Who was the Marine who had both of his legs shot off?" I asked the compartment at large.

No one admitted to the fact right away. Corporal Gregory raised his hand. "I was hit in one leg," he said. "Wasn't too bad, but I yelled for you, and I saw you coming toward me. Then we both got flamed by one of those Jack-bastards."

And that, of course, was an important distinguishing feature of ViRsims. *I'd* seen a Marine thrashing around on the beach with both legs completely gone, his combat armor guillotined shut across his thighs to maintain internal atmosphere. *He'd* experienced a minor wound, nothing serious at all.

They say that none of the witnesses to an accident ever remember the same events the same way. Maybe so, but that's nothing compared to what you get in a group-training sim download. There's literally no way to line up the facts about what actually happened, because everyone is getting a different feed.

Well, hey. Maybe that's not so different from real life after all, but it sure can be freaking confusing when a bunch of you are dissecting it later.

"What's the problem, Carlyle?"

It was Chief Garner. He'd walked up behind me and put a beefy hand on my shoulder.

"Nothing, Chief. Well . . . not really."

"Spit it out, son."

I glanced around the compartment, making sure no one else was close enough to overhear. "Shit, Chief. I'm *scared*."

"Glad to hear it. You wouldn't be human if you weren't."

"No . . . I mean I'm scared of fucking up."

"Doc Francis put the fear of God in you?"

I blinked. "You *know* about that?"

"What do *you* think?"

He would . have downloaded the report, yeah. And of *course* he would have been following Howell's case. Chief Garner was the enlisted department head for the whole company. Hell, there were probably AI recordings of the whole emergency up on B Deck. Garner had downloaded them, allowing him to literally watch over my shoulder the whole time.

I nodded. "I know. Look, Chief, I'm not FMF yet, y'know? I'm not sure I have what it takes."

"You've been through most of the training, Carlyle. You've missed, what? A training deployment to Europa, and your final boards. If you don't have what you need now, you *ain't* gonna find it."

"That's just it. What if I don't?"

Garner sighed. "And I don't have any answers for you." He got a kind of faraway look in his eyes for a moment, and I knew he was accessing records from somewhere. *My* records.

"You've been consistently top ten percent in your class," he said. "First in A and P. Third in exoenvironmentals. Fourth in nanotech applications." He pursed his lips. "Twenty-first out of forty in S and T. You could use some work there. You want to go greenside, you need to be up on your Strategy and Tactics. Third in biochem, though. That's *good*."

"Yeah. Like my head is so damned stuffed with crap it's going to explode. But my anatomy and physiology scores didn't help when I saw Howell at sick call. I gave him *aspirin*."

"I know," he told me. "There's a *big* difference between head knowledge and gut knowledge." He held up his hands, one forefinger pointed at his forehead, the other at his stomach. "That much, and it might as well be a hundred light years. But it'll come together for you, once you deploy for real."

I must not have looked like I was convinced. He grinned. "Put it this way, Carlyle. We've taught you everything you need to know for you to swim. Now we're going to toss you into the deep end, kerplunk. It's scary as hell, yeah. But the training *is* there, you *do* know what you need to know. You'll be fine."

I wasn't so sure. His analogy wasn't very comforting, because knowing how to swim isn't about knowing how to do the strokes or knowing that most people tend to float naturally. It's about knowing in your *muscles*, knowing in the autonomous portions of the brain. I knew what he was saying—that once I was on that fire-swept beach for real, the training—all of those sims and all of those hours of downloads—it would kick in and I'd find myself doing what I'd been trained to do.

But why the hell did I keep seeing Paula lying on the well deck of that sailboat in Maine, staring up at the unforgiving sky?

WE WEREN'T HEADING FOR BLOODWORLD. OUR FIRST STOP WOULD BE Gliese 581 VI.

In the earliest days of the great extrasolar planet hunt, back when we were just learning how to detect the planets circling other suns by their gravitational effects on their primaries, the International Astronomical Union had laid down the rules for cataloguing and naming new planets as they were discovered. Astronomers gave newfound planets lowercase letters to identify them, and did so *in the order in which they were discovered*. The star itself—in this case, Gliese 581—was listed as *a*; the first planet discovered in the system was Gliese 581 b; the second planet c, and so on.

I suppose it made sense to the astronomers of the IAU, but eventually, this led to an ungodly tangle that made no sense at all, especially once we began actually physically exploring those planetary systems closest to us. For Gliese

581, for instance, the discovery of its first planet, b, was followed by c and then d, all in nice, neat order from innermost to outermost . . . but then planet e was detected with an orbit *inside* that of b. Not long after that, planet g was picked up orbiting between c and d, and planet f was found well outside of d, so the planetary order ran, from innermost to outermost, e, b, c, g, d, and f.

It didn't help that planets g and f were, for several decades, unconfirmed, and official lists of the Gliese 581 planetary system kept losing one or both planets, then regaining them, and the whole issue wasn't settled once and for all until the first interstellar survey actually reached the star, early in the twenty-second century.

What made the old system even more confusing was the fact that the stars in multiple star systems were *also* given letter IDs. You might have a multiple star system, like Alpha Centauri, with the three stellar members designated as A, B, and C, and so the first planet to be discovered there would be labeled with a lowercase *d*. And when astronomers began detecting *moons* around all of those new planets, things *really* got twisted.

Which is why, by the time the survey ship *Human Endeavor* reached Gliese 581, planets were given *numbers*—expressed as Roman numerals—showing their order out from their primary rather than their order of discovery. The three suns of Alpha Centauri are A, B, and C, while Chiron is designated *Alpha Centauri A II* and *not* as *d*. Lowercase letters are reserved for the moons: Chiron's three satellites, Hippe, Chariclo, and Carystus, are therefore designated as *Alpha Centauri A II a*, *b*, and *c*.

Much simpler, and much more usefully practical. I understand that the IAU still protests the change from time to time, but then, that august body was the obsessive-compulsive bunch that raised such a furor three and a half centuries ago by declaring that Sol IX was *not* a planet. They're hardcore traditionalists, and the old naming scheme goes back to the letter IDs given to the individual rings of

Saturn as they were discovered, a mishmash that puts the E ring innermost, the D ring outermost, and the C, B, A, F, and G rings in between, an order that hasn't been changed in three hundred years because no one but the astronomers have to keep track of them.

And so MRF-7 slipped silently into orbit around Gliese 581 *VI* rather than f, a frozen ice giant the *Human Endeavor* Expedition had named Niffelheim.

At about 108 million kilometers from Sol, the planet Venus has been trapped in a runaway greenhouse effect that has resulted in a surface temperature hot enough to melt lead, and with a surface pressure of around 91 atmospheres. Gliese 581 VI is less than six million kilometers farther out from its primary than is Venus—for all intents and purposes the same distance—but its climate is startlingly different. Its primary has a luminosity of just 0.013 of Sol, that's a bit over one percent. As a result, Niffelheim is an ice giant, a smaller version of Neptune with about eight times the mass of Earth, with a solid rock core smothered beneath 1,000 kilometers of ice and ice slush, and a dense and frigid soup of methane and ammonia for an atmosphere above that. Its primary is a sullen, ruby disk slightly smaller than the sun seen from Earth.

Niffelheim has rings, though the light level is so low it's tough to see them, and it possesses a small coterie of moons; Niffelheim-e is as large as the planet Mercury back home, ice sheathed and big enough to hold an atmosphere, mostly of nitrogen and methane. The surface temperature stands at around minus 200 degrees Celsius.

Of particular interest is the fact that tidal forces between Niffelheim and Niffelheim-e keep the moon's deep interior hot. The heat works its way up out of the core, and warms the surface a bit more than would be the case otherwise. According to the initial surveys, there's an ocean down there, liquid water maybe 100 kilometers deep, more water than is contained in all of the oceans of Earth, locked away beneath an ice cap ten kilometers thick.

It turns out that Niffelheim-e, which we of course began calling "Hymie" before we even dropped into orbit, is a large version of Europa, one of the Jovian satellites back in the Sol system.

I wondered if there were local equivalents to the Europan Medusae undulating beneath the ice.

THE FLEET STAYED IN ORBIT AROUND HYMIE WHILE THE SUFACE EXPLO-ration team shuttled down to the surface in a Cutlass. Interstellar transports like the *Clymer* and the *Puller* and heavy cruisers like the *Tikki* are strictly orbit-to-orbit vessels, too clumsy and too massive to maneuver inside a planetary atmosphere. A second Cutlass carried forty tons of rawmat from the *Clymer*'s stores. We needed to grow a base on the surface, but the only building materials present were water ice, nitrogen, methane, and a few organics. We dumped the rawmat onto the icy surface and turned loose a few trillion nanocon 'bots; within a couple of hours, the 'bots had pulled carbon, iron, aluminum, and silica from the pile and grown them into a dome thirty meters across, complete with furnished interior compartments, including the lab, personal quarters and rec area, a heavily shielded power plant, and the big central moon pool. A portable nano air factory began pulling oxygen from water ice and nitrogen from the local atmosphere, until the dome was pressurized at one standard atmosphere.

We still all wore facemasks, though. There was a chance that there were toxins or free organics mixed in with the surface ice. The moon pool was a circular pit melted into the ice, perhaps five meters across and a meter deep.

"Why the hell do they call it a moon *pool*?" I asked. The exposed ice steamed in the warm air of the dome, though it was still so cold we didn't dare touch it with bare hands. The air inside the sealed chamber was frigid despite the efforts of the dome's power tap.

"It's an old term from back when they drilled for petroleum on the continental shelves," Chief Garner told me, his voice muffled a little by his mask. "The drilling platform or ship had an opening in the underside of its hull, see? The opening was filled with water, and they could lower the drill rig down through it. Some research vessels used them too, as sea access for divers or small submersibles."

"I pulled down a 'pedia reference from the ship's library," I said. "It talked about the title of some old book."

Garner nodded. "*The Moon Pool*, by Abraham Merritt. A very early example of twentieth-century horror."

"Horror?"

"Horror fiction. Really nasty things under the water pulled people down into the pool. And when they drilled through the ice on Europa, of course, they used a moon pool there inside the drilling chamber."

"And we found the Medusae."

"Exactly."

I shivered a bit, and not entirely from the cold. "Do you think there's anything like that here?"

Garner nodded in the direction of a heavy four-meter disk, a flattened cylinder suspended from gantry rails up by the ceiling of the compartment. "We'll know pretty soon, won't we?"

"I guess we will."

The stop at Hymie, I gathered, was so that our intelligence people could scope out the situation at Bloodworld from the covert safety of Niffelheim-e. At the moment, Planet IV was on the far side of the sun, but it would swing around to our side in another few days, allowing us to see what was going on around it from our base camp at Planet VI. In the meantime, the MRF's science department wanted to check out Hymie's iced-over ocean.

Our operational orders gave a couple of reasons for this. First and foremost, it was possible that the colonists on Bloodworld had established a secondary colony here. There were no records of such a thing, but it had been more than sixty years since Salvation's founding. It could have happened. If there was a human colony here, chances were good that it had been built beneath the ice, within the relative warmth and security of the world-ocean. When the Qesh arrived, such a colony could be expected to lie low and stay out of sight; by entering the ocean ourselves, we would be able to establish sonar contact with them in short order, and the MRF would be able to get some up-to-date intel from the locals.

But the second reason was the possibility of a new First Contact.

Since the final decades of the twentieth century, we've known that planets are shockingly common throughout the universe. Most stars have them; hell, the very first extrasolar planets we detected were orbiting neutron of a star 980 light years away from Earth. Apparently, they accreted out of the left-over debris from the supernovae that created the neutron star in the first place. If planets could form there, they could form anywhere.

And since the first manned expeditions to Mars in the mid-twenty-first cent, we've known that life is common as well. Right there in our own Solar System, we've found six different exotic biochemistries besides what's on Earth. There are the pseudobacterial mats beneath the Martian permafrost, which we first detected by the isolated puffs of methane they release into the thin air every once in a while. There are the aerial venerarchaea of the upper Venusian atmosphere, happily metabolizing sulfuric acid, water vapor, and sunlight. There are the Jovian aeoleaprotistae drifting on the high-altitude winds of Jupiter, with their enigmatic hints of more complex life farther down within the unreachable depths of the Jovian Abyss. There are the prometheaformes, digesting frigid methane lakes on Titan, and there are the vast and complex ecosystems discovered beneath the iced-over surfaces of both Europa and Enceladus.

And that's just what we've found so far; there are hints of other exotic ecosystems a hundred kilometers down within the liquid-water mantle of Pluto, and some inexplicable exotic nitrogen chemistry going on within the coldest real estate in the Solar System—Neptune's moon Triton. With seven—and possibly nine or more—examples of independent organic evolution just in our own system, it's clear that life will take hold in any environment where it has half a chance.

We discovered the third part of the equation in 2120, with the Olympus Expedition to Jupiter. Besides finding alien biomes in the Jovian atmosphere and beneath the ice of Europa, the Europan survey crew made first contact with what was *probably* another intelligent species.

Funny, isn't it? We *still* don't know for certain that the Medusae are sapient, at least in the way that humans usually define the term. We know they're thermovores, attracted by sources of heat. We know they appear to have a symbiotic relationship with something the survey team's survivors called ectoplasmic *kudzu*, which might be a different life form altogether, might be a kind of biological technology, or might even be something the Medusae exude from their own filmy bodies. *We just don't know*, even now, 125 years later.

Of course, ten years after the Olympus returned to Earth, the first AI translations of the Encylcopedia Galactica were published, and we discovered just how common intelligent life actually is across the Galaxy. The interesting thing was, however, that by far, the majority of the intelligent life out there does not live on planets like Earth. A lot of it is hydro-subglacean, meaning it lives in a layer of liquid water beneath the ice of frigid worlds and moons that are internally warmed either by tidal stresses or by the decay of radioactive elements in their cores.

Intelligent beings like *Homo sapiens*, evolved to live on the dry, open surface of their world, may in fact be relatively rare by comparison.

We don't know what the actual ratio might be; after all, very, very few subglaceans ever develop astronomy, radio telescopes, or space travel. The Encyclopedia Galactica lists a number of alien civilizations that live beneath the ice ceilings of their worlds—a few hundred, perhaps—but subglacean intelligence may outnumber other sapient life forms by many thousands to one. The Europan Medusae aren't listed on the EG, so far as we know, because they've never made their existence known to the universe at large.

Because of our own ignorance in the matter, the Commonwealth has made contact with subglacean intelligences a high priority. The base at Conamara Chaos, clinging upside down to the Europan ice cap above the sunless world-ocean abyss, has been studying the Medusae and their bewildering zoo of organic symbionts for a century, now. Conamara base had been the next destination for my FMF class, before the class was cancelled by events at Bloodstar. Our people and AIs there were still just trying to come up with a workable common language, and FMF students, among others, continued to work at trying to catalogue and understand the local biochemistry.

And now we were going to have a peek beneath the ice on Hymie, to see if there were similar exotic life forms down there. I think the Commonwealth government is lonely and looking for friends. We don't have many of those yet, out here among the uncaring stars.

"Okay!" someone shouted, her voice echoing within the moon pool chamber. "Lower away!"

The four-meter cylinder began lowering on its connector cables until it rested on the ice, nano-face down. A red light began flashing, together with the rasp of a Klaxon.

"Time to leave, Carlyle," Garner told me. "The drilling might release volatiles as the water ice separates. We don't want to be in here if it does, even with filter masks."

"How long will it take?"

The chief shrugged. "The nanodrill should descend at the rate of about four kilometers per hour. Seismic soundings suggest that the ice here is twelve kilometers thick. Do the math."

Three hours. "Well, I need to get outside and pull some samples anyway," I said.

"Stay warm," he told me.

STAY WARM. RIGHT. IT WAS MINUS TWO HUNDRED-SOMETHING OUT-side the dome. I grew myself an e-suit, stepped through the external lock, and trudged out across the surface ice. Calli Lewis went with me. Orders were strict. *No* one went outside alone. Our e-suits were tuned to bright orange, just in case someone had to come looking for us.

Niffelheim was a pale purplish half disk hanging above the horizon, imbedded in a deep ultramarine sky and illuminated by the bloody eye of its sun. A couple of smaller, inner satellites were visible as well, casting dark oval shadows against the cloud tops. The surface beneath our heavily insulated boots was ice beneath a few centimeters of snow. The stuff was loose enough to swirl around us in plumes and streams blowing on the thin wind.

What would happen, I wondered, if we *did* find intelligence in Hymie's under-ice ocean? If they were humans, a secondary colony spawned by Bloodworld, it would be a job for the MRF's intelligence people. But if we found nonhuman locals?

Then it would be a job for the fleet's science team—and for the Navy Corpsmen. First contact.

And my first chance at the xenotech my dad was so eager to acquire. The problem was, if we actually found anything important, wouldn't the government step in and take over, just like it always did?

"How far do we need to go?" Lewis asked me. She used her suit's laser com. We were under strict orders not to use radio or microwave communications. Someone might be listening.

"Far enough that we won't get false readings from the dome," I told her. When they'd released the nanoconstructors on the rawmat a few hours ago, some stray atoms and molecules would have spread out into the immediate environment around the dome, leftovers that might skew the readings I'd been sent to take. I needed my samples to be as pristine as possible. We were walking upwind into a gentle breeze in half an atmosphere.

Three kilometers out, I stopped and turned around. The dome . . . I couldn't even see the dome from here. Its outer surface was coated with reactive nanoflage, a layer of molecule-sized computers that sampled the surrounding light levels and re-emitted wavelengths that perfectly matched the shades and tones of the surroundings. It wasn't quite true invisibility, but it came damned close. If we went much farther, we might have trouble finding our way back.

"This ought to be good enough," I told her.

I opened a pouch on the front of my e-suit and pulled out an ES-12 environmental sampler. I squeezed it to open the tripod, and set it down on the ice. Then we backed away a few meters, so that the waste heat from our e-suits wouldn't affect the readings.

I brought up a display on my in-head circuitry, watching as the sampler pulled in trace amounts of atmosphere and began checking the composition, pressure, temperature, and so on. I then opened a copy of the *Clymer*'s electronic ephemeris and began cross-checking the results.

Download
Commonwealth Planetary Ephemeris
Entry: Gliese 581 VIe
"Hymie"

Star: Gliese 581, Bloodstar
Planet: Gliese 581 VI
Satellite: VIe
Name: Gliese 581 VIe, Niffelheim-e, Hymie, Niffie
Type: Europan; ice-covered world ocean, rocky core
   Mean orbital radius: 725,301 km; **Orbital period:** 25_d 3_h 11_m 23_s
Inclination: 0.0°; **Rotational period:** 25_d 3_h 11_m (tide-locked with primary)
Mass: 7.87×10^{25} g = 1.07 Luna; **Equatorial Diameter:** 4,924 km = 0.386 Earth
Mean planetary density: 5.372 g/cc = .973 Earth

Surface Gravity: 1.85 G

Surface temperature range: ~ -200°C

Surface atmospheric pressure: ~60 x 10^3 kPa [0.6 Earth average]

Percentage composition: N_2 91.5, CH_4 8.1, Ne 0.2, C_2H_6 23 ppm C_2H_2 5 ppm; others <5 ppm

Age: 8.3 billion years

Biology: Unknown; no surface forms present

Human Presence: None

So far as I could see, there'd been no change from the data collected by the *Human Endeavor* in the 2140s. Not that I'd expected any change, but you never knew. The universe is good at throwing surprises at us.

We were standing there, waiting for the device to do its chemical thing, when I heard a quick, sharp chirp over my helmet electronics.

"What the *fuck*?" Lewis said.

"Was that an emergency recall?" I asked her. The chirp was a tightly condensed packet of information, but I couldn't translate it at the moment because I still had the ephemeris data up on my CDF display.

"An emergency alert," she said. "Pick up your toy, fast!"

I knew better than to argue with her. The sampler should have completed its analyses by now anyway.

A second alert sounded, two chirps this time.

"Hit your nanoflage!" she screamed. *"Now!"*

Chapter Eight

I LANDED FACEDOWN IN THE SNOW AND LEWIS LANDED BESIDE ME. I thoughtclicked my nanoflage to active, and the eye-catching orange of my e-suit shimmered and melted away into dull white.

I turned my head to look at her. Her helmet was all white now, even the visor, which had shifted to one-way transmission. She held up one hand and wiggled the fingers, then clenched it into a fist.

I got the message: *close off all sources of radiation!* I thoughtclicked on the IR screen, and almost immediately began feeling warm.

It was mostly my overactive imagination, of course. I wouldn't be close to stewing in my own juices for an hour or two yet. Still, the insulation of those e-suits is good, *so* good that the biggest problem in wearing the things is getting rid of waste heat. It builds up as the human body sheds it; there's a heat sink in a unit at the small of the back, underneath the rebreather pack, but it can only hold so much before it needs to be purged.

Normally, excess heat is just dumped into the environment, but the alert from the dome warned that there were possible hostiles in the area, and to them our waste heat would show up like a couple of hot flares against the ice. We would have to stay very still, store what heat we could, and wait it out until the bad guys left.

Was it the Qesh? Or had the MRF decided that local human colonists qualified as hostiles as well? I lay there motionless for an agony of seconds, wondering what the hell was going on, what the threat was, and where the hostiles might be.

Motion caught my eye, and I lifted my helmet slightly, trying to track it. I wasn't sure what I'd just seen—a flicker of movement at the horizon, perhaps—but I'd glimpsed it against the dark sky. My helmet optics threw computer augmentation across my field of vision, searching for nearby sources of IR or radio wavelengths.

There . . . against the face of Niffelheim.

There were three of them, from my vantage point looking like flattened ovals with a bite taken out of each. I'd seen those shapes before.

Rocs.

The silhouettes passed across the planet's purple disk from bottom to top, obviously at high altitude and moving fairly quickly. One by one, they slipped off the face of Niffelheim and vanished; with image enhancement I could just barely see them against the dark of the sky near the zenith.

What were they doing here? A routine patrol of the other planets in the Gliese 581 system? Or had they detected the MRF?

We didn't know much about Qesh capabilities. We knew that their technology was superior to ours—the equivalent of as much as a century, though the rates of technological advancement in other technic species are always tough to judge. Given a century more of development, how good would our radar, lidar, IR, and neutrino scanners become? What other sensors might be developed? Something that can pick up the warping of spacetime caused by the Plottel Drive across a few astronomical units, perhaps? Or the trace leakage from a vacuum energy converter?

IR scanners can pick up the footprints of people who've passed through a room an hour before. Were those Qesh ships now passing almost directly overhead able to detect the heat of the footprints Lewis and I had left in the snow?

I tried to calm the panicky back-and-forth of my thoughts. Our boots were superbly insulated—they *had* to be to let us work in this environment, and the cold wind and the blowing snow should have erased any IR traces we'd left behind.

Should have . . .

I couldn't see the Rocs now, not without rolling over to look up and behind. I stayed huddled there on the ice with Lewis for minute upon minute, a literal freeze that dragged on for a good ten minutes, long after the Qesh patrol must have vanished over the horizon behind us. At last, though, a chirp warbled in my ear, another low-power, compressed-data transmission tight-beamed from the dome.

"All clear," Lewis said over the laser com at the same moment I decrypted the chirp myself. "RTB."

"You know, Louie," I told her as I rolled over, "we've really *got* to stop meeting like this. The rest of Second Platoon are getting suspicious."

"Fuck you, Doc," she told me, helping me awkwardly to my feet.

I would have come back with the traditional, "Any time," but didn't want to sound like Dubois.

QESH ROCS HAD BEEN NAMED AFTER THE MYTHOLOGICAL BIRDS large enough to carry off an elephant. According to Intelligence, they served both as spacecraft and as surface assault vehicles—somewhat smaller versions of the Daitya weapons platforms. I wondered if the habit of naming Qesh military vehicles after giant beings and creatures out of Earth's mythologies was necessarily a good idea. The damned things were scary enough without giving them code names like "Behemoth," "Leviathan," or "Roc."

The base was on full alert, of course, by the time we locked back inside. Chief Garner was waiting for us, and he was looking worried.

"So what's happening, Chief?" I asked him as I dissolved the e-suit. "Is the MRF okay?"

"They've gone," Garner said. "At least for now."

"Gone! Where?"

"The colonel did not choose to share that information with me," he said. He sounded almost disapproving. "Their options, though, would have been deep space—or into close orbit around Niffelheim. Someplace where Qesh EM sensors couldn't pick them up."

That made sense. If they'd stayed in orbit around Hymie, the Rocs would have caught them by radar or lidar as they approached the moon. They would have seen the approaching Rocs by their high-G drive signatures; by engaging their Plottel Drives at very low power, possibly while on the far side of the moon from the approaching enemy, they could have nudged themselves clear of Hymie and far enough out into space that, in all of that emptiness, the chances were good that the Qesh ships wouldn't see them. With enough warning, they might have finessed their trajectory to drop them into orbit around the nearby ice giant, where they would be lost in the planet's radiation belts, or blend in with the orbiting debris of its ring system. In space combat, the trick was always to detect the enemy before they managed to detect you.

Which begged the question: Had the Qesh picked up the fleet from Bloodworld? Or had that flight of Rocs been a routine patrol?

"So what are the Qesh doing now?" I asked.

"They appear to be searching the surface," Garner replied. "They're over the horizon now, but they could be back."

"Did we do something that attracted their attention?"

Garner shrugged. "Hard to say. They might have sniffed a whiff of our drive signature when we entered orbit. Or maybe they're worried that the Bloodworlders have other bases out here."

"So we just sit and wait them out, Chief?" Lewis asked.

"Exactly. They didn't see through the base nanoflage just now. If we lie low and keep quiet, we should stay off their radar. We'll be okay."

As we talked, we were walking into the dome's interior from the airlock, and entered the observation compartment overlooking the moon pool. A wallscreen gave a BTL view of the drilling operation. The pool now was a literal pool of black water, with the tunneler's support and program cables vanishing into the surface. As the nanodisassembler surface broke ice molecules into gaseous hydrogen and oxygen, most of it began recombining into liquid water, and the reaction released enough heat to keep the deep and water-filled pit liquid, despite the frozen sides of the tunnel. The technicians were helping the process along by pumping hot water into the pit, keeping it both full and open.

Somewhere down in the depths of that pool, the tunneler was continuing to eat through the kilometers of rock-hard ice.

"Is it possible the Qesh picked up on our operation here?" I asked.

"Don't see how," Garner said. "Not across hard vacuum, anyway."

"Yeah, but once they got here, they might detect the vibrations of the tunneler. Maybe they have surface monitors on Hymie somewhere."

"That's a bit far-fetched, isn't it, Doc?" Lewis said.

"Maybe," Garner said. He shrugged. "It's not all that likely, though. From what we know of the Qesh so far, they're not much for careful scientific exploration and measurement. They're more into smash-and-grab."

"I'm just saying that this operation could be putting out enough noise or vibrations or whatever that they could pick them up through the ice, or even through the air."

"Well, you know, Carlyle," Garner said, "we can't just hide under a rock because the Qesh *might* be able to pick up our heartbeats. At some point, we have to do what we need to do and to hell with what the bad guys could be capable of."

"Maybe the question," I said, "is whether we're really at war with the Qesh."

"I doubt that the Qesh understand what we mean by *war*," Garner said. "That's a distinctly human concept, you know."

I'D NEVER REALLY THOUGHT ABOUT IT, BUT THE CHIEF WAS RIGHT. Carl von Clausewitz wrote that war is a *political* instrument, a continuation of politics by other means. We'd downloaded a lot of von Clausewitz in our Strategy and Tactics classes at Camp Lejeune, and that line, from his unfinished *Vom Krieg*, may be his most famous quote.

But how relevant are the writings of von Clausewitz to modern warfare, or to alien politics, for that matter? Politics assumes that two governments have something in common, enough so that they can communicate with each other. When we humans entered the galactic stage, we learned that actually communicating with any of the myriad civilizations described by the Encylopedia Galactica was going to be a *lot* harder than anticipated. Ninety-five years ago, we encountered the Durga, at Delta Aquarii V, 160 light years from Earth.

The name Durga is drawn from Hindu mythology. The word is Sanskrit for, roughly, "difficult to reach." She was a goddess who existed, supposedly, in a state of *svatantrya*, meaning complete independence from the rest of the universe, an attitude that appeared to fit the introverted worldview of those hulking, 3-meter-tall siphonapterans. Since they used modulated sound rather than, say, tentacle waving or color changes on their abdomens, to communicate, we actually learned the principal Durgan language fairly quickly. After a century, however, we were *still* trying to figure out how they were using it, or how their peculiar and isolationist mental map of the universe aligned with ours.

The Encyclopedia Galactica shows only a bare-bones sketch of the races and civilizations it lists. The EG gives the dominant Qesh societal drivers as "clan/hunter/warrior/survival"—but what does that *mean*, really?

And what we humans really needed to know was what it meant to the Qesh.

We think we know what the concept of "war" means, at least to us—using military force to project our political will, or to defend our way of life, or to protect our herds, or even to settle political, territorial, or ideological disputes. Add to that modern refinements like "total war" or "limited war" or "rules of engagement," and things get really confusing, just within the boundaries of our own species.

The chances are good that the Qesh have a completely different meaning in mind, one that may have very little in common with strictly parochial human notions of warfare.

Learning exactly what it was that the Qesh were after, and why they were attacking us each time they encountered our colonies or fleets, was probably *the* most critical question Humankind now faced.

In the meantime, though, there were seventy of us inside the Hymie dome: forty-eight Second Platoon Marines under the command of Second Lieutenant Earnest Baumgartner, plus twenty-two technical and Hospital Corps personnel charged with deploying and running the ice tunneler and making contact with the locals, assuming we could find any.

Three hours and forty-eight minutes after deploying the tunneler, we broke through.

I WAS STANDING INSIDE THE TUNNELER CONTROL ROOM, WATCHING Chief Garner deploy the microsub.

"Watch that first step," his voice said over the viewall display. "It's a *hell* of a long way down!"

It was a little strange, listening to the chief's voice coming over the feed from the miniature submarine ten kilometers below our feet when his body was right there in the compartment with us, lying on a recliner and apparently dead to the world. His left hand was encased in the chair's contact array, giving him a direct neural connection through the cybercircuitry implants grown in the heel of his hand and in his fingertips.

I caught myself wondering—again—just where Chief Garner's mind was right now. Inside his physical brain? Or down there inside a remote probe the size of my fist?

The brain, you see, can't tell and doesn't care whether the signals reaching it from the eyes are crossing just a few centimeters of optic nerve, or the ten kilometers of cable from the dangling tunneler below all the way up the ice shaft to the moon pool, then over the internal network to the control room.

The viewall was showing us the view from the sub's cameras, and what Garner was seeing at that moment. There wasn't a lot to see, actually. Above, the sub's light illuminated the underside of the ice cap. Myriad dust specks caught by the light drifted like stars across our field of view.

The water swallowed the sun's light beam almost immediately; below the sub yawned the impenetrable night of the moon's ocean depths.

A long way down indeed. Our initial surveys from the dome had suggested that the ocean beneath Hymie's ice cap was more than 100 kilometers deep, almost ten times deeper than the deepest part of the Mariana Trench on Earth. The total volume of water down there exceeded the volume of all of Earth's oceans combined.

Even with Hymie's light gravity, the water pressure must be astonishing. I know they had the moon pool chamber sealed off now, with the air pressure inside raised to keep Hymie's ocean where it belonged. We didn't want an Enceladus-style geyser going off inside our dome.

"Okay," Garner's voice said. "We're testing positive for active biologicals. And a long list of salts."

"What kinds of biologicals?" That was Dr. Rutherford, one of several civilians in the compartment, and the head of the expedition's xenosophontology team.

"CHON."

Two of the civilians broke into applause and cheers, but stopped when they realized that neither their boss nor the military personnel had joined in.

Readouts began scrolling down one of the control-room monitor screens. I tapped into them with my in-head and read them there. High concentrations of ions, including sodium, chlorine, potassium, bromine, magnesium, sulfur. If anything, the percentage of salt in Hymie's ocean was running higher than Earth's average salinity: about four percent.

More exciting, though, was the positive result on the initial tests for biologicals. Garner was picking up traces of a number of amino and protein chains. There were far too many coming up through the list to sort out any details as to what kind of life there might be in that ocean, but it was clearly CHON—carbon based, with hydrogen, oxygen, and nitrogen at the top, followed by a scattering of other atoms all the way down the periodic table to iodine. CHON is what we have on Earth, though because of the ease by which carbon atoms form long-chain molecules, it's a pattern that we've found repeated elsewhere, including inside both Europa and Enceladus.

"I'm not getting any sonics," Garner said. There was a brief hesitation. "What do you say, Carlyle? You ready to assume the duty?"

"Absolutely, Chief," I replied. Strange to think that my words were transmitted electronically to the probe, then all the way back again to Garner's brain, by way of more than twenty kilometers of optical cable and the palm of Garner's hand.

Someone had grown a second recliner out of the deck next to Garner's. I laid back, settled myself in, and slipped my left hand into the armrest's cradle. "Coming on-line," I said through my in-head.

The duty roster had been set up days before. The idea was that Chief Garner, with the most experience, would run the initial tests when the tunneler broke through into the ocean, handle the probe's final sterilization—the chances were overwhelmingly good that none of our bugs would be compatible with any of Hymie's bugs, but you never knew, and protocol called for taking every reasonable precaution—and begin the first exploration pass with the microsub. But we expected to be searching Hymie's hidden ocean for quite a while, so ten of the Corpsmen attached to the expedition, including me, would be pulling rotating shifts piloting the thing.

And I was first up on the duty list.

For a brief moment, I sensed Chief Garner's electronic presence as he withdrew from the sub. There was an awkward moment of orientation . . . and then I was there, ten kilometers beneath the frigid surface of Niffelheim-e, adrift in a marine world of liquid water filled with pinpoint motes and flecks of debris.

"You have the con, Carlyle," Garner's voice said in my head.

"Aye, aye, Chief," I replied. "I have the con."

It was like *being* the microsub, rather than simply steering it. I was seeing through its camera array, mounted beneath the tiny but powerful light on the dorsal surface of the hull. I was hearing through its ears, and I could feel the tiny impacts of bits of muck as they glanced off the teleoperated vehicle, feel the rush of water about me as I surged forward. The ice ceiling blurred past overhead.

I could see better with sonar than with light. The microsub was sending out brief, high-frequency chirps, and the reflected sound waves created shadowy images around me, just out of reach of my light. I saw something big close by the ceiling, fifty meters away. It looked like stalactites hanging from the roof of a cave. Adjusting my course, I moved in that direction.

A shadow loomed at the touch of my light . . . grew sharper . . . resolved . . .

"You guys seeing this?" I asked. "I think . . ."

"My God," Garner's voice said in my head. "Is that what I think it is?"

"I think it's life," I said.

It looked something like terrestrial coral, branching and

blunt-ended—but it was growing upside down, rooted in the underside of the ice. The arms appeared fuzzy, as though the surface was coated with algae or moss; the color was dark gray.

"Definitely living." That voice was Dr. Rutherford. "Well done!"

I hadn't *done* anything, actually, except steer the microsub in the right direction, but the praise glowed in my thoughts nonetheless.

I brought the sub closer to the mass, probing at it gently. The fuzzy mass looked exactly like filaments of algae, but with all of the green washed out.

"Can you get us a sample, young man?" Rutherford asked.

"A small one," I heard Garner tell him. "That sub doesn't have much cargo capacity."

I extended a cutting arm, toothpick-slender, and snicked off a couple of millimeters from the end of a filament. There was no reaction from the organism; it looked like a plant, yeah, but with alien biota you just never knew. Backing away to be sure I didn't snare the sub in the gently waving forest in front of me, I stowed the sample, then let the microsub begin drifting lower.

I checked the sub's tether, a fiber-optic connector thinner than a human hair that was paying out from the tunneler, now a good half kilometer behind me. The tunneler nanufactured the stuff to order, growing it as a single *very* long-chain molecule rather than storing it on a reel; I should have a good eight to ten more kilometers in reserve, and we could always add to that from the surface. The problem was not limitations in range; it was in limitations of depth. The ice above me exerted an extraordinary pressure on the water beneath, despite the lower gravity and the fact that ice was less dense than water; the microsub was now enduring many tons of pressure on every square centimeter of its surface. While most of it was solid state, the specimen chambers would implode if I didn't make certain the pressures were well balanced.

No human-crewed vehicle would have been able to endure those pressures.

I wanted to go deeper, but none of us was certain about the device's crush depth. At some point, even solid-state circuitry would collapse.

Something caught my attention at the lower edge of my view forward. There was something there, ahead and deeper.

Whatever it was, the glare from my light was washing it out. Ceasing my forward movement, I cut the light.

"What are you doing, Carlyle?" Garner asked. "The procedure list calls for—"

"I know, I know. But I can't see. I thought I saw a light or something."

And then the stars came out.

In the 1930s, William Beebe and Otis Barton conducted a number of dives into the deep ocean off the islands of Bermuda, and became the first humans to observe the organic fireworks displays of bioluminescent creatures half a mile down or more. Their emotions upon seeing the denizens of this bizarre benthic zoo must have been similar to mine at that moment. Many of them looked like shooting stars streaking across my field of vision; others were flashes or pulses or ripples of pale light. The "Hymiean" world-ocean, it appeared, was literally *filled* with life, at least at its upper levels.

How far did the marine phosphorescence project underwater? That depended entirely on how cloudy the sea water was to begin with, and it would take a while to get accurate readings on that. But my impression, from the vantage point of the microsub, was that most of the light we were seeing was coming from organisms within a very few tens of meters.

"Aim your light at that one," Garner said, and a crosshairs pointer appeared in my in-head, indicating a long train of blue-green lights that gave the impression of a rippling chain of lighted portholes.

"No!" Dr. Rutherford's voice said. "Intense light can kill

organisms adapted to the deep sea on Earth! It might be the same here."

"Then how the hell are we supposed to get a look at them?" Garner demanded.

"I think they were avoiding the light when I had it on," I told them. "The bioluminescence didn't switch on until I turned the light off."

"That could just be because your brain wasn't registering the lower levels of light," Rutherford told me.

"Here," I said. "I'll try the sub's light, but at low intensity."

I switched on the light again, and very gradually increased its brightness. It *was* harder to see the surrounding luminescence with that thing on, and some of them did appear to be moving away.

But the light illuminated a couple of critters close up, and they were startling. The first was a jelly-worm thing a meter long, transparent as glass, imbedded with glowing embers.

The second was a fish.

Correction: it was something *like* a fish. The need for streamlined efficiency in a marine environment had shaped the thing—flat, finned, and with jaws at the front end. But it moved in spurts, like a squid propelling itself with jets of water, and each time it slowed, its narrow scales puffed out like fur, revealing that its body was sheathed in hair-thin tentacles that formed a kind of net around it. As far as I could tell, it had no eyes.

Which made me wonder. "If these creatures use light, they must be able to see it," I said. "I don't see any eyes, though."

"More to the point," Rutherford said, "is why they would ever evolve eyes—or light-producing organs—at all."

"Maybe they need to find mates," I suggested. Mating strategies drove a lot of the evolutionary choices made on Earth, after all.

"Yes, yes, a very good possibility. Or possibly—"

"Hang on," I interrupted. "What the hell is *that*?"

The nearby life forms were vanishing into the darkness, but there was something left behind. As I engaged my enhanced optics, a form began to take shape.

It was . . . titanic. At first, all I could see was a faint patch of hazy light, almost too dim to see, but as moment followed moment, the light became stronger, brighter, and it began to define a shape, a shape that literally filled my field of view, stretched out beneath me.

"Are you guys getting this?" I asked.

"We see it," Garner said. "Everything's being recorded. My God, the *size* of that thing!"

"How . . . how big is it?" Rutherford's voice asked.

"Ping it, Carlyle."

I did so. The echo told us the shape was still 800 meters beneath us. The edges, however, were out of sonar range. The thing was too big to measure, though what we could see was at *least* five kilometers across.

The fact that it was almost a kilometer away, though, meant an output of light that was starkly astonishing. Sea water on Earth absorbs almost all sunlight in the visible spectrum in the first ten meters, though photosynthesis can take place all the way down to about 200 meters. The regions beneath 900 meters, though, are referred to as the *aphotic zone*, meaning no light at all ever reaches that deep.

Something, a very *large* something, was glowing beneath the microsub. Individual lights seemed to pick out lines and clusters, like an aerial view of a brightly lit city at night. As I watched, the longest lines of illumination began pulsing in rhythmic waves; it took me a moment to understand that I was seeing something like the spokes of a vast wheel, picked out in blue-green radiance, and turning, moving across my field of view from right to left in an awesome and ponderous sweep.

Five hundred meters.

The thing was rising, getting closer moment by moment.

Chapter Nine

MY FIRST INSTINCT WAS TO TURN AND RUN. I COULD FEEL THE RUSH of displaced water as the giant shape rose. . . .

And then there was a sharp, hard shock, and once again I was lying in the recliner back in the dome on Hymie's surface. The control room was crowded with Marines, techs, and Corpsmen who'd come in to look over my electronic shoulder, as it were. Second Lieutenant Baumgartner was among them. "Welcome back, Petty Officer," he told me.

"It's . . . good to be back, sir."

"Probe terminated," Chief Garner said, looking up from his console. "Smashed against the ice. You okay, Carlyle?"

"I'm fine, Chief. A little shaken, is all."

A lot of people think that if your remote dies while you're teleoperating it, you die. I suppose they think the shock gets you, or something. The truth is a lot less exciting. It's like waking up from a particularly intense dream, disorienting, a bit confusing, maybe, but not deadly.

"That giant life form," Rutherford said, excited. "Did you get the idea that it was intelligent? Perhaps trying to communicate?"

I thought about it. "I really don't know, sir. It's possible, I guess. But . . . it was so huge! How likely is it that something that big would even notice something as small as the microsub?"

"Point. Still, I had the impression that it was reacting to you . . . to the sub's presence, I mean. Maybe to your light, maybe to your sonar."

"Yeah," Baumgartner said. "But was it saying hi, or was it coming up for a snack?"

Rutherford chuckled. "Well, that's the question, isn't it? We'll need to drop some more remote probes down the shaft, to see if we can establish meaningful contact."

"Just so 'meaningful contact' doesn't mean that thing comes up to the surface," Baumgartner said. "If we're going to talk to it, I'd rather it stayed put under the ice."

"In the meantime," Rutherford said, looking at me, "our young Corpsman here has just discovered three new species. The honor of naming them goes to him."

"Thank you, sir," I said, surprised. "I, uh, nothing occurs to me at the moment, though."

"No hurry, no hurry. Use the library AI to help you with the Latin, if you need to. And send your suggestions to my office, oh, in the next few days."

The idea of getting to name the critters I'd discovered during the sub teleoperation was an exciting one, and something I'd not expected. Generally, the scientist who first describes a new life form in a formal paper is the one who names it, and that would probably be Rutherford. I figured he would probably have some ideas in reserve, just in case I dropped the ball and couldn't come up with something suitable.

That evening, I linked in to the fraction of the *Clymer*'s library that had been copied and sent down aboard one of the Cutlasses. It was resident now, along with the expedition's AI, inside the dome. I called up the recordings I'd sent back of each of the creatures, opened a Latin dictionary, and got to work.

Scientists have been giving living organism double-barreled names for genus and species since Linnaeus, in the 1700s. Binomial nomenclature, it's called, and while Latin predominates, you'd better not call it the creature's Latin name, or the biologists will correct you. The names can be Latin, or ancient Greek, or be a person's name or the place where the organism was found, or even be taken from a pun or an in-joke.

The translucent tube-thing I'd seen I called *Tubivitrea pellucidus*, the "translucent glass tube." The odd fish with the odd scales became *Hymaeapiscis squamatopilus*, the "Hymean fish with hairlike scales."

The abyssal monster that had smashed the microsub against the ice ceiling was easy. I dubbed it *Luciderm gigans*, the "giant with light-emitting skin."

I transmitted my choices to Rutherford's mailbox, feeling somewhat fatalistic about the whole thing. I wasn't sure my attempts at Latin—even with the AI's help—would stand close inspection, and it was distinctly possible that the Academy of Xenobiology back on Earth would have different ideas. On the other hand, this was actually a step for me along the path of scientific recognition and legitimacy, something I knew would please my father.

One thing I did know. If we managed to straighten out the situation with the Qesh at Gliese 581, the xenobiologists would be back, and in force, to bring to the surface the secrets hidden beneath Hymie's ice.

The next day, the *Clymer* and the other ships of MRF-7 returned to Niffelheim-e.

"CALLAHAN!"
   "Yo!"
   "Cameron!"
   "Here."
   "Carlyle!"
   "Yup."
   "Colby!"
   "Yeah!"

The roll call was an old, old tradition for the military. Hell, by monitoring our implants, they *knew* we were all here—not to mention our vital signs, general state of health, and probably our attitude and what we'd had for breakfast as well. But the ritual of drawing us up in ranks and having us sound off as they read our names may have had a psychological aspect to it as well.

Somehow, it reminded us that we all were part of the team, that the familiar names and faces around each of us were brothers and sisters who were the real reasons we were fighting.

Not for ideology. Not to keep Earth safe for Humankind, or to rescue the Salvationists.

Brothers and sisters.

The roll call complete, we left-faced at Gunny Hancock's barked order, and walked single file through the open lock of the Misty-D waiting in the ceramplast embrace of its launch tube. *Clymer* boasted ten tubes, enough to launch an entire battalion in three waves. Today, only three misties—carrying the three platoons of Bravo Company—were launching.

Inside, we squeezed into seats just barely large enough to accommodate a Marine in full Mark 7 armor. A recon platoon consists of forty-eight Marines divided into three squads, all under the command of a second lieutenant. In our case, this was Earnest Baumgartner, already aboard and wired into his command block. Packs and weapons went into the overhead gear lockers, which were sealed from the command deck—and that included our sidearms as well as our primary weapons. Gunny Hancock checked on that part personally; a bored Marine fiddling with a charged weapon in the cramped confines of a Misty could put a *very* sudden halt to the festivities.

I jacked in the connectors that linked me to the D/MST-22's artificial intelligence and the platoon com channel. I could hear the Marines around me engaged in another ancient Corps tradition—griping.

"It ain't right, is all I'm sayin'." According to the ID, that was Corporal Randolph Gregory. "We was deployed already on Hymie! Why're they sending us out again?"

"Can it, Orgy," Sergeant Gibbs growled. "Hymie wasn't a deployment. It was a picnic."

"Yeah," Lance Corporal Andrews said. "Didn't you hear? They're gonna take it off our accumulated leave."

"Orgy's right," Private Kilgore said. "They still should've given it to Alpha Company."

"Fuckin' right," Gregory said. "Those assholes ain't done any *real* work since Tiantan."

I listened to them bitch and bicker for a while, then tuned in-head to the mission profile.

**Download
Mission Profile: Reconnaissance
Operation Blood Salvation/
OPPLAN#5735/28NOV2245**

[extract]

. . . Second Platoon will deploy by D/MST-22, entering the target planet's atmosphere on the nightside. Extreme care must be employed to avoid alerting Qesh forces to MRF presence in-system.

Landing will take place at LZ Red Tower, located at 1° 14' N, 179° 02' W, which will serve as recon advance outpost and headquarters. Mission commander will use best judgment in penetrating objective colony facilities and contacting local political or military authorities.

Unit will in addition to making contact with locals perform in-depth reconnaissance of objective area and report on Qesh presence, strength, and deportment.

There was a lot more, but those were the gist of our orders. Get in without being seen by the Qesh. Land at the sea's edge without being spotted. Slip some people into the human colony domes and make contact with the colony's leaders. Second Platoon would be at Red Tower; First Platoon would be coming down at LZ Red Sky, near the colony city of Martyrdom, 200 kilometers north of Salvation. Third

Platoon would be held in reserve at sea. Because smaller spacecraft were tougher to detect than large ones, we would board our Misties half a million kilometers away from Bloodworld and use stealth tactics for the final approach to our objective.

It promised to be a long, claustrophobic, and *very* uncomfortable voyage.

After studying our orders for a time, I moved on to the ephemeris breakdown of the Gliese system.

Download
Commonwealth Planetary Ephemeris
Entry: Gliese 581
"Bloodstar"

[extract]

Planet I
 Name: Gliese 581 I, Gliese 581 e, Surtr
  Mean orbital radius: 0.02845 AU; **Orbital period:** 3_d 3_h 34_m 05_s

Planet II
 Name: Gliese 581 II, Gliese 581 b, Logi
  Mean orbital radius: 0.0406 AU; **Orbital period:** 5_d 8_h 50_m 31_s

Planet III
 Name: Gliese 581 III, Gliese 581 c, Muspelheim
  Mean orbital radius: 0.073 AU; **Orbital period:** 12_d 22_h 3_m 30_s

Planet IV
 Name: Gliese 581 IV, Gliese 581 g, Bloodworld, Salvation, Midgard
  Mean orbital radius: 0.14601 AU; **Orbital period:** 36_d 13_h 29_m 17_s

Planet V
   Name: Gliese 581 V, Gliese 581 d, Nidavellir
     Mean orbital radius: 0.218 AU; **Orbital period:** $66_d\ 20_h$
      $52_m\ 48_s$

Planet VI
   Name: Gliese 581 VI, Gliese 581 f, Niffelheim
     Mean orbital radius: 0.758 AU; **Orbital period:** $1_y\ 69_d$
      $06_h\ 57_m\ 15_s$

When Captain Ludwigson and the crew of the *Human Endeavor* first explored the Gliese 581 system in 2143, they gave each of the six worlds names drawn from the Norse mythology of Ludwigson's ancestors.

Innermost was Surtr, airless, half-molten, and named for the fire-giant who ruled Muspelheim. Next out was Logi, "wildfire," the giant who represented fire to the Norse. After that, in order, came Muspelheim, Midgard, Nidavellir, and Niffelheim. Ludwigson had dubbed Planet IV, our destination, Midgard—"the enclosure"—the world of man balanced precariously between fire and ice. When the Neoessenists arrived in 2181, of course, they promptly changed Midgard's name to Bloodworld; no pagan gods or mythological worlds for *them*, thank you very much!

There's no record of what, if anything, they called the other worlds in the system. Presumably they renamed them all, but they haven't talked much with the rest of their species in the past sixty-some years.

As you can see from the ephemeral data, Gliese 581's coterie of planets is tucked in tight and cozy around the cool, dim primary. Surtr, airless and baked, and with a partially molten surface, is just .03 AU from the star, whipping around its primary in just over three days. Logi, a true monster, sixteen times the mass of Earth, is .04 AU out, with a period of about five and a half days. Muspelheim, with six times Earth's mass and a greenhouse effect worse than the one smothering Venus, is .07 AU from its primary—about

10.5 million kilometers—and has a period of just under two weeks.

Our objective—originally designated as Gliese 581 g— was a little more than three times Earth's mass, orbited 0.146 AUs from its star, and circled it once every 36.5 days. That distance, theoretically, placed it smack in the middle of Gliese 581's so-called habitable zone, the distance from the star at which water could exist as a liquid.

Habitable didn't necessarily mean *comfortable*, however.

Of particular interest to the habitability issue was the fact that Bloodworld was almost perfectly balanced between Muspelheim and Nidavellir, massive super-Earths each with about six times Earth's mass. On the inside, Muspelheim— planet III—frequently passed Bloodworld—IV— at a distance of 10.9 million kilometers. That sounds like a lot, but it's close enough to deliver a sizeable tidal nudge to planet IV, especially due to III's huge mass. About once every twenty days, then, Muspelheim passed Bloodworld close enough to be visible as a disk in the dayside sky—and close enough to cause seismic tremors, volcanism, and tidal waves.

On the outside was the orbit of Nidavellir, the other giant. Bloodworld passed Nidavellir at a distance of 11.1 million kilometers, once every eighty days or so.

So there was poor little Midgard-Bloodworld, caught between the push and pull of those two giants, kneaded like a ball of putty in a giant's fist. You find the same situation with Io, Jupiter's moon, squeezed and stretched in a similar tug-of-war between Jupiter and the other Galilean satellites. No wonder Bloodworld was seismically active! The other planets contributed to the tidally induced chaos as well, as did the local sun, but Muspelheim and Nidavellir were the main culprits.

The more I downloaded about the place, the less appealing it sounded.

But the *Clymer*, escorted by the two destroyers, had slipped through interplanetary space, closing with Bloodworld. Now, just half a million kilometers from the planet, we'd packed ourselves into the Misty-Ds, ready for drop and the last leg of our voyage. The *Clymer* would return to Hymie and await our call for pickup.

Jacked into the Misty's intel system, I could see a graphic representation of Bloodworld, circled by the bright red pinpoints marking the Qesh warships, each with an identifying block of text. We were reading forty-four ships at the moment, although one of them, the Jotun-class monster, was more like a ten-kilometer asteroid than a starship. We couldn't see it from half a million kilometers out, but the mass and energy readings were literally astronomical, and the light reflected from it at optical wavelengths was irregular and shifting, as if from a rocky surface.

An interesting coincidence, that. The Jotuns were the ice-giants of Norse mythology, which meant this one fit right in with the planet names suggested by the *Human Endeavor* survey.

Bloodstar glowed with sullen intensity ahead, its face mottled by black starspots. The nightside of Bloodworld loomed close by, a slender crescent of red-hued light bowed away from the sun.

The entire region around Bloodworld was blanketed by radar and lidar searching for intruders like us. The outer skins of our Misty-Ds, however, were coated in reactive nano, stealth screens that literally absorbed all incoming radiation just like the larger ships, and if we weren't reflecting any of that energy, we were effectively invisible. We had to keep the Plottel Drive idling at very low power, however, to avoid giving ourselves away by the wake the drive dimpled into spacetime. As we drew within 100,000 kilometers or so, our AIs cut the drives and we drifted in, silent and powerless.

The chatter in the compartment died away with the drive. There was no way the enemy could actually hear us, of course. Sound doesn't travel through hard vacuum, and our com channels were shielded, isolated form the rest of the universe. Maybe we were all following genetic programming laid down a few million years ago, when our ancestors stopped their screeches and calls as they hid in the foliage and watched the big hunter cats pad silently past in the night.

As hour followed hour, it started getting hot inside the Misty. If we're absorbing incoming radiation *and* keeping our own heat from radiating into space . . . well, there's only so much we can store up in the shipboard heat sinks or convert to electricity. After a while, the cabin temperature began climbing rapidly. We had our armor set to cool us, of course, but after about six hours, our suits were dumping so much excess heat into the crowded cabin that it became a vicious circle—our armor pumping out more heat into our surroundings to protect us against the increasing heat around us—and before long the heat sinks in our armor were maxed out and we were sweltering, stewing in our own juices. I used the platoon data channel to keep track of everyone's core temperatures, including my own. If *those* started climbing, we would have to start taking exceptional measures to avoid heat exhaustion or, far worse, heat stroke.

"Listen up, everybody," I said over the platoon channel. "Everyone set your autoinjects for a fifty milligram shot of 'lyte balance."

I punched in my own dosage on my armor's wrist control pad. In the old days, troops swallowed salt tablets to replace electrolytes lost to sweat. This was better—an injection of electrolytes plus nano, programmed to maintain a tailored isotonic balance. I felt the sharp sting beneath the angle of my jaw as the hypo fired the cocktail into my carotid.

Invisible, we drifted past the nearest of the orbiting Qesh giants, a Titan-class, as large as one of our battleships, at a range of just 500 kilometers. It was invisible to the un-aided eye, of course, but through enhanced optics, we could see it as a flattened dagger shape with flaring aft sponsons, painted in the distinctive red-and-white livery of the Qesh warships we'd encountered in the past. I don't know why they didn't bother with nanoflage hull coatings. They certainly must have had the technology to employ them.

Possibly they just figured they were the biggest and meanest kids on the block, and didn't need to sneak. That, or the warrior tag on their cultural profile meant that sneaking, for them, was the same as cowardice.

That's okay. I was happy to play coward if it meant we didn't get noticed by those bad boys. The Titan gave no notice of our presence as we glided past, entering the upper shreds of Bloodworld's atmosphere.

I imagined that we'd already inserted some spy-probes into orbit to get close-up imaging on whatever it was they were doing there, but the higher-ups hadn't told us anything about what they might have found. It did look like there was a lot of activity, though, with small ships—corvette sized or smaller—shuttling back and forth among the larger vessels, or in transit through the atmosphere, between surface and orbit.

The glaring red eye of Bloodstar dropped beneath the planetary limb, plunging us into darkness.

The nightside of Bloodworld, turned eternally away from the sun, was completely black and featureless to the naked eye. Under enhanced optics, though, we could see the ice sheets below, ragged, broken by mountain ranges and following the twists and curves of broad plains and valleys. For some reason, I'd been expecting the ice cap to cover the nightside of Bloodworld neatly and completely. In fact, ice covered only about two thirds of the dark-side hemisphere, giving way in places to empty tundra, in others to open ocean. Several hundred pinpoints of red-orange light glowed against the surface, especially in a broad ring near the edge of the planet's disk.

Volcanoes. Hundreds of them. Possibly thousands. The eons-long gravitational tug-of-war between Bloodworld, its sun, and the nearest giant planets kept them erupting on a fairly regular basis. I could see storms below, too, vast spiraling swirls of clouds hugging the dark surface. Most of the clouds were gathered around the periphery between day and night.

We felt a sudden shock . . . and then another, followed by the steadily increasing sensation of weight as we decelerated. We continued our descent over Bloodworld's nightside, doing our best imitation of a large meteor as friction ionized the thin air around us. We were certainly showing up on their sensors *now*, but hours ago our AI had nudged us into a path that let us enter the atmosphere at a flat angle, using aerobraking to sharply reduce our velocity.

The nearest Qesh warship, a cruiser-sized Leviathan, was now 900 kilometers distant, and didn't appear to be paying us any attention whatsoever.

We passed low above the vast sweep of a coriolis storm. In my in-head, I could see the clouds seemingly close enough to touch, illuminated from within, from moment to moment, by the silent pulses of lightning. Seconds later, we slid into the clouds, then punched through above open water and a deep purple sky. At the last possible moment, our AI kicked in the Plottel Drive and slowed us to a few hundred kilometers per hour, lowering us into the black water below.

The added weight first felt during deceleration continued to drag at us. Bloodworld had a surface gravity of almost twice Earth's. I weighed eighty-three kilos on Earth; here I weighed 153.

"Systems check, people," Gunny Hancock called. "Suit power!"

The order startled us, pulling us up out of a kind of waking sleep as we began running through our pre-debarkation checklist. Power. Life support. Communications. Suit AIs. Suit nanotechnics and fabricators. Exowalker. Jumpjet systems and meta tank. Weapon links. Even though our weapons were all safely stored in the lockers above our heads, we could activate the targeting links to make sure we could connect through our CDF links.

In my in-head display, I could see nothing but blackness outside, the watery depths of Bloodworld's major ocean. According to the data feed, we were under open water rather than ice, traveling at nearly 200 kph at a depth of 500 meters. This was a calculated risk, of course; the Plottel Drive created a kind of energy bubble around us that let us zip through deep water at high speeds, but we were still putting out a lot of noise from the interface—sound energy that could be picked up by underwater receivers hundreds, even thousands, of kilometers away.

But we were gambling that the Qesh couldn't think of everything, wouldn't cover every approach, and especially wouldn't think about an enemy coming in through space, then making the final approach under water. The Qesh might be advanced, but they weren't *gods*.

At least, that was the assumption being made by the planning staff for Operation Bloodworld Salvation. The alternative was to spend a few days or even weeks maneuvering in close, and we didn't have that kind of time available to us.

Two hours after entering the water, then, we surfaced. Every Marine inside that Misty-D was tuned in and watching, the stress inside that compartment palpable. We were all remembering that last training exercise.

"Thank God!" Gabrielle Latimer said. "No fucking Daityas!"

Several Marines laughed, and someone called out, "*Boo! Got ya!*"

Our D/MST-22 hovered, dripping, above the ocean swell, then drifted in slowly above a rocky beach. A volcano erupted noisily to the south. The wind shrieked outside, buffeting our craft.

"Debarkation in two minutes!" Gunny snapped. "Marines! Stand up!"

A bustle of noise sounded through the compartment as almost forty armored shapes unbuckled and de-linked, then stood up in the narrow central passageway. Our seats melted away, returning to the deck from which they'd been summoned.

"Marines! Break out packs and weapons!"

With more space in which to maneuver, we turned and

opened the lockers, retrieving our weapons and our back-packs.

There's still a popular fiction out there that says that Navy Corpsmen never carry weapons. Once upon a time, two or three centuries ago, before we entered space, combat medics actually weren't allowed to carry weapons. A series of international agreements jointly called the Geneva Convention laid out what nations could and could not do in warfare, according to the ideas of international humanitarian law at the time. Among other things, combat medics couldn't carry weapons, and they were required to wear helmets and arm-bands marked with large and prominent red crosses.

The trouble, of course, was that not every nation was a signatory to the Geneva Convention, and even some that were didn't always play by the rules. During the series of small wars, "police actions," and wars against terrorism that flared up during the last half of the twentieth century and the first half of the twenty-first, most of the rules went out the window. The United States Marines often found them-selves fighting opponents who would deliberately target the Corpsmen who were trying to save Marine lives. It became common knowledge that a lot of combat Corpsmen, as soon as they entered the war zone, removed the red crosses and acquired their own weapons; the records listing Corpsmen who won the Medal of Honor and other medals for heroism include quite a few who protected a fallen Marine by using weapons—either their own or their patient's—to hold off approaching enemy troops.

Once we entered the interstellar arena, "the enemy" tended to be individuals and governments who had never heard of the Geneva Convention, and who wouldn't under-stand it if they had. Every species has its own idea of what war is, what constitutes decency, fair play, or war crimes, and whether or not such attitudes are even sane in armed conflict. When you think about it, the idea of "playing fair" in a war where the survival of your species is at stake is sheer lunacy. That idea has always caused problems for proponents of the Geneva Convention; the accords say you never target civilian populations, that to do so constitutes a war crime, a crime against humanity—and yet from the mid-twentieth century until well into the twenty-first, nations routinely held vast civilian populations in the cross-hairs of their nuclear weapons. An all-out nuclear war would have killed tens or hundreds of millions of innocents, perhaps more. But for any one nation to risk unilaterally disarming on humanitarian or moral grounds would have been tantamount to suicide.

Nowadays, and facing nonhuman foes, Corpsmen *always* go into combat armed.

My weapon was a lightweight laser carbine, a Sunbeam-Sony half-megajoule-pulse Mk. 30 officer's model, accurate to line-of-sight horizon and massing just 4 kilos. My sidearm, of course, was a Browning Five, the 5-millimeter automatic magnetic slug-slinger that's been standard issue for the Marines for the past eighty years. The carbine went over my right shoulder, clicking home in the snap catches on my backpack. The Browning went into a thigh holster, right next to my M-7.

A moment later, we touched down with the crunch of hull on gravel, rocked slightly as the landing jacks extended and the bulkheads to either side began morphing open, as ramps extended from the deck down to the black stones of the beach.

"Second Platoon, *go!*" Gunny Hancock yelled, and thirty-nine Marines pounded down the ramps.

My first non-simmed footsteps on an extrasolar world.

Ooh-ra!

Chapter Ten

THE LOCAL STAR WAS HANGING ABOVE THE EASTERN HORIZON, FOUR times bigger than Sol as viewed from Earth. It was hard to remember that Bloodworld was a third the distance from its primary as Mercury was from Sol. A third the distance . . . but Bloodstar itself was less than three tenths the diameter of Sol, so that red sun actually appeared to be a bit smaller in the sky than Sol as seen from Mercury.

I saw why the mission planners had decided to call this LZ "Red Tower," though. Off to the north of the beach, a spire of rock, needle slim and at least a kilometer high, caught the perpetual late-afternoon sunlight, which gave it the appearance of being drenched in blood. A lot of the nearby rock formations had the look of the badlands geology of the American Southwest, iron-stained and rugged. The landscape was harsh, heavily eroded, with spires, pinnacles, and mesas of rock. Toward the south, I could see a sawtooth line of mountains, one of them beneath a mushroom pall of dark gray cloud.

"First Squad!" Hancock yelled. "Put up the perimeter! Second Squad! I want the HQ right over there, beside those boulders. Amphibious green blurs, people! Move it! Move it! Move it!"

We were using quantum-encrypted comms on low power, with thousands of frequency shifts per second spread over a fair part of the frequencies; we *should* be safe enough from high-tech eavesdroppers, though it was never a good idea to assume too much in that department. First Squad spread out into the surrounding rocks, setting up a defensive perimeter, including robotic gun positions and sentries, and sensor arrays. The rest of us started building the Red Tower headquarters.

"Headquarters" was contained in a five-kilo box the size of a large briefcase, which Sergeant Leighton set on a large, flat, bare expanse of basaltic rock fifty meters up from the water. The rest of us did a sweep across the rock, side by side, picking up loose rocks and tossing them away, clearing a work area ten meters across.

Working in the local gravity was a strain. I picked up one loose chunk of rock the size of my fist and it felt as heavy as a lump of gold. All of us were working in strap-on exowalkers, of course, frameworks embracing our armor that supported our legs, torsos, and backs, amplifying each move we made and taking some of the gravitational strain off. Still, 1.85 G made for slow and heavy going.

With the growing area cleared, Gunny Hancock triggered the box, which began releasing a steady stream of nanoconstructors onto the rock. It was a similar process to what we'd done on Hymie, except that here we were using local materials entirely—the basaltic rock, plus carbon, hydrogen, oxygen, nitrogen, and a long list of other elements drawn straight from the atmosphere. A few more necessary elements not available in the air were provided by a hose with an attached pump strung across the rock shelf and down to the water. Seawater on Earth has an amazing supply of elements—various salts, of course, but also gold, silver, copper, iron, tungsten, magnesium, even traces of platinum, iridium, and uranium. The seawater here on Bloodworld was richer in metals than Earth's oceans by far. The planet, remember, was 8.3 billion years old, almost twice Earth's age, and the constant internal stresses caused by tidal forces guaranteed that everything from hydrogen and helium to the heaviest natural elements were constantly getting squeezed up out of the planet's crust and churned into the sea. Bloodworld's seas were a thick, mineral-rich soup, heated from within and constantly stirred by fierce storms and savage tides.

Once the area was clear and the HQ dome was growing, I got to work on my planetfall to-do list, hauling out my sniffer and pulling in microsamples of the atmosphere. As expected, the oxygen here was running at just under twenty percent, with nitrogen at 75.5 percent. There were two red flags, however, again as expected. Carbon dioxide was showing 1.01 percent, while sulfur dioxide was a whopping .69 percent.

The CO_2 was actually fairly low and not immediately lethal. Normal levels on Earth average about 300 parts per million, or .03 percent. We could breathe this stuff for short periods, though some people experienced drowsiness at those levels. The SO_2, however, was deadly at over .5 percent. Five parts per million—that's 0.0005 of one percent—is the PEL, the permissible exposure limit, for even short-term exposure to the stuff. More than that causes respiratory difficulties and can result in death.

Appropriately charged filter masks would take care of that easily enough. Nanodisassemblers in the air intake break it into oxygen, a gas, and sulfur, which is stored in the mask's rejection bin as the familiar yellow powder. It's funny, though, how very close the atmosphere of Bloodworld is to being breathable by humans; that's the story on so many worlds throughout the Galaxy, even those generally considered "Earthlike." It doesn't take much to make the place unhealthy. I looked up toward the south and the distant, erupting volcano. Both sulfur dioxide and CO_2 are outgassed by volcanic activity, and there were thousands of volcanoes on the planet. It was pretty obvious where the high levels of poisonous gas were coming from.

The temperature here was an invigorating four degrees Celsius, the wind, relatively mild for Bloodworld, coming out of the nightside in blustery gusts of forty or fifty kilometers per hour. The deep purple thunderheads gathering off-shore suggested that rain was on the way. A beautiful spring morning on Bloodworld. . . .

Except that there were no seasons here. Trapped in a tidal lock with its nearby star, Bloodworld had no axial tilt at all. Both planetary climate and local weather were driven by the dayside-nightside atmospheric convection currents. Sub-solar temperatures dayside ranged as high as fifty Celsius—close to the hottest it ever gets on Earth. Hot dayside air rises and expands outward—a perpetual high-pressure system—sending currents of hot air streaming out toward the night-side at high altitudes.

Over the glaciers of the nightside, the air cools rapidly, the temperature dropping to around eighty below—close to winter in Antarctica. Cold air then moves back to the day-side, traveling a bit slower and at lower altitudes, and car-rying with it moisture picked up over the night-side oceans and ice fields.

Most of that moisture precipitates out at the twilight band, which was why the heaviest concentrations of clouds gathered there in the swirls and streams visible from space. The circulation makes sure that the day-to-night tempera-ture differences don't get too extreme, but it guarantees hell-ish storms and constant high winds. Air pressure, I noticed as I changed the settings on my sniffer, was falling quickly. A storm was on the way.

By the time I finished taking my readings and getting test samples of air and water, the HQ dome was nearly complete, rising swiftly as though being inflated from within. The base of the HQ dome had eaten nearly eight meters down into the solid rock, and its outer surface rippled and gleamed with an iridescent sheen as the external nano set into place. Like our ships and armor, the reactive nanoflage would closely imi-tate the surrounding light and tone. From the air, even from the ground just a few tens of meters away, it would look like an irregularly shaped mass of igneous rock.

I saw Baumgartner and the HQ staff making their way

from the grounded D/MST, and gathering near what would soon be the HQ dome's airlock. A second dome was being set up a little farther to the south; that would become barracks and supply building for the enlisted personnel.

Chief Garner was with Baumgartner. So were Doobie Dubois and Machine McKean, Gunny Hancock and several others. I joined them.

My suit clicked me into their private channel as I approached. " . . . and I want you to be damned sure you keep your people in hand, Chief," Baumgartner was saying. "No free-wheeling, no scrounging, no black marketeering, you understand me?"

"Yes, sir." Garner's voice sounded carefully neutral.

Baumgartner saw me. "Carlyle. Did you get your readings?"

"Yes, sir. The numbers are exactly what we thought they'd be."

"Well, it's a relief to know the planet's basic chemistry hasn't changed in the past sixty-four years. Lloyd? Did you pick up anything?"

Staff Sergeant Arnold Lloyd was one of Carter's people, a communications expert from Company S2.

"Negative, sir. I did a complete freak sweep. There's lots of radio noise from the local sun, of course, but nothing that sounds artificial. Of course, both the locals and the Qesh have quantum encoding. Anything they broadcast *will* sound like noise."

"I am aware of quantum communications technology, Staff Sergeant. What I need from you is results."

Second Lieutenant Baumgartner had something of a reputation in Bravo Company. Some of the Marines called him "Mommy" behind his back. He was fussy, a worrier, and something of a prima donna.

He was, frankly, the kind who doesn't last long in the Corps. You either learn to work *with* your NCOs, or you find yourself transferred to permanent desk duty Earthside, a sure-fire killer of any officer's career.

"Hancock? I want the first recon squad deployed in thirty mikes."

"I would suggest waiting twenty-four hours, sir," Hancock said, his voice dead level. "That'll give my people time to acclimate to the higher gravity."

"I will remind you, Gunnery Sergeant, that they are not *your* people. They are *my* people, *my* assets, and I will determine how best to utilize them." He turned back to me. "Carlyle!"

"Yes, sir."

"You will break out your bag of tricks and shoot up Second Platoon with G-boost. Supercharge 'em."

I hesitated for an uncomfortable moment. Had Dr. Francis given me that order—or even Chief Garner—I would not have had a problem. Second Lieutenant Baumgartner, though, was not medically trained, and could not prescribe medications.

"You have a problem with that, Carlyle?" Baumgartner demanded.

"Sir—"

"We'll take care of it, sir," Garner said, interrupting.

"Good. Gunny Hancock, you will take Second Platoon across country to the city of Salvation. Set up an advance OP, establish QB contact with Red Tower, and coordinate the approach of the rest of the company."

"Aye, aye, sir."

"You will not, repeat *not*, initiate contact with either the Qesh or the locals. You will wait for the approach of the main force. Am I understood?"

"Yes, sir."

And that seemed to be that.

But I couldn't help thinking about the old von Moltke adage: *no plan survives contact with the enemy.*

TWENTY MINUTES LATER, SECOND PLATOON'S SECOND SQUAD WAS forming up for the patrol, a total of thirteen Marines plus one Navy puke—me. Gunny Hancock was in command. They were breaking out the quantum flitters from the D/MST's cargo compartment and lining them up on the beach.

But I was having a few final words on a private channel with Chief Garner before we left. "Are you saying I just ignore a direct order?" I asked.

"Not ignore," Garner said, "so much as bend it, just a little. You don't want your Marines coming down with a crash."

"And *I* don't want to end up in the brig," I told him. "Baumgartner's been known to do that, y'know?"

I was thinking about that incident back at Lejeune, when an overstressed kid tagged by a training laser had lost his temper and snapped off something about "fuck the fucking ossifers" over an open channel, not even knowing he was on the air. Most officers would have ignored it; at most they would have had his platoon sergeant have a private word with him later about communications security. Not Mommy Baumy, though.

"You won't end up in the brig," Chief Garner told me. "I'll back you. Just hold off on the G-B injections until your people really need them. And you'll know when *that* is, believe me."

"E-Car!" Hancock bellowed over the platoon frequency. "Get your Navy ass over here!"

"On my way, Gunny!" I replied. I looked at Garner. "Thanks, Chief. Just keep the Man off my neck, okay?"

All Marines carry a few million Frietas respirocytes circulating through their bloodstreams—artificial one-micron cells that work like the body's own red blood cells, only far more efficiently. Natural systems that have evolved hit or miss over hundreds of millions of years tend to be pretty clunky compared to human engineering. Respirocytes are a lot better at carrying oxygen and removing waste metabolytes than RBCs; though they're one fifth the diameter, they can store and transport 236 times as much oxygen as a red cell, and deliver it to specific cell groups—in the brain, in the heart, in key muscle groups—with targeted precision.

It's been estimated that if the red blood cells in a human's circulatory system were completely replaced by respiroctes, that person would be able to hold his breath for over an hour—or sprint at top speed for fifteen minutes and never take a breath. We haven't reached that point yet—it brings us smack up against the Transhuman Debate and the Hopkins Declaration. But injecting Marines with respirocytes dramatically improves their endurance and physical performance, and we've been doing it routinely since the late twenty-first century.

G-boost, though, is different. It's a complex artificial protein that bonds with respirocytes already in the blood and jacks them up to a whole new operational level. Boosted respirocytes circulate through muscle tissue and suck up lactic acid and other metabolytes, supercharge the muscles with O_2-rich blood, and fine-tune the nervous system to improve the person's reaction time. The person becomes faster, *much* stronger, immune to exhaustion, and able to function in a relatively high-G environment for hours on end. Supercharging, it's called. Supercharged Marines no longer need to sleep, and they can carry two to three times more weight than before, going on for hour after hour without tiring. The stuff is illegal for civilians, but has been available for military use for about thirty years.

But the boost in performance comes with a price. We call it "G-crash," and it happens when the respirocyte addons begin denaturing after fifty or sixty hours. The person comes out of the boost phase exhausted, all but incapacitated, and there can be some nasty side effects to the nervous system as well. Even before the crash, some users can suffer from confused thinking; the Marine feels so great he can misjudge his actual condition—or try to do something stupid like fly.

Because of the potential side effects, G-boost is not a part of the Marine armor pharmacopeia, and can only be administered by doctors or Corpsmen. Technically, Baumgartner didn't have the authority to order those injections, though he could have discussed the possibility with competent medical personnel. I'd been about to tell him I needed Dr. Francis's say-so before I could carry out his order. Had I done so, I would have ended up on Baumgartner's shit list; enlisted personnel do *not* second-guess officers, even when they're right. Garner had stepped in and saved my ass.

Taking care not to fall in the high gravity, I did a slow and cautious jog across the beach to join Gunny Hancock and the others beside the flitters. Each was a flattened, nanoflaged, torpedo-shaped flyer with a kind of elongated dorsal saddle and grip-handles, and they hovered silently half a meter above the rock. Quantum flitters, like the various commercial fliers back home, adjusted the electron spin within the material of the ventral surface, allowing the device to react against the spin states of electrons in the ground as well as any local magnetic field. They didn't really fly, but they had enough lift to support an armored Marine and his equipment, they were silent, and they were fast.

And they would be getting us as close as possible to the colony dome of Salvation.

Private Colby helped me clamber onto my flitter, holding the machine as it bobbed beneath my weight. "Thanks," I said, and then gave him a searching look. "How's the leg, Colby?"

"All better, Doc," he said. "Good patch-up."

"Just be careful in this gravity," I told him, settling myself belly down into the saddle. "Don't go breaking it on me again."

He laughed and strapped me down. "Not a problem, Doc." He slapped my armored shoulder. "You're good to ride."

I linked into the controls; you steer a flitter through your in-head display, moving a cursor with your eyes to steer. That makes them highly maneuverable, but it takes a lot of practice getting used to them. They can be almost too responsive, especially at high speed.

"Okay, Marines," Hancock transmitted over the platoon channel. "Sound off! Andrews!"

"Yo!"

"Carlyle!"

"Yeah!"

"Colby!"

"Ooh-rah!"

He ran down the alphabetical list, and had gotten as far as Kukowicz when a piercing in-head alarm went off. "Native surface craft approaching perimeter," the platoon AI announced. "Repeat, native surface craft approaching perimeter, bearing two-six-five, range five hundred meters. . . ."

Red Tower had been set up above a shallow bay, and the HQ team had deployed robot guns and sensor arrays on both headlands, looking out to sea. The platoon channel was transmitting an image, now, of what looked for all the world like a sailing vessel of some sort, a low, lean hull with two sharply canted masts angled aft, with triangular sails. The boat was running ahead of the gusting, westerly wind. The horizon behind it was a purple-black wall of clouds, moving in swiftly toward the shore.

"Second Squad!" Hancock bellowed, taking the initiative. "Deploy to the beach!"

A thoughtclick on the control link, and I was in motion, gliding half a meter above the ground as we swung around and slid down the rock shelf toward the beach. We didn't stop at the water's edge, but kept on going, skimming above the water as the repulsor effect threw up roostertails of spray behind us. Quantum flitters can only skim above water if they're moving fast; if they try to hover in one place, the spin-repulsor effect starts pushing the water aside and the craft begins to sink into a hole of its own making. If it's moving, though, its flat body creates a bit of lift, and the spin-push can be directed slightly aft, allowing it to skitter above the water in a precarious balance between flying and drowning.

The critical speed necessary to stay up depends on the local atmospheric pressure, but on Bloodworld it worked out to about twenty-five kilometers per hour. I gunned it up to forty, following Tomacek's and Gunny Hancock's machines. I wasn't entirely sure what I was doing in the deployment, to tell the truth. My laser carbine was clipped to my back, of course, but that wasn't supposed to be the reason I was attached to the squad. I was a *Corpsman*, not combat infantry . . . but if any of the squad's Marines was hit in a firefight, his or her flitter would sink, and I'd have a hell of a time getting to him to render first aid.

The bay was quite shallow, west to east, more of a curved crescent anchored between two low cliffs than an enclosure. I could see the native boat up ahead now, in between incoming ocean swells. Two masts—main and mizzen, with the mizzenmast ahead of the con. That made it a ketch rig. The hull was about eight meters long; there was no way to tell how many people might be on board—or if it was, in fact, an AI craft of some sort. Colonies short on manpower often deployed robotic sailing craft to patrol nearby bodies of water, for fishing, or for the automated coastal transport of cargo.

I hit one of those swells. My flitter bucked up as it climbed the moving mound of water, but I still punched through the top, emerging in an explosion of spray. My first thought was a feeling of sheer exuberance; I *loved* being on the water again.

My second was an emotional supercrash; I could see Paula's face in my lap as I drifted off the ice cliffs of Maine, helpless, terrified, waiting for the med-rescue lifter to arrive as her life slipped away from me.

Angry, I focused on conning the flitter. The ocean swells grew a bit lower as we got away from the shore, farther out into deep water. I could see someone moving on the deck of the ketch, now, a ragged-looking figure with a cloak flapping in the wind.

"Second squad is under attack," the AI announced. What the hell? I hadn't seen or heard—

A geyser of water exploded from the dark surface to my left, five meters away. Damn it, they were shooting at us! I leaned right and skittered my flier to the side, then angled back the other way. If I zigzagged enough, maybe I could throw off their aim.

High-Mass and Hutch—Masserotti and Hutchison—were out at the head of our impromptu flying column, swinging now around to the far side of the ketch. A hole appeared low in one of the sharply laid-back sails.

"U.S. Marines!" Hancock's vastly amplified voice boomed across the water. "Put down your weapons and prepare to be boarded!"

Several more geysers of water appeared. I could see one of the people on the boat aiming something that looked like a snub-barreled plasma weapon . . . and then his arms flailed, the weapon went flying, and the man dropped back out of sight behind the gunwale. I couldn't tell which Marine got him. It was a hell of a shot, though, from the back of a bucking, skittering quantum flitter. I hadn't even bothered unshipping my laser carbine; I didn't see how I could keep steering the flitter *and* get off an accurate shot.

"U.S. Marines!" Gunny Hancock boomed again. "Cease fire! Drop your weapons and prepare to be boarded!"

There was some more confusion on board the ketch, and then I saw three men in the aft part of the boat holding up their hands. The sails above them were shortening, too, and the ketch slowed a bit, though it continued bearing down on the shore behind us.

"Tomacek, Colby, Gutierrez!" Hancock called over the squad channel. "With me! The rest of you keep circling!"

The four flitters slowed to just above the minimum velocity needed to stay aloft, edging in alongside the moving ketch. Nano-grapnels snapped out, fused with the hull, and pulled the flitters in tight to the boat's freeboard. Hancock went aboard first, scrambling up and over the gunwale and onto the deck.

"Drop it!" Hancock yelled, his voice carrying both on the squad channel and through the atmosphere. "I said drop it! All of you! Down on the deck! *Move!*"

There were a few seconds of silence as I continued to

follow with the Marines circling the ketch. Then, "Corpsman! Come on board!"

That was my cue. I cut out of the formation and came up
on the ketch from astern, cutting my speed back . . . back . . .
and then firing my grapnels when I was just a meter or so off
the ketch's starboard side. I released my safety harness and
scrambled up on board.

The ketch looked like a fishing boat. There were piles
of nets amidships, along with coiled lengths of cable and
neon-green buoys. Four crewmen were flat on the deck—
three getting their hands tied behind their backs by Colby
and Gutierrez, with Hancock and Tomacek keeping them
all covered. A fourth lay nearby, screaming, writhing in
pain, his right arm, shoulder, and part of his right torso
badly burned. It looked like he'd taken the fringe effect
from a plasma bolt, which meant he'd been tagged either by
Tomacek or by Leighton.

"We have a patient for you, Doc," Hancock said.

"Right."

I kneeled next to the man, pulling out my M-7. Like
the others, he was wearing what looked like brightly dyed
leather—all oranges, browns, and reds—with a filter mask
and a set of goggles that gave him an odd, bug-eyed look.
"Take it easy, fella," I told him. He wasn't wearing combat
armor, so I plugged ten ccs of anodynic recep blockers into
my hypo's receiver and dialed up its regular head. I pressed
it against his carotid artery under his jaw and fired in the
nananodyne.

"What are you doing!" one of the prisoners called out.
Flat on his stomach, he was arching his back, trying to see.
"What is that man doing?"

"Take it easy," Hancock said. "That man's a medic. He'll
take good—"

"No! No! *What is he doing to him?*"

I ignored the outburst and kept working on the wounded
man, pulling out my N-prog and monitoring the migration
of nanobots to his brain. Within a few seconds, the nanano-

dyne started taking hold, blocking out the pain receptors in the man's brain. He relaxed, sagging back to the deck with a sigh as he released a pent-up breath.

"Thank you, brother," he said. "*Thank you!*" Then he seemed to realize what was going on. "Wait, what did you just do? The pain is gone!"

"Shot you with nananodyne pain-blockers," I told him, studying the N-prog's screen. "They'll hold you until you can get to . . ."

He tried to grab me with his left hand. "*Satan! What did you put into my temple?*"

He couldn't get much of a purchase on my throat with my combat armor in the way, and his clawed fingers scrabbled ineffectively at my helmet. I punched in Program 2 through my N-prog. Half of the nanobots in the man's brains reprogrammed themselves and began shifting from the thalamus and the insular cortex to the hippocampus and prefrontal cortex, binding with the NMDA receptors and taking the patient down into a drowsy, half-aware state. He was still trying to fight me, though, so I injected another ten ccs of nanobots, programming them to join with the others in shutting down his consciousness. In another few moments, he slumped into coma, his eyes still open but his body completely anaesthetized.

I monitored his state for another moment through the N-prog, making sure his breathing, heart rate, blood pressure, and other vitals were sustainable. They weren't *good*; he was shocking fast. But at least they were holding stable.

The other three prisoners were screaming, raging against their bonds, and Gunny Hancock told the others to put them down with swifties.

And I focused all my attention on my patient.

Chapter Eleven

THE FRINGE EFFECT OF TOMACEK'S PLASMA BOLT HAD NEARLY burned through the wounded guy's right arm completely. Most of his humerus, between shoulder and elbow, was gone, and what was left was hanging on by straps of muscle charred to the consistency of hardened leather. His right torso, from armpit to hip, was deeply blistered. I estimated fifteen to twenty percent second-degree burns, with another five to ten percent third-degree. There was a very good chance that my patient would die within the next few hours if I couldn't treat him successfully.

First up was stabilizing him. His blood pressure was dropping as his heartbeat became weaker, fast, and thready. He'd lost a tremendous amount of blood and tissue fluids in an instant, which had put him into shock almost immediately. The nano I'd sent to his brain included some that was monitoring his cerebellum and medulla, but there was only so much they could do to control his BP. His arm had been cauterized at the shoulder, but he was leaking fluid, a *lot* of fluid, from the raw, blistered skin along his side. I pulled a packet of skinseal from my M-7, thumbed it open, and dusted the man's side with it. Skinseal is a type of first-aid nano used for superficial wounds, and also for wounds covering a large area of the body—scrapes and large burns. The nanobots link together to form a strictly temporary artificial skin, holding in whatever is trying to get out, and also acting as a local anesthetic. My patient didn't need further anesthesia, obviously, but the skinseal would stop the ooze of blood and interstitial fluid.

Another check on his respiration and pulse. Still falling. I gave him another shot of nanobots, these programmed to target his medulla and cerebellum to further stabilize his autonomic processes. What he needed most at the moment was intravenous fluids to replace the massive blood volume loss, but I didn't have any with me. We'd have to get him to our rough-and-ready sick bay on shore to deal with that.

"Okay, people," I heard Gunny Hancock call from farther aft. "Who knows how to steer this thing?"

I glanced up. I'd been so involved with the injured man that I'd momentarily forgotten just where we were: on board a two-masted sailing vessel running before an oncoming storm, with rocks and a rugged coastline a few hundred meters ahead.

"I do!" I called. "But I'm a little busy right now. Talk to the boat's AI."

"It doesn't *have* one, Doc."

I blinked. That was just crazy. Sailboats on Earth *always* had an artificial intelligence as pilot, able to step in and take over control of the craft if the pilot was disabled or found himself out of his depth.

But, then, this wasn't Earth, and we knew so damned little about the native human culture here.

"There still should be some kind of interface with the craft," I told him.

"If there is, I don't see it."

I looked aft. There was a wheel mounted on a post behind the mizzenmast, lashed tight with a line thrown around one of the handles extending from the rim. I pointed. "Unship that line on the helm. Then take the wheel and turn . . ."

I glanced up at the sails, then aft at the wall of purple clouds on the horizon behind us, then at the angle the ketch was pursuing across the water. There were three sails up, the jib all the way forward, and the main and mizzen, both billowing from multiple yardarms angled across masts canted so far back they were very nearly horizontal to the water, like wings. With no one at the helm, the ketch was angling more and more toward starboard—to the right—which was causing us to heel farther and farther to port as the wind gusted in from the open sea. At the moment, the boulders and sheer cliffs along the southern headland of the bay were directly ahead. If we kept turning into the wind, we might miss them—or we might slam into those rocks and all of us would end up in the drink.

"Take the wheel and turn it to port, to the left," I continued. "Keep turning until we're pointed at the beach again and hold it there."

Tomacek took the helm, releasing the wheel and grabbing the archaic handles. I was a long-time bedsheet sailor—I used to sail a little four-meter sloop all the time in the Chesapeake when I was a kid—but I was used to automated controls, with an AI constantly adjusting the sails and running rigging. This ketch was like something out of the days of Nelson and Decatur. From the look of it, you had to actually adjust the sails *by hand*, by hauling in or releasing the lines running between sails and deck.

As Tomacek hauled the wheel over, our bow began once again swinging away from the wind and toward the rocky beach where the Marine encampment was located.

"What the hell are you trying to do, Doc?" Hancock asked, the words quiet, mildly curious. "Run us aground?"

"Exactly," I told him. "We don't know enough about this kind of boat to actually *sail* her, especially with a squall coming in astern. I figure if we can beach her, we can get off okay." I shrugged. "It'll be better than slamming into those rocks on the headland, or maybe capsizing when that squall hits us."

I was pretty sure that the crew of the ketch had been planning just that. They'd been at sea when they'd seen the storm moving in, and had turned in toward the shore to find a bay offering at least a little shelter from the blow. Given the high winds on this planet, I was amazed that the locals engaged in old-style bedsheet sailing at all. A submarine would have been more appropriate.

The ketch kept swinging toward the left until the beach was dead ahead. To either side, the Second Squad Marines still on their flitters paced us like dolphins, skipping along the swells as we barreled in toward the beach.

We were moving fast, too damned fast. "Gunny!" I yelled, and pointed. "Use your lasers to cut away the mizzen and the mains'l!"

Gunny Hancock gave orders to Colby and Gutierrez, who both were armed with standard Corps-issue megajoule-pulse Mk. 24 laser rifles. Calling those things rifles was a bit of a misnomer, of course; they fired bolts of coherent light, and so didn't have the grooved rifling that gave the old slug-poppers their name. They identified the points on the yards and the sail itself where the running rigging held the mainsail down against the mainmast, and began firing with careful precision. There was a crack, followed by a sudden thunderous flapping as the mainsail boomed and fluttered wildly on the wind. A moment later, the mizzen sail did the same, fluttering hard as the ketch shuddered.

The two Marines fired again, and both sails parted from the yards, snapping and twisting in the wind as they flew forward and into the water. We were now being carried along solely by the jib, a small, triangular sail stretched from the top of the mainmast to the end of the bowsprit forward. It continued to draw wind from astern, but the sail area was so reduced, now, that the ketch slowed from a headlong race before the wind to a lumbering, shuddering plod.

I focused on my patient for another moment; pieces of his leather costume—and there was a lot of plastic in there as well—had melted in ragged patches to his skin. I couldn't pull them free without opening fresh wounds, but they would also be a major source of infection in this guy if I couldn't get them out. Debriding the wound, it's called.

I used a surgical laser scalpel to first cut through the charred tissue that still connected his right arm to his shoulder. The charring and bone loss was far too great for any hope of it healing. I cut the arm away, used more skinseal to stop a few small, leaking blood vessels at the shoulder, then began concentrating on the patches of melted plastic and charred leather imbedded in his side.

"Hang on, people!" Hancock yelled. "We're coming up on the beach!"

An instant later I both heard and felt the vessel's keel grind along the bottom. I snapped off the laser to avoid cutting too deeply, and then the deck lurched beneath me with a long and drawn-out rumbling crunch. The mainmast swayed alarmingly, and for a moment I thought it was going to fall, but the standing rigging held. The deck canted slightly to starboard, as incoming swells rolled and broke past her bulwarks.

"Masserotti! Kukowicz! Andrews! Gregory!" Hancock snapped off the names of four more Marines who were still skimming above the water on their flitters. "Get your asses up here and give a hand with these prisoners! Doc? How's the patient?"

"Not as bad as he could be," I said. "We need to get him to sick bay stat."

I packed up my med gear as the other Marines swarmed on board. The ketch had come to rest about a hundred meters offshore. The water was waist-deep, perhaps a little more. Two Marines each took an unconscious prisoner, lifting him between them in a two-handed seat-carry, hands joined behind shoulders and beneath knees. Thank God for the exoskeletal walkers strapped to our armor; they would have been hard-pressed to carry those men in Bloodworld's 1.85 G.

My patient was a different matter. We might have killed him, trying to lift and awkwardly manhandle him down the side of the boat. Hancock called to the Marines ashore and had them bring a stokes out on a floater pad.

The floater was a quantum-lift device like the flitters, but with lateral pontoons so that it floated on water. Staff Sergeant Abrams and Sergeant Gibbs brought it out, along with the wire-basket stretcher known as the stokes. Hancock helped me get the patient into the wire basket and strapped down, and together we lowered him over the side to the waiting Marines below.

I left his severed arm on the deck.

Golfball-sized hail began rattling around us—a few stones at first, followed by an avalanche of hard, icy projectiles snapping out of the purple sky and smashing against the deck, or lashing the water around us into a white torrent of spray. Mixed with the hail came torrential rain, huge drops plummeting with twice the speed they would have had on Earth, and the wind began gusting so hard it was difficult to stand.

Our armor kept us dry and breathing, but it was still a long and difficult wade through surf and storm back to the beach. Somehow, we made it with all four locals up the beach and into the HQ dome. Chief Garner led Hancock and me through the freshly grown corridors and into the compartment designated as the sick bay.

You can only program so much into nanoconstructors when you build a facility like this one, and the sick bay was little more at the moment than walls, lights, tables, and ten bare-pad beds. The banks of diagnostic equipment, sensors, and medical gear would have to be brought in later. At Chief Garner's order, Leighton made the trip through the storm out to the D/MST and brought back a case of artificial blood, BVEs, and IV gear. Together, we got the patient onto a bed and hung a bag of BVE solution from the frame overhead. A BVE—blood volume expander—was essentially a colloidal-salt-and-protein solution that would help stabilize the guy's falling blood pressure, quick and dirty. The artificial blood was a perfluorocarbon-based emulsion that mimicked blood in transporting oxygen through the circulatory system. We needed to test the patient for perfluorocarbon sensitivity

first, though, and that meant reprogramming some of the
'bots in his system.

I did that while Garner began working at debriding the
burns again. I transmitted the program, then studied my
N-prog's screen for a few moments. "Huh," I said.

"What's 'huh'?"

"The nanobots I shot into this guy out there?"

"Yeah?"

"Those are the *only* ones in his system. He's not carrying
any artificial biologicals at all."

Garner shrugged. "Not all civilians have internal prostheses," he said. "He's obviously not military."

"Yeah . . . but a civilian living on a planet like this one?
I'd think they'd be bioteched to the gills."

Back on Earth, of course, there's a broad mix of biotech
usage, everything from nothing at all—natural biology—to
the tech-savvies who've replaced their blood cells with respirocytes and gone the cyborg route with artificial limbs,
eyes, cerebral implants, and advanced genetic prostheses.
Nanomedicines routinely cure everything from cancer and
coronary artery disease to colds and old age, and most
people have a population of programmable 'bots patrolling their bloodstream, watching, diagnosing, cleaning, and
healing.

And colony planets tend to be high tech. It stands to
reason, since none of the worlds we've colonized is a perfect double for Earth. Here on Bloodworld, I would have expected to see fairly elaborate nanomedical systems in use to
filter sulfur dioxide and heavy metals out of the lungs, nasal
passageways, and circulatory systems, to protect the eyes
from radiation and atmospheric contaminants, even to help
them digest native-grown foods. But this man was a natural,
meaning no nanotechnic or genetic prostheses at all.

What was it he'd yelled at me, before I put him under?
What did you put into my temple? Yeah, that was it.

Curious, I ran "body as temple" through the base library,
and got back a Bible reference, something in I Corinthians 6.

*19. Or do you not know that your body is a temple
of the Holy Spirit, who is in you, whom you have
received from God, and that you are not your
own? For you have been bought with a price.
20. Therefore glorify God in your body.*

It seemed a strange sentiment, but so damned little was
known about the Neoessenes, especially the bunch that had
left Earth to build a God-centered theocracy at the Bloodstar. I did seem to remember something about them being
Luddies, opposed to high-tech, although getting on board
a starship to make the move to a new planet twenty light
years away seemed to be about as tech-intensive as you
could get.

Did the Neoessies forbid the use of nanomedical technology? It wouldn't be the first time religions had rejected medical technology. The Jehovah's Witnesses, I knew, refused
blood transfusions because, for them, that was the same as
"eating blood," something forbidden by the Laws of Moses.
And the Christian Scientists and some of the more extreme
Christian fundamentalist sects rejected *all* medical treatments, on the grounds that only God could heal.

Shit. Anti-tech fundies? That could be a problem, and I
said as much to Chief Garner.

"Well," he said with a philosophical shrug, "everyone's free to go to hell in his own way, including the crazy
people." He continued working on the debridement, deftly
slicing away bits of raw tissue adhering to scraps of melted
clothing with his scalpel. "We'll just take it a step at a time."

"Yeah, but what if what we're doing to this guy is taboo
in their culture?" I asked.

"What if it is? Our job is to save lives the best way we
can, *any* way we can, and we're not responsible for what they
believe, or how they think. Or *don't* think. . . ."

"Well, this guy doesn't show perfluorocarbon sensitivities," I said, studying the N-prog screen. "So, do we do it?"

"What, 'tube him with perfluoro? Of course."

"Even though it may be against his religion? I think we need to find out more about that."

Garner shook his head. "Uh-uh. First we save his life. *Then* we worry about his immortal soul."

EVENTUALLY, THE DEBRIDEMENT WAS DONE, AND I WENT BACK TO THE barracks. The rain, sleet, and hail outside were so heavy that someone had rigged a guideline between the HQ and the barracks dome. The sea, I noticed, had come inland, and was already ankle deep around the buildings. That wasn't a particular problem; those domes were designed to survive being completely submerged, and similar structures were used as sea-bottom research facilities. But the fury of the wind had lashed up a storm surge that had all but completely submerged the beach.

Adding insult to injury, we felt our first seismic quake during the storm. It seemed unlikely that the storm had triggered a 7.5 temblor, but it did seem as though Bloodworld was throwing everything at us that it could.

At least we were off the operational hook for the moment. Although Baumgartner fumed and fussed a bit, there was no way we were going out on our patrol in that storm. We stayed inside either the HQ dome or the barracks, getting used to the local gravity, catching up on our sleep, and having something hot to eat—a luxury we'd not been able to enjoy during the hours-long flight out from where the *Clymer* dropped us off.

And twenty hours after we'd boarded the ketch, Gunny Hancock called me back to the HQ dome, where they were bringing one of the prisoners around.

"I thought you'd like to be here for this," he told me. "I heard you were concerned about local taboos."

Garner must have told him. "It helps knowing what we're up against," I told him.

Baumgartner was there, along with Staff Sergeant Lloyd and another member of his staff. He was deep in a quiet discussion with the two of them and didn't notice when I came in. I was amused. Second lieutenants are at the bottom of the totem pole when it comes to chain-of-command among the officer types, and don't generally have their own staff. Our little expedition boasted thirty-nine combat Marines out of a contingent of forty-eight. The leftovers included Baumgartner, four Corpsmen, and an operational staff of two communications-intelligence specialists and two tech specialists.

Baumy looked like he was in his glory.

Doob Dubois was working on the unconscious prisoner. With his goggles and respirator off, we could see that he was a young man, probably in his twenties, with dark hair and eyes and pasty white skin. That made me wonder about something right there. Was his skin so pale because he was never exposed to the local sun's direct rays, to ultraviolet radiation especially? I made a mental note to check both his vitamin D levels and his bone density.

Dubois was using an N-prog to revive him. People who'd been swiftied could be unconscious for anything from minutes to hours; when we'd gotten them back to shore, Hancock had ordered one of the other Corpsmen to inject the prisoners with nanobots and so we could switch them unconscious, simply because we didn't have the manpower to guard them full time.

"Why the hell is it called a swifty, anyway?" I asked. I could have downloaded the answer from the library, of course, but it was meant to be a rhetorical question. It seemed like such a strange term.

"Early twentieth century," Hancock told me. "There was a series of kid's books, *The Adventures of Tom Swift*, all about a genius inventor who came up with some gadgets that seemed pretty far-out for their time. *Tom Swift and His Aerial Warship. Tom Swift and His Bicycle.* That sort of thing."

"Okay. . . ." I'd never cared much for twentieth-century literature in school, and gotten away with downloading as little as I could.

"Sixty or so years later," Hancock continued, "a NASA researcher invented a non-lethal weapon that delivered an electrical charge to the target. He called it the Taser, after one of the adventures of his childhood hero—*Thomas A. Swift's Electric Rifle*."

"Thomas A. Swift . . . oh, I get it."

"Exactly." Hancock drew his swifty from its holster, a HiVolt 3mm stun gun that fired sliverdarts built around ultra–high-density batteries carrying a charge large enough to incapacitate a man. "Tasers didn't knock people unconscious, usually, but later weapons did. Hence, 'swifties.' "

The man on the table groaned and opened his eyes. "Where in His name am I?"

"You're safe," Hancock told him. "We're U.S. Marines, and we're here to investigate reports that the Qesh have attacked your colony. Who are you?"

"Hezekiah," the man said, sounding a little uncertain. "Hezekiah two-fifty-four of Green-two-three. My brothers . . ."

"They're safe as well," Baumgartner told him. "The one who was wounded . . . what is his name?"

"Ezekiel. Ezekiel oh-four-nine of Green-two-four. How is he?"

"I'm told he should pull through."

"He lost his arm. . . ."

"Easily fixed, Hezekiah," Dubois said. "Either regenerative therapy or biomechanical prosthesis will—"

"No!" The man looked terrified. "That's not the Way!"

"Easy, there," Hancock said. "You say he's your brother?"

"All of the Temple are my brothers."

"I see. Why did you fire at us?"

An eloquent shrug. "You obviously weren't of the Temple Brotherhood. We thought you might be demons."

Hancock grinned. "Not quite. We can actually be very nice folks if you don't get on our bad side. By shooting at us, for instance."

Hezekiah spoke English. According to the little we knew

about them, the original Neoessenes had first appeared in Southern California, then spread across the Southwest—Arizona, New Mexico, and Sonora. For a time they'd been based in Chihuahua, and a lot of them spoke Spanish as well.

" 'Demons,' " Baumgartner repeated. "Do you mean the Qesh?"

"Demons," the prisoner said, speaking slowly, with great conviction, "are *any* who stand against the Way."

"So what were you doing in that boat, anyway?" Baumgartner asked.

"The Qesh-demons came to Salvation," he said with a shrug. "Some of us were attempting to reach Redemption . . . that's a city south of here, on the Twilight Coast. But the *sirocco frio* was blowing up, and we needed to find shelter. And then you attacked us."

"We weren't *attacking* you," Baumgartner said. "You fired on us first."

"It looked like an attack to us." He hesitated. "On the boat, you . . . one of you, was putting something into Ezekiel's body."

"That was me," I told him, taking a step closer. "He was in a lot of pain. I gave him a nananodyne blocker."

His face darkened. "That is . . . what?" he demanded. "A nanomedicine?"

"Yes. They're programmed to break down into harmless constituents in—"

"Satan!" the man howled, and he came up off that table like a rocket, his arms stretched out to grab me.

Hancock stepped in front of me, grabbed and twisted him sharply, and pinned him in a shoulder hold. "Dubois!" he shouted as the prisoner raged. "Drop him!"

Doob punched a code into his N-prog, and Ezekiel slumped into happy-happy land.

"A little touchy on the subject of intrusive nanotechnics, are we?" Baumgartner observed as Hancock and Doob hauled him back onto the table.

"At least," Staff Sergeant Naomi Hernandez, one of

Baumgartner's technical people, said, "their lack of nano-technics means we'll be able to Clarke them."

Arthur C. Clarke, a writer and a promoter of future high tech of two or three hundred years ago, had been responsible for one of human technology's most famous aphorisms: *Any sufficiently advanced technology is indistinguishable from magic.* You don't generally see the actual technology nowadays; the infrastructure is invisible behind the effect, and that certainly can look like magic—growing furniture out of a solid deck, for instance, downloading data directly off the local net into your brain, or using invisibly minute robots to clean the cholesterol out of your arteries. When you "Clarke" someone, you get the advantage on them by using technology that they don't even know is there.

"You're thinking of microprobes?" Baumgartner asked.

"Yes, sir. It should be easy enough to get a cloud of gnat-bots in there, and have a look around. If they don't know about nanotech, they'll never know they're there."

"Put it into the operational plan, then," Baumgartner told her.

"Aye, aye, sir."

"Christ!" Baumgartner said, looking up as a deep-voiced rumble sounded, and the room began to shake. "Not again!"

It was another seismic quake, a bad one—this one shaking us at about 7.1 on the standard modified Mercalli scale.

"Earthquake," Hancock said. "Or a Bloodworld-quake, I guess I should say."

Well, between the flooding and the seismic events, at least Baumy would be off our cases about getting an early start.

Of course, I felt sure that Hancock already had gnatbots in mind for the patrol.

EVENTUALLY, THE STORM BLEW ITSELF OUT, THOUGH FOR ABOUT FIVE hours there, we were all stuck in whichever hab dome we happened to be in at the time because the storm surge deepened the water outside to almost 4 meters.

As the storm abated, though, the water level went down, and pretty soon the beach was only a little truncated from the way we'd found it. The D/MST-22 was still there, anchored by nanograpnels to the rock. The ketch, however, was gone.

Fortunately, the Marines had brought in the quantum flitters and secured them inside the storeroom. We broke them out and saddled up in a deep, purple twilight. The sun had dropped below the eastern horizon, though the sky still carried some light.

After a final check of armor and equipment, we strapped onto our waiting flitters. Hancock gave the signal. "Okay, Marines! Route formation! Move out!"

We'd practiced this type of deployment endlessly, of course, both on Mars and through in-head sims. Corporal Masserotti and Private Hutchison were out ahead on point, with Gutierrez and Andrews on the left flank, Kilgore and Lewis on the right, and the rest of us strung out in a raggedly staggered column down the middle. I was flying just aft and to the right of Gunny Hancock and ahead of Sergeant Tomacek, who was one of Second Squad's two plasma gunners. There were fourteen of us—a typical Marine squad of thirteen, plus me. We also had one robot, a big cargo flitter hauling expendables, sentry, and perimeter gear, and a 100-megajoule plasma cannon all disassembled and stowed inside.

"I still say it's Alpha Company's turn for this shit," Randolph Gregory grumbled as we got moving.

"Can it, Orgy," Tomacek said. "You heard the man. We're just gonna go have a look-see. No gun play. Sweet, slick, and simple."

"We pulled the *easy* duty for a change," Calli Lewis added.

"Yeah, right."

We began picking our way inland, navigating toward Salvation.

Chapter Twelve

ACCORDING TO THE MAP LOADED INTO OUR PERSONAL RAMs, Salvation was thirty kilometers north along the coast, while Redemption was fifty-five klicks to the south. There'd been some discussion between Hancock and Baumgartner, I knew, about switching targets, but Charlie Company was handling Redemption and our original target was still Salvation. There'd also been talk about waiting until we could get more information about the target from our nautical "guests," but we couldn't really afford the time to interrogate them, especially since Ezekiel had been showing little interest in cooperating with us. We set off knowing only that the Qesh were already in control there.

The trip north was uneventful. Once we got up and off the beach, we climbed onto the high plateau beyond, open, rolling ground shrouded in the rubbery, black-leaved vegetation that seemed to cover most of the open ground here. With both armor and our vehicles nanoflaged, we blended into the black background perfectly; I couldn't even see the Marines flying closest to me, just a few dozen meters up ahead.

Our top speed in this gravity field was limited to about fifty kilometers per hour, but we often had to move much more slowly than that as we negotiated what amounted to forests of bushy, black, house-sized masses of vegetation with whip-thin tendrils ten meters high.

Eventually, though, about two hours later, we began to get close.

We *heard* it first. In Bloodworld's dense atmosphere, sound carried very well. Even five kilometers back in the jungle, we could hear the grinding shriek and thunder of some sort of large machinery.

A short time later, we reached the tree line looking out across an open plain that I recognized from our briefings. A trail, a path beaten down into the earth, ran along the edge of the woods, where we took cover in the underbrush. From here, we could see the city wall.

Eons ago, some massive seismic event had thrust these basaltic cliffs into the sky along Bloodworld's western twilight zone. The cliffs here rose in two sections, the first from the turbulent sea, rising perhaps fifty meters from the water to the relatively flat plain that, inland, gave way to soil and the thick growth of the forest where we were hiding.

The second section rose from this plateau another twenty or thirty meters up, creating a massive black wall off to our right and about a kilometer away. The city of Salvation appeared to be growing from the sheer face of this second black cliff. It was dark, with Bloodworld's curious half twilight beneath a deep purple sky. There were no lights from the city itself, but a number of high masts mounted spotlights that bathed the surrounding dark rock in an intense glare.

All of us remembered the scenes in that early briefing of Qesh Rocs blowing up buildings. That had been over by the spaceport, somewhere behind those cliffs; from here, we couldn't see much damage at all.

On top of the plateau beneath the city wall, close to the drop-off into the sea, dust or smoke boiled from what looked like a broad, open pit several hundred meters across, only to be caught and tattered away by the stiff wind blowing out of the west. The dust appeared to be illuminated from beneath, from within the pit, by a deep and flickering red glow.

With Bloodstar still below the horizon, it was too dark to see much at optical wavelengths. By low-light optics, we could see what might have been movement around the pit, including something squat, black, and enormous along one side. Under magnification, and by shifting to infrared, we could see armored vehicles or figures moving around on the ground . . . and we could see a row of humans, eight colonists, apparently tied together in a string and held motionless at gunpoint at the very edge of the crater. Armored Qesh, grotesque, centaur-shapes with hot power units glowing on their backs, patrolled the line, weapons at the ready. A number of enormous machines appeared to be devouring the ground nearby; on closer inspection, much of the dust came from these.

I increased my visor's magnification all the way up, zooming in on the nearest machine. The thing must have been the size of a city block back home, shaped like a flattened egg with a low-arched opening across the entire front end that seemed to be devouring the ground in front of it. The machine appeared to be enlarging the open pit, grinding up rocks in a thunderous cacophony of raw and violent noise as it crawled slowly but inexorably across the ground.

There were five other similar machines—no two identical in detail, but all squat and monstrous—working around the edges of the pit.

It looked like the Qesh were strip-mining the surface.

Silently, Second Squad spread out among the trees along the edge of the plain. Sergeants Leighton and Tomacek began recording what they could see for burst-transmission back to Red Tower. I pulled out my sniffer, a palm-sized ES-80 environmental sensor, and began a sweep for radiation or other background effects.

I immediately got a ping on my IHD.

"Gunny?" I said over a private channel. "I'm picking up nano-D effects."

"Shit. How bad?"

"Very, very low. Ten to the minus three. Our suits can handle it fine. I'm not so sure about those poor bastards beside the pit, though."

Nano-D—short for nanotechnic deconstructors—is the basis for all modern deconstruction techniques. Nanobot machines the size of large molecules, around a hundred nanometers or so, cover a target surface or material in a thin sheen and break it apart, atom by atom. Basalt, for instance, is about fifty percent SiO_2, with the rest made up of iron and magnesium. Depending on the precise type of basaltic rock, there might be other elements present as well, calcium, sodium, aluminum, and so on—including even traces of scandium, vanadium, and titanium, and others.

The Qesh evidently believed in going the full-scale industrial route. Those huge rock-eaters were carving or breaking off massive chunks and grinding them up first, increasing the surface area so that the nano-D could break it down faster. The pure elements would be separated out and stored, somehow, possibly in those huge canisters lined up close to the city.

From over a kilometer away, I couldn't see the actual process, but my sniffer was reporting random hits by deconstructor nanobots. While most would be contained beneath the rock eater, a few, inevitably, would escape with the billowing dust and scattered across the landscape on the breeze. Whatever they chanced to land upon, they began eating—but doing so a molecule at a time, which was far too slow to cause any real damage. At that range, the background radiation was doing a lot more damage to us.

Closer to the mining operation, however, the concentration of deconstructor nanobots would be higher, perhaps *much* higher. Without armor, those natives standing along the edge of the pit might be taking enough hits to hurt them, even to kill them over time. What the hell was going on over there, anyway?

I tried zooming in close on the humans. I couldn't see much detail at this range; they appeared to be wearing the same garb as our prisoners back at Red Tower; it looked like their hands were tied behind their backs, and their necks joined by three-meter lengths of rope or cable. Their guards towered over them, armored centaurs with heavy, oddly curved crests on their helmets. One of the prisoners, trembling violently, collapsed in line; one of the guards picked him up with one arm and planted him back on unsteady feet.

An alarm sounded inside my head.

"Heads up," Hancock warned over the quantum-scrambled squad channel. "We've got company. From the south."

I twisted around, trying to see into the dark forest at our backs. A moment later, I saw movement . . . and then a column of humans emerged from the shadows. They wore black cloaks and hardened leather, and their faces were concealed by that same combination of breather mask and bug-eyed goggles we'd seen on the crew of the boat. There were five of them; they carried antiquated laser rifles with heavy, external battery packs slung over their shoulders. They didn't see the Marines nanoflaged in the underbrush, but passed us by, moving along the tree line toward the east.

"That last one in line," Hancock's voice said in our heads. "Masserotti! Gibbs! Get him, but *quietly*!"

Two dark, armored shapes rose from the underbrush behind the native, who was following his companions up the path. A hand closed over the man's mouth, an arm circled his waist and dragged him backward. Masserotti pulled the laser rifle from him and tossed it aside, as Gibbs kneeled in front of the man and held a finger to the lower part of his opaque helmet visor, miming silence.

"U.S. Marines," Sergeant Gibbs said. "We're from Earth. We're here to help you."

Gibbs used audio, rather than radio or laser communications. Our squad AI hadn't yet sorted out or analyzed the native freaks. We were using tight-burst, quantum encoded communications among ourselves, but we had no idea as to what kind of communications technologies the human colonists of Bloodworld might have. Judging by those battery packs, they were at least a century out of date in terms of general weaponry.

"Where . . . where did you come from?" The native said, his voice slightly muffled by his filter mask.

"Like I said, fella, Earth."

"What's your name?" Masserotti asked.

"Caleb. Caleb three-one-one of Orange-one-oh."

"Well, Caleb, we need you to tell us what's going on here."

"The demons!" he spat. "They arrived a little less than a year ago! They told the elders that the Bloodworld was theirs, and that we now belong to the Qesh! Lies of Satan! We belong to God, and none other!"

"They're coming back, Gibbs," Leighton said.

"My brothers!" the native said.

"You want to introduce us to your . . . brothers, Caleb?" Hancock asked.

Caleb nodded, and the two Marines let him go. A moment later, the four other natives who'd passed us by a few moments earlier came up the path once more, obviously searching for their missing "brother."

"Malachi!" Caleb called out. "Albiathar! God has sent His warrior angels!"

Then four stopped, their laser rifles raised. "Take it easy, people," Hancock said. "We're friends. We're here to help you."

"We need no help," one of them said, "for God is with us! *He* is our help!"

"How about lowering your weapons," Hancock told them, "and considering the possibility that God is helping you by sending *us*?"

"Matthew!" one of the others said. "It's possible! These could be the promised angels of the Rapture!"

I'd never heard of Marines being referred to as *angels* before, but it seemed like a promising start.

The truth was, we needed a fresh start with the locals. Obviously, the colony here had some sort of religious taboo or prohibition against nanomeds, and it was possible they rejected all medicines. I knew of several sects besides the Jehovah's Witnesses and Christian Scientists who'd rejected at least some medical technology; the Apostles of Light, for instance, who believed relying on mere human medicine showed a lack of proper faith.

We needed natives who could fill us in on the current tacsit, and who might be willing to get us into the city. And if we could avoid violating any of their taboos long enough to get to know them, these five might be the ones.

WE GREW A SMALL FIELD HUT THERE AT THE EDGE OF THE WOODS TO serve as our forward observation post, taking care to mask it with a heavy sheathing of nanoflage. The OP had a two-person airlock that meant we could at least take off our helmets inside. It was big enough for ten or twelve Marines with a bit of crowding, but at least half of the squad would be outside at all times, keeping an eye on the activity on the far side of the plain.

We also opened up the cargo flitter and broke out several robot sentries and the big plasma cannon as a support weapon. The cannon was self-assembling, and in a few moments was up and running, its muzzle aimed at the nightmare lights and noise in the distance.

Our new guests were Caleb, Albiathar, Samuel, Malachi, and Matthew, members of a patrol sent out to attempt to contact some of the other colony cities in the area. Matthew five-three-one of Orange-one-oh was the leader. He was an older man, though just how old depended a lot on Bloodworld's medical technology, or lack of one. He *looked* like he might be around two hundred, but without cybertelomerics and other rejuve processes, he might have been only fifty.

Their names, frankly, worried me. Each had a common name apparently drawn from the Bible, but since such names were fewer than the total number of colonists, each was followed by a number and by a color plus a number, which seemed to refer to a particular district or perhaps a section of the city. The system felt dry and static, even repressive, and I was beginning to think Salvation might in fact be a theocratic dictatorship of some kind.

Those could be nasty.

I was inside the hut with Gunny Hancock, No-Joy Leighton, Orgy Gregory, and High-Mass Masserotti, and our five guests. We were off to a rocky start when we began with a very basic misunderstanding.

"You say the demons came almost half a year ago?" Hancock asked. "That doesn't seem possible."

"Have they been inside Salvation itself?" Leighton asked. "Have they figured out how to translate your computer files?"

I knew what was worrying her. That secondary objective to our mission—to keep the Qesh from getting navigational data that might lead them to Earth, that was on all of our minds at the moment. Earth had received word of the Qesh arrival at Gliese 581 six days later, or so we assumed. A second ship had arrived a day later with an update. Then it had taken us six days and some to get there—for a total of two weeks, max. Or so we'd assumed.

Two weeks was bad enough—plenty of time for the Jackers to take over Salvation and hijack the computer records, which just might still contain all the data necessary to lead them straight to Earth. If they'd been here six months, though, we were lucky they weren't already in Earth orbit delivering an ultimatum.

"Just a minute," I said. "Matthew, how many *days* ago did they arrive?"

"Do you mean lights? One."

"Do you still measure time with weeks?"

"Of course," Albiathar said. "But only for *sacred* time, to remember the Sabbath."

"The Elder Council computer measures sacred time by hours and seconds," Matthew said. "There are one hundred sixty-eight hours to the week, the first twenty-four of which—"

"Right, right. So the Qesh, the demons, have only been here about two weeks, then?"

Matthew nodded. "Yes."

I nodded at Hancock. "Local terminology, Gunny," I said. "Bloodstar's year is thirty-six and a half days long. *Our* days. Since the planet is tidally locked to its star, one 'day' here, one 'light' or one diurnal period, would be one libration cycle. The sun rises and sets two or three times in one local year, depending on the orbits of the nearby planets."

"Thank God," Hancock said. "I thought—"

"Thou shalt *not* take the name of the Lord thy God in vain!" Matthew snapped, pointing a finger at Hancock. "It was the wholesale breaking of the Commandments that led to the Sacrifice!"

"If the demons hear," the one called Albiathar said, "they will come!"

"They are drawn by evil," Caleb added. "By Commandment-breaking, by evil thoughts!"

"Take it easy, brothers," Hancock told them. "I'm sorry if I offended you, but—"

"You are *not* our 'brothers,'" Samuel pointed out. "You are from the Evil World, which means you are evil yourselves! Fallen creatures in league with the demons!"

"No!" Malachi said. "They are Angels of the Rapture!"

"Of that," Matthew said, eyeing Hancock coldly, "I am not so sure. We need the discernment of the Elders on this."

"The Elders," Massarotti repeated. "Is that like your government?"

"Our *government* is the Church in its holy union with God," Matthew replied, as if talking to a six-year-old. "But the Elder Council speaks for the Lord, yes."

"We would like to talk to this Council," Hancock said. "Are they in Salvation? Or have they gone elsewhere?"

"Where would they go? They are in Salvation, yes."

"And the demons?" I asked. "Are they in Salvation as well?"

"Sadly, yes." Caleb shook his head. "A few of us got out before they forced their way in. We've been trying to contact the other cities, to organize a defense, a resistance. We've not had much luck so far."

"Hush, Caleb," Matthew ordered the younger man. "Until we know these . . . these newcomers better, it's best not to say too much."

"Will you take us to see your Elders, then?" Hancock asked.

"No," Matthew said, with an abrupt shake of his head. "No, it's too dangerous."

"So," Hancock said, thoughtful, "why are you five out here? To contact those other cities?"

Matthew looked at him for a long moment before replying. "No. The nearest city is many kilometers to the south, and it's safer to send our messengers there by boat. We came out of the dome to see if we could find a way to rescue the prisoners."

"The prisoners," I repeated. "That line of people in front of the pit?"

"Yes."

"Hostages for your good behavior?"

"Those eight, and others, resisted the demons when they first arrived," Samuel told us. "They are to be held there until they die of the poison from those machines. As they die, one by one, other . . . resisters are dragged out to take their place."

"My daughter is among them," Matthew said. The pain behind those words dragged at his face, his bearing.

"So, if you succeed in rescuing them," Hancock said, "what happens then? The demons take more resisters?"

"The demons know some of us are out here," Caleb said. "They've been hunting us. If we can free the prisoners, others may be staked out there to die, but at least *some* will have been saved."

"We might be able to help you," Hancock said.

That startled me. Our orders were not to get involved, not to risk having the Jackers find out Marine Recon Seven was on the planet.

Matthew looked at Hancock sharply. "Could you? *Can* you?"

"Possibly. We'll need your help to plan it, though."

"Perhaps," Matthew said. There was a new light behind his eyes, though, a look of hope. "We will need to talk with them first, to see if we can get you inside."

"That," Hancock said, "will have to do."

"How can you help us free the prisoners?"

"By answering a few questions for us," Hancock said. "We'll start by finding out about the demons' numbers. . . ."

"GOOD CALL, E-CAR," LEIGHTON TOLD ME LATER. I WAS OUTSIDE ON the perimeter, looking toward the construction—the *de*-construction, I should say—taking place in front of the city of Salvation. In the past couple of hours, the six huge rock eaters had widened the pit considerably, taking the edge close to the foot of the cliffs upon which the city of Salvation uncomfortably rested. Another seismic tremor had struck about an hour before. It looked like all work had stopped for a time until the dust had settled once more.

"What call was that?"

"Picking up on their year being only five weeks long or so. That was pretty sharp."

"Pretty obvious, you mean. It's interesting that they still measure out twenty-four-hour periods so they can keep the seventh day holy—but for them a 'day' is the rising and setting of the sun above the eastern horizon every two weeks or so."

"I imagine they had to make a lot of adjustments when they migrated out here."

In the distance, one of the prisoners, silhouetted against the glare from the pit, collapsed. A centaur standing close by picked the figure up with its single upper arm, shook it once, tried to set it back on its feet. The bound human collapsed again. Using its upper arm together with the next two in line, the Qesh centaur detached the human from the cable binding it to the prisoners to either side, then picked up the body and without ceremony flung it into the pit.

I stifled a shudder. It was damned hard not to think of

those alien things as evil, deliberately torturing those prisoners to death by forcing them to stand in the deadly wash
of nanodisassemblers.

We were going to go in there and rescue them soon. I
knew Gunny Hancock was working out a plan now as he
and the squad's sergeants questioned the Salvation colonists.
The question was how we were going to pull such a raid off
without alerting the Jackers to our presence on Bloodworld?
I could see three . . . four . . . no, five of the centaur shapes
near the line of prisoners, two of them carrying what looked
like weapons.

As I watched, a sixth centaur led another human out from
a small, squat polygon near the base of the cliffs beneath the
city and forced him—no, her—into the place in line recently
vacated.

I thought about Matthew five-three-one, and his evident
pain at the death sentence placed on his daughter.

Gunny Hancock materialized out of the darkness behind
us. "You two ready for a bit of an outing?"

"I thought we were already having one, Gunny," Leighton said.

"Maybe, but this one's about to get interesting."

I pointed. "Gunny, you see that small building to the
right? Below the city cliffs?"

"Yeah."

"They just now brought another prisoner out of there.
Either that structure is a gate leading into the underground
part of the city, or it's what the Jackers are using for a holding cell for the prisoners."

"You think there are more prisoners there, Doc?"

"Either there, or that's where they're bringing them outside from the city. From here, though, it looks like a building."

"It's a building," Hancock said. "Our guests drew a map."

"If we're going to rescue those eight there beside the pit,"
I said, "we should at least make a try at releasing the prisoners inside the jailhouse."

"That about cubes the difficulty of the original assault. You sure there are prisoners in there?"

I pointed to one of the robotic scanners we'd set up on the perimeter, aimed at the city. "It's probably recorded. Check it and see."

Hancock stood motionless for a moment as he accessed and downloaded the video from the scanner collected over the past few minutes. I did the same, fast-forwarding to the part where you could just make out a centaur walking up to the building. "File seven, frame nine-eight-two-eight," I told him. The time stamp showed about three minutes earlier.

"I see it."

Together, we watched the Qesh go inside the building, and emerge a moment later half dragging, half carrying a struggling female figure.

"Shit," Hancock said at last, as the woman was secured to the cable between two other prisoners. "I think you're right."

"Just how are we going to get in there and do this without tipping the Qesh to our being on the planet?" I asked.

"A little thing Marines call strategy and tactics, Doc."

"I know, I know. I was twenty-first in my class of forty. I'm working on it, Gunny, okay?"

"Well, you're about to have a remedial class, Doc. Check out the boys and girls for combat. Full stim."

"Aye, aye, Gunnery Sergeant. G-boost too?"

"Do it."

There have been a number of drugs and, later, nanomeds in the military's arsenal, some going back to the turbulent years of the twenty-first century that have been used to fine-tune the warrior's P and P, his psychology and physiology. The oldest and most basic obviated the need for sleep. More modern nanomeds, like stim, let a Marine go without sleep for seventy-two hours or more with no adverse effects, while G-boost actually improves human reaction times, tunes up the body's ability to transport oxygen and carry away metabolites, strengthens muscular response, and allows the brain to think faster and more clearly.

One by one, I visited each of the Marines in the squad, snapping vials of stim and G-boost into the drug locks in their armor, and keying in the appropriate codes. It would take about ten minutes for the new nanobots to link up with the Freitas respirocytes already in each Marine's circulatory system and begin boosting their performance.

Last of all, I gave myself the injections, feeling the sharp but momentary sting as my armor's injectors fired a thin spray of nanobots through my skin and into my blood.

"All squared away, Doc?" Gunny Hancock asked me.

"They're good to go," I told him.

"Okay, Marines, listen up!" Hancock said over the squad channel. "Here's the plan. . . ."

Chapter Thirteen

WE MADE OUR APPROACH ON OUR QUANTUM FLITTERS, OUR NANO-flage reproducing the blacks and dark grays of the rocky plain between the woods and the mining pit as black dirt and vegetation gave way to bare rock. We went in slow, painstakingly slow. Nanoflage can't provide true invisibility; if you're a sentry and know what you're looking for, you can see movement, a kind of ripple against the background as the nanoflaged Marine approaches your position.

We got around this in two different ways. Move slowly enough, and you won't trigger the motion-sensing program of any watching AI. And if you move *directly* toward your objective, there's less of a side-to-side ripple effect to catch the eye or the electronic sensor.

The closer we got to the pit, though, the greater the chances for discovery.

Our biggest problems were the six Qesh rock eaters below the city. Each one appeared to have several weapons turrets mounted on its upper deck and flanks, and the Salvationists assured us that they were heavily armed with heavy beam weapons. At least there were no Rocs or Daityas overhead. Gunny's plan would have been impossible if any of those monsters had been about.

As it was, with only a poor understanding of Qesh sensor capabilities, we were taking a horrendous chance. There are times, though, when you have to realize that the enemy is only human—even if he, she, or it has seven limbs and looks like a cross between a Greek centaur and a rhinoceros on steroids. Organic beings get tired, they get bored, they get distracted. At night, their optics are adapted to the pool of light within which they work, not to the purple darkness surrounding them.

Machines—artificial intelligences—have the potential of doing a lot better as watchmen than do organic species. We had no idea as to how sharp Qesh computers or AIs might be. We weren't even sure they had computers, as we understood the term, though their Encyclopedia Galactica entry gave them a data storage/transmission history, a DS/T, of more than nine thousand years, which pretty much guaranteed that they had the technology.

That didn't tell us whether or not they'd created their own AIs, however. Some species—hell, some *humans*—preferred not to create machines that could think for themselves.

Well, perhaps we were about to find out.

We'd left the five Salvationists behind in our forward OP, and Kookie, Lance Corporal Kukowicz, was with them, partly to keep an eye on them and partly to serve as overwatch with his accelerator rifle. Through our robot scanners on the perimeter, he could keep an eye on activities in and around the pit that we might not notice once we got in close. He could also relay warnings, if any, from our guests, and serve as sniper, if need be, from more than a kilometer away.

The flit from our OP to the pit seemed to take forever. Our brains, under the influence of the combat nanomeds, were receiving and processing data at something like five times the normal rate, at the very peak of electrochemical efficiency. I felt cool, collected, and sharply focused, but the ten minutes or so it took our flitters to make that crossing passed in what felt like almost an hour.

That pit was enormous. It stretched more than a kilometer across, from just in front of the city cliffs to a point less than a kilometer from the tree line, and the six rock eaters were busily enlarging it as we watched. There was activity in the depths of the pit as well, though we couldn't see down inside as yet. Whatever was down there was illuminating the belly of the rising dust clouds with deep, ruby light, giving the hole the look of a broad, gaping gateway into hell.

What, I wondered, did the hyper-religious Salvationists think of that sight?

For that matter, why were the Qesh carrying out their strip-mining operation here? The city appeared to be un-damaged, at least so far, despite the images we'd down-loaded days before suggesting the contrary; with the vast majority of Bloodworld's surface uninhabited, why were the Jackers digging here, within full view of the captured city?

Was the city captured? The Salvationists back at the OP said it had been, but there were still too many questions about what the Qesh were doing here, and why.

As we approached the area lit from overhead by the mast-mounted spotlights, we began to disperse into two assault teams. I stayed with Colby, Masserotti, Kilgore, Lewis, Gregory, with Sergeant Leighton in charge, maintaining a slow but steady creep toward the line of prisoners by the pit. Gunny Hancock took the remaining five Marines with him off to the right, circling around the enemy perimeter, closing on the small building where more prisoners were being held.

In a sense, there was an additional, unseen, Marine with us—the squad AI, which was resident within all of our in-head CDF circuitry, coordinating our movements, guard-ing our quantum-scrambled communications channels, and scanning our surroundings through the sensors in our armor and within our skimmers. So far as we could tell, there were no Qesh sentries, no perimeter defenses, no force fields or other barriers around the area. We had to assume, at the very least, that they'd deployed microsensors of some sort. If they had nanodisassemblers, they had the technology to build microscopic sensors that could detect movement, magnetic moment, or even the air displaced by our silent passage. We had such devices, and the Qesh were nine millennia beyond us in terms of electronic wizardry.

"I am detecting comnet transmissions," our AI's voice said, speaking to all of us at once. "Activity suggests a full alert."

"Right!" Hancock's voice added. "Gun it! Go to the assault!"

I gunned it.

A comnet is the many-node communications network linking a sensory net. Our AI had just picked up the telltale surge of energy through the Qesh perimeter that said the enemy's sensors had detected something and were sounding the alert. At that point, a stealthy approach becomes more or less useless; we went from what the Marines refer to as "sneak and peek" straight to "shoot and scoot," springing our attack.

I covered the last hundred meters of open ground in seconds, my skimmer sliding centimeters above the bare rock in a programmed zigzag designed to confuse enemy sensors and to avoid the zigzags of my companions. I'd already unshipped my carbine and mounted it to the prow of my skimmer, though my primary focus was not going to be on combat. Calli Lewis fired first, her Mk. 24, sending a megajoule pulse of coherent light into one of the armed Qesh guards.

One megajoule represents about the same energy as two hundred grams of exploding TNT. The intense bolt of energy causes such sudden temperature change in the target that it will gouge out a double-fist-sized chunk of solid steel. Part of the target will vaporize, and what's left will suffer massive shock damage.

And when that bolt hits organic tissue, the results can be even more spectacular.

The side of the Jacker guard's helmet flared a dazzling white, erupting in a sudden, expanding cloud of mist. The figure reared up on its hind legs, turning, and then two more laser bolts caught it with explosive bursts side by side on its upper, ventral, surface. Its weapon spun away through the night as the Qesh toppled over backward, vanishing into the open pit behind it.

Contrary to most entertainment downloads and VR interactives, you can't actually see a laser pulse, even when there's lots of dust and smoke in the air, as now. It's light, after all, traveling at the speed of light, and a pulse with a duration of a hundredth of a second is just too brief to register on human vision. What I could see were more and more explosive bursts scoring against the armored giants standing around the line of human prisoners. Two were down . . . then three. A fourth opened fire, but wildly, sweeping a long-duration beam, slicing through the dust cloud in a brilliant thread of green. The shot was high and well off to the left; an instant later, the Qesh gunner collapsed as its chest armor exploded in a gout of white light and molten metal.

The firefight erupted with what seemed to be a surreal unfolding of events in slow motion. I angled my flitter toward the line of prisoners, leaping off the machine as I approached, shouting, *"Down! Down! Everyone get down!"*

Gregory cut down another Qesh guard with a burst from his laser, then dropped to one knee, mounting guard. "Get the civilians outta here, Doc!" he yelled.

I pulled my cutter from its sheath—a Marine-issue nanoknife. The active surface was coated with disassemblers that sliced through damned near anything, and it snicked through the heavy cables strung from collar to collar of the prisoners, then cut the shackles binding their wrists.

"Who are you?" one bearded man cried as I freed him.

"Marines," I told him. "From Earth! We're here to get you out, okay?"

He nodded through his terror. "Thank God!"

I pointed back across the rocky plain toward the distant forest. "You have some friends waiting for you in that direction," I told him. "Can you make it on your own?"

"I . . . I think so."

"I can't walk," a young man nearby said. He was bare-
foot, his pants torn off at the knee, his feet and legs showing horrible sores and ulcerations. High concentrations of
nano-D in the air can do terrible things to unprotected skin.

"Kookie!" I called over the squad channel. "Send me the
cargo flit!"

"On the way, e-Car."

The cargo flitter was four meters long and one wide, with
spin-reversal lift enough to haul several tons.

"You people!" I yelled at the civilians. "Get down and
stay down! We're going to get you out of here!"

The civilians sat or lay in a small huddle, as the Marines around them continued to blaze away at Qesh warriors
whenever they showed themselves. Laser fire snapped from
the nearest of the titanic rock eaters, exploding against black
rock. Joy Leighton raised her plasma gun and triggered a
bolt at the huge machine's right-flank turret.

The man-portable M4-A2 plasma gun uses a high-energy
laser to excite a tiny mass of highly compressed hydrogen
gas into a plasma state. At the moment it fires, a laser beam
drills a straight-line tunnel through the air, through which a
magnetic field accelerates the plasma bolt to high velocities.
Whatever that bolt hits suffers serious thermal shock and va-
porization plus the kinetic impact of the fast-moving plasma
mass, making the weapons far more destructive—and
heavy—than lasers. Every Marine squad has two plasma
gunners; they're the equivalent of squad machine guns back
in the old Corps.

The M4-A3 packs a five-MJ punch—the equivalent of
one kilogram of TNT. The explosion shredded the rock
eater's turret and left a crater in the metal, white-hot and
furiously steaming. Leighton slammed several more rounds
into the machine's tower, which loomed ten meters above
the vehicle's broad deck, then shifted targets to the next-
closest machine, which was slewing about on its tracks, now,
to bring its own turrets to bear.

A beam struck Private Kilgore, kneeling near the edge

of the pit. I saw him twist and flop over backward, heard Gregory's shrill yell of *"Corpsman!"*

Reaching for my M-7, I jumped up and ran.

Dave Kilgore was dying.

I knew it as soon as I saw the front of his combat armor. The enemy beam had struck him low on his torso and to his left. A twenty-centimeter chunk of armor from his hip to his waist was gone, vaporized, and much of what was left was half melted. Skin and muscle had burned away above the lower left quadrant of his abdomen, releasing a mass of intestines and mesentery tissue that had spilled onto the ground, some charred black, some blood-wet and glistening.

There was a *lot* of blood, bright red and pulsing with the rapid beat of his heart.

I cleared his visor so I could see his face. His eyes were wide open, glassy, unseeing. Thank God he wasn't feeling it, but I suspected he'd already lost so much blood he'd gone deep into shock.

"Hang on, buddy!" I told him. There was a chance that he was aware behind that glazed-over stare. If he was, I didn't want him to slip away on me—and I wanted him to know he wasn't alone. I keyed in a jolt of nananodynes through his armor, just to make dead certain he wasn't feeling it.

The actual wound was borderline for field first aid. Under different circumstances, I would have been able to pack his belly with an instant dressing, stabilize his blood pressure, and call in an emergency medevac. In a hospital, even in the *Clymer*'s sick bay, he would have had a good chance—say ninety-five percent—of coming back.

But there were two major problems here. First of all, he was bleeding badly—badly enough for him to exsanguinate in the next handful of minutes. Worse, though, was the medevac problem. The *Clymer* was some tens of millions of kilometers away, and with the Qesh in control of local space around Bloodworld, there was simply no way we were going to be able to get him to a decent medical facility.

I wondered what might be available inside the city of Salvation. They would have hospitals there, but if the locals didn't go in for nanomeds or microintervention, I didn't think the chances of helping him would be very good.

And if we couldn't get him to a decent medical facility within the next few hours, he had no chance at all.

First things first. I needed to stop that bleeding or he wouldn't survive the next five minutes.

No time to inject nanobots or attempt to track them on my N-prog. My gloved fingers probed through the intestinal spill, moving the mass aside as I tried to see. *There*, just visible as a pool of blood drained away, I could see the throb of an artery—the left external iliac, I thought—a severed end pulsing bright arterial blood.

I reached in and pinched the end between my left thumb and forefinger. It's damned tough doing that in combat armor, because the pressure receptors in those gloves aren't really as good as what we have in our fingertips. Besides, what I was trying to grab was *slippery*, and it had a life of its own as Kilgore's heart kept beating.

With my right hand I fumbled in my M-7 for my hemostatin foam. The stuff comes from a push-nozzle applicator the size of a pencil, and when it meets blood it gels into an inert plastic that binds with living tissue. It's way better than a clamp for sealing off leakers.

Kilgore's external iliac was no longer bleeding, but there was still blood coming out of his belly, a *lot* of it. In school, you download hundreds of millions of bytes describing and showing every vein and artery in the body, but somehow the reality *never* looks like the textbook images. Hell, even if it did, the Qesh weapon had done a hell of a lot of damage. The heat had cauterized a lot of blood vessels, but others had simply torn. I kept probing, trying to find where the fresh blood was coming from. The abdominal descending aorta appeared to be intact, thank God, but there was a lot of bleeding coming from higher up in the body cavity, possibly the superior mesenteric.

"Corpsman!"

The new shout brought my head up. I'd been so involved with Kilgore that I hadn't been watching what was going on nearby. Corporal Hugh Masserotti had been hit.

I opened a med channel from Masserotti as I kept working on Kilgore. One of the worst nightmares a Corpsman can experience is having multiple casualties going down when there's only one of him. *Triage* is a term we all hate. It means having to make a judgment—often a snap judgment—as to who we can help and who we're gong to have to let die.

Okay. Masserotti had taken an energy bolt of some kind in his right shoulder. It looked bad, but not immediately fatal.

The key word there was immediately. Any wound can turn critical on the battlefield in moments. What I was facing now was the realization that no matter what I did, Kilgore's chances were slim, while Masserotti had a good chance of pulling through *if* I took care of him now.

I still couldn't find that second bleeder.

"Who's with Masserotti?" I called.

"I am!" That was Colby.

"Make sure his suit medsupport is triggered!"

"It is!"

Good. Marine armor has a lot of built-in first aid technology. Besides monitoring your pulse, respiration, BP, and other stats, it can constrict certain parts to restrict blood flow. By tightening on legs and belly, it can help prevent shock. With bleeding from an arm or a leg it can close down tight enough to serve as a tourniquet, or in extreme circumstances—like a mangled limb in hard vacuum—it can cut off the limb and cauterize the stump, saving both blood and air supplies. It wouldn't work with severe damage, like what had happened to poor Kilgore, but it should keep High-Mass alive until I could get to him.

Damn it, I still couldn't find that bleeder! I was pretty sure now it was up under the part of Kilgore's armor that had only partly melted, tucked away inside the more-or-less intact part of his left abdominal cavity. The superior mesenteric supplies blood to the head of the pancreas and the transverse colon . . . but I couldn't reach it to find out if that was the source of the blood, not without nano probes and more time than I had right now.

The vitals feed from Masserotti was showing in the upper right corner of my in-head display—heart rate 150 and BP at 190 over 105—both elevated but steady.

"High-Mass!" I called over a private channel. "How you holding out?"

"It goddamn fuckin' *hurts*, Doc! . . ."

"Colby!" I said. "Open High-Mass's ACP!"

"Got it!"

"Punch in one . . . five . . . seven . . . three . . . enter!"

"Got it!"

Entering that code into Masserotti's armor control panel, mounted behind his left shoulder, would direct his suit to autoinject a dose of nananodyne into his carotid artery. The nanobots would converge in the cingulate cortex of his brain and shut down key pain receptors.

While Colby was doing this, I was working quickly to seal off Kilgore. I fired enough hemostatin foam into the gaping body cavity to close up whatever was still bleeding, scooped up the mass of spilled intestines and mesentery and packed it back into Kilgore's body, then squirted a generous blast of skinseal across the wound. That would hold him together until we could get him into surgery, whenever that might be.

And there was one thing more.

Jacking into his armor, I opened up the CAPTR application resident within his helmet. I noted the last backup time stamp—three days ago, while we were still at Niffelheim-e—and engaged the CAPTR software.

We call it the life preserver, or LP, after the old flotation rings they used to throw to people who were drowning. CAPTR stands for cerebral access polytomographic reconstruction, a mouthful that means that a living brain— together with neural states, synaptic pathways, chemical equilibria, even quantum spin states—can be recorded in a kind of electronic snapshot of brain activity.

With that recording, it's sometimes possible to pull off a reboot and bring a person back.

It doesn't always work. There are those who argue that the original person is still dead, that a CAPTR implant at best provides a kind of sad, pale imitation of the original, that within a few minutes of clinical death, the brain tissue deteriorates enough that it can no longer hold the implant data.

Others see CAPTR technology as the golden promise of immortality.

Whatever you believe, the technology isn't quite there yet, but the military has been working on it. Some day, we might have backups on file for every person, the way we do for AI personalities now. By using the CAPTR software on Kilgore, we were in essence preserving his training and recent experience, a record for debriefing later, and, just possibly, a means of providing closure for his family.

I tried not to think about Paula.

With Kilgore packed up and brain-recorded, I hurried across open rock to Masserotti. He was lying propped up on his bad arm, holding his laser rifle with the other. The firefight was petering out now, with all of the Qesh in the area dead or out of the fight. The six rock eaters had pulled back and were no longer trading shots with us; either Leighton's covering plasma fire had knocked out their weapons or they'd elected to disengage. Leighton, Colby, Gregory, and Lewis all were keeping up a fairly steady volume of fire, however, snapping away at the huge machines to keep them at a distance.

A hundred meters away, Gunny Hancock and the other Marines of the second assault group were filing out of the small building and heading our way with a ragged group of perhaps twenty civilians.

Masserotti's arm didn't need a lot of additional treatment. The nananoynes had switched off the pain, and his suit was both controlling bleeding and keeping the slightly toxic Bloodworld atmosphere out. I took a look at the wound; the Qesh beam or energy bolt had grazed his shoulder, vaporizing some of his pauldron and melting about half of the rest of his armor. It didn't look like the beam had actually touched him, but droplets of the molten titanium-ceramic composite had melted through the underlying buckyweave layer and burned into the flesh. The outer part of his shoulder was charred black and interlaced with blobs of cooling alloy. The inner part of the wound was raw and bleeding; I could see part of the glenohumeral joint beneath burned flesh.

I checked High-Mass's nananodyne level, sealed off the bleeding, and sliced away the worst of the half-molten blobs of composite before they could burn their way deeper into bone and soft tissue. After that, I packed Masserotti's shoulder with skinseal and coded his armor to immobilize his right arm.

"Damn it, Doc!" Masserotti said. "I can't move my arm!"

"That's right, Marine. I don't want you doing more damage trying to use it."

He gestured with the weapon in his left hand. "Just so I can still pop the bastards!"

The cargo flitter drew up to our perimeter. Lewis began waving to the waiting civilians, getting them to clamber on board.

"How's Kilgore?" Hancock asked on a private channel. He would, of course, have been following the biofeeds from the entire squad.

"If we could get him back to the *Clymer*," I said, "maybe . . ."

"Do what you can for him."

"A lot of the prisoners are hurt," I told him. "Nano-D concentrations here are pretty high."

"That will have to wait. I—"

And then the alarms went off.

A Qesh Roc drifted in out of the east, huge and black and

dimly seen against the night sky, but our AI illuminated it
on our combat displays. An instant later, beams from the
winged disk drifting 30 meters above shot across the ground
in coruscating bursts of raw light, as the civilians screamed
and scattered.

Masserotti snapped off a number of shots one-handed,
without any effect that I could see. Leighton stood almost
beneath the thing, firing her plasma gun straight up into its
belly. Two of the prisoners freed by Hancock's team were
caught in a high-energy blast that vaporized them both.

Then the prow of the drifting Qesh craft exploded, sending a shower of white-hot fragments scattering across the
landscape. The flier lurched, listing heavily to one side; a
second blast savaged its smooth ventral surface. The fire, I
was pretty sure, was coming from our OP—from the portable robot plasma cannon we'd set up there. The stricken
aircraft kept drifting across our position, nosing down.
High-energy beams lanced out toward our OP, and then
the craft slammed wing-tip first into the rock, cartwheeling
slowly, coming apart in flame and ragged debris.

"Everyone saddle up!" Hancock shouted. "We're getting
the hell out of Dodge!"

I helped several of the injured prisoners clamber up onto
the cargo flitter, and made sure that Kilgore was strapped
down safely on the deck. Kilgore's flitter folded up and went
into the cargo compartment; Masserotti was stubborn and
insisted on riding out on his. Since you can control the things
through your in-head, and don't need physical strength or
a good right arm, I let him. Our AI was warning of more
Qesh aircraft approaching from the south, so we hightailed
it, moving fast to clear out of the combat zone before bad-
guy reinforcements arrived.

I did take a look inside that infernal pit before mounting
up, though, because I was wondering what the hell the Qesh
were doing in there. The pit, I saw, was about 50 meters deep,
and there was something like a building growing down there
in the center, dome-shaped and squat. There were more ma-

chines eating away at the rock, but much of the floor of that pit was seething, molten lava—liquid rock with a black, crusty surface and with hot orange light gleaming from underneath. That was the source, I saw, of the eerie, shifting glow on the dust clouds rising above. On the far side of the pit, the curtain of rock separating the pit from the cliffs dropping to the ocean had been eaten through, and streams of lava were oozing out, falling into the ocean, where fire and water exploded into billowing clouds of steam.

I recorded the whole scene with my armor, then hopped onto my flitter and arrowed away after the rest. The downed Qesh flier lay halfway between the pit and the tree line where our OP was located.

And that's where we found the Qesh pilots.

Chapter Fourteen

THE QESH FLIER HAD A COCKPIT SECTION THAT HAD BROKEN FREE from the wreckage. As we steered past, I could see two Qesh strapped belly-down to what looked like narrow benches. One was motionless, but the other was thrashing about, trying to get free. The main body of wreckage was on fire close by, burning fiercely in the planet's high-oxygen atmosphere.

"Gunny!" I called. "I'm going to help them out!"

"Colby!" Hancock said. "Give Doc a hand!"

"Aye, aye, Gunnery Sergeant!"

I hadn't really thought about the pros and cons of helping the aliens. Corpsmen have a long tradition, though, of helping *anyone* who's hurt in a war zone, even the enemy. Your own people come first, of course, and you're not supposed to jeopardize the mission with heroic gestures—but damn it, I didn't want to see those Qesh burn.

"Watch for boobies, Doc," Hancock warned me.

"Roger that."

Boobies—booby traps—were always a threat. In this case, the danger went a bit deeper. We knew pathetically little about the Qesh, and there was every possibility that they wouldn't mind triggering an explosion and killing themselves if it meant taking a couple of us with them. Marines—and the Corpsmen who were with them—have faced that kind of insanity before, and not always with alien species on alien worlds.

I let the AI probe the cockpit wreckage before I got close. It reported no electrical activity, which wasn't a sure-fire guarantee, but it reassured me a little bit. I jumped off my flitter and jogged up to the wreck.

Neither Qesh was wearing much in the way of armor, and this was the first time I'd seen one in the flesh, as it were.

I'd assumed, based on the armored Jackers I'd seen already, that they had huge heads. That wasn't quite true. Rising from the anterior end of each of their bodies was a pair of massive horns, one curving up to meet the other, which curved out and forward. The structure looked vaguely like an immense claw, a meter or more across. Below and to either side were armored turrets like those possessed by African chameleons on Earth; there were two eyes to a side, four in all, each of them large, deeply set, and jet-black. And as with the chameleon, they appeared to track separately. The thrashing one settled down and watched me as I approached, but there was no way to read the emotion behind that gaze.

"Take it easy there," I said. I had no way of knowing if they understood English, nor did I know whether what for me was a soothing tone of voice would be soothing or calming to them. I got close enough that I could reach the leg of the motionless one and slap on a blank nano patch. Then I stepped back and pulled out my N-prog. There was a lot of blood around the motionless one, pale-green but turning darker.

After studying the readouts for a long time, I slapped a second nano patch on the active one.

Okay. This was more like it. The first one, I was fairly sure, was dead.

The thing is, we knew nothing about the Qesh except for what was listed on their EG entry—cold and emotionless facts that said little about what these creatures truly were. I knew their vision extended a lot further into the red end of the spectrum than did ours—well into the infrared, in fact, but they couldn't see the colors blue, blue-green, or violet. Their hearing was better than ours at the low end of the registry, but they couldn't hear higher-pitched sounds that were easy for us. Humans can hear up to around 10,000 Hertz; Qesh can only hear up to about 6,000 Hz. Instead of DNA, they use TNA for genetic encoding—threose nucleic acid, which on Earth is a precursor of RNA. For blood they have copper-based hemerytherin proteins circulating in something like polyunsaturated vegetable oil.

None of which helped me when the injured Qesh waved its top arm at me and gave vent to something that sounded like a kettle drum solo.

I used a laser scalpel to snick through the restraint harness holding the Qesh to its padded platform. I would have liked to have studied it more, but the fire was spreading and the idea here was to keep it from being incinerated. I stepped well back, watching as it shrugged out of the harness and crawled clear of the wreck.

It didn't seem badly hurt. Through my N-prog, the nanobots circulating through its body were giving me an interesting look at what appeared to be two massive hearts, a brain considerably larger than a human's, and a number of organs whose purpose was utterly beyond me. Since I had no idea what readings were normal for a Qesh, there was nothing I could do for it. For blood pressure, I was getting alternating values of 200 and 300 for the systole, but nothing at all for a diastole, and what the hell did *that* mean? No readings for pain at all, but we measure pain by taking a reading of cortisol, norepinephrine, and other stress hormones in the blood; this critter didn't have cortisol, or any other stress hormone I recognized.

And even if I'd gotten a reading, I knew zero about a Jacker's central nervous system, about pain receptors, or about how it registered pain; I could as easily kill the being as cure it if I interfered.

It tried to rise up on its rearmost set of legs, and collapsed.

Ah. *There* was something I could recognize. As the nano-bots spread through its circulatory fluid, they were showing me more and more of the being's internal structure on the N-prog, including its skeleton, massive and alien.

But not *that* alien. If you have an internal skeleton and you have legs, there are only so many ways the bones can grow, only so many body plans that work. This guy's legs were digitigrade—meaning the Qesh essentially was stand-ing on its toes, that its lower leg was actually an elongated foot. Lots of non-primate mammals on Earth—dogs, for instance—have the same arrangement. So do birds. I could see the shadows of bones in the Jacker's legs, and the long one in its upper right leg, just above the rear-pointing "knee"—the equivalent of the tibia in a human—was broken clean through.

"Give me a hand, Colb," I told the Marine. "We need to get him away from that fire."

"Right. Damn it, Doc. He's *heavy!*"

Heavy was right. The Qesh massed between 400 and 450 kilos. On Bloodworld, that translated to nearly 800 kilos—a good four fifths of a ton.

Colby and I could get a fair amount of leverage with our suit walkers, letting the servo motors do the work, but there was no way we could drag such a weight across the broken and uneven ground. Fortunately, the Jacker itself was able to get its good legs under it and, with our help, hobble clear of the fire. We managed to get it fifty meters from the blaze and the three of us collapsed in a heap, the Qesh thundering a string of bass drum rattles. The skin of its face beneath that massive, double horn, I saw, was true skin rather than leathery plate exoskeletal armor. It had appeared dark gray at first, but I noticed now that it was flushed a deep, rust red, and that in places it was flaring bright orange in complex, rippling patterns. Jackers, I remembered from the EG down-load I'd seen, communicated both by sound and by changing color patterns. This one obviously was trying to say *some-thing* important to us, but I had no idea what that might be.

"Doc!" Hancock's voice sounded in my ears. "Hurry it up! We got incoming!"

"Just a sec." I looked at Colby. "Get back to the others," I told him.

"Negative, Doc. I'll cover you."

I didn't argue. Using my N-prog, I zeroed in on the Jacker's broken leg, then punched in a series of commands. The two ends of the bone shifted, then slowly began moving together.

I was working almost completely in the dark. The Jacker wasn't wearing combat armor, so I couldn't use it to generate an electrical field either to promote healing or to aid the 'bots swarming around the two broken ends of the bone. And since I couldn't give the being a jolt of nananodyne, if the thing's pain physiology was *anything* like ours it would be in agony now.

"What the hell is taking so long, Doc?" Colby asked. "What are you doing, anyway?"

"Our friend here broke his leg. Just like you on Mars, except that he snapped *his* clean through. I'm setting it the same way I set yours, but the nanobots only have muscle to push against, and the muscles have pulled the ends of the bone past each other."

Guided by the program from my N-prog, the nanobots inside the Jacker's leg were linking to one another, creating a kind of thin scaffolding around both ends of the bone. More nanobots flooded into the area, connecting the two end caps, and applying force to first push the ends apart, then to bring them together in line with each other.

Qesh were powerfully muscled—so much so that I suspected they were from a high-gravity planet. Curious, I pulled up the Encyclopedia Galactica entry for the Qesh and glanced at the published planetary parameters.

Sure enough. The EG listing showed $G = 25.81$ m/s^2, which translated to about 2.6 times Earth's gravity. Evolution on their home planet had favored heavily muscled beings that could walk against a surface gravity that would cripple a human in moments.

Two—no, three—of the being's four eyes had swiveled to stare at me. They really did remind me of a chameleon as they flicked back and forth, glancing now and again at Colby or our surroundings, but always snapping back to focus on me. The EG data said that the Qesh homeworld had been the sixth planet of an F1 star. *F1* meant young and hot.

It was odd, though. The upper eyes on either side were small, about the size of a marble; the lower eyes, however, were deeply recessed inside a kind of pit within each turret and were much larger—the size, apparently, of a baseball. Both sets, large and small, were a deep and lustrous black, suggesting that I was seeing only the equivalent of the pupil.

A life form evolving beneath an F1 star, I thought, would have vision that took advantage of the shorter wavelengths of the spectrum—blue and violet and even ultraviolet. The smaller eyes seemed designed for that type of environment.

And yet the EG entry suggested that the Jackers' visual range was in the longer wavelengths, from what humans see as green all the way down well into the infrared. Larger eyes would have evolved for capturing long-wavelength radiation.

Curious. Was the EG entry for the Qesh incomplete? Or was there something else going on here that we just didn't understand?

My patient rumbled another drum solo, the skin on its face flaring orange and yellow now. I was beginning to think that the color show might provide an emotional content to its speech—or it might be the Jacker equivalent of a groan of pain.

But slowly, and with great deliberation, the major muscles bundled around the broken bone were relaxing. The Qesh was actually *helping* me, somehow sensing what I was doing inside its leg and isolating the muscles, relaxing them in a manner that would have been impossible for a pain-wracked human.

And the nanobots began pulling the broken ends of the bone together.

The break, I was glad to see, was relatively clean. The bones appeared to be made of calcium within a kind of interwoven mesh of copper, an arrangement that seemed to give them tremendous strength.

I tapped a final command into my N-prog, sealing the nano sleeve around the broken area of the bone.

"Okay, big fella," I told it, knowing the sounds I was making were meaningless. "You're good to go." The Qesh gently flexed its leg.

"Let's get the fuck out of here, Doc," Colby told me. "This thing's friends are on the way."

"Right."

I packed away my N-prog and dropped back onto my flitter. The massive Qesh watched me without anything I could identify as emotion as the two of us slid away toward the woods.

"You know, e-Car," Colby told me, "that if that thing tries to follow us, we're gonna have to kill it."

"Maybe. But I wasn't going to let it burn."

"Sure, but you didn't have to patch its leg, either."

"So maybe it'll tell its friends humans aren't so bad."

I wanted to review the recordings I'd made through the N-prog of Qesh anatomy. There were several things about it that were puzzling me.

Above the city in the distance, three more Rocs had just appeared, drifting slowly in from the sea as if they were surveying the damage.

Colby and I got under cover just in time.

"*WE DON'T WANT YOUR DEMON-SPAWN MEDICINE!*"

We'd folded up our dome and moved several kilometers back into the forest. The Qesh didn't appear to be searching for us aggressively at the moment, but we wanted to be well hidden from any of their sensors that might pick us up through the thick masses of black vegetation. So we dismantled the OP—what was left of it. The plasma cannon had been smashed to hell by the fire from the Roc before it had crashed. We grew five new nanoflaged domes. Which provided space enough for us, and all twenty-six of the rescued

Salvation prisoners—plus the five we'd left at the OP—to squeeze inside, until we could be sure any search by the Jacker forces had ended.

The dome I was in was crowded—four Marines and six Salvationists, plus me. Hancock had ordered two Marines to stay outside and watch for any enemy activity, and told the rest of us to take it easy and get some rest.

I took the opportunity to check both Kilgore and Masserotti. High-Mass seemed to be doing okay, but Kilgore was in a very deep coma, showing very little brainwave activity. That was okay. I could keep him on nanosuppression for a long time, so long as I could keep some high-O_2 circulation going to his brain.

When I started trying to treat one of the wounded Salvationists, though, it elicited a major problem.

"Look," I told them, trying to be reasonable, "do you know about nanobots? Nanodeconstructors? The Qesh were using clouds of them to deconstruct the rock, and those of you who were being held beside the pit got a lot of them—on your feet and legs, and I think they may have slipped through your filters, too. If they did, you've got some in your lungs, and they're eating away at you from the inside! Now will you let me—"

"We are *human*!" one of the former prisoners yelled, "and made in God's image!"

"We will not be defiled!" a woman added.

Their response was both bizarre and unsettling, and I had to think about it for a moment. There *had* to be a way. . . .

"Look, you people are *already* defiled," I told them. "You've all picked up a dose of Qesh nano-D, and if you don't let me do something about it, it's going to kill you!"

"We will not take more nanotech evil into our bodies!"

I pulled a small spray nozzle from my M-7, clipped on a vial of dark liquid, and held it up. "This," I told them, is *not* nanotech."

I was lying of course.

Neutranan is an aerosol propelled by nitrogen gas. The

active ingredient is nothing more than carbon atoms arranged in C_{60} spheres—buckyballs, as they're popularly known—but with a Cruz impeller and a quantum-state computer encapsulated inside the structure. The nanocomputer and the microdrive make it just smart enough to let it track the by-product signatures of nano-D 'bots. The buckyball fullerenes home in on individual D-'bots and surround them, acting like antibodies with outer surfaces too smooth to eat. The end effect of the stuff is to instantly disable nano dissassemblers. While buckyballs are found in nature, QS computers and microdrives most assuredly are not; they're assembled atom by atom, and that makes them nanotechnology of the first order.

It was also the only thing that would save these people from being very slowly eaten alive.

One of them was a young woman, probably in her mid-teens, who said her name was Miriam two-nine-two of Orange-one-oh. "If it's not nanotechnology," she said, "it should be safe enough. . . ."

Matthew was there with her. "Is this your daughter?" I asked him.

He nodded, and put his arm around her shoulder. Miriam's feet and lower legs were a mass of red, oozing sores. If you looked closely, you could see the inflammation steadily growing worse.

"If you don't let me treat her," I told him, "you are condemning her to a *very* nasty death."

"That can you're holding . . . it does not have nanotech?" he asked. His voice broke on the final word.

"I promise. It's a very, very fine aerosol powder that will kill the nanobots infecting her."

"*Please*, Father!" The girl looked terrified. She couldn't have been older than fifteen.

Reluctantly, he nodded. "Perhaps God *has* brought these people to us." He said. "Praise and glory to His name!"

"Praise and glory to His name," the other locals echoed.

Quickly, before any of them had time to change their

minds, I sprayed the girl's feet and calves with the neu-tranan, coating them with a dark powder that rapidly van-ished as it melted into her skin. Then I had had her stand up, turn about for me, and finally lift the tattered hem of her skirt high enough that I could be certain to get all the sores.

"Why are you people so set against nanotechnology?" I asked as I applied the spray.

"Our people," Matthew told me, "are against *anything* that defaces the divinity of the human form. We are, all of us, created in the image of God. To change it, to corrupt it with machines made by the hand of man . . ."

"There is no sin greater than defiling the image of God!" one of the others said.

"Uh-huh," I said. I could think of quite a few "sins" that were worse, but I wasn't about to get into a theological debate with these people. Sometimes all you can do is smile and nod and agree with the crazy people. "Can you lift your skirt a little more, miss? I need to get a spot on your hip. Like that. Good."

"Miriam!" her father warned. "Decency!"

"Sir, I am a medical professional and I am trying to save your daughter's life," I told him. "Let me see your hands, now. Good. Spread your fingers . . . now turn your hands over. . . ."

A proper job would require putting her through a full-body scan. Many nano-D types are self-replicating and will keep on multiplying and spreading until they reach their program endpoint. And with Qesh technology, we didn't know yet how their programs were organized, or if they *had* an endpoint.

"Okay," I told the girl. "That should do you. If you notice any sores or redness, though, you tell me or one of the other Corpsmen, okay? It's important."

"Yes, sir."

"Have you noticed any problems breathing? A cough? Pain in your face, your throat or your chest?"

"A little pain here when I breath," she told me, laying her hand at the base of her throat.

"Okay." I broke out an inhaler, charging it with neutranan.

"What is that?" Matthew asked, instantly suspicious.

"Exactly the same stuff I sprayed on her legs," I told him. "I'm going to have her breathe some of it to neutralize any nanobots that might have gotten past the filters in her breathing mask." I saw him hesitate, and added, "Don't your doctors use inhalers for patients with asthma?"

"We don't *have* doctors," he said.

Ah. Nothing to deface the image of God, which at its worst included pain, disease, and death.

I handed Miriam the inhaler. "Breathe out as completely as you can," I told her. "Then put that opening in your mouth, squeeze this button, and take a deep breath. Okay?"

Matthew was not convinced. "I'm not sure about . . ."

"Look, Matthew!" I said, angry. "Those masks you wear. They have, what? Five-micron filters?"

"Three."

I nodded, privately amused. The main purpose of their masks would be to separate out certain toxic gasses in the atmosphere like sulfur dioxide, and that wasn't done with a mechanical filter. Instead, it used some rather sophisticated nanotechnology that identified molecules by their mass, popped an electron off of each to give it a charge, then shunted it back into the atmosphere. In other words, these people depended on nanotechnology just to live and work on the surface of this hellhole planet—but evidently, they either deliberately overlooked that part, or they flat-out didn't know. Such masks could also filter out things much larger than molecules of SO_2—from dust and allergenic grains of pollen all the way down to large bacteria.

"Three microns," I said. "That's three millionths of a meter. Typical nanobots run anywhere from one micron in diameter down to, oh, a hundred nanometers or so. That's one thousand times *smaller* than one micron. I don't know yet what the Qesh are using for their disassembler technology, but it's a good bet that your filter masks don't even slow them down."

While I was talking, Miriam took a hit on the inhaler. She coughed, once, and handed it back to me.

"How do you feel?"

She nodded. "Okay. My legs are still burning, though."

"I've got something for that, too."

"No more!" Matthew said. "You . . . you've done enough!"

I held up another vial, and shook it. "Skinseal," I told him. "It will stop the bleeding, and keep the wounds from becoming infected. It's just a spray-on bandage." I glanced at him. "You *do* use bandages, don't you? If someone is bleeding?"

He refused to rise to my gibe. "What's in it?"

"CHON."

"What is that?"

"Carbon, hydrogen, oxygen, and nitrogen. A few other things, like phosphorous and calcium. Exactly the same stuff God turned into *you*."

"It's . . . natural?"

God preserve me from fanatics who think something is "unnatural" just because we can grow it in a lab, or produce it commercially in a nanufactory.

"As natural as you are."

He was still reluctant, but he gave me permission. I thought that if I could win this crowd over with a practical demonstration of medical technology, it might stand us in good stead with their leaders when we met them later on. I carefully didn't tell him that there were local nananodynes mixed in with the skinseal, to block pain-receptor nerve endings and lessen the pain, plus an antibacterial agent to kill any organic infection.

I sprayed a light layer over the sores on Miriam's legs. She smiled. "It feels good. Kind of cold."

"Is the pain gone?"

"Most of it."

"Good. That layer will be absorbed by your body after a week or so. Just leave it alone, and it'll be fine." I looked up at the other Salvationists, who were sitting around us in a tight, intently focused circle. "Okay, who's next?"

I treated two more of the rescued locals, as Miriam, Matthew, and Ezekiel looked on. Neither of them was anywhere close to being as badly burned as Miriam, but I dusted them with neutranan anyway, and made them both take a hit from the inhaler, just in case.

As I finished the last one, I looked at Matthew. "Thanks for understanding what I'm trying to do," I told him. These people made me furious with their dark-ages attitude toward technology, but I knew that the only way I was going to get them to cooperate was to be as diplomatic as possible. I would have to get them to work with me, not challenge their beliefs, not get into arguments, and not make fun of them. If I had to, I would lie through my teeth in the name of a higher and greater good.

"I could use your help in the other domes," I went on. "Will you come with me, explain what I'm doing?"

"Are . . . are you sure you're not releasing a gray goo plague?"

I had to think about that one. At first, I wasn't sure what he meant, but a quick check of my CDF RAM turned up the phrase, something from back in the twentieth century.

One of the early pioneers of nanotech thinking back then had been John von Neumann, who hypothesized the use of self-replicating robots that might land on a planet and begin using local materials to manufacture exact copies of themselves. If the process were to run out of control, more and more replicators would devour more and more raw materials until all that was left would be a swarm of hungry replicators.

It's the nightmare scenario of exponential growth. Start with one replicator the size of a large protein molecule. It pulls in atoms from its environment and is able to make an exact duplicate of itself, right down to its programming, in one thousand seconds. Those two build two more in another thousand seconds, those four build four, those eight build eight. After ten hours, one replicator has become 68 billion. In less than a day, the mass of replicators weighs about one ton; in less than two days, they outweigh the Earth—or *would*, if they'd not used up Earth's entire mass some hours before.

Another early nanotech pioneer, Eric Drexler, had coined the phrase "gray goo," though he later regretted ever having done so. Somehow, the public became focused on the idea, and the development of nanotech was held back for years by the doomsayers.

In fact, von Neumann's replicators were not at all a realistic scenario. True, nanodisassemblers and other nanotechnic tools were designed to manufacture copies of themselves, but they had to be programmed to do what they did, and an integral part of that programming was the endpoint, the line of code that read "Stop! Don't make any more!" Most nano-D was designed with a fairly short life span; an internal clock within each quantum-state computer ticked off the milliseconds until the nanobot ran out of time, then quietly disassembled itself into its component atoms.

"Gray goo" would not necessarily be gray, nor, most likely, would it be gooey. The term was meant to refer to *anything* artificial that might out-compete organic life forms. A better term was *ecophage*—something that devoured the local ecosystem.

But the captivatingly alliterative term remained fixed in the public consciousness for the next couple of centuries. There was some major social disruption back in the early 2100s, when the Luddies tried to turn back Humankind's technological clock. The Neoessene Messianists, I knew, were the philosophical offspring of the neo-Luddite movement.

If they thought that nanotech might result in that kind of runaway doomsday scenario, hell, no wonder they were afraid of the stuff.

I chuckled. "I promise, no gray goo."

Yeah, I was going to have to be careful and keep my technological bag of tricks well hidden while I was on planet.

If I didn't, we could be facing a whole new Luddie revolution.

Chapter Fifteen

"**W**HAT THE FUCK WERE YOU *THINKING*, E-CAR?"

Gunny Hancock didn't sound angry, exactly. It sounded more like exasperation, the frustration of having an already difficult task made unbearably complicated. We were in armor, standing outside of the cluster of nanoflaged domes where we could have a private conversation beneath the black canopy of the forest. It was windy, with the promise of another storm.

"It seemed like a good idea at the time, Gunny," I told him. "Look, if I hadn't treated those people, they would have *died*."

"They've got their own medical facilities inside their city."

"I don't think they do. Matthew told me they don't."

"Shit."

"They certainly don't have the medical technology to deal with a nanotech infection."

"So what kind of time frame were you looking at with the nano-D? How long before things got serious?"

"They already *were* serious. That girl, Miriam, she would have been dead in a few hours if the Qesh nano had anything like the turn-over rate for replication that we have. Even if it wasn't replicating, the nano-D infestation on her legs would have started opening major blood vessels in another hour or so."

"You were careful about contamination?"

I nodded. "I sprayed down everyone when I was done. Including myself. And the dome interiors."

"Did you get samples?"

"Oh, yeah. I was able to pull some out of the air here." A close examination of the Qesh nanobots would tell us a *lot* about their technology, though we didn't have the equipment to do a work-up here. That would have to wait until we got back to the *Clymer*.

"Okay. So far as the locals are concerned, I guess we'll just have to hope for the best."

"What's the problem, anyway?" I asked. "Like I said, I told them I wasn't using nanotech on them. Yeah, it was a lie, but—"

"It was a damned transparent lie, and their Elder Council is probably going to be more savvy about things like that than these yahoos. *And* more suspicious. We know they have some kind of governing computer. If they suddenly realize you fibbed, there could be hell to pay."

"I don't get it," I said. "Getting eaten alive a molecule at a time is no fun at all. You'd think they'd be grateful!"

"Doc, people are *never* grateful when you challenge their religious assumptions. You can't convince them with logic. You can't convince them with emotion. And if you convince them by tricking them, they tend to get upset as hell when they learn the truth."

"So was I supposed to just let those people die?"

He sighed. "No. You did what you had to do. But, damn it, we have enough on our plates right now without inviting a new round of Luddie riots. From now on, leave the locals to the care of whatever they have in the way of their own doctors."

I wondered if Gunny Hancock could possibly be serious. If the locals didn't use nanotech, how were their doctors—assuming they even had any—going to deal with nano-D infections?

"I'll try to keep that in mind, Gunny," I told him. "I'm sure prayer is an *extremely* effective antidote for nano-D."

"Shit-can the sarcasm, Carlyle."

"Sorry, Gunny."

"How's Kilgore?"

"Bad. I don't think he's going to make it."

"Okay." Hancock nodded, accepting my prognosis. "Matthew is getting ready to take his people back to Salvation," he said. "If there's any final scan or check you need to do with any of them, now's your time."

"Aren't we going with them?"

"We're following orders and waiting for the rest of the platoon. They should be here in a few hours, though. Then we'll see. The thing is . . . we need to be prepared in case there's some sort of backlash over your . . . medical philanthropy. We'll have to move the OP again, just in case."

"Gunny, you have a nasty, suspicious mind."

"Out here, Doc, it's the only way to go."

THE SALVATIONISTS WE'D RESCUED AND TREATED DEPARTED A SHORT time after that, returning to the city. According to them, there were ways into the city the Qesh didn't know about—though so far, they'd refused to share them with us.

The Qesh started looking for us a few hours later.

We'd expected some sort of backlash, of course, and I gathered that Gunny had gone over the possibilities with Matthew and the others before we staged our raid to free the prisoners above the pit.

The chances were good that Baumgartner was going to be royally pissed that we'd gotten involved—hell, that we'd gone in and actually attacked the Qesh mining operation in front of the city. Too damned bad. The fact of the matter was that there'd been precious little we could learn from the OP. The *only* way to get hard intel had been to talk to the locals. Matthew and those with him had seemed suspicious and divided about us, and rescuing the prisoners had seemed a reasonable way to get into their good graces.

It had been a calculated risk—but Matthew and the others had indicated to Hancock that there was at least a low-level military resistance to the Qesh, despite the enemy's hostage-taking and terror-murder of civilians. The Salvationists, we'd learned, *did* have a military, at least at a low and fairly basic level, that was probably more for self-policing than for beating off a Jacker invasion. While their laser weaponry was more primitive than front-line gear currently used by Earth forces, a laser is a laser, and we knew that the Qesh wouldn't be able to tell from the traces we left behind whether the raid had been carried out by us or by renegade natives, like Matthew and the others. Even if they spotted our armor, dramatically different in design from the leather and lightweight ceramic the locals used, they'd be more likely to assume we were natives with previously unseen equipment than Marine recon.

The important thing was for us not to get captured. That wasn't as big a risk as you might think. Marines do *not* leave their own behind.

So now the Qesh had their Rocs crisscrossing the night sky above the forest near Salvation. They would not be looking for sophisticated nanoflage shielding, though. Probably the biggest problem raised by our attack was the possibility that the Qesh would retaliate, hard, against the civilians in the city. They had foot patrols out too, groups of seven armed Jacker centaurs in heavy armor obviously searching for some sign of the hostage-freeing raiders—us. We watched one patrol pass within ten meters of our OP domes, but they never saw us or the Marines we had on sentry duty hidden in the forest outside.

I spent the next several hours going over the electronic data I'd collected during my examination of the Qesh pilot.

All of it tended to support and confirm the Qesh entry in the Encylcopedia Galactia. The nano I'd shot into the two of them had transmitted details of their biochemistry to me. They were actually fairly close to humans in most ways, though they required more sulfur than we do in their metabolic processes. Humans utilize sulfur in two amino acids—cysteine and methionine—and it's also found in hair, connective tissue, veins, and as a part of the chemistry of insulin, but the Qesh appeared to use it in their basic metabolism. One interesting point: the air of Bloodworld turned out to be almost identical to what we knew of their homeworld's atmosphere. It raised a possible motive for what they were doing here.

It was just possible that this was a Qesh colonizing expedition.

What didn't fit were the eyes. The small, upper-turret eyes appeared to be perfectly adapted for the world of a white F1V star, heavily armored against the ultraviolet radiation released by such suns. The lower eyes, though, were adapted for life beneath a cooler, redder sun—a red dwarf like Gliese 581, for example.

There was a problem with stellar age, too. If the Qesh home star was a type F1V, it seemed unlikely that any planets would have had time to develop life as highly evolved as the Jackers. F-class stars aren't on the main sequence for long. They're so bright and so massive that they burn through their stores of nuclear fuel quickly—a billion years for type F0, a bit longer, maybe two billion years at the absolute outside for an F1, and that was stretching things.

And I had the idea that the Qesh might be very highly evolved indeed.

It was that set of horns or claws they had on their heads, and the fact that they seemed to have started off as bilaterally symmetrical and then gone in a different direction entirely, when their ancestors developed *seven* limbs instead of six or eight. While it was always hazardous to speculate too far about species as alien as the Qesh, their appearance had me wondering if their ancestors had been octopods—eight legs—but that somewhere along their evolutionary path one arm had fused with the body, vanishing except for the remnant of two massive claws that became the ornamentation atop their heads. There are species on Earth that have evolved in a lopsided fashion like that. Look at the fiddler crab, with one massively outsized claw for fighting rivals and attracting the ladies, and a smaller one for eating.

Imagine if the larger arm had been absorbed into the body, with only the massive claw remaining as part of the crab's body, while the lesser arm migrated to a more central position.

But that kind of evolution takes a long, *long* time—hundreds of millions of years. And I was suspicious of even such ordinary bilateral critters as humans evolving from the planetary ecosystem powered by a star less than a couple of billion years old.

I could only think of a couple of possible ways around the discrepancy.

First off, there was a theory that said that hotter stars, emitting higher levels of background radiation, kicked the evolution taking place on any of their planets into high gear, accomplishing in ten million years what might have required a hundred million years on Earth. So maybe the Qesh *had* leaped up out of the primal soup in the time it had taken Earth's biome to figure out how to go from single-cell loners to multi-celled communities.

Alternatively, the Qesh might be examples of deliberately directed evolution. They, or the Galactic overlords whom they worked for, could have tinkered with the original Qesh genome for God alone knew what aesthetic or practical reasons in order to create the modern Qesh artificially. Very little was known yet about the R'agch'lgh Collective and less still about their motives, their ethics, or their worldview, but there were whispers within the EG suggesting that they liked to play God with the species they thought of as their inferiors—rumors of entire sapient species having been bio-engineered for unknown purposes.

There's so damned much we didn't understand. So far as the Qesh were concerned, I was up against a major mystery about their biology and their origins, and I didn't have the data necessary to solve it.

I was inside one of the domes, the one we'd set up as an operational HQ. The grow-program that created them had included a set of big viewwall screens, and these were displaying images transmitted back from a variety of microbots inserted into the area around the city of Salvation. During our raid to free the hostages, Gunny Hancock had released a small cloud of surveillance drone floaters close to the city wall. They had me riding the board because Corpsmen are trained in the use of microprobes.

At least a thousand times larger than nanobots, microbots are tiny, autonomous machines ranging in size from the thickness of a human hair—say, around 100 microns—up to a millimeter or so, which is about the size of a grain of sand. Microscopic charged-couple devices—CCDs—can record light at optical wavelengths and transmit images with a maximum range of several hundred meters; a larger field robot, about the size of my fist, collects these transmissions, recompiles them, and sends them along as quantum-state scrambled bursts. Without the necessary keys, the enemy wouldn't pick up anything but noise.

The images were pretty low-res—grainy—and they were in black-and-white in order to preserve bandwidth, but they were good enough to give us close-ups from a number of viewpoints of the pit and the Jacker machines working on it. Qesh warriors in battle armor and lugging massive personal weapons were everywhere, newly arrived, it appeared, on several Roc assault craft that were now hovering motionless in the sky. There was something else in the sky, too, floating above the Rocs, so much larger than the other fliers that it dwarfed them—a gleaming Daitya weapons platform.

"When did *that* show up?" Hancock wanted to know. He'd been outside checking on our sentries, but came in when I told him there was something on the monitors he might want to see.

"Just a couple of minutes ago," I told him. "The bad guys look pretty stirred up."

"Looks like we managed to kick over the hornet's nest," Calli Lewis said.

"Any sign of reprisals?" Hancock wanted to know.

We were all worried about that. After freeing the hostages, it was a fair bet that the Qesh would simply grab some more, maybe a *lot* more, and promptly start executing them. What was curious was that Matthew and the other Salvationists with him hadn't seemed that concerned about the possibility.

"No, Gunny." I told him. "But we did see this."

I brought up a segment of video recorded about half an hour before. We had thousands of such segments individually beamed back to our OP. Only our AI could monitor all of them and single out the particular ones that might be of interest to us.

This particular sequence had been captured by a microbot stuck to the side of one of the spotlight masts rising near the city wall.

Most microbot surveillance drones, smaller than a speck of dust, drifted on currents of air in the same way that biobots moved through circulatory fluid. We didn't have a lot of control over them—you can lock them into a local magnetic field and steer them a bit that way, but with the equipment our squad had been able to pack along, we were pretty much limited to what we could pick up by chance.

Worse, microbots were subject to the wind. You can release a cloud of them over an enemy encampment, but if there's any wind at all, the cloud will be dispersed to hell and gone before you can get much in the way of recon data. And the wind on Bloodworld was fiercely unrelenting, gusting constantly from dayside around to night, except when thermal storms happened to send countercurrents from the wintry night across to the day.

This wasn't a major limitation for simple surveillance; out of some hundreds of millions of 'bots released into the wind, a few could be expected to hit convenient rocks or other structures, and most were designed with nano-reactive pads that let them adhere to convenient surfaces. With enough samples to draw upon, our AI could usually pick up images of what we were interested in, selecting them from the flood of data coming back from the relay.

"That," I told Hancock, using the AI program to isolate and zoom in on the interesting part of the picture, "looks like the bad guys' head honch."

We were looking down at an oblique angle on a procession of Qesh warriors. Most were encased in heavy armor and carried weapons that looked big enough to take on a Commonwealth Mk. 4 hovertank. Their armor showed scuffs, dents, and dings as though it all had seen long and rough usage.

One of the Qesh below, however, was wearing what could only be called *elegant* armor. We couldn't guess at the color in those images, of course, but this one individual's armor looked like it was richly engraved, with a mirrored polish that gleamed in the glare from the mast-mounted spotlights. If the battle armor of the average Qesh troopers was utilitarian and well-used, *this* guy's armor was strictly ceremonial. It looked lightweight, not much heavier than the Qesh's own exoskeletal plates.

"That Jacker," I told Hancock, "is either a general or a politician. And maybe both."

The chasing on the Qesh leader's armor reminded me of the ornate engraving on some samples of medieval parade armor—the sort worn by kings and dukes and the wealthiest of knights, gear far too precious to be worn into actual battle.

I was particularly interested in the fact that the Qesh seemed to go in for this sort of thing. Marine combat armor shows absolutely no difference between that worn by a general and that worn by a private; emblems of rank, of combat distinction, and of tradition—like the centuries-old eagle-globe-anchor device—are displayed only during full-dress parade. In combat, you don't want the enemy to be able to pick out your officers for special consideration.

A warrior culture might be expected to have lead-from-the-front officers with highly visible regalia. That sort of thing doesn't make much sense in modern combat, at least not as humans understand it now, but the Qesh weren't remotely human, and their society and history might have emphasized a markedly different set of traditions.

This particular Qesh leader was approaching a small structure built into the rock of the city wall, surrounded by a retinue of more conventionally armored soldiers. The structure opened in front of them—it appeared to be a doorway into a large airlock—and the group filed inside.

"Interesting," Hancock said. "I wonder if they'll come out again later with a new bunch of hostages?"

"I was thinking, Gunny . . ."

"What?"

"We might be able to use Jackers to get a look at the inside of the city. Maybe we could see what's going on in there."

"Hitch a ride, you mean? Instead of gnatbots?"

"Exactly."

"It's certainly worth a try," Hancock told me. "Do it."

So I did.

We had a supply of gnatbots with us, of course, but they would be all but useless over Bloodworld's windy surface. To deploy them effectively, we would have to get inside the city ourselves. Until we heard back from Matthew and his people, we were stuck outside.

Gnatbots are, literally, the size of gnats—perhaps a tenth of a millimeter long and just barely visible to the human eye *if* you're focused right on them. They dance through the air on tiny wings and can be directed either by a human controller or by a simple on-board program. The police use them a lot for general surveillance on Earth—and especially for security surveillance inside sealed structures on Earth, the moon, and Mars. In the wind-gusted environment of Bloodworld's twilight zone, though, those wings were next to useless. We needed to find another way of getting camera-carrying 'bots inside the city gates.

What I had in mind was using standard microbots attached to an individual Jacker's armor, and letting *him* carry the surveillance drone inside. A gram or so of programmed nano could assemble itself at the scene into a camera and transmitter too small to see without optical magnification.

The problem was finding a way of safely putting the microbots on the armor. We didn't have any special-grown nanobots like that on hand, and would have to program our own. I plugged my N-org into a console, brought up the programming base chart on-screen, and then asked Kookie to join me.

This would be a job for a Marine sniper.

"YOU SHOULD HAVE BUGGED THAT QESH PILOT, E-CAR," SERGEANT Leighton told me. "Would've been more certain."

"Not really," I told her. "Chances are he got shipped back up to orbit as soon as his friends picked him up. No reason to think they would have dragged him inside the city."

"I guess that's true."

I'd actually considered at the time bugging my alien patient, but had decided against it. It might have been useful having a spy-cam on board one of the Qesh capital ships up in orbit, but there were some major disadvantages as well. For one thing, if the Qesh were the suspicious sort, they would assume that one of their troops given medical treatment by the enemy would carry bugging devices of some sort, and so would screen him extra closely. In fact, I fully expected that as soon as they got the Qesh pilot back to one of their medical facilities, they would deprogram the nano I'd put into him, and shoot him up with their own, including something to wipe out any enemy alien nano that might still be in his body.

And for another, I'd not had the appropriate base nano on hand. The medical 'bots I carried with me in my M-7 needed substantially different programming than I could normally provide through my N-prog, with most of the code written by an AI. I could have managed something, but it would have taken longer than I'd cared to remain out there in the open, with bad guys closing in.

We were in the OP dome with two viewall displays above us, one showing the view from the microbot glued to the spotlight mast outside the city gate, the other giving us a vid feed from Lance Corporal Ron Kukowicz's M-440 accelerator rifle.

Kookie had slipped out of the OP encampment and stealthily made his way back to the edge of the forest over-looking the plain beneath the Salvationist city. The camera mounted on his MAR was zoomed in on several Qesh warriors; they appeared to be making their way toward the gate.

"Try for that one," I said, indicating one of the Qesh warriors in front of the others with a red dot. A crosshair reticle appeared against the Jacker's side.

"Range one-one-four-five meters," Kukowicz said over the squad channel. "Wind, variable at two-eight-five degrees, at my back with a slight drift to the right, between thirty and fifty kph, gusts to eighty-five. Selecting for twelve thousand Gs of acceleration."

I watched the data dropping into a column on the right side of the display. The paintball-bullet could steer itself to a certain extent, but needed input on windspeed, acceleration, and direction.

"You're cleared for the shot," Hancock told him.

"Roger. On the way."

I'd programmed a "paintball," a term that once referred to a marker used in target practice and a non-lethal combat sport but that now referred to a useful means of inserting nano cameras into hostile territory. The round consisted of a tiny slug of programmed 'bots packed into a steel jacket so that it could be gripped by the magnetic field of a gauss accelerator weapon and launched at extremely high velocity. Boosted at 12,000 gravities down the one-meter-long barrel of Kukowicz's accelerator weapon, the round would exit with a muzzle velocity of 490 meters per second, giving it a flight time of 2.337 seconds. The projectile was designed to hold an aerodynamic form briefly, and to use lift and steering to actively compensate both for wind and for the better than 43-meter drop between the time it left the muzzle and the instant it struck the target two and a third seconds later in this gravity. Just before impact, it would shed the steel jacket and the round's inner packing firing it forward, in order to kill its speed an instant before it struck the target, with as small a projectile as possible.

What actually struck home massed less than a gram. The Jacker probably didn't even feel the impact or, if it did, it would assume that its armor had been hit by a bit of wind-blown debris. From Kookie's vantage point back at the edge of the woods, it didn't look as though the Qesh we'd targeted had noticed anything.

Good.

There was a nervous silence for several seconds, as we waited to acquire the probe's transmission. A lot could go wrong with a mag-inducted round; a miss was possible despite the high-tech gimmickry, and too hard of an impact could damage the microbots to uselessness.

But within a few seconds, a new image came up on the monitor, transmitted from the newly grown nano camera now riding on the Jacker's side just above its right middle leg.

"Good picture," Leighton said.

"And a very nice shot, Kook," I added. "Bang on."

"Thanks. RTB."

Returning to base. "Come on in," Hancock told him.

I watched the show on the main monitor. After a few flashes and pixilation blizzards, the image from our paint-ball grew sharp and clear, rocking from side to side with the pace of the Qesh warrior it was riding on. This transmission, unlike the mass generic broadcasts of the gnatbots, was in full color, and included a sound feed as well.

We heard something like rumbling drums—an exchange of speech among several of the Qesh. Ahead, past the armored being's front shoulder, I could see a white door dilating open, leading into the side of the city cliff.

A number of Qesh filed into the airlock; it was crowded inside, with at least twenty of them packed in flank to flank as the outer door irised shut, the local air pressure bled off to Earth-normal, blower-filters pulled out the last of any toxic gasses, and an inner door opened up.

We'd been wondering if this was a Qesh assault team, moving into the city to seize more hostages or to otherwise punish the locals for the attack of a few hours before.

We were quite unprepared for what we actually saw and heard.

Chapter Sixteen

THE QESH TROOPERS ENTERED A LARGE, WELL-LIT CHAMBER BEYOND the airlock door, a chamber large enough to have served as a concourse for some thousands of people. I'm not sure what I expected the interior of the city of Salvation to look like. I *did* know that, whatever the Salvationists might think about nanotechnology in general, the city itself—the buildings and the infrastructure, including air purifiers, life support, power generators, and everything else that went into making a city live—would have been created through applied nano-technic engineering.

When the Salvation of Man colony had been put down on Bloodstar's World in 2181, the engineering department of the Commonwealth Colony Ship *Outward Venture* would have employed large-scale nanotech to tunnel out vast caverns going deep into the rock, and to have used native materials to create the life-support infrastructure, everything from power generators to furnishings in the living quarters. An entire city grown from native rock, using the techniques we'd pioneered back when the summers had stopped coming and the glaciers of the New Ice Age had begun their southward march. The hall we were looking at now had the look of nanarchitecture, with highly polished stone walls and a mirror-bright reflective floor of a deep, lustrous, semitrans-parent green stone. One far wall was dominated by an im-mense floor-to-ceiling portrait of a bearded man in black robes, though I couldn't tell whether it was supposed to be Jesus or some other, more modern, religious leader or guru. Oddly out of place, something like a shallow swimming pool occupied the center of the room.

Waiting for the newly arriving Qesh were a number of other Qesh, including the one we'd seen earlier with the richly engraved ceremonial armor. With them were perhaps a hundred humans, those in the forefront wearing ornate red robes with rich and elegantly detailed silver and gold embroidery. The fanciest robes belonged to a white-bearded man who looked like he was well past two hundred, though again, without anti-aging treatments he might have been only seventy or so.

And that whole thronging crowd appeared to be the best of buddies. The humans, many of them, were sipping from spherical drink containers. The head-honch Jacker held a mug of something steaming with his top arm, and sipped at it from time to time with what might have been a mouth, a puckered, upside-down *Y* located well down below the upper arm. His helmet was off, his armor open in the front, and he wasn't armed. Lots of the Qesh behind him had their helmets off as well. It was impossible to read expressions behind those flicking, turreted chameleon eyes, but they didn't appear to be particularly anxious or on guard.

And neither did the humans.

"What the shit?" Hancock asked. "They're having a fucking *cocktail* party in there!"

We heard a drumming sound, as the Qesh carrying our camera-and-microphone combo said something to Head Honch. The richly armored Qesh drummed something back, then turned to the white-bearded human. "My subordinate tells me that my troops have not found the bandits as yet. They will do so, however. Of this I promise you."

The Jacker's voice was pitched in a deep and rumbling bass register, but it had a flat affect to it, sounding almost mechanical. He must have been wearing some sort of electronic translator.

That was disturbing on several levels. For a Qesh translator to work, they would have to have access to English and, possibly, to other human languages. I strongly doubted that they could come up with the means for a running Qesh-English translation in less than two weeks.

And conquerors rarely troubled to learn the speech of subject peoples. Usually, at least as it had played out countless times on Earth, they made conquered populations learn the masters' tongue.

What the hell was going on?

"You have my assurance," the human said, "that the raiders will be rooted out. If they're in this city, we'll find them. And when we do, we will hand them over to you."

"It is important," the Qesh said, "to present the . . . how do you say . . . the *people* with an object lesson immediately, to prevent similar banditry in future."

"Of course, Lord."

Lord. So this was a conversation between the conqueror and his subject after all.

I made sure everything was being recorded. Several of the Qesh were not wearing armor at all, and this was a good opportunity to glimpse something of their physiology. Their mouths appeared to be slits shaped like an inverted *Y* located between the uppermost paired legs. More slits—two pairs on either side partially concealed by leathery flaps of carapace—were probably for breathing. I could see them rippling open and shut every few seconds. The rattling and booming speech of the Qesh appeared to be generated by a pair of large tympani on the upper part of the body, and they appeared to add emphasis to their speech both with color changes to the gray, blank area of leathery skin between their four eyes, and by clicking and grinding the tips of their two enormous horn-claws together.

Qesh speech, I decided, must be extraordinarily complex, combining fast-shifting color patterns with the sounds made by two plate-sized drum heads and the screech and clack of rubbing claws. No human could reproduce that blend of voiceless sounds, to say nothing of the colors. Maybe they spoke English with the Salvationists because the humans were simply incapable of reproducing "spoken" Qesh—not without a kettle drum and a few other instruments in an orchestral percussion section.

We all wanted to hear more of the conversation between Head Honch and the bearded human, but the Qesh carrying our spy-cam boomed something at the leader, then turned and walked off with several of his fellows.

Over the next several hours, we saw a number of the rooms and underground spaces that made up the city, and glimpsed lots of the inhabitants, but it was difficult to attach any sense to what we could see.

Our overall impression, however, was that the Qesh were solidly in control. There were armed guards standing at several busy intersections, and small groups of them patrolled the corridors like cops on a beat. The humans we saw watched the patrolling Qesh with expressions ranging from boredom to terror; no one tried to talk with the invaders, and for their part, the invaders didn't seem predisposed to interfere with the human crowd.

About ten minutes passed before we started getting signal breakup, and then the image dissolved into pixels and winked out. The transmission, shifting around randomly across tens of thousands of frequencies each second, probably couldn't be monitored by the Qesh, but it *could* be blocked, by tens of meters of solid rock if nothing else. True quantum communications would use quantum entanglement to connect sender and receiver without passing a signal in between; such a signal could not be intercepted and it could not be blocked, because the signal exists only in the transmitter and in the receiver, not in the space in between. We haven't figured out that trick, however, and so thick basalt walls still serve as a barrier.

What we received before that happened, though, had been useful.

And disturbing. If the human leaders of Salvation were cooperating with the Qesh, had they already given the invaders access to their computer records?

Had the Qesh already learned the location of Earth?

And how could we find out if they had?

SECOND LIEUTENANT BAUMGARTNER SHOWED UP WITH THE REST OF the platoon a few hours later. As expected, he was furious that Hancock had gone ahead and carried out a raid on the Qesh landing force.

"You've exceeded your authority, Gunnery Sergeant," he told Hancock, "and jeopardized the entire operation!"

The two of them were in an office space just across from the compartment we'd set up as a small sick bay. I was in there with Dubois, Garner, Masserotti, and a still comatose Kilgore, and we could all hear Mommy Baumy shouting next door. Those quick-grown habitats are pretty good, but they can't provide a hell of a privacy.

The soundproofing *was* good enough that we couldn't hear Hancock's answer, if he gave one.

"Do you realize," Baumgartner continued after a moment, "that the Qesh could have figured out that we were on this planet? If nothing else, they might have run into Marines on other planets they've already attacked. There were Marines at Cernunnos *and* at Athirat! If the Qesh had seen Marine armor at either of those places, they might make a connection if they saw it again here!"

"I saw an opportunity, sir," Hancock said, his voice rising just enough that we could hear his reply in sick bay, "to make a solid connection with the local humans. We were careful not to let the bad guys get a good look at us."

"And you know as well as I do that things *always* go wrong in combat! Your orders were to set up an OP and observe, *not* to get involved in a firefight!"

I was pretty sure that Baumgartner was just pissed because Hancock had spotted that opportunity and taken advantage of it without deferring to him. Not that Hancock could have asked for permission. Quantum-scrambled radio or laser communications can work over long distances but is strictly line-of-sight, though the lowest frequencies can penetrate obstacles to some degree. We didn't have any communications satellites up, for very obvious reasons, so we really had been totally on our own until Baumgartner showed up with the rest of our people.

"You are skating on damned thin ice!" Baumgartner went on. "I am *not* going to tolerate any more of your gung-ho old-breed nonsense! Do you understand?"

We couldn't hear Hancock's answer, but I assume it was a precise and clipped "Yes, sir."

So . . . Baumgartner didn't want any more gung-ho old-breed nonsense, did he? I'd heard about things like this, how every so often young, up-and-coming Marine officers somehow got the idea that this was a *new* Marine Corps, a *modern* Corps, and all concerned would be well advised to adopt the new and modern ways. The "old breed," originally referring to the old China Marines of the 1930s and later a nickname for the 1st Marine Division, unaccountably became a term of derision or even contempt.

Somehow, fortunately, the twisted attitude never lasts.

Don't get me wrong! Marines *do* change, adapt, and evolve. They hardly ever board and storm sailing vessels nowadays. Ah, well, maybe once in a while they do, but the capture of that Bloodworlder ketch a couple of days ago was decidedly an exception to the rule. Marines no longer use muskets or bayonets, or wear the high, stiff, sword-deflecting leather collars that gave them the name "Leathernecks" four and a half centuries ago.

But "gung-ho" has been a tradition with the Corps long before the phrase entered the lexicon during WWII. It was an Anglicized term, from the Mandarin *gong he*, and meant "work together." Somehow, "gung-ho" had become a battle cry for the Marines, an expression of Marine determination, dedication, camaraderie, and esprit.

The up-and-comers tampered with such time-hallowed institutions at their peril.

"Baumgartner," Masserotti said quietly, with grim emphasis, "is cruisin' for a bruisin'." He was lying on a treatment table, as I adjusted the framework of the EM cage embracing his arm.

"Belay that, Marine," Garner told him. "He'll learn."

"He'd fuckin' well better!"

"I think he's feeling his oats out here on his own, out from under Captain Reichert's thumb," I observed. "He'll learn, or he'll screw up . . . and then heaven help him!"

"The problem," Doob said, "is that if he screws up, we're *all* screwed! So heaven help *us*!"

I suspected that Hancock would have disagreed, that had he been a part of the conversation he would have pointed out that survival in the Corps doesn't depend on any one man, but on everyone working together.

Gung-ho.

I was getting ready to go inside Masserotti, so I quietly dropped out of the discussion. Once the EM cage was functioning, I settled back in a neurolink recliner and checked the connections. I'd already injected him with the necessary nano. All that remained was letting our AI make the final link that would take my virtual point of view down to the micrometer scale.

"You're all hooked up, e-Car," Garner told me. "You're good to go."

"Roger that," I said, closing my eyes. I brought my hand down on the contact plate, connecting the chair's electronics with the neuroimplants in my palm. "I'm going inside. . . ."

There was a brief, all-consuming instant of static . . . and then I was rushing through Masserotti's right thoracoacromial artery, a blood vessel branching off from the larger axillary artery high in the Marine's right shoulder, just above his collarbone. From my new perspective, I seemed to be drifting at high speed through a vast, dimly illuminated tunnel filled with myriad tumbling shapes. The tunnel walls, their glistening surface divided into irregular polygons, flashed past, but slowly enough that I could make out details of cell nuclei and organelles.

Much of the view was blocked by the red cells all but filling the murky fluid through which I was moving. The RBCs surged past me in pulses, each surge marking one beat of Masserotti's heart.

My point of view was now being relayed directly into my brain from an NV-340 microbot, a streamlined robotic vehicle some fifty microns long—ten times the width of the flattened, disk-shaped red blood cells drifting through the plasma. Light from the microbot's prow provided illumination, a blue-violet haze casting weirdly tumbling shadows from the translucent cells around me. In the distance, several large and amorphous masses appeared to be seeping into the arterial wall, passing among the cells—granulocytes, or white blood cells, each two or three times larger than the RBCs around them.

The cells were slowing, and I reduced the microbot's velocity. Blood flows at various speeds through the body—fastest as it emerges from the left side of the heart and into the aorta, slowest within the fine web of capillaries connecting arteries with veins, where red cells nudge and jostle along in single file, like dancers in a conga line. Here in Masserotti's shoulder, the typical speed of the blood flow was around fifty centimeters per second—a blisteringly fast pace for cells just five millionths of a meter across. The microbot was actually traveling considerably slower than the blood through which it moved; the electromagnetic cage around Masserotti's shoulder provided the microbot's motive power, as well as power for the light and for the high-energy laser built into the hull.

I was approaching the damaged area of Masserotti's shoulder, however, and the blood flow was slowing sharply. Ahead, red cells were piling up into a vast, dark red mass, a shadowy, hazy mountain of darkness as platelets reacted to the injury and began causing the red cells to clump—a blood clot. I could see numerous platelets along the red cells around me; red cells were flattened disks with depressed centers; platelets were spherical, roughly half the size of an RBC, but when they were activated by a nearby injury, they formed pseudopods over their outer surfaces, becoming stellate, and began clumping together to begin clot formation.

I wasn't here to interfere with the clotting, however. The clot had stopped the bleeding in and around Masserotti's wound, as it was supposed to do, and was by now releasing various chemicals to encourage the formation of fibroblasts from the surrounding tissue to promote healing. Instead, I was interested in a particular patch of endothelial tissue, the inner lining of the blood vessel, and I guided the 'bot through the surging red cell tides toward the arterial wall.

"I think I'm just about in position," I said, adjusting the craft's drive to hold its place against the current. Red cells thumped and rumbled against the craft's hull, generating a steady, agitated trembling. "Check me, please."

Words appeared in my in-head display. "The tracker shows that you're in the right place. Go for it, e-Car."

Conversations with the outside world were moderated through our AI. I was working on A-Time, now, accelerated time; my time sense had been boosted in order to slow the rapid pace of events around me to a manageable—and comprehensible—rate. A-Time was generated by initiating software resident in our CDF implants and speeding up our brain chemistry. It was like G-boost, no, *better* than G-boost; it was like stepping into a whole new world, a world slowed down to a crawl, at least from my skewed perspective. Had we been using ordinary radio for communications, the voices of the others would have seemed ponderously slow and dragged out to my ears, while my replies would have sounded like a rapid, high-pitched buzz or chirp to them. So the AI ran interference, letting me read their statements rather than hearing them.

"Initiating program," I said.

Turning the 'bot to face the arterial wall, I triggered a millisecond pulse from my laser, punching a tiny hole between two of the epithelial cells a few microns in front of me. Next I used the microsub's manipulator arm to insert a canister in the puncture. This done, I adjusted my 'bot's position, and punched another hole a couple of microns above the first.

I continued working in a circle, creating a pattern of punctures perhaps 200 microns across. The punctures, together with the canisters containing an MMP precursor, would tell Masserotti's body exactly where to begin angiogenesis—the formation of new blood vessels. MMP—matrix metalloproteinase—degrades the proteins that keep blood vessel walls solid, allowing endothelial cells to escape into the interstitial matrix for sprouting angiogenesis. By choosing precisely where to start the new arterial branch, we could both hasten and control the growth of new blood vessels, bypassing the clot and ensuring that healing nutrients reached the wound area.

The work could have been done by robots, sure, but every human body—and every network of blood vessels—while similar to one another in gross detail, is uniquely individual in the fine. That's why you can use mapping software of the human retina as a means for identification; no two networks of vessels are precisely the same. Robots need a lot of autonomy and very good AI to handle that sort of work, and while the platoon AI we had was adequate, its medical coding was fairly rudimentary. Most times, it's actually safer and surer to have a human teleoperator make the decisions and manage the operation.

I completed three more circles, marking the beginning points for three more blood vessels, before I decided I was getting tired and needed to pull out. I thoughtclicked the bail-out icon on my in-head, and woke up in my recliner.

"How you doin', e-Car?" Garner's face leaned over mine, his voice low and slow paced.

"*Everythingwentfinenoproblems,*" I chirped. I stopped, took a deep breath, and tried again. "Everything went fine," I repeated. "No problems." It sometimes took a few moments for the synapses associated with speech and thought to readjust back down to a slower level after kicking out of A-Time mode. My body was sore all over, like someone had worked me over with a ball bat. Accelerated mode also speeds up the natural pace of random muscular contractions, and can feel like the equivalent of running a 100-meter dash.

I glanced over at Masserotti. "How you doing, Marine?"

"No problems, Doc. My shoulder got kind of warm there for a while. Uh . . . what happens to the submarine?"

"The microbot? It'll break down into component parts, just like the smaller nanobots you have in your system. Basically, it'll dissolve into your blood, and either get filtered out or metabolized. There's nothing in it that can harm you in microscopic doses."

"I just want to make sure you guys clean up after yourselves in there, know what I mean?"

I grinned at him. "Your insides are already a mess, High-Mass. Nothing we could do could possibly make them any worse."

I climbed off the chair and hit the STOW key, folding it into a small, flat package that merged once again with the deck. Its pattern was stored in the hut's memory for recall whenever it might be needed again, but usually free space was more important.

"Can I get up yet?"

"Stay put for another hour or so, Mass," Garner told him. "The EM field is pulling in more 'bots to work on growing arteries. Let's leave the cage where it is for now."

Baumgartner chose that moment to walk into the room, along with Staff Sergeant Lloyd. "We're officially on full alert, people," he told us. "We're moving out in two hours."

"What's going down, sir?" I asked. "We get an invitation to meet with the Salvationists?"

"In a manner of speaking."

What the hell did *that* mean?

"What we need," Garner said, "is the opportunity to plug into the Salvation computer network."

"Exactly," Baumgartner said. "And that's why we're going in by the back door."

IT TOOK LESS THAN AN HOUR TO RETURN THE DOMES BACK TO ROCK and dirt by reprogramming the nanoconstructors in the walls and decks to debond and go inert. The rest of the two hours allotted by Baumgartner was spent getting the flitters packed up and ready to go. We strapped both Kilgore and Masserotti to the deck of the big cargo flitter; the rest of us mounted our personal quantum flitters and began filing out of the clearing that once had been our camp.

We circled west, then south, skirting a region of open pools of lava steaming and thundering in the semidarkness. Twice, we went to cover, hiding beneath our nanoflage under the breeze-rippled cover of Bloodworld's forest canopy of tendrils and feathery branches as Qesh Rocs passed in the distance. We still couldn't be sure how good Qesh technology was when it came to detecting quantum-pulsed communications, so we maintained radio silence throughout the entire journey, using direct line-of-sight laser-com transmissions for any necessary exchanges.

Eventually, we got clear of the lava pits and began moving east, then north. We had to ground again when another severe seismic disturbance set the ground beneath our skimmers to jolting and rippling. In the distance, a vast chunk of ice calved off of a nightside glacier and thundered into an arm of the sea.

By the time we once again approached the city of Salvation, the sky was definitely lighter, taking on an emerald-green glow at the eastern horizon beneath a turbulent wrack of storm clouds. Bloodworld's ponderous nodding back and forth was bringing it to forth, and soon, we knew, the red sun would again rise above the horizon.

I'd recognized the basalt plain in front of the northern side of the city we'd seen before, but this view of Salvation was familiar as well. Ahead was the colony's small spaceport in front of the southern side of the city. As on the far side, mountains rose precipitously above plain and surging ocean, but there were many more buildings scattered out across the bare rock bordering on the spaceport.

A number of the buildings were blackened ruins; this was the vantage point, I realized, of the vid from the Marine Specter probe they'd showed us during the briefing on board the *Clymer* shortly after we'd left Earth orbit. A Roc hovered above the port, and we could see several armored Qesh in the distance, moving among the buildings and wreckage. This appeared to be the focus of the Qesh attack.

"This way," Hancock told us. The laser-com units in our suits linked all of us together, a transmission from one of us automatically relayed across our network to all nearby receivers, with the signal strength deliberately kept so low that the Qesh couldn't pick up any stray IR laser flashes—we hoped.

"Where the hell are we going, Gunny?" Lewis asked.

"That way," Hancock replied, pointing. "To the left, down that rill and in among those buildings. That damaged pyramid there is our way in."

"And how do we know *that*?" Gregory asked.

"We bugged one of the natives," Baumgartner said. His use of the word "we" was a little self-important, since he hadn't even arrived yet when Matthew and his people had left our camp. "Now shut up, all of you. Necessary comm only."

That made sense. It would have been easy enough to tag one or several of our guests with gnatbots or other microscopic hitchhikers, and track their movements back into the city. Such devices would not have been able to maintain radio or laser contact with our base, of course, but Hancock likely had dispatched a robot relay to follow them. We had several such devices in our arsenal, including the spider-legged RV-90, which is a nanoflage-black sphere about the size of my fist, striding along on slender legs that hold it perhaps thirty centimeters off the ground. The spider would have followed the short-range pulses from the gnatbots, recorded the path by which our guests had entered their city, then skittered back to base, where the entire path could be downloaded and analyzed by our command team.

Of course, no one had bothered to tell the rest of us what we were doing. No matter. We were here now, and it looked like we had a means of getting into the city . . . *if* we could slip past those patrolling Qesh.

Five of us would make the descent—Hancock, Hutchison, Leighton, and Gregory, with me along as tech support. The rest would stay with our wounded and equipment at the top of a barren ridge overlooking the spaceport.

Using an eroded gully for cover, we edged our way down the hill and into the wreckage bordering the port field, achingly aware of the disk-shape with the bite taken out of it hovering 100 meters overhead. We moved slowly, to avoid tripping any motion sensors they might have up there, focused on the ground below. We knew the Salvationists had made the same trip, however, and they didn't have nanoflage to cover their movements. Either the Qesh weren't keeping an especially close lookout for trespassers, or the Salvationists had figured out just how slowly to move to avoid being picked up by their automated scanners.

Possibly, the Qesh simply didn't care. The Roc might be parked up there simply to intimidate the local population, or to declare their spaceport off-limits. The port didn't have much in the way of space-capable assets; I could see the wreckage of two orbital craft, possibly there to service the communications satellites that would be vital for a terrain-divided colony like Bloodworld, but nothing larger, and certainly nothing interstellar, of course. Ships capable of star travel are *big*—bigger than that whole starport—and usually weren't designed to set down on planetary surfaces. Besides, the Salvationists appeared to be an insular, isolationist bunch, utterly disinterested in contact with anyone else. I wondered what could drive a community to embrace that level of isolation, on a world of storms, temperature extremes, and rumbling volcanoes.

Once among the buildings, we froze in place, as three Qesh walked past, fifty meters away. They were carrying what were obviously weapons. Again, though, their search didn't appear to be terribly focused or intense. I was becoming more and more concerned about what we'd seen so far— an apparent collaboration between the Qesh invaders and the ruling faction of the human colonists.

The fact that the humans were divided into factions at all was also worrying. Until we knew more about the local politics, we would have to proceed very carefully indeed.

The pyramid-shaped building, a squat, truncated structure about ten meters high, rose from the debris and rubble a few meters ahead, its upper surface blackened by a Qesh energy bolt.

We were halfway to the door when it irised open directly in front of us, and leather-clad humans began filing out. The one in the lead spotted us almost at once.

"Halt!" he called, his old-fashioned laser rifle snapping up to cover us. "Fallen ones! Drop your weapons!"

For a horrible moment, the five of us stood facing ten of them, our weapons trained on one another. Hancock took the initiative.

"Hold your fire, Marines," he said over our private laser-net channel. "Put your weapons on the ground . . . slowly. Then raise your hands."

"Hancock!" Baumgartner snapped at us from his vantage point on the ridge behind us. "What the hell are you doing?"

"Getting into the city," Hancock replied. "Trust me, sir. . . ."

Chapter Seventeen

As we laid our weapons down, the Salvationist soldiers crowded around us, poking at us with the muzzles of their rifles. I actually doubt that those obsolete lasers could have burned through our Mk. 10 combat armor—not unless they were able to hold a steady beam on one spot for several seconds. I glanced up at the Roc overhead, but they didn't seem to be taking notice of us.

Or had they seen us in our approach down the gully, and dispatched a Salvationist patrol to pick us up?

Too many unknowns. We would have to play this one damned carefully.

"Inside," the presumed leader of the native patrol barked, gesturing sharply. All of them were thickly swaddled in the local equivalent of environmental gear—breather masks, heavy goggles, and brown and gray leather outerwear and boots. I wondered if the leather was synthetic—did their dislike for industrial chemistry extend to clothing? And if it was real, what kinds of animals did they have, to provide the hides? There might be native animals capable of providing skins that could be tanned by traditional techniques, but more likely they'd brought the fertilized ova of various species from Earth. Somewhere beneath that mountain there must be grazing areas large enough to accommodate herds of gene-tailored neocattle or measts.

One of them nudged Hancock along with the butt of his rifle.

"Easy there, fella," Hancock said over his external speaker. "We're not your enemies."

"You are Fallens," the leader said, using the word like a name. "We're willing to suffer hell for you, but we will *not* listen to your lies! Drop your pistols as well!"

"We're not Fallens," I said. "We're Angels of the Rapture!"

"That remains to be seen. You will be judged by the Council of Elders. *They* will determine your relevance to sacred scripture!"

Once we were disarmed, they herded us into a fairly large airlock, and I watched one of them operate a control that shut the outer door. I could hear pumps operating somewhere overhead, replacing the outside air, laden with sulfur dioxide and sulfuric acid, with Earth-normal air.

"Heads up," Hancock said over the laser channel. "After they open the inner door for us . . ."

The inner door began to dilate open.

"Now!"

Five of us, against ten of them. What happened next took almost no time at all.

They outnumbered us, yes, but four of us were Marines extensively trained in hand-to-hand combat. In the centuries since the U.S. Marine Corps has become the principle space-capable combat infantry force for the Commonwealth, Marines have honed their close-quarters combat techniques to an amazing degree—necessary, if they are to conduct VBSS operations—visit, board, search, and seizure—against potentially hostile ships. In the close confines of spacecraft or orbital stations, you often don't have enough room to employ ranged weapons like lasers, and certainly not high-energy weapons like plasma guns. Close quarters combat generally comes down to hand-to-hand, employing heavily modified jujitsu and tae kwon do to pin and disable opponents, even in zero-G.

FMF Corpsmen learn some of the basic stuff, though we're not the masters that the Marines are. I brought my elbow up and into the throat of the Salvationist directly behind me, and snatched his rifle as I shoved him into a second man nearby. Fortunately, we weren't in zero-G; fighting hand-to-hand is *real* tricky in an environment where every punch, every movement has an opposite-but-equal reaction that can send you tumbling backward, out of control. My zero-G training had been pretty much limited to just learning how to maneuver through the dark and tangled interior of a disabled ship without becoming hopelessly disoriented, leaving the actual grappling and fighting to the Marines.

And this, of course, was anything but zero-G. At 1.85 Gs, we were reliant on our exoskeletons to keep us moving without falling and breaking something. Our opponents didn't have that advantage. All of them had been born and raised in this environment, however, and as a result they were heavily muscled.

But they were *slow*, their movements honed by lifetimes of moving carefully and with deliberation in high gravity, even when their reflexes were quickened by the fact that things fell almost twice as quickly here as on Earth.

With the two Salvationists behind me dancing with each other, I took the laser rifle I'd wrested away from one and slammed the other in the face with the butt, shattering his goggles. The rifle was connected by a flexible metal cable to a backpack worn by the first man; I looped this around his throat and yanked him off his feet. He pounded at me with leather-gloved fists, but I couldn't even feel the blows through my armor. By the time he hit the deck, hard, perhaps three seconds after Gunny Hancock had given us the word, the fight was over. The deck was covered by writhing, groaning Salvationists. It took another ten seconds for us to cut their lasers from their backpacks, rendering them useless, and making sure they weren't carrying any other hardware.

"Tie 'em up," Gunny said. He found a small surveillance

camera mounted above the inner lock door up near the over-head, and disabled it with his knife. "Use the cables. We don't want to be interrupted."

Several of the bad guys were in bad shape after being manhandled by the Marines. I slapped nanopatches on the worst of them—giving them doses of generic nananodynes that would kill the pain and send them into a twilight happy-land for twelve hours or so. They protested, of course, loud and angrily, and I threatened to zap all of them if they didn't sit still and keep quiet; I could *not* understand their issues with medical nano.

We took their breath masks so they couldn't warn anyone else, and left them tied hand and foot inside the airlock. Beyond the inner hatch, a hallway slanted down into dark-ness; evidently, this outbuilding wasn't much used and the passageway was not lit. However, bundles of piping along the overhead showed the path of some major electrical con-nections. Following these down the corridor led us within a few tens of meters to a junction box—and the telltale jacks for a computer connection. They weren't the same size as the ones we use, but they showed us we were in the right spot.

"Major bingo," Leighton said.

"Yeah?" Hutchison shot back. "Who's he?"

"Okay, Doc," Hancock said. "It's all yours."

"Right." I stepped up to the input jacks, found a panel re-lease, and opened it. Inside were circuit panels and cables . . . and a configuration totally unlike what we used on Earth.

"Non-standard config," I said. "Jesus, it looks like they've been patching it with spit and duct tape."

"Let me see, Doc," Leighton said. She was a whiz with all things electrical, one reason she'd been volunteered for this mission. She pulled a multitool from a pouch and probed at the wiring for a moment before pulling a red and a blue free. "These two," she said. "I think they feed into a fiber-optic data cable through that converter."

"Let's see if you're right." I'd opened up a panel on the

left forearm of my armor and pulled a pair of wires free. This was definitely the old-tech way of handling things, but sometimes old tech is *simple* tech, and less prone to failure than the shiny and the new.

I hardwired the connection, then opened the link for the AI mod.

I'd downloaded it from the platoon AI back at the OP—a stripped-down version made by copying the original and trimming off all of the unneeded extras—like code for keeping track of supplies and logistics, or personnel health records, or tactical decision making. What was left was a low-functioning AI with some newly written code piggy-backed into the body, code designed to enter a strange computer network, explore it, and find certain very specific data files.

Since the beginning of the information age, we've had software constructs like this. They've been called agents, netbots, or simply computer viruses, and over the centuries they've become extremely sophisticated—as good as Marines at infiltrating hostile and well-defended places.

Words appeared on my in-head: INITIATING PROGRAM. MAPPING O/S.

Seconds passed. The Marines spread out around me, kneeling on the deck, watching both directions for the approach of hostiles. "Hurry it the fuck up, e-Car!"

"The agent is inside, Gunny. I can't do anything to hurry it."

O/S IDENTIFIED. INCORPORATING O/S SHELL.

"Okay, I said. "It's figured out the colony's operating system. It looks like a variant of Core 1230."

"Shit, that's ancient. Will it support the AI?"

MAPPING TARGET SYSTEM.

"It ought to. We had AIs running on computer nets long before the Neoessies packed up and moved out here."

SEARCHING TARGET SYSTEM.

More seconds passed, seconds dragging into minutes. What was happening inside the Salvationist network was very much like a virus scan on a non-AI system. As it identified each file, it explored it, looking for certain key strings of characters. Information about Earth and the location of Sol might be encrypted, but more likely it was resident within the computer's memory banks in the same format and with the same identifiers as when the Neoessies arrived on Blood-world sixty-four years ago.

Of course, it was unlikely that the agent would find something with a nice, neat name like "Navigation data: Sol." It would keep poking around, though, looking for any of a number of possible matches. Whatever was stored in there might be something as simple as a string of coordinates. Such a string wouldn't do the Qesh a bit of good, however—not without some sort of nav table or algorithm that would relate our standard coordinate system, with Sol at 0, 0, 0. Bloodworld's coordinates on our computers, for instance, were RA 15_h 19_m 26_s; Dec -07° 43' 20"; D = 20.3 ly, which identified a precise spot in Earth's night sky, plus the distance of just over twenty light years. The coordinates would be meaningless to the Qesh, unless they could convert it to whatever system of celestial navigation they used.

NAVIGATIONAL FILES IDENTIFIED.
SEARCHING NAVIGATIONAL FILES.
HISTORICAL FILES IDENTIFIED.
SEARCHING HISTORICAL FILES.

The process actually was proceeding fairly quickly, faster than I'd expected. On Earth and the other worlds of the Commonwealth, nearly all computers—some hundreds of thousands to millions of them—are linked together by system nets, with thousands of local systems overlapping and interconnected to create what amounts to an electronic nervous system for an entire world. This means the network is everywhere, and that every citizen can be connected to the local net through the hardware grown inside his own brain, with in-head CDF displays and internal-voice links with anyone else on the web with whom he wishes to converse.

On Bloodworld, they seemed to have pursued a different way of doing things. So far as my agent had been able to determine, there was only one computer in Salvation, with connections to a number of dumb terminals. One *big* computer, then, rather than millions of separate ones tied in together.

TARGET STRNGS FOUND IN SALVATION LOCAL NETWORK:
NAVSTELLEXE9386
NAVSTELRECORD284279.
NAVSTELRECORD284534.
NO FURTHER LOCAL SYSTEM ENTRIES FOUND.

Like the lady said, *Major bingo!*

I pulled up an abstract of the file listings. The first was the algorithm for creating a representation of three-dimensional space, listing all of the stars visited by humans when they colonized Bloodworld sixty-four years ago. The next gave the position of Sol in Bloodworld's night sky, using Bloodstar as the central coordinate, 0, 0, 0. The third was the position of Earth on an absolute map, showing all of local interstellar space out to about fifty light years from Sol. Using those three together would make it easy for the Qesh to find Humankind's homeworld.

"Hurry it up, Doc!" Hancock said. "Someone's coming!"

"We're nearly there. . . ."

I sent another search command through, looking for the last time those files had been called up, or the program executed. I was enormously relieved when I saw the answer come up: 1217:10, 15 November, 2181. That appeared to be the date when Salvation's computer went on-line, and they hadn't bothered with the information since.

It made sense. The Salvatonists weren't interested in staying in touch with Earth, or even finding it again. Mostly what it meant, though, was that the Qesh hadn't found it . . . yet.

"Got it," I told the others. "Permission to delete."

"Do it," Hancock told me.

I sent the command to delete all three files.

"Hostiles!" Leighton called.

"Engage at will!" Hancock replied.

I heard the shriek and crack of Leighton's M4-A2 firing in the close confines of the passageway. Hancock was beside her, firing his laser.

As the system did so, my agent was identifying portals and connections to other computer systems.

CONNECTION GATE IDENTIFIED: MARTYRDOM.

CONNECTION GATE IDENTIFIED: WIDE THE GATE.

CONNECTION GATE IDENTIFIED: RESURRECTION.

CONNECTION GATE IDENTIFIED: SCRIPTURE'S TRUTH.

Other cities on Bloodworld. On Earth, computers were tied together through orbital relays up at Geosynch. Here, they seemed to be tied together by landlines—probably fiber-optical cables. Odd. I would have thought that satellite relays would be less prone to disruption by, for instance, massive seismic quakes or lava flows or tidal waves, all of which this crazy planet had in abundance. As I thought about it further, though, I realized that satellites might not be that secure either, not with periodic gales of charged particles blasting in from that too-close red dwarf sun.

"Damn it, e-Car! Move it!"

"I'm scanning the systems in the other cities, Gunny. I can't rush it. . . ."

ENTERING MARTYRDOM LOCAL NETWORK.

SEARCHING TARGET SYSTEM.

I tried to remember how many separate colony cities there were on Bloodworld. About twenty, I thought, though there might be several that were missed by the earlier probes. If we did find and delete information about Sol's location in the Salvation database, how could we be sure it wasn't also on some of the other computers on the planet?

ENTERING RESURRECTION LOCAL NETWORK.

SEARCHING TARGET SYSTEM.

TARGET FILE STRINGS NOT LOCATED IN MARTYRDOM LOCAL NETWORK.

The colony city of Salvation had been established first. As secondary colonies had been built, the programmers had either copied the first set of files in their entirety and installed them on the new systems, or they'd copied *just* what was needed and installed that. The first method was lazy but common, the second more efficient, especially when the local systems didn't appear to have AIs to manage the data.

The disadvantage of the second method was that there were no off-site backups, so if something happened to Salvation, the data might be irretrievably lost.

TARGET FILE STRINGS NOT LOCATED IN RESURRECTION LOCAL NETWORK.

It was beginning to look like the Salvationists had done things efficiently, but without worrying about backups.

Excellent.

Whoever had been coming up the passageway appeared to have backed off.

I kept working, directing the stripped-down specialist AI to keep searching. The negative results kept coming back, and I directed my agents to do a second full sweep, just to make sure. As nearly as I could tell, the system was clean. The Qesh would not learn Sol's location here.

Of course, there was always the chance that someone had backups of the data on a separate drive, or in an inaccessible data vault someplace. But for that matter, the Qesh might learn where Earth was by any of a number of other possible means. Hell, all it would take would be for one Salvationist to tell one of his Qesh pals that humans had come to Bloodworld from right *there*, a dim yellow star in Bloodworld's sky when the sun was below the horizon, located in the constellation of Taurus, a few degrees south of the Pleiades, just twenty light years distant.

But our mission here had been to eliminate any reference to Sol's position in the Bloodworld computers, and we'd just accomplished exactly that. I spent another few moments uploading some additional virus-agents to the system, downloaded some additional records that looked interesting, and then unjacked from the box.

"We're good to go," I told Hancock.

"Right. Everyone, fall back to the airlock."

We began retreating up the corridor.

I wondered if the Qesh ship parked overhead was watching for us.

THE PROBLEM, IT TURNED OUT, WASN'T THE ROC SO MUCH AS THE squad of Qesh. They were waiting for us as we emerged from the Salvationist building, guns leveled. One boomed out a drumroll, and we heard the translation behind it. "Rebels! Stop! Under authority of your God!"

"Not *my* God!" Leighton shouted. "Back off!" No-Joy, I recalled, was Reformed Gardnerian, just like my parents, but this was the first time I'd ever heard her go public with her faith in a firefight.

I don't know if the Qesh understood her reply or not. They opened fire in the next instant, shooting wildly. No-Joy triggered her plasma weapon with deadly accuracy, burning through the armor of one of the Qesh warriors outside.

Hutchison stood in the doorway beside her, firing his laser, and then a Qesh energy bolt slammed into the building close beside the door, buckling the wall in a hot wash of white flame.

Mark 7 armor runs an electrical field over its outer surface, a charge designed to deflect incoming plasma bolts. The Qesh handheld weaponry fired bolts of positively charged plasma similar to our M4-A2 squad heavy weapons, but they had a *lot* more punch behind them. The kinetic impact of the incoming round picked up both Leighton and Hutchison and slammed them back into the airlock.

I ducked forward, kneeling next to Hutch. "You okay?"

"I'm okay! I'm okay!" He was scrambling back to his feet, scooping up his weapon. We were in fearfully tight quarters, an airlock filled with bound prisoners, and it was impossible to move without tripping over them. Part of me was yelling at myself that I needed to move the prisoners back into the building, get them out of the firefight, but my first concern was for my Marines. Leighton waved me off as I turned to check on her. Her armor was scorched, the nanoflage burned clean off in a crinkled gray swath across her side and upper torso, but she appeared to be otherwise intact. Leaning around the shattered outer door of the airlock, she began pumping bolts into the Qesh outside. I saw one rear up on its hindmost legs, its upper five limbs pinwheeling wildly as the heavy helmet covering its crest disintegrated in hot metal and bone. Qesh armor appeared to be less effective than ours at turning aside charged rounds.

The other Qesh scattered for cover. I saw another one go down, and realized they were taking heavy fire from their rear, from up on the ridge where we'd left Baumgartner and the others. The rest of the platoon was pouring it on, catching the Qesh in a deadly enfilade.

"We can't let ourselves be trapped here!" Hancock shouted, firing his laser through the door. "C'mon! Before they get themselves squared away!"

Hancock led the way through the door, bent low and running as fast as his exoskeleton-braced armor could drive him, firing his weapon as he ran. Hutchison followed, the two of them zigzagging across the plain, making their way toward the gully in the ridge perhaps fifty meters away. I heard a loud clank behind us. The inner airlock hatch was closed, but someone was hammering at the other side. More Salvationists, probably.

Gregory exchanged a look with me and Leighton. "Who's next?" he asked.

"You," Leighton told him. "Then you, Doc. I'll bring up the rear."

"Now wait a minute—" I began, but No-Joy cut me off.

"Just shut the fuck up and *do* it, e-Car!" she yelled. "You have the stuff you downloaded off the Bloodworld system!" She patted her plasma weapon. "And *I* have Betsy! So I bring up the rear!"

I'd never known she'd named her weapon. "Yes, Sergeant," I said, angry. Women have been serving with the Corps since Nancy Brewer on the U.S.S. *Constitution* in the War of 1812, though no one at the time realized it. I was well aware that chivalry has no place in the military, that I was supposed to see Joy Leighton as a *Marine*, not a woman. But, damn it, I didn't want to run and leave her behind.

Another explosion rattled the building, bringing down a section of the overhead and eliciting yells and screams from the bound prisoners. Someone was still hammering on the inner hatch; they would have to take care of their own people.

I gave my Mk. 30 carbine a quick check, gripped it in both gloves, and ducked through the outer hatch and into the open. The sky was almost at full light now, though the sun wasn't visible yet. Or maybe it was being blocked by the wreckage around the Salvation starport. The Roc still hung in the sky overhead, looming and terrifying, and I could see three tiny turrets in its belly tracking back and forth as they poured fire out against the ridge and the building both. A brilliant flash lit up the craft's belly, followed closely by a second; those had been 100-megajoule plasma cannon rounds. The Qesh had destroyed the one we'd brought to the OP on the other side of the mountain, but Baumgartner had two more. He must have set them up on the ridge, and was using them to engage the Roc. I could see some gaping holes in the Roc's belly now, and one of the weapons turrets had been knocked out of action.

I stopped watching the sky and focused on running. I ducked around the corner of a ruined starport structure—a wrecked crane, I think it was—and came face-to-face with a Qesh warrior.

It was one of those frozen-time moments—like being on G-boost and A-Time together, with your thoughts racing like lightning while your body was frozen by the chains of physics. I brought my carbine up, trying to aim, but my arms were moving so *slowly*. The Qesh was moving too, trying to twist its torso around, trying to bring its own weapon to bear. . . .

I started snapping off rounds even before I had the carbine lined up with the Jacker, but I continued dragging the weapon up and over, trying to aim for the helmet. I'm not sure I was thinking things through at that point, but I knew on an instinctive level that the helmet was vulnerable. Qesh helmets, like ours, didn't have visors that were always transparent, but they did have a black strip that was probably an optical sensor of some sort. A half-meg pulse might not pierce that body armor, but burn out its optics and it would be blind.

The Qesh triggered a round. It missed, slamming into something at my back, the blast propelling me up off my feet and to one side as I continued to mash down the firing stud on my carbine, continued trying to align my weapon with the armored monster's helmet. I landed on my side in the dirt at the same instant that the Qesh's helmet flashed, the optical strip exploding with the thermal shock of my last laser pulse.

I scrambled to my feet. The Qesh, holding its weapon with its upper arm, used its front two leg-hands to reach up and pull off the blinded helmet. Maybe it thought I was dead. I wasn't, and my next shot burned through the Jacker's unprotected face between its two upper eye turrets.

"Come *on*, Doc!" Hancock yelled. "Quit playing with the neighbor kids and get your ass up here!"

I stood, looked around for Sergeant Leighton . . . and saw her armor crumpled on the ground halfway between me and the airlock, perhaps ten meters away.

"Marine down!" I yelled. And then the world around me exploded in nova light and raw noise.

Chapter Eighteen

THE ROC WAS FALLING.

Its two remaining belly turrets continued firing, plasma bolts slashing across the ruin of the starport and up the face of the ridge. That last blast had been a round meant for me, but it had hit the wrecked crane instead, toppling the length of metal struts and girders, sending them crashing to the ground. A beam struck me as I tried to get up, knocking me onto my back. From that vantage point, I watched the Roc sliding past overhead, one wingtip dipping low . . . and then it slammed into the center of the port's landing field a few hundred meters away, erupting into white flame, burning fiercely in Bloodworld's oxygen-rich atmosphere.

I was pinned. I *had* to get up. I planted my hands beneath the girder and pushed, but couldn't budge it. I wasn't hurt, but the high gravity was working against me.

Adjusting my position, I managed to reach down and trip the release contacts for the exoskeleton embracing my right leg. It was awkward, working in a tight space like that, but I managed to pull the part free, then wedge it in between the ground next to my hip and the underside of the girder holding me down. I checked to make sure the power feed was still connected. Normally, the exoskeleton operated automatically, picking up my natural movements and amplifying them, but this time I thoughtclicked an icon in my in-head, switching the right leg to manual, then ordered it to flex and straighten.

I kept it braced with both hands, feeding extra power to the unit. I heard the servomotors shrilling, and then, as I flexed it once more, felt the girder shift slightly to one side.

That left me just enough time to edge out from underneath. Free!

The exoskeleton servos in the knee appeared to be blown, but I didn't care. I could manage to move around in the higher gravity without having both legs braced, so long as I was careful not to come down hard on the unprotected side.

Joy Leighton was lying nearby, unmoving. Picking up my carbine, I jogged toward her immobile form, my gait thrown into an unsteady limp. My right leg hurt with the effort, and I had to be careful not to tear something in my knee, but I made it to her side, dropping flat. "No-Joy!" I yelled. "Hey, Marine! Can you hear me?"

No response.

I switched her opaqued visor to see-through. She looked like she was asleep—deeply unconscious. I fired a jolt of nananodyne pain blockers into her carotid artery just in case, though, followed that with a large dose of nanobots, then began checking her suit.

Not good. There was a ragged tear in her armor, on her right side just above her waist, and the edges were still hot. There was a hole the size of my fist there, and fragments from her armor had sprayed through, burning into her flesh. There wasn't a lot of blood; the wound had been cauterized by the white-hot plasma. But just looking at it I knew there was bad damage inside.

How bad? I jacked into her armor and called up a full scan. CDF windows opened in my in-head, showing a thermal image of her entire body.

She had a reverse pressure leak going, of course, the thicker atmosphere outside seeping into her holed suit. The higher O_2 in the atmosphere was good, the CO_2 and sulfur compounds not so much. I checked to make sure her neck seal had triggered and that nothing was forcing its way up into her helmet. Good.

She was bleeding from a deep, incised wound in her side and back, the hot spot stark on the thermal image. Heart rate 168, thready and very weak, BP 96 over 44 and falling, respiration 35, quick and shallow, with elevating adrenaline and noradrenaline. Cooling at the extremities as blood started pooling in her core; she was already deep in shock. I told her suit to manage that—kicking on the internal heaters. The fact that the seal was closed at her neck might restrict the blood flow to her brain slightly—not a good thing. I decided that she could handle a little sulfur dioxide and elevated CO_2 in her breathing mix, that good circulation in her brain was the more critical factor of the two.

Pulling out my N-prog, I ordered the nanobots in her system to diffuse through her torso. I needed to see the deep extent of her injury. Within a few seconds, shadows began to form, then to solidify, outlining her bones, internal organs, and major muscle goups.

Oh . . . *shit*!

Her spine was broken, snapped clean through between T11 and T12—the eleventh and twelfth thoracic vertebrae, both of which were cracked and broken, and with the four floating ribs dislocated. There was a hell of a lot of internal damage. Her right XI rib had been snapped in two, and half of it driven down into her liver, and there was extensive bleeding—probably from the hepatic portal vein, though it looked like one or more of the major hepatic veins had been severed as well.

I had a few minutes at most to save her life.

The internal bleeding was the most immediate problem. The hepatic portal system isn't a true vein, because it doesn't carry blood directly to the heart. Instead, it drains blood from the whole gastrointestinal tract and from the spleen into the liver. The hepatic veins, by contrast, drain from the liver into the inferior vena cava, which takes the blood straight back to the heart. You can bleed out faster if you take damage to a major artery like the aorta or the femoral, but not by much.

Using my N-prog, I began programming the diagnostic nano in her torso, switching it to radical emergency hemostasis. It was her only chance.

"Doc!" Hancock's voice called. "How is she?"

He would have seen on his in-head display that she'd been hit.

"Not good!" I called back.

"Can you get her up here?"

"Not without fucking killing her!"

Some millions of nanobots were converging on No-Joy's liver now, riding the currents of blood feeding into her hepatic portal system. When they hit the ruptured area, they found intact blood vessel walls and latched on, forming a lattice framework upon which more 'bots could latch on. I could see the framework growing, thickening, strengthening, on the N-prog screen. The question was whether the microscopic robots could fight the current of blood rushing into her abdominal cavity, and find the other end of the vein in order to join the two severed ends together.

The 'bots were having trouble getting around the fragment of floating rib still lodged in her liver.

Once, battlefield emergency first aid was enormously simpler. You stopped a major bleed-out by applying pressure, lots of it. If you could *see* the bleeder you could pinch it off with a hemostat, or between your thumb and forefinger if you had to. There's a story on record of one Army medic who closed up a spurting femoral artery with safety pins.

And if the bleeding was completely internal, like this, you applied pressure to the abdomen, treated for shock, and hoped for the best. Whether or not the patient survived depended mostly on how quickly they could be transported to a well-equipped field surgical unit, and then back to a hospital stateside.

Nowadays, we had a lot more tools at our disposal. The bad news was that the line between emergency first aid and surgery was now *very* fuzzy, bewilderingly so. Medical technicians had *lots* more ways to save a wounded Marine's life than in the old days, when their medical kit held some gauze, a few lengths of roller bandages, morphine and antibiotic powder, some pins and hemostats, and not a hell of a lot else. Corpsmen then, as now, still had to balance their available tools against the situation. Could you physically transport the patient back to a safe area in the rear? Would the patient survive the trip? Were you actually under fire while you tried to save the Marine's life? How quickly could you stabilize the wounded Marine's medical situation?

One fact had not changed between the old days and now.

Time was everything.

I kept following the progress of my nanotechnic surrogates. I had two options that I could see. I could order the 'bots already attached to the ends of the veins to link together and close off, essentially sealing the bleeders shut. Joy would probably lose her liver, but she could grow a new one easily enough once we had her back in civilization, and the endcaps on her vessels would stop her from bleeding out. The other option was what I was trying to do now—to actually reconnect the severed ends, creating an artificial bypass across the damaged area.

The first option—capping off the flow—was faster and more certain if it worked, but those swarms of one-micron 'bots in there were up against an almost insurmountable problem—Joy's blood pressure. The blood was still coming through her hepatic portal system so fast and hard that the nanobots simply couldn't hold against that surging tide. Her heart was still beating—her heart rate was up to 190 now, trying to keep up with her rapidly falling blood pressure. As her BP continued to drop, the 'bots *would* be able to complete the pinch-off, but by then her pressure would be so low that she would be looking at serious brain damage on top of everything else.

And so I'd decided on the slightly longer option— rechanneling the flow through a nanobot bypass, literally

growing a centimeter or so of artificial blood vessel to keep
her blood flow contained.

Had I made the right choice? The 'bots were struggling,
fighting the current as they tried to complete the linkup.
This sort of work was a *lot* easier with smaller blood vessels.

Almost there . . . yes! The nanobots made the connection.

The latticework now formed a complete tube . . . and then
I watched the structure dissolve again as a few tens of thousands of the 'bots lost their hold against the tide.

They were failing. Heart rate 205 . . . blood pressure 70
over 30.

I had one more option, one more thing to try, but it was
hellishly dangerous.

"Doc!" It was Hancock again. "Doc, heads up! You've
got bad guys moving toward your position!"

As if I didn't have enough to worry about. "Where?"

"On your left. Fifteen meters!"

I looked. The body of the wrecked crane was there, providing some shelter but blocking my view. Well, if I couldn't
see them, maybe they couldn't see me. . . .

I could hear the sounds of the firefight all around me,
the lightning-bolt crack of lasers superheating tubes of air,
creating miniature thunderclaps as the vacuums collapsed,
the deeper *whoosh-bang* of plasma bolts. The Marines up
on the ridgetop were firing at everything that was moving
down on the spaceport, but they wouldn't be able to keep
it up for much longer. The Roc had been swept out of the
sky, but more and more enemy troops were converging on
the area, and before much longer the Marines would have
to withdraw.

"Doc!" That was Baumgartner. "You need to get out of
there. *Now!*"

"I can't move my patient, sir," I replied.

"*Capture* her then, and get her out of there!"

"*Not fucking yet, damn it!*" I shouted back.

Shouting obscenities at your commanding officer is never
a good idea, not if you want a healthy career in the military

illuminated by good quarterly reports and a lack of non-judicial punishment. On the other hand, he was up there, while I was down here.

A Qesh trooper came around the side of the ruined crane, coming straight toward me. I think he was more surprised than I was, because he came to an abrupt halt when he saw me, fumbling with his weapon.

Dropping the N-prog, I rolled half a meter to my right, scooping up Leighton's plasma weapon and dropping it across her legs as I took aim and triggered it all in one motion.

The bolt of charged plasma slammed into the armored giant right at the level of his upper arm, shattering his weapon and peeling open his armor in a blossoming flower of raw energy and vaporizing plastic and metal. The Qesh tumbled to the side and collapsed, dirty smoke pouring from the charred crater punched into his plastron.

I left Joy's weapon braced across her legs and went back to work on her wounds. Despite her falling blood pressure, I needed to further reduce her BP so that the nanobots in her side could finish their work. Short of letting her damn near bleed to death, there was only one way I could think of to do this quickly enough to make a difference. If I could just manage to switch off her heart . . .

Well, switch it *half* off, anyway.

The heart is an amazing organ. It keeps on beating completely independently of any and all nervous influences and hormone shifts with what cardiologists call intrinsic automaticity. Those heart-muscle cells with the fastest rate of electrical depolarization capture the depolarization rate of every other cell in the heart's muscular walls, causing all of them to contract, relax, and contract again in perfect synch. The pacemaker for the entire system is the sinoatrial node, or SA, located in the right atrium. It's this patch of cells that responds to signals from the autonomic nervous system or to certain drugs like adrenaline or halothane to change the rate of the beating heart.

I reached into my M-7 pack and pulled out a fresh vial of nano. I clipped it into the receiver on her left shoulder, snapped the panel shut, and fired it into her neck.

I keyed Program 5 into the N-prog, limiting the input to about half of the new nano. The rest I sent down to her liver to help out the 'bots still struggling to stem the bleeding.

Program 5 sent a few hundred thousand nanobots straight to Joy's sinoatrial node, following the currents of bioelectricity playing across her heart membranes.

There were other tricks I could have tried. You can slow a patient's heart drastically by stimulating the vagus nerve, which causes the heart rate to decrease, a condition called bradycardia. You can also suppress the signals coming from the sympathetic nervous system, which also induces bradycardia, or I could just wait for her blood volume to drop enough that it triggered her Bainbridge reflex, which drops the heart into bradycardia naturally.

Both of those would take too long, I feared, and both were harder to reverse. I needed to drastically slow her heartbeat only long enough for the nanobots in her liver to finish their work, then switch it back on again.

Program 5 switched off the sinoatrial node, which meant the heart muscle's pacemaking duties would be picked up by atrioventricular or AV node. The heart's ventricles will keep on beating with their own inherent and much slower rhythm. This rhythm, called nodal or junctional rhythm, usually comes in at a rate of around thirty to fifty beats per minute.

Almost at once, the numbers for her heart rate and blood pressure began plummeting. I had two main questions at that point: Was the drop in time, and was it going to be too much?

The fresh nano reaching her belly was reinforcing the original 'bots now. The framework of artificial blood vessel walls was reforming, knitting itself together, first as an open framework, then filling in the spaces between until they created a solid tube anchored deep within the natural vessel walls.

Heart rate 35 . . . deep in nodal rhythm. Blood pressure . . . shit, I wasn't getting any blood pressure. Zero over zero.

At this point, Joy's brain was being starved of blood; we had about three minutes before irreversible damage set in. Some of that might be corrected through surgery, including transplants of newly grown brain tissue, but when parts of the brain die off and are replaced, the new brain is different.

The person is *changed*, usually forever.

I looked up at Joy's face through her transparent visor, so I could see it, her eyes still closed, her skin a pasty, scary white.

I was thinking about Paula Barton, damn it.

You see, for the past year, ever since she'd suffered that stroke off the Mount Desert glacier, I'd been thinking of Paula as *dead*. It was easier that way. . . .

The truth was a lot tougher to deal with.

PAULA *HAD* BEEN DEAD WHEN THE MED-RESCUE LIFTER HAD HAULED her body up out of that sailboat and flew her back to Portland Medical. They'd hooked her to an artificial heart during the flight, but by that time she'd been dead for a good twelve to fifteen minutes. Life support, yeah, but no life to support.

But what that really meant was that the brain had started starving when her heart stopped. By the time blood flow had again been restored, large areas of her brain were dead, some from the direct effects of the stroke, some from the inevitable results of no heartbeat.

At Portland Medical, they'd used surgical nano to carve out huge, dead chunks of her brain, and they'd filled them in with new tissue grown from Paula's own stem cells. A few months of physical therapy and heavy reprogramming of her in-head hardware had gotten her walking and talking and thinking again. They'd brought Paula Barton back from the dead.

Only . . . she didn't remember me. She didn't remember the years we'd had together. She was perfectly healthy . . . and she was a different person.

I'd met with her once. She didn't want to have anything to do with me—a common-enough response when the doctors are telling you that this stranger beside your bed is the guy with whom you spent several years of your life.

Having a stroke can change a person's personality, change the way she feels about others, even rewrite memories.

And it's even worse when half of your brain has been regrown.

You can see why it was easier for me to think of her as dead.

THREE MEN CAME AROUND THE SIDE OF THE WRECKED CRANE, AND for just an instant I thought they were three Marines. Then I saw the clumsy leather armor, the bug-faced goggles and breather masks, and I knew they were Salvationists. My immediate question—were they from the faction that was with us, or the one that was with the Qesh?—was answered immediately when one of them raised his cable-bound laser to his shoulder and fired at me.

The pulse of coherent light was absorbed by my armor, and I rolled back into place behind Joy's plasma gun. They were almost on top of me, so close, I hardly even needed to aim; I squeezed the trigger and the blast of white-hot plasma burned through the leader's center of mass and kicked him back off his feet and squarely into the two behind him. I triggered the weapon twice more; all three Salvationists were down, portions of their leather on fire.

I could hear the comm chatter of the Marines over the combat channel as they tracked targets and brought them down.

"Over there. On the right. Two Impies!"

"Tracking . . . firing . . ."

"Good shot!"

"There's another. Twenty degrees west of the first!"

"Got him!"

"Bring that cannon around! Give him some cover!"

"Aye, aye, sir!"

"Range two-five-oh! On the way!"

Something slammed into the other side of the crane body, sending metal fragments hurtling into the sky, then raining back to the ground in plinks, clanks, and thumps.

I kept monitoring Joy. The restructuring of her hepatic portal vein was complete now, and the repair on her hepatic artery very nearly done as well. Fifty seconds had passed since her blood pressure had dropped to nothing. She probably had more than the three minutes of the deadline I'd given her; her heart *was* beating, and blood *was* flowing to her brain. But I didn't know how to calculate a safety margin for this procedure. Hell, I'd never done it before, not even in simulation. I'd read about it in one of my Hospital Corps download texts, but I'd never slowed anyone's heart before, not like this. There were so freaking many variables and danger points—the problems of too much pressure, of too little, of nanostruction in a high-volume flow, of shock, of exsanguination, of renal failure, of stroke, of cardiac arrest . . .

The list seemed to go on forever.

But the vessel repair was complete. It was time to bring her heart rate back up to speed.

If I could.

I reprogrammed the nanobots clustered over a particular spot on the wall of her right atrium, giving them the signal to fire a minute electrical charge into the tissue and trigger her SA node. I saw the feedback from the jolt, but nothing happened. I reset, then fired it again. And yet once again . . .

Her SA node responded, firing her heart muscles in unison, and then her heart was beating harder and faster as her SA node took over from her atrioventricular node, her heart rate swiftly rising from thirty-five to fifty . . . to seventy . . . to ninety . . .

I had a BP on her again!

Correction: I had her systole, the first number in a BP reading, but I wasn't picking up the second number, the diastole.

Systole is a measure of the highest pressure inside the arteries, at the moment the heart contracts and forces blood out into the body. Diastole is the lowest pressure, measured between the heart's contractions. I was getting a systole of thirty and a diastole of nil. Not good, not good by several hundred light years, but a hell of a lot better than a flatline zero over zero. At least I had something to work with now.

And the pressure was coming up. Heart rate at 103, BP 45 over 20. *Come on!*

I wasn't sure what to shoot for as an endpoint. Joy had lost a hell of a lot of blood, and I might not be able to get her pressure much above, say, 100 over 50. But if I could at least get it *stable*, that would be something.

While I was waiting, I engaged the CAPTR software in her armor, uploading the data to the Marine network, essentially giving it into the care of the platoon AI. If Joy died in the next hour or two, at least something might be recovered.

I also did something I should have done earlier—upload the data I'd pulled from the Salvation computer to the platoon net as well. That was to ensure its survival in case something happened to me, a distinct possibility with the firefight swirling closer and closer around me.

And then something slammed into my left side, knocking me away from the Marine. What the hell . . . ?

A Qesh warrior had emerged from the ruins fifty meters away, to my left and behind me. His plasma bolt had struck rock directly beside me, the shock slamming into my armor and kicking me to the side. I couldn't reach the plasma gun; my laser carbine was on the ground where I'd dropped it, just within reach. I scooped it up, twisted around, dragging the targeting cursor projected into my in-head display across the Qesh's body and triggered three quick rounds.

I hit him below the helmet and just above the upper arm, saw the bolts, with all of the explosive power of a firecracker's snap, absorbed. Damn!

The Qesh fired again; I managed to not be where the bolt was by rolling to my left, and when I brought the laser up again, I tried to target the enemy's optical sensor strip. Again and again, I mashed down the trigger button, slamming pulses of coherent light into that walking tank as fast as I could. I couldn't tell if I was hitting anything vital or not, and shifted my aim to the Jacker's weapon, hoping to buy myself some time by disarming him.

His helmet blossomed open, metal and ceramic torn and half melted. But a second Qesh was emerging from behind the crane's fallen cab, and my carbine was warning me that I'd drained its capacitors, that it would be a few seconds before the battery packs could recharge.

I tossed the carbine aside and scrambled back to Joy and the plasma gun resting across her thighs. An enemy shot grazed my left leg, a savage shock. I ignored it and grabbed the weapon, swinging it around and opening fire. The second Qesh ducked back behind the crane wreckage.

It looked like sheet metal, crumpled and propped up by a part of the crane's framework. I took a guess at where the Qesh might be hiding and put a bolt through the sheet. A half centimeter or so of corrugated iron offered about the same resistance to hot plasma as silk to a Marine nanoknife. The sheet sagged, glowing red-hot around the hole melting through the center, and the Jacker behind twisted and fell with the impact.

Joy's heart rate was at 120, her blood pressure 90 over 30. The hepatic vessel repairs seemed to be holding, and her heart was solidly back into its normal sinoatrial rhythm.

I took a close look at her spine, sending some of the remaining free nanobots into her back to outline the broken bones and tissues on my N-prog display. It was clear that the T-11 and T-12 vertebrae had been displaced far enough that her spinal cord was torn apart, and that alone was damage that I couldn't even think about addressing here. Maybe, back on board a ship with a decent surgical suite . . .

The most serious problem that I could do anything about was the possibility of doing more damage. I had to move her, and when I did, those bone fragments—especially those jagged lengths of broken rib—might puncture something else. It looked like another rib fragment was pressing up against her diaphragm; if it shifted, it might punch right through that thin sheet of muscle, and go on to puncture her right lung.

Programming the nano from my N-prog, I directed them to form ligatures—slender but tough threads insinuating themselves through damaged tissue, binding bone to bone, holding the fragments in place. I was tempted to try doing the same for the two severed sections of her backbone, but the damage was too severe. Instead, I popped open her suit controls and keyed in some coded instructions. The torso of her combat armor was damaged but still functional enough that the central torso section could tighten around her waist, then lock itself into rigid immobility.

Her combat armor would serve as a kind of rough-and-ready body cast, immobilizing her spine while I tried to move her.

Tried to move her. That was the operative phrase.

I was up against a major logistical problem now.

Joy massed 64 kilos; her armor massed 25. That was what they would weigh on Earth. Here, together, they weighed nearly 165 kilograms.

My normal weight on Earth comes in at around 90 kilos; here, and wearing full armor, I weighed almost 213 kilos.

I was faced with hauling a total of over 378 kilograms across 200 meters of open ground, much of it rugged, broken, and uphill.

I would have been hard-pressed to pull off that kind of feat back on Earth. Even on Mars our combined weights would have been only a little less than 80 kilos. Combat armor compensates somewhat, of course, and the exoskeleton bracing, legs, back, and arms would have let me get away with it.

But my exo-unit was useless, the right side removed to jack up the wreckage that had landed on me earlier, the left side shredded by a Qesh plasma bolt. There was no way in hell I could carry Joy out of there, not on my own legs. I needed a quantum flitter . . . or a spin-repulsor sled or stretcher. I had neither.

Briefly, I considered removing her exoskeletal unit—the legs, at least—and putting them on me, but that wasn't an option, not a good one. It would take time I didn't have, and those units are carefully balanced to provide a constant overall support, with feedback from the armor itself. That kind of gear wizardry was a job for a Marine armorer or a Navy roboticist, not for a simple Corpsman.

Even so, I had to try.

Simplest would have been just to drag her—preferably feetfirst, which would have put less pressure on her injured spine. The ground was rough enough, however, that I wouldn't be able to drag her far, and once I started trying to make it up the rough and stone-strewn gully, it would be hopeless.

Joy was on her back; I stretched her arms out to the sides, then lay down beside her, on my back, on top of her left arm. Grabbing her left hand in my left, I reached across her chest and grabbed her right wrist with my right hand, then rolled to the left, coming to my knees as I did so. Once I was on my knees, I held her wrists at my throat with my left hand, supporting myself on my right. Her weight was draped over my back, her legs hanging down limp over mine.

I started to crawl.

I wouldn't have been able to make it ten meters if it hadn't been for the armor. Even without the exoskeletal support, the armor on my legs adjusted to the stress and the pressure, and helped brace me—but each meter forward was a slow agony, the pain shrieking in my lower back and shoulders.

Each breath came as a gasp. My arm was trembling with the effort of supporting myself and the Marine on my back. I wasn't going to make it. . . . *I wasn't going to make it. . . .*

And then I glimpsed movement to one side, and froze. *God, freaking no!* I'd left both weapons beh nd—there was no way in hell I could have carried them *and* Joy—and if those Salvationist bastards were closing in on me now, it was pretty much up. I had a pistol and a knife.

"Let her down, e-Car," Colby's voice said. "We've got her!"

"You okay, Doc?" Hancock asked. "You look a little shot up."

Half a dozen Marines dropped into firing stances around me, facing outward, as Colby and Hancock took the weight from my back.

I dropped full-length on the ground for a moment, sobbing with relief.

Chapter Nineteen

WE GOT THE RECALL ORDER LESS THAN AN HOUR LATER.

We were on top of the ridge overlooking the Salvation-ist spaceport, waiting out the heaviest, most savage seis-mic quake yet. The ground trembled and bucked, sending numerous landslides clattering down the slope, and sev-eral of the wrecked buildings below collapsed. The enemy troops—both the Qesh and the Salvationists—seemed to have abandoned the chase. We weren't sure yet whether that was because of the ongoing seismic quake, or because they simply weren't that interested in us.

They seemed to think we were rebels, rather than a Marine recon force, a mistake very much in our favor.

Lance Corporal Andrews had just pointed out something unusual against the glowing, ruby face of Bloodstar. From the top of the ridge, we could see about three quarters of the slow-rising sun, hanging against the horizon. Among the chains of black starspots, the ragged patchwork of stellar storms that covered a good ten percent of the star's visible surface, was a single, perfectly round, black disk. At first, some of us had been wondering if it was a large Qesh space-craft approaching out of the sunrise, but as minute followed minute, it didn't move.

What the hell *was* that?

Calli Lewis finally hit upon the explanation.

"It's a planet!" she cried. "It's a planetary transit!"

Damn. *I* should have spotted that. I was still pretty shaken by my near escape down at the starport, though, and wasn't thinking clearly yet. I knew at once that she was right, however, as soon as she pointed it out.

"Muspelheim," I said. "It's Planet III, the next planet in from Bloodworld."

Gliese 581 III—formally Gliese 581 c—orbited its star at a distance of .073 AUs, almost exactly half of the distance of Bloodworld from its star. At its closest, Muspelheim passed within 11 million kilometers of Bloodworld. That's almost thirty times the distance between the Earth and the moon, but with six times the mass of Earth, Muspelheim could still give Bloodworld a serious nudge when it passed the outer world, about once every twenty days or so. Even at 11 million kilometers, the giant inner planet was large enough to appear as a visible disk as it slid across the face of Gliese 581.

The seismic thunders rolled on and on, as the orange glare of distant volcanoes lit the western horizon, off toward the nightside. The recall order came in from the *Clymer*, but it had taken a while to reach us.

The only way to be certain that the enemy wasn't picking up our communications was to use lasers. The *Clymer* and her escorts were waiting out the mission in orbit around Gliese 581 V—Nidavellir—currently 22 million kilometers outside of Bloodworld's orbit, and about 30 million kilometers ahead of Bloodworld's current orbital position—a straight-line distance of some 37 million kilometers. If they knew our precise location, they could send a modulated laser beam to us in a direct line-of-sight transmission.

The problem with this was that they couldn't know the platoon's *exact* location unless we sent up a transmission of our own. Worse, when we were as close to the enemy as we were now, well . . . laser beams tend to spread out a little with distance. At a range of 37 million kilometers, it was more than likely that the Qesh in and around Salvation would pick up at least the fringes of that incoming beam, and know that someone was carrying out high-tech interplanetary telecommunications in the area. Coherent light is not normally a natural phenomenon; it's kind of a dead giveaway that there's some high technology operating close by.

That was one reason we'd established Red Tower as a secure advance base some distance from our objective. From Nidavellir, the *Clymer* could pinpoint the location of Red Tower and send a laser-com beam there with little chance of interception. The *Clymer* could also communicate with the Misty-Ds, which were submerged offshore at three different sites along the Twilight Coast. On a regular timetable, the landing ships were supposed to extend an antenna mast above the surface, listening for messages from the *Clymer.*

Of course, that still left the problem of getting the message out to the Marine recon forces in the field. Quantumburst transmission were fairly safe—at least we'd seen no evidence yet that the Qesh could detect the ultra-fast pulses of channel-shifting data—but Red Tower was below the horizon for us, meaning the transmissions had to bounce off the local ionosphere to reach us. That was okay much of the time, but the charged particles streaming in from the nearby star could play havoc with the Heaviside layer. Especially during daylight hours over the Twilight Zone, the stellar wind pressed the Heaviside layer close to the planet's surface, rendering over-the-horizon signal reflections difficult or impossible.

It was a lot more certain sending a robotic messenger.

Once again, we employed the spidery-looking RV-90 robots, the same devices we'd used to track Matthew and his friends back to Salvation's back door. Stilting along at a steady ten to twelve kilometers per hour, never needing rest and recharging from their environment as they moved, they could cover the thirty kilometers between Red Tower and Salvation in a little under three hours.

The robot had arrived while we were inside the starport building, bringing word from Colonel Corcoran.

**Download
Mission Recall Order
Operation Blood Salvation/
OPPLAN#5735/28NOV2245**

[extract]

   . . . All platoons will break off immediately from current operations and fall back to the advance bases at Red Tower and Red Sky. MST/D retrievals will take place at advance bases Red Tower and Red Sky, initiating redeployment to *Clymer* and rendezvous prepatatory for return to Earth. . . .

There was more. Evidently, First Platoon had run afoul of Qesh and local human forces at Martyrdom, in the north, and were fighting to break free. Third Platoon, in reserve, had already deployed to help them.

So much for avoiding contact with the enemy.

We didn't yet know, however, if the Qesh had twigged to the fact that warships from Earth were in-system. They might still think we were "rebels" and planet-bound, though we couldn't count on that fiction holding for very much longer. The fact that the Salvationist government, at the very least, was collaborating with the Qesh vastly complicated things, and made it certain that sooner or later the Qesh and the Council of Elders would compare notes . . . that, or the Qesh would learn the truth from rebel prisoners.

I assumed that Colonel Corcoran had issued the recall because the Qesh fleet might know human ships were in-system now, and might even be searching for them. He would want to pull the Marine Recon forces off-world as quickly as possible, and then get the hell out of Dodge. Or perhaps it was simply that Baumgartner had flashed the word back to the fleet that it was mission complete, that we'd penetrated the Salvation computer files and deleted any and all navigational data pertaining to Sol.

I didn't know and didn't much care. The most important

thing for me was knowing that we might have a chance of getting both Kilgore and Leighton back to the *Clymer*'s surgery suite.

And the platoon had been running for a good forty hours now on G-boost. In another ten or twenty hours, we would crash—and we did *not* want to be anywhere within reach of the Qesh when that happened. I was glad when Hancock passed the order down.

We did take some time to pull Kilgore's exoskeleton out of a storage locker and adjust it to my armor. By that time, I could barely walk in Bloodworld's gravity; doing so was begging for a serious knee or ankle injury, and I would never be able to keep up with the others if we had to go any distance at all on foot.

That last, long seismic disturbance gradually faded away at last, and we started our trek back to Red Tower.

Our Misty-D was waiting for us on the beach when we got there.

KILGORE DIED ON THE WAY UP TO THE *CLYMER*.

There wasn't anything I could do to stop it. He'd been slipping away the entire time, going deeper into shock, and hemostatin foam could only do so much. Once on board the Misty, I tried giving him both BVEs and perfluorocarbon-based artificial blood from the ship's med locker, and I started trying to use medical nano to seal off more of the mesentery leakers, but the damage simply was too extensive, too deep, too serious.

Maybe if I'd been able to get him medevaced sooner . . .

Well, we had his CAPTR data, for whatever *that* was worth.

Joy Leighton was in medical stasis—a deep, nano-induced coma—and appeared stable, however. So was Hugh Masserotti, though his condition never came close to being as critical as the other two.

I was thinking a lot about the ethical problems of modern medical technology. It was the *Book of Salvation* that got me looking at that.

The *Book of Salvation* was one of the religious works that defined the Neoessene Temple movement. It had been written by the group's founder, Yehoshua Michelson, in the 2120s—though, like Joseph Smith's *Book of Mormon* three centuries earlier, it was now accepted as divinely inspired scripture, at least among believers. A copy was on file in the Salvation computer records, and I snuck a look at it after we reached the *Clymer*.

Gods. How can people believe such crap?

When Michelson wrote the thing in its really bad imitation of King James English, replete with all of those "thees" and "thous" and "verilies," claiming the thing to be a translation of a lost Greek text, the New Ice Age had been under way for just about a century, and glaciers were starting to form in Maine, Canada, Scandinavia, and elsewhere.

I say "New Ice Age," of course, because that's what the newsfeeds all call it. In fact, the climate change was pretty much localized to eastern Canada, New England, and northwestern Europe, because of the failure of the North Atlantic Conveyor. At the time, there'd been a lot of talk about the imminent extinction of the human race. At the same time, however, there was a countercurrent to the discussion, which held that technology was going to see us through. The Cayambe Space Elevator had been up and running for a couple of decades by then, and numerous plans to push back the ice— by covering it with black powder, by beaming microwaves at it from space, by turning specialized nanodisassemblers loose on it, by pumping massive amounts of carbon dioxide into the atmosphere—were being enthusiastically discussed and massively underfunded. There were also calls for the wholesale abandonment of Earth. The Plottel-Alcubierre Drive had been demonstrated in the first decade of the twenty-second century, and the Chiron colony had been established soon after. If Earth became uninhabitable, why not just migrate to other worlds?

But by 2100, there'd been a savage backlash against technology, at least within some religious sects and political minorities. Neo-Luddite philosophies were popping up everywhere, especially as reactions against nanotechnology and genetic engineering. Michelson had been neck-deep in the Luddie movement; he'd been imprisoned for a time for his role in the attempted bombing of Cayambe.

According to him, Humankind was doomed.

The *Book of Salvation* had predicted the end of human civilization in ice, you see, and it was all our own fault. Neoessenes pointed to 2018 and the collapse of the North Atlantic Conveyor—a current bringing warm water into the North Atlantic—as the human-caused beginning of it all. Believe it or not, 250 years ago, most people were convinced that we were entering a period of what was called global warming, and that the warming trend had been caused by human industrial activity dumping high levels of CO_2 into the atmosphere. By warming the planet enough to melt the Arctic ice sheet, they claimed, humans had catastrophically tipped the balance. Cold, fresh water from the melting ice had derailed the Conveyor current, causing mean temperatures in North America and Europe to plummet. That, coupled with a new cycle of low solar activity—a new Maunder Minimum—had resulted in the Century Without a Summer, and the inexorable growth of the ice sheets.

Humankind, then, was doomed, at least according to the Neoessenes. Our attempts to control our environment, to rebuild ourselves, to conquer even death itself all had merely hastened God's final judgment.

Of course, the Neoessenes themselves were special.

The original Essenes were a Jewish sect dedicated to daily baptisms and communal living in ancient Israel. The Neoessenes had started off as a fundamentalist Christian cult, and were still at least nominally Christian, believing that God had called them out from the "Breakers of the Covenant," the fallen, apostate Church. According to Neoessenist doctrine, it was they, the elect of God, who had the *privilege* to suffer the fires of hell in order to redeem the rest of a doomed humanity.

That, it seemed, was why the Elders Bryce and Pierson had chartered the *Outward Venture*, packed a few thousand Neoessenes on board, and headed for the planetary system circling Gliese 581. The Commonwealth Colonization Bureau had made it relatively easy and inexpensive for distinct social groups to plant colonies on other worlds, in the name of social and cultural diversity. But so far as the Neoessene colonists were concerned, they were embarking for a literal hell—a marginally habitable world right out of the pages of Christian mythology, a place where their sufferings somehow could save a portion of the human population left behind on Earth.

The joke, of course, was that they'd just wanted to go somewhere where it was *warm*.

Pretty much the whole idea was laid out in another of the documents I pulled from the Salvation files—something called the Covenant with Hell. By voluntarily living in hell, the sinless believers of the Temple could redeem an apostate Christian Church. It sounded screwy to me, but no worse, I suppose, than some of the stuff in the traditional Bible about blood sacrifice and redemption. Why anyone would volunteer to live in hell to save others was beyond me, though, in fact, Bloodworld wasn't *that* bad. You couldn't breathe the air, the storms were horrific, the volcanoes and seismic quakes were nearly constant, the gravity dragged at you like the weight of a large child constantly riding on your shoulders, and the sulfuric acid in the atmosphere gnawed at everything constantly, but you *could* live there with only minor technological help. From the little we'd seen from our robot camera, people inside the cities had a pretty good life; it was only when they ventured outside that they needed technological help.

And that, I gathered, was important. The Neoessenes hadn't been able to discard *all* technology, but they were doing their best to banish what they could.

The *Book of Salvation* had a lot to say about nanotech and genetic engineering, especially when they trespassed on what it meant to be human, the "image of God," as the Salvationists liked to say. Reading the passages about "medical abominations" brought me a little closer to understanding why the Bloodworlders were so fanatically opposed to nanomedicine. Tinkering with God's original design, clearly, was arrogance in the highest degree—and that included everything from artificial blood to nananodyne pain relief to synthetic bone replacement. Same for CAPTR technology, of course, but it also extended even to nanotechnically chelated brain enhancements and implants. The Neoessenes wanted to draw a sharp, absolute dividing line between Mark I Mod. 0 organic humans and machines.

The trouble is, the line between humans and machines is already fuzzy, and it's getting fuzzier every day. If you reject Freitas respirocytes, do you also reject old-fashioned blood transfusions as well? If you refuse to accept an injection of nananodyne 'bots, do you also refuse aspirin or other drugs? Do no cranial implants also mean no cochlear implants to correct deafness? How about eyeglasses instead of retinal transplants? *Where do you draw the line?*

Theoretically, the Salvationists accepted technology in other, non-medical areas. They used nanotech to grow their breather masks, and to treat their leather survival suits and boots. Their cities had been grown with nanoconstructors brought from Earth. The trouble is, once you accept one technological aid to life, it's damned hard to reject others as they come along. And once you ban one type of technology, you tend to become suspicious of *all* technology, rejecting more and more until you no longer use electricity, Net access, or e-cars. The Salvationists appeared to be in an awkward trap between high tech and low, needing the high tech to survive on Bloodworld, while desperately clinging to what they thought made them human.

Things had really gotten strange when the Qesh showed up.

The records I'd pulled off the computer net confirmed that there were two factions now—the Acquiescenists and the Militants. Acquiescenists believed that the Qesh were literal demons newly arrived to take over this particular corner of hell. As demons, they belonged here—they were part of the package. The Acquiescenist Council of Elders had surrendered moments after the Jackers had opened fire on the spaceport two weeks before, creating the Covenant with Hell to explain and justify the decision. If the demons belonged here, the Salvationists had to deal with them—ideally, in such a way that the Qesh didn't obliterate them.

The Militants, on the other hand, felt that demons were still demons, and it was the Neoessenes' duty to fight Satan's kingdom in every way that they could.

Both groups appeared to believe in divine beings called "the warrior angels of the Rapture," angelic creatures who would arrive to rescue the Salvationists and destroy hell at the very end of all things. "The Rapture" was an old idea, apparently first expressed by Puritan preachers in the seventeenth century, an interpretation of several verses in the New Testament suggesting that Christian believers would be caught up into the air before a final, terrible judgment on Earth. Since the Salvationists—this group, at any rate—was no longer on Earth, the doctrine had changed somewhat, applying now to the faithful who'd entered the tribulation of hell. According to some rather fuzzy prophecies from the Book of Salvation, warrior angels would arrive in the nick of time to save the faithful and transform hell into paradise.

The documents I saw didn't mention how the Acquiescenists expected to obey God by negotiating their survival with invading demons, and they didn't mention how the Militants expected to survive if the Qesh decided to drop relativistic projectiles on the human cities.

Nor was there any clue as to what the Qesh thought about all of this.

I turned all of the information over to the company's S2. Let the spooks figure out what it all meant. I was just happy that we'd made it off of that miserable hellworld, and were on our way back to Earth.

TWO DAYS LATER, WE WERE ACCELERATING OUT-SYSTEM, HEADING IN
a direction well off from the actual direction of Earth, in
Taurus. If the Qesh were tracking us, we didn't want to draw
a line for them pointed straight back to Sol.

The Qesh certainly knew we were there, but they
were . . . busy. While we'd been playing our sneak-and-peek
games outside of the city of Salvation, the Commonwealth
3rd Interstellar Fleet had arrived in the Gliese 581 system,
and was now engaging Qesh naval forces. The battle was
still going on four days later, though the combatants now
were spread out across a vast volume of space. When we
linked into the *Clymer*'s external cameras, though, we
could still see occasional silent, brilliant flares of light as
nuclear weapons detonated, or as relativistic projectiles
packing the same destructive energy as a nuke slammed
home.

I was in the squad bay with a couple of dozen Marines
and Corpsmen, watching the show, a little awed to realize
that with each flash, men, women, and Qesh were dying out
there. The larger ships had shields strong enough to absorb
or deflect the energy of a megaton nuke or a mass driver projectile moving at near-*c*, but the smaller vessels could only
rely on their speed and maneuverability to avoid being hit.
My God, *thousands* must be dying out there.

I wondered who was winning.

"So why," I wondered out loud after a time, "did the government decide to send in a fleet? I thought they were trying
to avoid a confrontation."

"They were," Chief Garner said. "But I think it's just hit
home how close the Impies have gotten."

"That's right," Hancock said. "Take a look at the history
of our engagements with the Qesh."

I'd downloaded that file during the trip out from Earth.
There'd been that first disastrous encounter with them at
Gamma Ophiuchi. After Gamma Oph, there'd been four
more encounters with the Qesh before they'd turned up on
our front porch, so to speak, at Gliese 581. I'd used *Clymer*'s

navigation AI to plot the positions of all those stars, and the distances between them.

Gamma Ophiuchi was eighty-four light years from Earth. Our next encounter with them was at Psi Serpentis, and that's the one everyone remembers, of course. An Earthlike world around a Sol-like star seventy-one light years away. Cernunnos, a joint European-American colony at Psi Serp III had been established there in 2198, and just seven years later, the place got smacked by a near-c planet killer. Fifteen thousand people incinerated in an instant, and a world—so much like Earth, it ached—was transformed into lava fields and glaciers.

That's when we began to realize just what it was we were up against.

The next encounter came in 2220, when the Commonwealth's 5th Fleet bumped into Qesh raiders at Eta Ophiuchi, sixty-three light years from Earth. Twelve of our ships were vaporized before the rest could disengage. We ran into them again two years later at another sunlike star, HD 147513, when they destroyed the research colony on Athirat, sixty light years from Sol. Once again, a relativistic projectile whipped in at near-c and took out damned near half the planet. Seven years later they showed up at Gamma Serpentis, where a Commonwealth deep-space recon base managed to get off a message drone an instant before it was annihilated.

That last brought them to within just 47 light years of Earth, and the Commonwealth military was becoming deeply concerned. The guess was that all of those incidents involved the same Qesh warfleet, and that over the past fifty-nine years they'd been getting closer and closer to Earth.

Notice the star groupings in which those stars appear as seen from Earth: the constellations of Ophiuchus and Serpens, along with HD 147513 in Scorpius, and Gliese 581 in Libra . . . all four constellations are tucked in right next to one another in Earth's summer-night sky.

I ran a plot on those six stars in order, and calculated the

jumps from system to system. Gamma Ophiuchi to Psi Serpentis: 45 light years. Psi Serp to Eta Oph: 33 light years. Eta
Ophiuchi to Athirat: 29 light years. Athirat to Gamma Serpentis: 49 light years. Gamma Serp to Gliese 581: 29 light
years. The bastards were zigzagging back and forth across
the sky, but every jump brought them a little closer to Sol.

The pattern raised two big questions. First: what was
taking them so long between jumps? It took them nineteen
years to get from Gamma Ophiuchi to Psi Serpentis, and
fifteen to get from there to Eta Ophiuchi. What were they
doing in all those years? Admiring their handiwork, maybe?

It only took them two years to cross almost thirty light
years to Athirat, but then seven years for the forty-nine
lights to Gamma Serpentis.

And that had been sixteen years ago. Had it really taken
them that long to make the twenty-nine light-year passage
from Gamma Serp to Gliese 581?

Surely, the Commonwealth, which could cover the
twenty light years from Sol to Gliese 581 in six days, didn't
have better starship technology than the Imperial Qesh. Our
fastest warships could manage to peg something like four or
five light years a day, and transports like the *Clymer* and the
Puller were only a bit slower. At that rate, the Qesh could
have jumped from Gamma Ophiuchi to Sol in sixteen days.
It didn't make sense.

The second question was even more urgent, but required
some serious guesswork on our part. Those zigzags through
three-dimensional space looked for all the world like a
search pattern, Ophiuchi to Serpentis to Ophiuchi to Scor-
pio to Serpentis to Libra.

If so, what were they searching for?

Us, perhaps?

A FEW DAYS LATER, WE DROPPED BACK INTO THE SOL SYSTEM, AND I
was surprised at how good it was to see that familiar, brilliant, and above all *yellow* sun gleaming against the endless
black of space.

The scattering of sunspots across the solar disk was reassuring. For four centuries, now, Earth's daystar had been in an extended solar minimum, like the Spörer and Maunder Minima that had ushered in the Little Ice Age of the Renaissance. For the past century or so, sunspot activity had been on the increase once more, raising hopes that the grip of the New Ice Age might be about to be broken at last.

It was still an open question as to whether Humankind's technological efforts were accelerating the warming, and I wondered about the Salvationist disdain for high tech. Humans are characterized by two apparently opposing characteristics. We are supremely adaptable; witness the Salvationists turning life on Bloodworld, even life under the invading Qesh, into a moral imperative, a duty for their God. And at the same time, we are supremely technic, remaking our environment to suit our needs, even our whims. We don't like the shifting climate on Earth? *Change* it. . . .

It was a matter of making the best of things versus making things better, a choice that shadowed so much of modern medicine. Where should the line be drawn between saving life and saving *dignity*—preserving the essence of what it means to be human?

I didn't know. I didn't even know where to begin.

But apparently I'd made some fair guesses on the op we'd just completed, because Colonel Corcoran called me into his office a day before we arrived at Geosynch Starport.

It seemed they wanted to give me a medal.

Chapter Twenty

Ward Citation: HM3 Elliot Carlyle (FMF)
Operation Blood Salvation/
OPPLAN#5735/28NOV2245

For extraordinary heroism on 2 through 3 December, 2245, in performance of his duties as a Medical Corpsman, Bravo Company, First Reconnaissance Regiment, First Marine Division, Fleet Marine Force, Petty Officer Third Class Elliot Carlyle is hereby awarded the Silver Star.

During a reconnaissance in force of the target area on Bloodworld, Gliese 581 IV, Petty Officer Carlyle was instrumental in rescuing a number of human colonists captured by Imperial Qesh troopers and arranging for their evacuation from the combat area. During the firefight, one Marine was seriously wounded, and Carlyle managed to render first aid despite heavy fire from the enemy. When a second Marine was wounded, Carlyle directed another Marine to render aid to the new casualty while continuing to give aid to the first patient. He managed to stabilize both casualties, and proceeded to evacuate them from the fire zone. During the evacua-

BLOODSTAR 275

tion, he additionally rendered aid to the injured pilot of an enemy combat flier, uncovering as he did so information about Qesh biology previously unknown to Commonwealth Intelligence.

Later in the operation, Petty Officer Carlyle participated in the infiltration of a human colony facility, extracting important intelligence from a hostile computer network. During the extraction at the conclusion of this raid, a third Marine was seriously wounded. Petty Officer Carlyle again rendered first aid, stabilizing the wounded Marine's condition. Despite being wounded himself, when hostile forces, both Qesh and human, attempted to overrun his position, he held them off with accurate fire, killing several of the enemy and saving the life of his patient.

Petty Officer Carlyle's actions were in the highest tradition both of the Navy Hospital Corps and of the Fleet Marine Force.

That was what the official citation download said, anyway. Not a word about how half the time I'd been scared witless—and how the rest of the time I'd been furious at the locals for their technophobic nonsense.

And there was not a word in that citation about me getting stuck out there, unable to drag Joy to safety, or about our having to get our asses freaking rescued by a detachment of Marines.

Medals, I'd long ago become convinced, were nice as an official acknowledgment by the brass that you'd done what you were supposed to do without screwing up *too* badly, or that you'd been lucky—but their importance didn't come close to the acceptance of your brothers and sisters, the people you actually worked with day to day.

Four weeks had passed since our return from Gliese 581. The Solstice Festival had come and gone, as had the changing of the year. They gave me the medal at the Geosynch Military Assembly Hall, located within the Synchorbital

Wheel, which was turning at twice per minute to provide spin gravity. The assembly hall could physically seat a thousand people. According to the records, something like five times that number were linked in virtually, through electronic implants, and that didn't include coverage by the various news media. There were some civilian VIPs there—a congresswoman from Virginia and the director of the FMF. The medal was given to me by Captain Victor Schmidt, commanding officer of the Fleet Marine Force Training Center—FMFTC Camp Lejeune. That was the *real* thrill of the full-dress ritual at Synchorbit that morning.

You see, besides giving me the medal and confirming my immediate promotion to Hospitalman Second Class, they also graduated me from the Fleet Marine Force training program.

I was no longer under probation. I could now include those three cherished letters—*FMF*—in parentheses after my name, rank, and rate.

And . . . okay. So I hadn't come back with that next big bit of xenotechnology that was going to put General Nanodynamics on the map. Right then, I didn't care about *that* at all. . . .

An entire bulkhead in the Geosynch Military Assembly Hall was set to show Earth, gleaming a dazzling white with ice sheets and continent-spanning loops and whorls of cloud. It was winter in the northern hemisphere—or nearly so . . . not that those regions north of Chicago had much in the way of any other season. The image was slowly rotating as the Wheel turned, a quietly hypnotic effect. Four Marines got medals as well—two Bronze Stars, another Silver, and the Navy Cross to Staff Sergeant Carolyn Hayes, for holding off a Qesh charge at Martyrdom long enough for the rest of her unit to withdraw. *Her* medal was awarded posthumously, and her image was thrown up on the big display screen while Captain Schmidt read off the citation.

And when the ceremony was over, Gunny Hancock was there to say "Congratulations, Doc," and shake my hand.

Doc. To the Marines, all Corpsmen are "Doc," but this time there was something special in the way Gunny Hancock said it. I'm not sure what the difference was . . . except, possibly, that now I *knew* I belonged, a proven part of the team. It felt damned good.

Masserotti was right behind him, his shoulder as good as new. He used his newly grown right arm to shake my hand. "Good job, Doc!"

My face fell just a bit when I saw who was with him.

David Kilgore.

"I know, Doc," Kilgore said, shaking my hand as well. "It's weird for me, too. All I can say is . . . yeah, it's really *me* in here."

"Of *course* it is," I managed to say through a plastic grin.

But I didn't believe it, not for a moment. They'd repaired Kilgore's shattered body at GNMC, Geosynch Naval Medical Center, including growing a new brain and installing a whole new CDF suite, and then they'd installed the CAPTR data I'd recorded on Bloodworld. It was just like downloading and running new software on a refurbished computer.

Was it really Kilgore? I decided I didn't even want to think about it.

Had the newly revived Paula Barton been the same person as the Paula I'd loved? *Still* loved?

Well, the critical difference was that Paula's brain had deteriorated pretty far before they'd pulled a CAPTR on her in Portland. Kilgore's brain had still been alive when I'd copied it. But where do you draw the fucking line?

I noticed that Kilgore was wearing civvies, rather than class-A full dress. There was a reason for that. Marines who'd been CAPTR-revived were never returned to their original units. Instead, they were integrated into other units, usually into a completely different division, one where no one knew them. It had to be that way. Marines could be superstitious, especially about death. And they had a word for CAPTR-revived Marines.

Zombies.

It was completely unfair, of course. The Kilgore standing there in front of me was as human and as alive as I was—and so far as his memories were concerned, he was the same Marine who'd been burned down by a Qesh particle beam beside the mining pit on Bloodworld, the same Marine whose life I'd tried to save. Tried and failed.

"They assign you to a new duty station yet?" I asked him, trying to keep my voice light.

"Not yet," he admitted, shrugging. "I'm still in limbo."

It was some time later that I realized that it had been a joke: "limbo"—for most Catholics a kind of in-between holding area after death, neither heaven nor hell.

I wished him well, and wandered off in search of the buffet table. Doobie was there. "What we're gonna do, my man," he said with a shit-eating grin, "is go celebrate by getting ourselves drunk!"

"None of your damned hooch," I told him. "I kind of want to keep my eyesight!"

"Hey, I *told* you, I only nanufacture the very best pure C_2H_5OH, right?"

"So you say. But I've heard your stuff is on the list of internationally banned weapons of mass destruction, right up there along with nerve agents, planet busters, and nano-D anti-organics."

"Lies! Lies and slander! But actually, I had something a little different in mind . . . something along the lines of the Free Fall."

My eyebrows went up. "I dunno, Doob. That's pretty rich for my blood."

The Free Fall Lounge was definitely a half dozen points higher on the classy-meter than the Earthview . . . an exotic play-lounge more for Geosynch's rich civilian tourists up from Earth than for the likes of us. It costs ten e-creds just to walk in the main access hatch, fifteen for a cheap drink, and some of the meals on the menu would cost a third class most of a week's pay. If you've got a hot date along, though, there's *nothing* like the hydrosphere.

At least, that's what I'd heard. I'd never been to the place, and never expected to go.

"Aw, c'mon, e-Car! You deserve it! We all do! I'll round up some of the other guys, and we'll have a real hyperbolic blowout to celebrate."

"Okay," I said. "But you'll have to treat me with more respect, Doob. I outrank you now."

In fact, Doobie had passed his test for HM2 and was on the promotions list, but it wouldn't take effect until next February. They'd made my promotion effective as of that day, as a part of the medal ceremony. I had that long to lord it over Doob before his promotion took effect.

"*Sir*, yes, *sir*!" Doob replied, and I realized I also had that long to endure his sarcasm. "Treat the newbie petty officer second class with all due courtesy and respect, *sir*!"

"Right," I said. "So . . . we've got three months of this nonsense to go through, huh?"

THE FREE FALL WASN'T A PART OF THE WHEEL, WHICH USED THE Space Elevator as its rotational axis, but was part of an independent orbital facility—the Hilton Synchorbital. You got there by boarding a fling pod on the rim of the main wheel, which cut you loose with a tangential velocity of just less than 47 meters per second at *precisely* the right instant so that you drifted into the embrace of a rotating catcher at your destination twenty minutes later in free orbit, 940 meters distant. The receiving catcher snagged the fling pod in a magnetic field, brought it to rest, then maneuvered it into the Hilton's receiving lock, which provided transport cars up to the zero-gravity lobby.

You entered the Free Fall through the hotel lobby, moving hand over hand out into the sphere at one pole of its axis. The Free Fall was an immense globe, fifty meters across and rotating once every fifteen seconds to provide a respectable four tenths of a G around its equator—a shade more than the surface gravity of Mars. The sphere's poles, of course, remained in zero-G, but your weight slowly climbed as you rode one of the inclines down the inside curve toward the equator. The equatorial region, from about latitude 30° north to 30° south on the sphere's inside surface, was where the chairs and tables were, with one part closed off to hide the kitchen and other support facilities. There was a nicely appointed bar as well, and a lot of soft lighting and lush tropical vegetation that gave it the look of a magical jungle, a green maze within which groups of tables were nestled, with flowing streams and small ponds and waterfalls. Genengineered koi swam in the larger ponds, their scales shimmering with constantly changing iridescence. At the higher latitudes, large viewall panels looked out into space and the spinning moon, sun, stars, and Earth, and you could look "up" across the sphere's interior to the other side, to see diners calmly enjoying their drinks or diners upside down relative to you.

But the big attraction, of course, was the hydrosphere.

The hub of the Free Fall sphere is in zero-gravity—well, *microgravity* is the correct term, but everything at Geosynch is in free fall around the Earth, completing one orbit in twenty-four hours. Farther down the space elevator, you actually feel weight, because you're moving slower than is necessary to stay in orbit. If you were to step out of an airlock you would take a *very* long fall straight down to the Earth. Above Synchorbit, on the other hand, the centripetal force of the elevator is trying to throw everything out into space, since the upper half of the structure is traveling *faster* than it needs to move in order to stay in orbit, and is, therefore, whipping around the Earth like a ball on the end of a whirling string. The ball, in this case, is a small asteroid anchored 35,000 kilometers farther out, providing the dynamic tension that locks the elevator system in place and keeps it stretched out taut. Geosynch, orbiting at exactly 35,786 kilometers above Mount Cayambe, in Ecuador, is at the halfway point, balanced between falling down and falling up, and so remains at zero-G.

Which is what made the Free Fall's hydrosphere possible. It was about ten meters across, a bubble of water floating at the exact center of the larger sphere which rotated around it four times a minute. The water, warmed to 40°C, was kept hot, fresh and circulating by inflow and outflow piping coming into it along the larger sphere's axis. Internal lighting gave it a shifting, constantly changing illumination— pink mingled with an emerald green. Waves and ripples constantly spread across its surface, adding to the exotic and ever-changing lighting patterns across the larger sphere's inner surfaces.

And people were swimming in it. Swimming, and . . . other things.

THERE WERE EIGHT OF US IN THE LIBERTY PARTY—ME, DOOBIE, AND Machine McKean; Carla Harper and HM3 George Gomez, both from *Clymer*'s medlab; HM2 Kari Harris and HM3 Tomas Esteban, from *Clymer*'s medical cryo unit; and HN Ken Klinginsmith, from Medical Imaging. Doob said he'd also invited Chief Garner, but the company's senior Corpsman had pled more pressing duties.

That was just as well; even within the Hospital Corps, which tends not to be as formally rank conscious as the rest of the Navy, chief petty officers are both a law and a social order unto themselves. A chief, not to put too fine a point on it, is *God*—exactly the same as a gunnery sergeant in the Marines. We would all be a little freer, a little more comfortable, if Garner wasn't there with us.

But we did have the three rifle-company Corpsmen, plus the lab, cryo, and MI techs. It promised to be a hell of a party.

We all wore civvies—conservatively dark, two-toned skinsuits for the gents, and formal glittersprays for the ladies. Carla was wearing blue light as well, for a formal-gown effect, but Kari had left her breasts bare, which allowed for some *very* nice things to happen to her anatomy while we were moving in zero-G.

A human hostess met us at the incline and led us to a table. Like the Earthview, this place had a *human* waitstaff, part of what made it so pricey. I honestly couldn't tell if she was wearing a high-tech skinsuit, a light coating of programmed nano, or animated tattoos, but her skin color kept rippling and shifting through shades and dappled patterns of sunlight and green, in keeping with the rain-forest theme of the place.

A waiter in similar camouflage took our orders. "What will you ladies and gentlemen have?" he asked. The rotation of the Free Fall meant that sunlight spilled through each set of viewwalls in turn, creating an ever-shifting patchwork of light and shadow, and his skin appeared to be responding to the changing light.

Remembering how good that drink at the Earthview had been, I ordered a hyperbolic trajectory.

"So," Klinginsmith said, "you all hear the latest scuttlebutt?"

"About what?" Doob asked. Rumors were always flying on board ship, and even more so at bases like the Geosynch Starport, where you had a *lot* more input of gossip, rumor, and wild speculation.

"The Commonwealth is going to take down the Qesh at Bloodworld!"

"Says who?" I asked. I was skeptical. The Jackers had been in that system in major force, *big-time*. It was going to take a major invasion fleet to knock them loose from the place.

"Just a girl I know up in Ops," Kling said with an affected nonchalance. "She's on the TT."

"The Tactical Team?" Esteban asked, and then he shrugged. "Fuck, those guys are always running sims on possible operations. Just in case, y'know? Doesn't mean shit."

"That's right," Harris said. She giggled. "They probably run sims for a Navy-Marine invasion of *Earth* every morning, just for practice!"

"Why wouldn't we send an invasion force to the Gliese 581?" Harper asked. "I mean . . . those are *people* on Bloodworld. Humans! And the Qesh are doing *horrible* things to them!"

"I'm not so sure about that, Carla," I said. "The Salvation government was working with the Qesh. It was the militant rebels who we saw being tortured."

"But they *were* being tortured," Harper insisted. "The Commonwealth *has* to go in and save them!"

"Actually, no," Doob said. "Unless there's some sort of treaty or agreement in place, we can't go in unless we're specifically invited."

"That's right," Harris said. "We might *call* Bloodworld a colony, but it's not, really—not in a political sense. It doesn't belong to the Commonwealth, and we don't have a say in how they choose to govern themselves."

"The only reason we went out there at all," Gomez added, "is because Earthport was afraid the Qesh were going to find out where Earth is."

Earthport—better known as Porto de la Tierra—sprawled across the Andes at the bottom of the space elevator; it had been the capital of the Commonwealth government ever since New York City and the old UN had become so cold that the delegates voted to move.

"Well, I still don't think it's *right*," Harper said.

I was about to say something to Harper about "right," but changed my mind. Carla Harper was a sweet gal, full of fun and, if some of Doobie's squad-bay anecdotes were to be believed, fun to fill. But she had some strange ideas about how the world, how the *universe*, actually worked.

"So who gives a shit about *right*?" Harris said, laughing, saying the same thing I'd almost said.

" 'Right' doesn't have anything to do with it, Carla," Klinginsmith added. "Still, Earthport's found *some* reason to go in."

"Well, you know, Kling-on, I'll believe that when I download the orders," McKean said. "There's just no reason for us to tangle with the bastards, y'know?"

Our waiter showed up with our drinks. Our table asked us

for e-creds, and we fed it from our in-heads. The hyperbolic trajectory here didn't have quite as much of a kick as the one at Earthview, but that was a *good* thing. I wanted to stay conscious and upright through more than three drinks tonight.

I took a sip, then heard a loud shriek and splash from twenty meters overhead and looked up. Someone had just jumped in, caroming into the water in a cannonball. Particularly spectacular splashes in the hydrosphere could send water droplets flying out toward the restaurant floor. Most were intercepted by the vegetation, but occasionally you felt a gentle mist falling at your table. It added to the tropical ambiance.

"Well, there is *one* good reason for us to go back out there," I said, taking a second sip from my drink. I'd been thinking about it for weeks, now, and didn't like my conclusions.

"Yeah?" Esteban said. "What's that?"

"The Qesh are now twenty light years from Earth," I told them. "Maybe Earthport decided they were just too damned close."

"How do you figure that, e-Car?" Doob wanted to know.

I told them about the reconstruction I'd done with *Clymer*'s navigation software, how it looked like the Qesh had been running some sort of long-term search pattern across the sky, quite possibly looking for us. "They've known we were out here somewhere in this general volume of space ever since they ran into the *Zeng He*," I concluded. "That was, what? Sixty years ago?"

"I don't buy it," McKean said. "You're talking about a volume of space a hundred light years across—that's a hundred *million* cubic light years . . . maybe, what? Two hundred thousand stars? That's not a needle in a haystack. It's more like a drop in the ocean."

"What the hell's a haystack, anyway?" Klinginsmith wanted to know.

"It's *highstack*," Esteban told him. "An old slang term for the space elevator."

"Well," I said, "they don't have to stop and look at every star."

"Maybe not," Gomez said. "But sixty years to get from ninety-something light years out to twenty? That's not a search. That's a slow amble, slow enough to enjoy the scenery."

"Yeah, e-Car," Dubois said. "If they were searching for us, they would have found us a few weeks after Gamma Oph."

"The fact remains," I said, stubborn, "they're only twenty lights away now. And if they decide to come in and check out the local node for the Encyclopedia Galactica . . . well, that's at Sirius."

"Shit, he's right," Gomez said. "The Sirius library node is designed to attract attention. And we have the big research complex there."

"It's worse than that," I said. "Look."

Our table had a 3-D projector built into it. I accessed the system and uploaded a small interactive graphic I'd been playing with. Stars appeared in a sphere hovering above our drinks. A red star at one side winked red.

"Gliese 581, right? Twenty point three light years away." A straight white line connected the red star with a yellow near the center of the projection sphere. "Sirius is here." A white star flared brightly on the opposite side of Sol from Bloodstar, slightly offset from the white-line axis. I drew a blue line from Bloodstar toward Sirius, extending it past Sol.

"See?" I went on. "To get to Sirius from Bloodworld, they'd have to pass *real* close to Sol. Five point seven light years—I did the math. Spitting distance . . . assuming Qesh spit."

"Shit," Dubois said, staring into the projection globe. "They'd be just about certain to pick up IR and RF leakage from our civilization."

A couple of centuries ago, there'd been a lot of talk about the dangers of radio and television broadcasts spreading out through local space and alerting anyone out there who might be listening. The idea was that hostile aliens might pick up reruns of old-style TV and radio programs and home in on Earth. Once we started listening in on the EG and found out about all of the predarian cultures spreading out in the wake of the collapse of the R'agch'lgh Collective, the worry over hostile ETs discovering Earth became even worse.

Well, that's the newsfeeds for you—vividly sensationalist and often inaccurate. In fact, research had already shown that modulated radio signals tend to degrade over a relatively short distance, thinning out as the volume of space they fill increases and becoming nothing more than white noise in as little as a light year or two, a fraction of the distance to the nearest star.

But that detectable distance is not a hard line. *Exactly* how far out it lies from the sun depends on the technology of the receiver. I don't know about you, but I wasn't willing to bet my planet on the Qesh not being able to pull *some* information out of noise at a range of, oh, six light years, say. At twenty light years, getting anything at all out of the background hash was probably impossible—which was why the pre-interstellar searches for extraterrestrial civilizations were so disappointing. At some point between about one and ten light years, any remaining data is irretrievably lost in the white-noise racket coming from the rest of the Galaxy.

But what about a distance of less than 6 light years? We couldn't be sure about that. At certain radio wavelengths, our Solar System *shines*—not from old television transmissions, or even from modern Net communications, most of which are tight-beam anyway, but from high-energy radar—especially *military* radar—as well as asteroid trackers, navigation beacons, and the radio traffic among the system colonies. And at infrared wavelengths, our deep-space industrial complexes stand out like an anomalous cluster of tiny, hot, IR stars.

Yeah, chances were *very* good that the Qesh would spot us if they happened to be passing by on their way to the Sirius library node.

"Well, I don't know about you guys," Harris said as I switched off the projection, "but *I* didn't come here to talk shop! Let's eat!"

"Second the motion," Gomez said, slapping his palm down on one of the table's interface panels. "They have *real* food here!"

Genuine meat was hellishly expensive here, since it had to be shipped "up-el" from South America. Cultured meat, grown in the nanufactories there at Geosynch, was less so . . . costing only an arm instead of an arm *and* a leg. The problem was that I knew where a lot of the carbon and other organics in the growth vats came from. While I was rationally aware that the stuff was completely sterile—carbon atoms are carbon atoms no matter *where* you get them from, and we're talking about the *complete* nanodisassembly of waste products, here—I'd always felt a bit squeamish about that sort of thing. My father always said I was atavistic—and as I think about it, I suppose my foible is as weird in its way as the Salvationists rejecting nanomeds.

The hell of it is, guess where a lot of the food we eat on board ship comes from, or the rations we carry with us in the field? I generally try not to think about that part.

But at the Free Fall, I decided I could indulge both in my foible and in a real celebration, so I ordered the unicorn filet with hydroponic tots and veggies. I'd had unicorn once in my life—when I completed my primary download series—and I'd loved it. It was just about the sweetest genengineered protein-on-the-hoof available.

The price tag made me go a bit faint as the blood drained from my brain to my eccount—eC78.90—but, hey, what the hell? I'd been living on shipboard crap for weeks, and the promotion to second class brought a nice boost in the pay. Why not?

I was about to upload my order when I felt a hand on my shoulder.

"Hey!" Doob said, looking past me. "Look who's here!"

It was Sergeant Joy Leighton. She was in a dressy skin-tight with animated iridescence flowing up and down and around her curves, and she looked stunning. "No-Joy!"

"Not tonight, e-Car," she told me. "Tonight it's *Joy*."

"When did they let you out?" I asked. She'd been transferred from *Clymer*'s cryo unit to the Naval Medical Hospital at Geosynch when we'd returned to port. I'd heard that they'd successfully regrown her spinal cord and put her ribs and vertebrae back together, but hadn't learned anything more, save that she was "prognosis favorable."

"Just this morning," she said. "That's why I couldn't attend the ceremony. They were still checking me out in the big med scanner."

"How are you doing?" I gave her a quick optical examination—purely professional, of course. "How's your back?"

She turned, twisting, her movement sending a cascade of color rippling delightfully across the curves of her hips and buttocks. "Good as new!"

"Osteofusion is a *good* thing," I said. They would have knitted the broken bones together with nanobots, then literally grown new bone over them molecule by molecule, cementing the fragments into place.

"*You're* a good thing, Doc," she said, twinkling. "They told me what you did. I wish I could have been there this morning when you got your medal!"

"The medal's nothing," I said, shrugging.

She considered me for a moment, then reached out and took my hand. "How about a swim?" she asked.

There was no possible way I could have said no.

Chapter Twenty-One

JOY LED ME UP THE INCLINE TO THE FREE FALL'S NORTH POLE. AT that point, we were in zero-gravity, and we had a choice. There were hand-overs along the inflow-outflow piping leading into the glistening, rippling sphere of water twenty meters away, in toward the center, but there was also a broad, round platform encircling the entrance to the rotating sphere, a kind of porch or balcony giving access to the restaurant inclines, but also allowing the more daring patrons in the place to enter the water by means of a long, high dive.

"Game for a jump?" she asked me.

"If you are," I said. I was feeling less than certain, though. I *don't* like heights, though I can't say I actually fear them. From our vantage point up there on the polar porch, the inner surface of the Free Fall dropped away on all sides, with the floor at the equator thirty-five meters away and rotating fairly rapidly around the center, once in about every fifteen seconds.

Though we couldn't feel up or down there, with our feet on the porch, the hydrosphere glowed and shimmered directly "above" us. "So what happens if we miss?" I asked.

"Nets," she said, pointing past the hydrosphere. They were hard to see—nearly invisible above the jungle—but they'd rigged fine-mesh netting to catch jumpers whose aim was so bad that they missed the water. The target, the ten-meter rippling sphere of pink-and-green water, was actually pretty big, spanning about 23 degrees across the Free Fall's center, but swimmers who'd had too much alcohol or were otherwise impaired might easily misjudge angles or become disoriented.

Joy touched a spot on her left wrist, and the shimmering iridescence covering her body disappeared, the minute particles going inert and drifting away in the air. It *had* been a nano coating after all. She floated there in front of me, gloriously nude, wonderfully inviting. Damn, she had to be the most gorgeous Marine I'd ever seen.

"Well?" she asked, and that twinkle returned.

I touched a pressure point on my skinsuit, up just beneath the hollow of my throat, and the fabric gently dissolved into gas and fine dust. Joy flexed her knees, placing her bare feet against the porch deck, her arms stretched taut above her head, and she kicked, hard, launching herself into space.

I followed, a bit less gracefully.

My trajectory was directly astern of Joy, sailing through 20 meters of open air, following her feet in toward the water. She hit with a splash, sharp and clean, and a couple of seconds later I hit the water as well, plunging deep into the luminous emerald depths.

The water was 3 degrees above body temperature. There was no need to breathe. The Freitas respirocytes in our systems would keep us oxygenated for a good ten minutes or so. As I moved inward, the water slowing my velocity, Joy turned, opening her arms and legs to receive me. I collided with her gently, the impact putting us into a slow and gentle tumble. We pulled in close to each other, her mouth seeking mine. . . .

Eventually, we *had* to breathe, so we disentangled and made our way to the nearest surface. How you saw the surroundings depended on how you told your mind to see them. For a dizzying moment, it felt as though I'd just poked my head out of the bottom of the hydrosphere, with the surface of the Free Fall's interior sweeping past directly below.

My stomach gave a small lurch, and I made myself think I was looking *up* instead. The floor of the Free Fall restaurant now passed serenely overhead, the clusters of tables like stars arranged in tight little constellations. Joy surfaced beside me, holding me.

In microgravity, we didn't have to work at staying afloat. In fact, with a little effort, we could have paddled our way out of the water entirely and hung there in midair, just "above" the water's surface. I'm not at all shy, but I preferred to stay in the water, engulfed by the warmth. After I'd taken a breath, Joy pulled at my legs, drawing me back into the emerald glow.

The hydrosphere was thinly occupied at the moment. There were three other couples embracing within the depths, barely visible in the water, and a couple of teenagers who appeared to be racing each other back and forth across the sphere.

"I wanted to thank you, Doc." Her words both appeared on my in-head display and sounded within my ears as she subvocalized them and sent them through her own cerebral data feed, which transmitted them to me. The system is as good as telepathy; we could talk and be understood even though we were underwater.

"For what?" I asked, playing dumb. Her eyes, centimeters from mine in the clear water, were hypnotic. Her hands were on my back, her legs wrapped around mine. Somehow, I wanted that moment to last forever, and I was afraid that if I just said, "You're welcome," she would let go.

"For saving my life. For fighting off the bad guys. For not leaving me there when the order came down for you to bug out. *Lots* of reasons."

"Well we don't leave our own behind," I told her. "And the rest was just . . . just doing my job, y'know?"

"*Doing your job*," she told me with a hard edge to her voice, "would have meant pulling a CAPTR on me. Turning me into a fucking zombie!"

"Yeah . . . well, that's kind of a last resort, if there's no other way." I desperately wanted to change the subject. I kept seeing Kilgore in her eyes . . . and then his face was replaced by Paula's. I ran my hand up the bare curve of her spine. "Hey, this really *does* feel good as new. They did a good job!"

"Not even any scars."

Playfully, I let my hand move lower, well below the level where her spine had snapped. "You feel this?"

"Perfectly," she said, laughing.

"I just want to make sure they grew your spinal cord back properly."

She giggled in my mind. "It's nice to have a *professional* opinion."

Her left hand was still at the small of my back, pressing me close. Her right had moved, was moving up my thigh. I could feel myself becoming aroused, a tingling warmth, but there was a thin, reedy flutter of panic there as well. I almost pulled away. . . .

It wasn't that I was being faithful to Paula, or any such romantic nonsense as that. I'd certainly thought about finding a fuck buddy, even just for a night—Carla Harper, for instance, if I could ever pry her away from Doob for an evening. I'd been tempted more than once by Kari Harris— smart, quick, and pretty, though the word was that she was in an exclusive relationship with a woman working in Supply. There was that waitress at the Earthview . . . what was her name? Masha, yeah. Even if she *had* expected a cred-exchange for the privilege. The point was, it had been a year since I'd lost Paula. Time to get over it and move on, right?

So why couldn't I? . . .

Joy's hand moved higher.

"You, ah, don't have to do this," I said. *God*, I felt clumsy!

"It's not about *have*," she said. "Maybe I want to. Maybe I just want *you*. Does this feel good?"

Yeah, it did. So far, though, my arousal was purely internal. Impulsively, I went to one of my in-head menus and switched off my CC-PDE5 inhibitors.

Oh, yeah. It started feeling *real* good. . . .

PDE5—phosphodiesterase type 5—is a naturally occurring enzyme in the human body, where it's found especially in the retina of the eye and within the *corpus cavernosum*, the smooth muscle responsible for penile erection. By constantly breaking down the nucleotides responsible for relaxing smooth-muscle tissue and controlling certain specific blood vessels, it makes it possible for men to wear skinsuits or layers of nanoclothing without accidentally and constantly proving to the world how *manly* they are.

With shipboard skinsuits as revealingly formfitting as they are, male military personnel routinely have nanobotic CC-PDE5 inhibitors circulating within their corpus cavernosa, allowing fashion statements that have long been common in the civilian world as well. There are, of course, civilians who *do* want to make those manly statements, but on board ship such statements can too easily get in the way or get caught on something.

Centuries ago, they used chemical PDE5 inhibitors like sildenafil to treat erectile dysfunction. Nowadays, it's easier and surer to use nanobots to suppress the local effects of PDE5 while selectively enhancing the effects of those vasodilatory nucleotides at will. Whenever the man decides to hell with fashion, that he *wants* extra blood flowing to certain parts of his anatomy . . .

Which was precisely where I found myself at that moment. The actual biochemistry takes only a few seconds to complete. Within moments, I was ready for her.

And, oh, yes, Joy was ready for me.

Like nudity, sex in public wasn't the social taboo it once was. Most parties and cocktail gatherings nowadays involved orgies, at least in a back room, and it wasn't unusual to see couples making love on the beach or in a public park. Why should there be taboos over something so completely natural, so essentially *human*?

Human or not, it's interesting to see how modern technology has crept into this most basic of human pastimes. I found myself thinking again of Private Howell. And there were men, I knew, who used nanotechnology to put that manliness I mentioned on deliberate display, either to advertise for a willing partner or just to show off. There was one group, the "Pole Vaulters," who went around sporting public erections all the time.

Quite apart from what the military had to say about such demonstrations, that sort of thing wasn't for me. Like I said, I wasn't shy, but I found I *was* a bit reluctant about showing off my passion to the whole restaurant as it circled around the two of us. Under the water, though, the two of us were simply shadows entwined with each other. We could see those three other couples in the distance—no, one of them was a ménage à trois, it looked like, not a couple—but in any case they weren't paying any attention to us, any more than we were watching them.

For a long time, all I could look at were the depths of Joy's eyes. Once in a while we would surface for air, then drift again deeper into the glowing depths.

Gods! Was Private Howell's o-looping better than *this*?

I lost all track of time, lost all track of others in the water with us, lost all track of *everything* except her.

LATER, SHE JOINED US AT THE TABLE FOR DINNER AND THEN DRINKS. "Hey, No-Joy," Doob said as she took a seat. "Thanks for joining us!"

I read his grin, and the laughter in his eyes. "You son-of-a-bitch," I said. "You invited her, didn't you?"

"You have a problem with that?"

"Hell, no! I just feel ambushed, is all."

We'd picked up skinsuit patches at the Free Fall's pole after we used the axis handholds to pull ourselves out of the water. You transferred a few e-creds through a palm contact and picked up a fist-sized ball of goo that spread out over your body when you slapped it against your chest. I used my in-head to program mine in the same conservative two-tone pattern I'd been wearing before, black and maroon, with a gold filigree design over my left shoulder and down my arm. Joy programmed hers differently, though—nothing but bare skin on the right side of her body, but with rainbows of liquid light swirling up from left ankle to the top of her head. *Damn*, she was beautiful!

"That's the Marines for ya," Harris said, laughing. "You never know when they're going to strike!"

"They're always alert for targets of opportunity," Klinginsmith added.

"Fuck *that*," Joy said, growing another seat out of the deck and sitting down. "This ambush was deliberate, well planned, and with malice aforethought. Hey, that looks good."

In our absence, the others had gone ahead and ordered their meals. Carla Harper had ordered the silversweet, a genengineered delicacy, part meat, part fruit, grown here in orbit, and Joy decided she would have some as well. I stuck with the unicorn, and called up another trajectory.

"So Doobie tells me you've been accepted for FMF," Joy told me.

"That's right. Don't tell anyone I dragged your ass out of a firefight under false pretenses, okay?"

"Don't worry, Doc. You can drag *my* ass any day!"

I laughed. I was curious about my own feelings at that point, and probed at them a bit, half expecting to get pain reflecting back. There was a twinge . . . but maybe I was finally accepting that I'd done the best I could for Paula, that sometimes there was *nothing* you could do, that your best simply wasn't good enough. I'd done my best for Joy *and* for Dave Kilgore. Both of them were alive, and that counted as a success in anyone's book. One of them was a zombie—like Paula—and nothing I could have done in the sailboat's well deck or beside the Qesh pit on the Bloodworld could have made a difference there.

So far as the two of them were concerned, each was the same person as before the CAPTR, whatever the hell that actually meant.

And I was now HM2 Elliot Carlyle (FMF), and officially a part of the team. It felt damned good.

"Here," Doob said, extending his hand. I took it, and felt the flow of incoming data, palm to palm. "You kids enjoy this."

"Kids?" I said. "You're younger than I am, youngster." He was, too, by six months.

Then I opened his electronic package. It was two nights' stay for two at the Rabu Hoteru, a high-end Japanese Geosynch orbital hotel complex catering to newlyweds and sex tourists. It was Friday night, shipboard time, and weekend liberty didn't expire until 0800 Monday morning. Joy and I had until then to . . . get better acquainted.

Most hotels in zero-gravity catered to people who wanted to try out sex in microgravity, but the Japanese had pioneered the field a couple of centuries ago, and the Rabu Hoteru was supposed to be something special. Among other things they offered was a shared sensual net that let you feel what your partner was feeling in addition to your own sensations, *and* you could edit them on the fly, as it were.

Man, Private Howell never knew what he was missing.

I WAS DEAD TIRED ON MONDAY MORNING WHEN I CHECKED IN. FOR some reason, Joy and I hadn't caught all that much sleep by the time we caught a fling pod for the Wheel, then made our transfer back to Starport and the *Clymer*. We'd kind of been out of the loop so far as both official news and scuttlebutt were concerned, so we hadn't heard.

The Commonwealth was organizing an invasion fleet to take Gliese 581 back from the Qesh.

Ships were marshalling for the deployment there at Starport, though most were in free orbit nearby, rather than docked, as the troop ships were. The battleships *Lütgens*, *Montcalm*, *Garibaldi*, *Sinaloa*, and *Pennsylvania*; the star carriers *Constitution*, *Spirit of Earth*, *Magna Carta*, and *Droits de l'Homme*; the heavy cruisers *Suffren*, *Jianghu*, *Godavari*, *Almirante Villavicencio*, *Antietam*, and *York-*

town; the heavy bombardment vessels *Turner* and *Slava* . . . the list ran on and on, with almost two hundred ships already in Geosynch orbit, and more arriving all the time.

We'd pinpointed only forty-four Qesh ships in the Gliese system, not counting the Rocs, which appeared to be for planetary surface combat rather than fleet actions. In terms of mass, however, and possibly of technology, we would be heavily outnumbered. The biggest ships we could muster were the system monitors *Sentinel* and *Europa*, and the Jotun-class monster that was probably the predarion flagship was five times more massive than either of them.

The scuttlebutt was that Admiral Talbot's orders were to attempt to contact the Qesh without initiating a fight, to overawe them, perhaps, with a show of force that would convince them to go find easier pickings elsewhere.

From what we'd seen of the Qesh battlefleet, I wasn't sure that *overawe* would be the operative word. The Commonwealth was using predator psychology against the Qesh, but no one knew whether they would be thinking like the predators we knew from our limited and strictly parochial experiences on Earth.

Terrestrial predators, you see, won't attack a target if there's a good chance that they're going to be injured in the process, not unless they're damned hungry and have no other options. A pack of wolves might bring down a healthy adult reindeer, but if one of them is injured in the process it will die. Better to stay at the fringe of the herd, watching for an easy target, one that is itself injured, sick, or young, and separated from the others.

Talbot, according to what we were seeing on the Monday newsfeeds, was counting on the presumed unwillingness of the Qesh to risk losing a significant portion of their fleet. Since the fall of the R'agch'lgh Collective, they'd been limited in being able to acquire new ships, or new crews to operate them. Forty-four Qesh ships might well obliterate the largest fleet we could send against them, but at what cost? The Commonwealth Planetary Security Bureau was hoping they would back off, and go raid prey that couldn't bite back.

That was the idea, anyway. Like so much else in military operations, things didn't develop according to plan. The Qesh were warriors, and they had a certain disdain for scavengers, as we later learned.

The Qesh did *not* normally back away from a fight.

THE GRAND COMMONWEALTH FLEET BROKE ORBIT A FEW DAYS LATER, accelerating out-system on their Plottel Drives until local space was flat enough that they could wrap space around themselves and begin chewing through the light years at something like three and a third per day. A week later, we dropped back into normal space a bit over three astronomical units out from the Bloodstar. Unlike the last time, we didn't play it sneaky, and made no effort to hide our arrival. We decelerated into Gliese 581's inner system on our Plottel space drives, broadcasting our intent to talk if we could, to fight if we must.

We'd heard one Qesh, at least, speaking English during our sneak-and-peek. We knew they must understand us.

But there was no reply from the titanic warships clustered around Gliese 581 IV. They were ignoring us—or waiting for us, and it was hard to tell which was more unsettling.

Throughout the transit to Gliese 581 and during most of the final approach, I occupied myself with the usual round of duty and watch standing. There's no such thing as day or night on board a starship, so although we operate on Starport time, which is Greenwich plus five, roughly half of the ship's crew and passengers were up and about at any given time. The company Corpsmen stood one in four watches to cover the night shift, their duty primarily that of holding sick call for Marines or naval personnel who hurt themselves or who'd come down with the creeping awfuls.

So things were pretty slow the night Sergeant Leighton came down to sick bay. She was off duty, and I was making up nanosurgical packs and stowing them for the upcoming op, a mindless task handled by the sick bay's robots that didn't require much in the way of human attention. "Hey, Doc."

"Hey, beautiful. What brings you down here?" She didn't look ill.

"I heard you had the duty, thought I'd stop by."

She was wearing standard Marine utilities—olive drab skintights, but considerably less revealing than what she'd worn at the Free Fall . . . and *not* worn at the hotel later. I thought longingly about the tube-racks in the sick bay's small hospital section, and there was one in the duty room, too, but using one would have been very much contra-regs while on duty. You never knew when the OOD—the officer of the deck—might wander through, and besides, the AI running the sick bay would make a record of everything done or said.

"I'm glad you did," I told her. "I've missed you."

"Yeah, well . . . it's been crazy, y'know? Heavy on the training sims."

The Corpsmen had been going through simulated training sessions as well. As a Marine Recon battalion, the only unit with actual surface time on the Bloodworld, the Black Wizards would be serving as guides for the rest of the Marine invasion force. Bravo Company, once again, would be hitting the city of Salvation, only this time we would be coming down smack in the middle of the ruined spaceport.

"You worried about the landing?" I asked. Hell, I knew I was, and I hadn't been shot up the way she'd been.

"Nah," she said. "It's all pretty soppy."

Soppy—military slang for standard operating procedure. A planetary invasion was never that, but it was something for which the Marines constantly trained.

But I could tell Joy was anxious about something.

"So what's nagging you?"

"I'm worried about the Salvationists," she said. "The Bloodworld colonists. Have you seen the latest briefing download?"

I nodded. "I pulled them off their computer net, remember? And I looked through some of the stuff on the way back."

"By living on Bloodworld, they think they're suffering for the sins of the whole Earth. All of Humankind."

"Not *my* sins," I said. "*I* never signed up for that."

"Neither did I."

"It doesn't make any sense!" I shrugged. "There's one religion that's been around since the eighteen hundreds. Among other things, they made a practice out of baptizing people after they're dead."

She made a face. "What, they dunked dead bodies?"

I laughed. "No. But they would look up the names of ancestors, and then baptize them by proxy. They thought that baptism was absolutely necessary if someone was going to get into heaven."

"So the people getting baptized didn't have a choice."

"Right . . . though I suppose the people in that sect thought they were doing them a favor. I think some religions are just a little too anxious to help other people, though, and don't pay attention to their own problems first."

"I still don't see why the Salvationists would choose to live in a place like Bloodworld."

"Religious history is full of examples of people who became hermits living out in the desert, who gave up sex, who used knotted cords to whip themselves bloody, who gave up everything they owned, who castrated themselves, who massacred whole populations, who gave up technology, who blew up buildings full of people, who had themselves crucified, who joined in mass suicides. All in the name of Jesus, or to please God or to get into heaven or to . . . I don't know. Get other people to stop sinning and join them, I guess."

"That's crazy."

"That's religion. People who really, *really* believe can be pretty scary. I'm not saying belief is wrong . . . but you need some real-world common sense, too."

"You're Reformed Gardie, like me, aren't you?"

"My parents were. I'm not sure what I believe." I thought about it. "I guess what's important for me is the idea of respecting others. Doesn't matter how crazy they are, or exactly what they believe. They've got the gods-given right to believe what the hell they want. Just so they return the favor."

She nodded. "The Gardnerian's Rule. 'Whatever you send out comes back to you three-fold.'"

"So how do you handle that, Marine?"

"What do you mean?"

"*I* wouldn't care to be the plasma gunner in a squad and have three times my firepower coming back at *me*! Is that what happened to you on Bloodworld?"

She shrugged. "Things can't always be taken literally."

"Right."

"I know that's rationalizing. . . ."

"Doesn't matter. Humans are great at taking strange beliefs and rationalizing them, twisting them around until they can live with them. Look at the Salvationists."

"You think their living on Bloodworld is a rationalization?"

"I think believing that they're living there to save us is. I think they didn't know just how bad the place was—or maybe they went there thinking God would provide a miracle, tame the winds, calm the seismic quakes, plug up the volcanoes, make the air breathable. When that didn't happen, they had to explain to themselves why things were so bad."

"They could have come home."

"Maybe not. Not if their leaders had burned the bridges behind them when they boarded ship at Starport. People in positions of leadership, of *power*, are the biggest rationalizers of all. They'll believe anything—or make others believe it—if it helps them keep their power."

The briefing download Joy had mentioned had included a psychological profile of the Salvationists, based on their

Book of Salvation and some of their other writings. Religio-social mania, the briefing called it, with the warning that even the rebels, the Salvationists we'd been helping and who had helped us—could not be trusted. Our operational orders were to establish contact with human colonists where they initiated it, but to avoid them otherwise. The key problem seemed to be that the Salvationists thought that anyone who'd taken nanobots or other high-tech medical gadgets into their bodies *were no longer human*.

Working with the demons of hell, the Qesh, was one thing. Apparently, working with humans who were no longer "pure" in Salvationist eyes was quite something else.

"I just want to know if we're going to have to fight both of them," Joy said, "the Qesh *and* the Salvationists."

"Maybe it won't come to that," I said, "if the Qesh back down."

"Maybe," she replied. She shook her head. "You have it easy, Doc."

"How's that?"

"*You* just have to heal them. The Marines have to sort them out."

"Who was it who said, 'Kill them all, let God sort them out'?"

"A religious fanatic," Joy said, "like the damned Salvationists."

Hours later, we decelerated into battlespace to engage the predarian fleet.

Chapter Twenty-Two

WE HIT THEM GOOD GOING IN.

We didn't learn the whole story until later, of course. Even with all of the optical scanners and AI integration, with viewwalls and cerebral downloads and in-head displays and all the rest of the technologies that let humans link in to the flood of data moving around them, the ancient darkness we call the fog of war still guaranteed that we would see only a tiny fraction of what was going on. The advanced AIs managing the battle, Admiral Talbot and his command staff and tactical planners . . . maybe *they* knew what was going on.

But at the time, they didn't bother telling us.

Admiral Talbot, it turned out, had pulled a sneaky, a tactical coup with which to open the battle.

First of all, he'd divided the fleet. All of the downloads on fleet tactics declare that you should never do such a thing, but he did it.

A diversionary force, designated Force Glacier, continued decelerating in-system, falling past the orbit of Niffelheim and heading directly toward Bloodworld and the Qesh fleet, continuing to broadcast demands to parlay across a range of EM frequencies known to be used by the enemy. That diversionary squadron consisted of eight destroyers and frigates, plus the two largest warships we had, the two system monitors, *Sentinel* and *Europa*. These were massive bombardment ships grown out of a pair of small planetoids, semi-mobile fortresses originally launched to keep watch over the dark outer marches of the Sol System. Only recently, however, they'd been uprated with Plottel initiators that turned them into capital ships, which let them keep up with the rest of the fleet. Talbot had sent both of them in manned by skeleton crews, piloted by artificial intelligences copied and downloaded from the heart of the Primary Command AIs.

The balance of the fleet, however, our main force consisting of 266 ships, had re-engaged their Alcubierre Drives and, so far as the Qesh were concerned, disappeared.

The Jackers knew we were there, of course. They must have picked up our drive signatures as soon as we emerged from Alcubierre Drive the first time. But we'd emerged at more than three astronomical units out—and it took light, and the EM signatures of our drives—nearly half an hour to crawl in-system to their receivers. After they picked up our emergence from Alcubierre Drive, some twenty-five minutes after we'd actually done so, they would have been focused on that one small patch of sky where the fleet had first dropped into normal space.

What they didn't know, what they couldn't know, is that Talbot had taken the main body in a long, wide swing around the Gliese 581 system, re-emerging into normal space on the far side of the star. It was a dangerous maneuver, since by that time we were well inside the accepted safe limits for Alcubierre travel in the vicinity of something as massive as a star. Gliese 581 was a midget, so far as stars were concerned, with a hair more than three tenths the mass of Sol, but it was enough to gravitationally warp local space, making faster-than-light Alcubierre travel risky at best.

Four of our ships failed to emerge on the far side of the star from Bloodworld—a Brazilian heavy cruiser, the *Mato Grosso*, the French planetary bombardment vessel *Duquesne*, and the destroyers *Murakumo* and *Boyevoy*. The rest dropped into normal space with the Bloodstar between us and Bloodworld, accelerating hard, while a scattering of battlespace drones kept us apprised of unfolding events close to Bloodworld.

For the record, the Qesh opened fire first, sending volleys of relativistic projectiles streaking through our diversionary squadron while they were still minutes out, turning the destroyer *Rochambeau* and the frigate *Gravina* into dazzlingly brilliant minor suns as the rounds vaporized first one, then the other, in flaring bursts of kinetic energy. *Sentinel* took a grazing hit as well, but kept coming in.

At the moment the *Rochambeau* exploded, the organic crews of both monitors had jettisoned in lifepods; the Commonwealth assault at the Battle of Gliese 581 was initiated by computer AIs.

With the *Europa* trailing the *Sentinel* by 10,000 kilometers, the pair swung around Bloodworld and into the midst of the waiting Qesh war fleet. From our electronic vantage point, in *Clymer*'s squad bay, it appeared that the swarm of red icons representing the enemy ships were closing in around the *Sentinel*, surrounding her, concentrating fire against her. Both monitors had been constructed in and on kilometer-wide planetoids, and were mostly solid lumps of nickel iron bristling with particle beam turrets and missile launchers. It takes a *long* time in combat—whole *minutes*—to smash and burn through that much native shielding.

Sentinel fought back, giving a good impression of a manned ship attempting to maneuver and fight against desperate odds. A Qesh Leviathan was badly damaged and one Titan was destroyed before *Sentinel* began to come apart in tumbling, semimolten chunks.

Europa entered the hornet's nest of Qesh fire an instant later. By now almost all of the Qesh warfleet's attention was focused on the two monitors.

And *that* was the second part of Talbot's tactical one-two punch. The largest, most massive vessels in the Earth Commonwealth's fleet were, from the Jacker perspective, clearly the most dangerous, the biggest, most serious threats. All of their attention was, for a critical few moments, devoted to eliminating those two vessels.

And that's when the bulk of the Commonwealth fleet arrived, skimming past the star, hurtling through that final fifteen hundredths of an AU into the volume of battlespace around Gliese 581 IV, and slamming the Qesh fleet with kinetic impactors, high-yield nuclear weapons, and particle beams. Both of the monitors were destroyed by then, but the diversion had pulled most of the enemy ships out of position and focused their attention on a relatively small volume of space out beyond Bloodworld's nightside. Pulses of nuclear light, starcore-hot, flared among the Jacker vessels, and enemy ships began to die.

By that time, however, 1st Battalion was loaded into the *Clymer*'s compliment of Misty-Ds, strapped in, making the final preparations for trans-atmospheric deployment. We hadn't seen the close passage of the main body past the mottled red-and-black face of the Bloodstar, hadn't seen the final approach of the fleet as we came in out of the sun, closing on the Qesh defenders from their rear, our approach masked by the star's glare. We were receiving tactical feeds, still, through our implants, but those were limited in the amount of data they could provide.

At that point, I imagine things were pretty confusing, even on the bridge of Admiral Talbot's flagship, the heavy carrier *Spirit of Earth*. The battle for Gliese 581 had been joined.

And all the Marines on *Clymer* and the other troop transports could do was prepare to play their small role in that titanic clash of arms.

"HEY, GUNNY!" PRIVATE COLBY CALLED OVER THE PLATOON NET. "What happens if the fleet gets vaped?"

"Then we have a long walk home," Hancock replied. "Now shut your fly trap and finish your weapons check."

I could feel the shudder through the bulkheads as our

D/MST-22 dropped into atmosphere and tried not to think about Colby's question. Talbot was breaking another of those fleet tactical rules besides the one that said not to split your fleet in the face of an enemy force. If you're going to invade a planet, *make sure you've secured the space around it first.*

Ideally, the combat vessels would have moved in first and destroyed the enemy fleet or put it to rout, and only then would the transports have come in, sent the Marines down to grab the appropriate real estate, and declared victory. Sometimes, though, the real universe doesn't work the way the tactical download briefings say it should.

In this case, Talbot wanted to grab the low ground.

Ancient military dictum emphasized the *high* ground. If you have a defensive position on top of a hill, looking down on an enemy who's forced to charge uphill to reach you, you've got a significant tactical advantage. Crécy, Gettysburg, Dushanbe, Noctis Labyrinthus—all places where the infantry grabbed the high ground and held on. In space combat, space itself is seen as the high ground, with planetary defenders trapped at the bottom of a gravity well. The attackers, literally, can drop crowbars on them from orbit, and the defenders can't do a damned thing about it.

But long-standing military wisdom eventually had to give way to planetary energy weapons and fusion cannons.

Major General William Craig, commander of One MarDiv, had presented the plan to Talbot. Put a Marine force down on Bloodworld large enough to hold a patch of ground against all comers, and have them grow a planetary defense battery. Do it while the fight to dislodge the Qesh is still raging around the planet, and Bloodworld becomes in effect a very large system monitor, one big enough to take out even Jotuns.

It was that part about holding against all comers that was going to be tricky. The issue that Colby had raised was one that probably every marine in the division was wondering about just then. If the Commonwealth fleet got "vaped"— vaporized—those of us on the surface of Bloodworld would be trapped: stuck on a hostile planet with no way off and no way home.

The Misty-D shuddered again, harder this time. I'd already checked both my Mk. 30 and my Browning Five as well as my M-7, and knew I was as ready as I would ever be. The platoon tactical feed was showing a detailed graphic of the planet's surface ahead and below. We were coming in low above the Twilight Ocean. A chain of volcanoes was erupting to the south; the city of Salvation emerged from solid rock above the black, basaltic cliffs directly ahead.

The area around the city had been smashed moments before by a heavy railgun bombardment by the *Ceres* and the *Juno*; Navy trans-atmospheric strike fighters off the carriers *Spirit of Earth* and *Constitution* had followed up with low-altitude passes, loosing cluster-D munitions and volleys of laser and missile fire. Our Misty was vectoring in toward the wrecked spaceport, just to the left of the main city.

There were no Qesh Rocs or other heavies that we could see, thank God. Maybe the bombardment had swept them out of the sky.

"Ten seconds, Marines!" Hancock barked. "Stand ready!"

The Misty swooped in, nose going high, and we felt the sudden, hard deceleration as the landing craft bellied down, jacks extended, egress hatches already swinging up and open as the debarkation ramps came down. I was a little surprised to see that it was dark out, the sun having dropped below the eastern horizon. The data feed had been enhanced, and looked like broad daylight. I turned up the illumination in my in-head, and daylight returned.

Hancock was screaming at us. *"Go! Go! Go!"*

I pounded down the starboard ramp and out onto the ruin of old tarmac. My platoon data feed was throwing graphics up against my vision—identifying buildings and showing a path, picked out in green, toward a city entrance. I took a closer look, then nodded to myself. The entrance was the same one we'd visited before, where we'd found the computer interface and downloaded the goods. Wreckage was strewn everywhere, and the spaceport surface was heavily cratered; some of the pits were twenty meters across and four deep.

We spread out across the ruined tarmac, getting clear of the grounded Misty. The landing craft had been configured for gunship mode, with a couple of turrets on its dorsal hull that were whipping back and forth, seeking targets. As the last Marine came off the cargo deck, the craft lifted into the air once more, drifting clear of the LZ to provide covering fire over the whole area. Fighters howled low overhead as well, Marine A/S-40 Star Raiders off the *Spirit of Earth,* the *Constitution,* and the *Tarawa*, providing close ground support.

Above the fighters, where clear sky peeked through patchy clouds, brilliant pulses of light flared and faded— nuclear detonations strobing among the desperately battling fleets out in space.

I ignored the far larger battle going on overhead. There was nothing I could do about that, and my attention was completely focused on what was going on immediately around me. We were taking fire from the city itself—energy weapons of some sort, firing from turrets or open ports high up among the cliffs from which the city of Salvation grew— and the Marines of Second Platoon, Bravo Company, were going to ground, taking cover behind tangles of wreckage or inside the rims of craters punched into the tarmac.

I couldn't tell if the fire was coming from Qesh inside the city, or from the city's human defenders. It hardly mattered. Ten seconds after my boots hit pavement, Sergeant Tomacek yelled "*Corpsman!*"

It was Lance Corporal Andrews, sprawled on his back in the bottom of a crater. A beam had sliced into his right leg just below the knee, melting armor and severing the limb; I saw it, his foot and lower leg, still encased in armor, the knee-end still smoking and molten, lying a few meters away.

He was shrieking, rolling on the crater floor, hands gripping his right thigh.

"Easy there, Bennie," I said, linking in for a diagnostic. "Let me see whatcha got."

In fact, his armor had already done a lot of my work. A guillotine seal had come down just above his ruined knee, amputating the damaged part cleanly while firing a high dose of nananodynes into his carotid, sending them flooding through his system and blocking key nerve bundles. His screaming was probably less from actual pain at this point than it was from realization: the sheer, mind-ripping horror of seeing a piece of yourself burned away.

Sure, we can grow new arms and legs and graft them into place, no problem—assuming you don't want a *better*-than-human prosthetic instead—but the more primitive parts of our brain tend to lose it when we take that kind of damage. For the better part of half a million years, almost the entire span of *Homo sapiens'* existence, that kind of injury had meant crippling deformity at best, a horrible death by gangrene at worst, assuming you didn't just bleed out and die on the spot. The reassuring knowledge that we can grow a new leg when we need one hasn't filtered down and through to the brain stem yet.

His blood pressure was 190 over 110, almost certainly a fear response.

I sent a second jolt of nanobots into Andrews' brain, programming them to move into his limbic system and, especially, to a tiny lump at the end of his caudate nucleus called the amygdala. It actually looks something like an almond, which is what *amygdala* means in Greek, and is the center of the fear network that connects key parts of the brain—the hippocampus and medial prefrontal cortex, especially. The nanobots began dialing down Andrews' level of fear by damping out some of the chemoelectrical activity within the amygdala, and also began working to interrupt his epinephrine response, slowing his breathing and relaxing his blood vessels, which, in turn, would bring his blood pressure down. I also told his suit to treat him for shock, but with an override to keep his diastole below 130.

"Man, Doc . . . what the hell hit me?" Andrews asked.

"Fear," I told him.

"What the fuck? That's not in the Corps' job description!"

"No, it's part of being human. Don't sweat it, Bennie. You're going to be fine."

I checked his vitals again, then tagged him for medevac. The nano I'd given him ought to hold him until we could get him back to the *Clymer*. The wound appeared to have been sealed both by the suit's guillotine valve and by the beam's cautery effects; no need to peel him open and use skinseal.

"Corpsman! Corpsman front!"

"They're calling me, Bennie," I told him. "Gotta run."

"I'm doing . . . okay, Doc. Thanks."

"Sure you are. Just hang tight and pretty soon you'll be asking Ms. Wojo for a date."

An OR nurse on *Clymer*'s surgical ward, Lieutenant Andrea Wojowicz was a stunning woman who served as inspiration for a lot of the Marine shipboard bull sessions and shared fantasies. Scuttlebutt had it that she'd provided the personality matrix for a popular ViRSex model, though I tended to believe that that was wishful thinking on the part of some sex-starved Marines.

Bennie Andrews just gave me a thumbs-up. "She's a class-A babe. Be sure to introduce me to her when I'm awake, Doc."

"Absolutely." I was already scrambling out of the crater and getting a line on my next patient. Gunnery Sergeant Roger St. Croix was the senior NCO in Third Platoon. I'd seen him around a lot, but didn't know him well. It didn't look like I was going to get a chance to, either; he'd taken a plasma bolt square in the chest.

His Mk. 10 armor had taken the brunt of the impact, bleeding off both heat and kinetic energy. The overload had managed to burn through, however. I could see charred tissue and burnt ribs behind a hole in his plastron the size of my fist. Not good, not good at all. My God, I could see his *heart* beating in there, a rapid, quivering pulse beneath sheets of translucent red tissue.

I thought at first he was unconscious, but as I sprawled out flat next to him, his left arm reached over, his glove closing tight on my wrist. "Take it easy, Gunny," I told him. "I've got you!"

There was no verbal reply, not by audio, not through my in-head. I didn't know if that was because his transmitter was dead, or because he *couldn't* say anything. He was shaking, though, trying to writhe against my touch when I laid my hand on his chest, and his breath was coming in short, hard, paroxysms, like hiccoughs.

Damn. He was in agony.

Corpsmen aren't generally called upon to handle open-chest surgery, but I didn't have much in the way of options. St. Croix's chest was wide open already.

His armor had already fired nano into his system to counter the pain, but right now his brain was getting so many major pain messages from so many sources that the nananodyne blocks were being overloaded or bypassed.

A plasma burst howled past, detonating against tarmac a few meters away. There wasn't a lot I could do about that right at the moment; St. Croix was in a *very* bad way, so bad I couldn't take the time to move him, not without stabilizing him first.

I linked into his suit diagnostics. His BP was low—80 over 30—and his heart rate fast and weak. Pain readings off the scale. Those spasmodic hiccoughs suggested a problem with his phrenic nerves—the nerves supplying his diaphragm. His thoracic mesothelium and endothoracic fascia, the thin sheets of tissue shrouding the cavernous space containing his lungs and heart, had been burned through in places. I guessed that droplets of molten armor had spalled off the inside of his suit and were lodged, now, somewhere deeper in his thoracic cavity.

It was *only* a guess—the hole was rapidly filling with blood and I couldn't see—but I was pretty sure that most of the pain must be coming from his parietal pleura. The lungs, you see, are surrounded by two membranous sheaths collectively called the pleura. The inner layer is the pulmonary pleura, the outer the parietal pleura. That inner layer doesn't have much in the way of nerve endings, but the parietal pleura is innervated by both the intercostal and the phrenic nerves. I double-checked my stores of data on the central nervous system—the intercostal nerves arise from the thoracic spinal nerves, which emerge through the vertebrae all the way from T1 through T11, while the two phrenic nerves come in from higher up, from C4, though in humans they're also fed from the 5th and 3rd cervical nerves, at C3 and C5. Got it.

Another burst of high-energy plasma shrieked through the air above me. I ignored it.

I sent a massive dose of nano into St. Croix's carotid, programming it to shut down sensory input all the way from C3 down to T11. I had to be especially careful to target *only* sensory nerves. His diaphragm was entirely run by motor impulses from his phrenic nerves, and if I shut *those* down he would stop breathing.

I followed through with a second jolt of nananodynes targeting the cingulate cortex of his brain, to shut down his major pain receptors. After a few more seconds, he shouldn't have been feeling anything at all, but anodyne blocking is not as precise a science as we would like to believe. I redirected a portion of the intracranial nanobots to his hippocampus and prefrontal cortex with orders to shut down his NMDA receptors. St. Croix's struggles grew weaker . . . weaker . . . then dropped away as he slipped into deep anesthesia.

I hated doing that. A battlefield, in the middle of a firefight, is *not* the best place to take a patient into anesthesia, but I had no choice at the moment. Pain management was critical, but by dealing with that by knocking St. Croix out, I had new and urgent problems to deal with.

For one thing, he stopped breathing.

For another, his left lung was collapsing.

I'd tried to be careful with the phrenic nerves, hoping to keep his diaphragm working, but when the hiccoughing stopped, so did his breathing. The lung collapse was pneumothorax—what happens when the pleura are pierced and air gets into the pleural cavity. This was especially serious with the Marine's chest open to the Bloodworld's atmosphere; with a surface pressure more than one and a half times greater than Earth's, the local air was forcing its way into St. Croix's lungs through his chest wound, forcing his left lung into a smaller and smaller volume.

The injury is sometimes called a "sucking chest wound," and it's serious. In the old days, battlefield medicine took a brutally pragmatic approach: Navy Corpsmen would slap the cellophane wrapper from a pack of cigarettes over the wound, and the suction would hold it in place, preventing further air from getting inside. I had to look up "cigarettes" when I first downloaded that bit of history; it's astonishing what people used to do to themselves.

On second thought, I suppose it was no worse than o-looping.

I didn't happen to have a cigarette wrapper handy, and it wouldn't have been big enough to seal the hole in St. Croix's chest in any case. I pulled a cylinder of hemostatin foam from my M-7 and squirted it directly into St. Croix's chest. The stuff hit the blood and congealed, sealing over the wound.

"Corpsman!" someone yelled. "Corpsman front!"

"Wait one!" I yelled back. Damn it, I couldn't leave St. Croix now.

"I've got it, e-Car!" That was Dubois. Bless him.

St. Croix was bleeding, but not too badly, not as much as you might think with his chest torn open. The major blood vessels emerging from his heart—the aorta, the pulmonary veins and arteries, the venae cavae—none of them had been nicked, thank God. All of the blood appeared to be seeping from ruptured vessels in the layers of skin and muscle over his burned-open sternum and ribs, and the hemostatin sealed them off at once. It would also provide an airtight seal over his chest.

Through my link, I ordered his suit to up the pressure on his air feed, and also to dial up the O_2 mix to 50 percent. That would help force the Bloodworld air out of his pleural cavity and into the surrounding thoracic cavity, would stop the lung from collapsing further, and if I got lucky, might even partially re-inflate it. The richer gas mix would help his respirocytes do their thing even though he wasn't actively breathing, and help boost the efficiency of his lungs *if* I could get him breathing again.

For that, I needed to take some of the nanobots on analgesic duty and redirect them to St. Croix's medulla—his brain stem, the portion at the very base of the brain leading to the spinal cord—which was what controlled his breathing, heart rate, and blood pressure, among other things. There was a column of neurons tucked away inside the medulla called the dorsal respiratory group, or DRG, and they were the primary center in the brain for initiating respiration. The nanobots entering his brain stem began infiltrating the DRG, feeding them a trickle charge that mimicked the neurochemical impulses from his apneustic center, the part of his brain that told him to breathe. At first, nothing happened . . . and then St. Croix's chest jerked up off the ground, and he drew a tremulous breath.

Next I had to get him out of there. We were out on a relatively flat and open part of the spaceport field, nakedly exposed. Enemy plasma gun and laser fire continued to snap around us, kicking up bursts of flame and spinning fragments as they struck the tarmac. A larger explosion—an incoming rocket, I think—detonated five meters off to my left and showered me with rock.

Ten meters behind me, a crater gaped in the field, three meters wide. Several Marines were already crouched inside, taking shelter from the storm of high-energy bolts sleeting overhead. I grabbed a handhold on St. Croix's backpack, directly beneath his helmet, and started crawling in that direction. I couldn't stand up. The incoming fire was too heavy, and once I started moving, I seemed to be attracting a lot more of the stuff. An explosion went off three meters to my right, slamming me to the side, spraying my armor with chunks of tarmac. St. Croix plus his armor massed about 110 kilos, but on Bloodworld they weighed closer to 200, damned close to a quarter of a ton. The ground was rough and hard, and the friction from trying to drag him over the tarmac wasn't helping.

I was in the same situation I'd been in with Joy at a spot just a hundred meters or so from here, needing a quantum spin-floater of some sort. "Logistics!" I called.

"We hear you," a voice came back. "Whatcha need, Doc?"

The logistics staff consisted of three Marines in the Company HQ platoon tasked with getting combat expendables and other supplies to the Marines and Corpsmen who needed them—fresh battery packs and recharges, ammunition for the slug throwers and plasma guns, and spin-floater stretchers for casualties. "I need a stretcher out here! Stat!"

I started broadcasting a homing signal. The logistics people were somewhere back *there*, on the other side of a tumbledown spaceport structure. They generally debarked inside an armored supply vehicle, which gave them some maneuverability, but usually they stayed hunkered down in a firefight, doing their best to stay inconspicuous under a layer of nanoflage.

The stretcher arrived about ninety seconds later, skimming in a few centimeters above the ground on its spin-repulsors, guided by an onboard robot and propelled by a miniature jet engine strapped to its underside. I caught it as it drifted up, keyed the control that dropped it to the ground, and proceeded to get it underneath St. Croix.

That's not as easy as it sounds, especially in a surface gravity of 1.85 Gs. I had to tell St. Croix's armor to go stiff, then lever the Marine like a flat, heavy log over onto his left side, nudge the stretcher into place, then let him, rigid armor and all, roll back onto the floater's surface. I keyed the controls again, and the stretcher levitated; frictionless, the stretcher could be guided with one hand. I could give him a shove and get him started moving in the right direction.

But not easily when I was lying down flat. I rose to my knees to give him a shove.

That's when I got hit.

Chapter Twenty-Three

SOMETHING STRUCK ME IN THE BACK OF MY LEFT LEG, STRUCK ME *hard* and knocked me down. It didn't hurt, but the shock jarred me, smashing me forward, and an instant later I was sprawled facedown on the tarmac, with red warning icons flashing across my in-head.

I rolled over and looked at myself. The walker framework and the armor encasing my lower left leg was a tangle of half-melted ceramic, plastic, and titanium, and appeared to be attached above my knee by a ragged twist of metal as thick as my finger. There was a *lot* of blood, and it was still spurting, bright arterial orange-red, all over the pavement; as I lay there, staring at the damage, something went *snick* inside my leg, a few centimeters up from my thigh, and the lower leg and what was left of my knee dropped off. My armor, sensing both the loss of blood and the inflow of higher-pressure air from outside, had decided to guillotine me, amputating my leg.

So far, all I felt was a dull, heavy, throbbing sensation in my leg . . . and I needed to take care of St. Croix. When I'd fallen, his stretcher had skittered away, and was drifting free now, ten meters away.

I started crawling.

Okay, okay, so I wasn't thinking real straight just then. The iris valve that had cut off my leg wasn't pressed as tightly against the stump as it could have been, and blood was still pouring into my armor. I tried to tighten the tourniquet by telling my armor over my in-head to constrict, but I was having trouble bringing up the right menu.

It felt as though the damned planet was dragging at me, pinning me to the broken tarmac. I raised my head, trying to spot the drifting stretcher.

There . . .

It might as well have been on the other side of the planet, so far as I was concerned. The in-head menu connecting me to the stretcher's engine was still open, at least. Somehow, I managed to use it to engage the engine, and set the stretcher moving toward the crater I'd spotted a moment before. "Logistics!" I called. "Take control of the stretcher! I'm hit!"

"Copy that, Doc. How bad is it?"

"Sucking chest wound," I told them. "His chest's open. I've packed it and—"

"Not him, Doc. *You!*"

About then was when the pain hit, searing, shrieking, excruciating.

Gasping, I rolled over onto my back. I used my in-head to access my suit controls and trigger an injection of nanobots, half earmarked for pain control, half to travel to my leg and start sealing off blood vessels.

"Not . . . good."

My big problem at the moment was the common femoral artery, or CFA. One branches off from each of the iliac arteries in the abdomen, one entering each leg at the groin, moving down to divide above the knee into the deep and the superficial femoral arteries. They were big and they carried a *lot* of blood, at high pressure. I could easily exsanguinate—bleed to death—in just another few minutes if I didn't get the damned bleeding under control. I was feeling dizzy and nauseated, my blood pressure was dropping past 90 over 40, and my vision was starting to blur. God, had I lost *that* much blood already?

The injury was similar to Bennie Andrews' wound.

I'd patched him up in a couple of minutes, no sweat.

I was having trouble doing the same to myself.

The pain began to fade somewhat. At least, the screaming agony in my leg was losing some of its edge as the nananodynes began shutting down nociceptors in my leg—the neural receptors responsible for transmitting pain. I could have done a better job at pain management if I'd begun diverting nano to my brain, but I didn't trust myself to do it right. I was feeling *very* fuzzy.

I used my N-prog to follow and to control the repair efforts in the stump of my leg. A cloud of nano was moving down the left femoral artery, the individual bots linking physically one to another in order to form a tightly woven net spanning the lumen—the interior diameter—of the artery. The problem was that the pressure of the blood flow there was so great, carried along in massive spurts, that there was a danger that any patch was going to tear free before it could slow the bleeding.

The guillotine blade, though, was pressed up hard against the severed end of my leg, applying pressure, and the wall of the armor around my thigh had automatically constricted, tightening to form a tourniquet. That's what had saved Andrews' life a few minutes ago. His wound, however, had been cauterized to begin with, so he hadn't bled out as much as I had when the guillotine blade irised shut. I had already lost a lot of blood by the time my suit amputated my leg, and quite a bit more had seeped into the armor enclosing my thigh afterward.

So my attempts to staunch Andrews' bleeding had been pretty straightforward and quickly successful; I was still bleeding despite the tourniquet, proof that no two first-aid procedures *ever* work out quite the same way. No two people are precisely the same anatomically or in the way that they respond to drugs or programmed nano.

I fumbled with my N-prog. I needed to increase the amount of nano trying to close off my left femoral artery.

I couldn't see the screen. . . .

"Take it easy, e-Car. I've got you."

It was Dubois.

I tried to follow what he was doing on my in-head, but I was having trouble focusing on the windows open in my mind. Numbers and words jittered and flickered there, at the very edge of my comprehension, but I couldn't make them snap onto focus.

Blood. I'd lost too much. My brain wasn't getting enough of the stuff.

I mumbled something incoherent at him, felt him jacking into my armor.

They say that Hospital Corpsmen make the very worst medical patients in the cosmos, although I suppose the same thing could be said about doctors, nurses, or civilian emergency trauma techs. I was trying to tell Doob that I needed BVEs, that I was still bleeding, that my BP was dangerously low—all stuff that he already knew.

"Nothing wrong with you, my friend," I heard him say. His voice sounded like it was coming from very far off. "You've just been at my hooch supply again, is all."

The pain was starting to return. Possibly Doob had redeployed some of the nananodyne 'bots to other duties, like stabilizing my BP or helping to tie off my femoral artery. Or maybe the pain signals were finding other ways past the blocks and into my brain. Funny. I could still feel my left leg, which was hurting like hell all the way down to my toes.

"I'm sending you off to sleepy land," Doob told me. The words were faint, far-off and coming at me out of a vast, roaring cloud of static.

And Paula was there, looking up at me in the well deck of our sailboat. I could feel the bite of the cold wind off the glacier, feel the pitch and roll of the boat. Her eyes were going glassy. Damn, I was losing her! *Losing* her!

Paula's face faded, replaced by . . . what the hell? I was looking down on someone in Mk. 10 Marine armor, lying flat on the ground. Another armored figure lay next to the first, jacked in through a couple of slender cables connecting helmet to helmet. The first figure's left leg was gone from just above the knee.

With a heart-stopping jolt, I realized that I was looking down at *me*.

You know, my family had always been pretty serious about the Gardnerian stuff. Reincarnation, the migration of the soul from body to body, hell, the *existence* of the soul . . . something, some noncorporeal part of us that is more than and distinct from the mere chemical and biological machinery that we call *us*.

So I'd heard all about NDEs—near death experiences—growing up. My medical training had mentioned the phenomenon, but relegated it to the realm of the psychochemical and the hallucinatory. Blood loss, neural shut-down, anoxia, and other stimuli—or perhaps the *failure* of neural stimuli—could create hallucinations that were remarkably similar across thousands of case histories. There was the sensation of leaving the body, of looking down on your own body from a vantage point somewhere overhead, of feeling peaceful and happy. There was the iconic tunnel of light, the experience of moving toward the light, of joining loved ones long dead somewhere *up there*, of meeting beings or a Being that the mind interpreted as the departed or as angels or gods or a divine and immortal part of the Self.

And there are arguments, based on the records of thousands of personal near death experiences, that what happens is *not* hallucination. There are so many stories of non-medical people who were able to describe in detail medical procedures on their own bodies after they were revived, procedures that they couldn't possibly have seen except from a vantage point located somewhere outside their own bodies.

The problem is that those are all *just* stories—purely anecdotal. People undergo surgery or traumatic medical procedures, they wake up, they talk about a tunnel of light or of listening in on the surgical team's conversation, but where is the *proof*? We know that people often hear things even when the bedside instrumentation says they're in deep coma, and possibly the descriptions of surgical procedures is something similar.

If what I was seeing was hallucination, it was a damned convincing one.

Dubois had picked up my N-prog. I could peer down at the screen, watch him keying in an operational code.

He was setting the device to run a CAPTR.

I tried to tell him *please* not to do that.

I'd had my brain CAPTRed before, of course. All military personnel have their brain patterns backed up, just in case. It's routine for personnel about to deploy into combat. My own was already in electronic storage on board the *Clymer*, and there was an earlier version back at Starport as well.

A lot of people don't like the idea of being backed up, however. The Marines, with their half-superstitious prejudice against zombies, are a case in point. I didn't think of myself as superstitious, but the idea of dying, then waking up with all of my memories intact *only up to some earlier part of my life* seemed horrible. Creepy.

The issue opened some fascinating aspects of philosophy, not to mention medical ethics. For a start: is there such a thing as a soul?

If there is, is the soul the same as the personality? The ego? Or perhaps the mind?

They used to think that *mind* was what they called an epiphenomenon of the brain, that it was a sense, even an *illusion* of being that arose from the electrochemical processes taking place within the lump of gray jelly medical science knows as the physical brain. According to this model, when the brain dies, when the neurons stop firing, the illusion we call "mind" ceases to be.

If that's true, then there is no such thing as "soul," no noncorporeal part of the self that survives death. No afterlife, no reincarnation. Sorry, Mom . . . Dad . . . but dead is dead.

But here I was, floating above the battlefield, hovering above my own dead body watching my best friend trying to bring me back. It didn't *feel* like a hallucination. It felt . . . well, it was what I *wasn't* feeling that was important. There was no pain, none at all. Oddly, I was no longer afraid. I was simply detached. Quite literally detached, in fact. No longer connected with my broken body. Interested . . . even intrigued.

There was some resistance. A part of me still didn't want Doob to CAPTR my brain pattern, but I was having some trouble now remembering *why*. Was it because I didn't want to come back as a zombie? Or was it something simpler than that?

Did I simply not want to come back at all?

I was still skeptical enough to at least consider the possibility that when Doob had hit my brain centers with anesthetic nano—sent me to sleepy land, as he'd put it—I'd managed a dissociation somehow. That still begged certain key questions. How was I seeing what I was looking at now? How was I aware of anything at all?

I suppose I could have accepted that it was simply an elaborate dream based on what I knew must be happening, but the evidence I was getting now, hallucinatory or not, was so damned vivid I didn't have much choice but to go along with it.

I watched Doob hit the ENTER key, initiating the CAPTR program.

Something went SLAM behind my conscious awareness.

And I tumbled back into my body.

I WAS ASLEEP FOR A LONG TIME.

When I blinked out of it, I was in a microgravity tube on board the Navy hospital ship *Consolation*, looking into the face of a ward nurse.

"How long was I out, sir?" I asked him.

"Five days, and a bit," he replied. He grinned at me as he floated closer and peeled the stick-tight cuff from my arm, through which they would have been feeding me both respirocytes and BVEs.

I wondered what my ratio of respirocytes to red cells was

now. I glanced down at my leg, and was not surprised to see a stump capped off by a plastic and metal hemisphere. There was no pain but, curiously, my missing leg *itched*, right about where the ankle and the top of the foot should have been.

Then more memories came flooding in: the pain, the fear. They seemed remote, however, held at bay, their sting blunted. My brain probably was still riding nanomeds that kept my emotions in check.

"Am I . . . am I . . . ?"

Shit. I didn't know how to ask it.

"Are you a zombie?" he asked, and gave me another quick grin. "Does it matter?"

"Hell, yeah, it matters!" Then I remembered I was talking to an officer. "Sir."

"You have all your memories? You remember yourself as a kid? Boot camp? Corps School?"

I remembered floating off the ice-locked Maine coast, cradling Paula's head in my lap. "Yeah . . ."

"Then you're the same person you were. It took—I think they said three hours to get you back up to the *Clymer*. They had a heartkeeper in you sooner than that, though. Maybe ten minutes after you died."

Heartkeepers were inserts that kept the heart beating and the blood flowing. Once they managed to get BVEs and a load of Freitas respirocytes into my . . . corpse, the heartkeeper would have kept me alive.

It really depended on how much brain damage there'd been when the blood had *not* been circulating.

I did still feel like "me."

"Your medical report says there was some minor brain damage, easily corrected in surgery," the nurse went on. "I'm no philosopher and I don't know what the theologians would say, but I'd say you're the same person."

"That's . . . good."

"Whoever you are, you've become something of a celebrity, you know."

It took a moment for the nurse's words to sink in. "Wait a minute. Celebrity? What do you mean?"

"Once the Marines seized the planet and grew a couple of planetary batteries, the Qesh fleet pulled back out of range, then asked to parlay. They wanted to know who the human was who saved the life of their lord high muckety-muck when he got shot down on Bloodworld. Admiral Talbot ran through the computer records for the op so far, and your name popped up."

That Qesh pilot I'd pulled out of the downed Roc. He'd been some sort of Jacker big shot? It was news to me.

"We were going to let you sleep until we could grow your new leg," the nurse went on, "but we've had a formal request from the Qesh."

What the hell? "A formal request?"

"We've been negotiating with them for four days, now. And they insist they want to meet you."

This was all going a bit too fast for me. "Wait, because I rescued one of their warriors?"

"Don't ask me." The nurse shrugged. "I just work here. But you seem to have impressed *someone*."

I wondered if that meant another damned medal.

I'D SPENT A LOT OF TIME THINKING ABOUT THE QESH.

The Encylopedia Galactica entry on them lists their dominant culture as "clan/hunter/warrior/survival." That means, as I understand the JKRS classification code, something like this:

J: The dominant society arose out of clan relationships, family groupings built around interrelated reproductive groups. Clans, in turn, built networks of alliances and political support groups supporting a dominant clan or family.

K: The species arose from more primitive hunter cultures, meaning they were organized around clan collectives working together to bring down and kill prey animals to feed the social group. The skill of individual hunters almost certainly served to enhance the political status of the clan leaders.

R: The dominant culture has survived through or has encouraged participation in warfare. Concepts such as honor, courage, and duty might well play an important part in clan focus and standing.

S: A key concept within the cultural mindset is *survival*, which could mean that they felt threatened by other cultures, or simply that other cultures that *might* pose a threat should be eliminated in the name of societal survival.

At least that was our best guess. It's always difficult to translate alien experiences, alien emotions, alien evolution into terms understandable by humans—and for "difficult" read "damned near impossible." Popular fiction sims and downloads are filled with characters who supposedly hail from "alien warrior cultures," and these generally turn out to be thinly disguised Celts or Romans or Vikings or similar *human* civilizations, cultures pulled out of Earth's history, and have little to do with societies that have evolved elsewhere, on alien worlds, and beneath alien suns very, very different from ours.

Ever since we first met the Qesh back in 2186, we've been trying to get a handle on them, trying to figure out what makes them tick. Calling them a "warrior culture" might help us understand their obvious militancy, their warlike nature, their love of titanic warships, their willingness to turn the surface of once-habitable worlds into glass.

But we don't really *understand* them.

I think that point really drove itself home for me when I saw those human prisoners on Bloodworld, tied together and lined up at the rim of the crater the Qesh were nano-devouring into the rock. At first, I tried to work it through by thinking in terms of warriors and hunters, but somehow that approach just didn't work. For humans, *warrior* generally carries the connotations of honor and duty, the image, perhaps, of Rousseau's noble savage. Deliberately torturing prisoners to death has more in common with Attila's Huns—or Torquemada's Inquisition—than with noble savages. In the same fashion, *hunter* generally assumes sportsmanship, patience, and skill, or the sleek beauty of a leaping jaguar—not the bleak institutional horror of Hitler's death camps.

What made the Qesh tick? The question was gnawing at me there on the ward—*had* been gnawing at the back of my brain since that first battle outside Salvation.

I was beginning to think that I might see a little of the pattern.

Suppose the Qesh saw themselves as superior to other species, superior to humans, in the same way that humans saw themselves compared to dogs—and that, in turn, meant that human worlds and humans themselves belonged to them, that they could do to us what they wanted. From the Qesh perspective, we would have no rights.

Hell . . . the concept of *rights* is purely human, a holdover from a simpler time when a beneficent deity bestowed unalienable rights upon His creation. Why would a species as alien as the Qesh think in terms of *rights*?

Especially for the likes of us?

I remembered what one of the human natives, Caleb, had told us. *"They told the elders that the Bloodworld was theirs, and that we now belong to the Qesh! Lies of Satan! We belong to God, and none other!"*

But I retained in my mind two contradictory images of the Qesh—the Qesh herding helpless human prisoners into line above the nano-D pit, allowing them to be slowly and horribly dissolved, and the Qesh I'd seen inside the city of Salvation—one of them even speaking English. The first were treating human prisoners like animals, *worse* than animals. The second group had been mingling with humans, *talking* with the Salvation rulers with the help of an electronic translator, evidently helping the human government put down "banditry."

In human history, hunters started off as nomadic clans following the herds, but eventually they settled down. And they learned to domesticate livestock.

No, I didn't think that the Qesh were domesticating

humans as food animals. Again, that's one of the sillier tropes of popular download fiction—that and alien-human hybrid babies. Qesh and humans are just too different biochemically. The fact that they incorporated so much copper in their bone and muscle chemistries certainly meant that their flesh would be highly poisonous to us; I would need to do a full biochemical workup on them to be sure, but the chances were good that humans would be toxic to them as well.

But suppose that the migratory Qesh had simply been looking for a pliable population that could be coerced into subservience?

The Salvationists were convinced that they were living in the mythical Christian hell, serving time for the sins of Humankind. When the Qesh turned up, they proved to be reasonable stand-ins for demons or devils—whatever the ancient Christians thought were supposed to populate such a place.

I remembered those spy-cam views of the interior of Salvation, of Qesh in battle armor patrolling passageways, of humans off to the side, some looking bored, some looking scared. Curious, I sent a search query through my in-head RAM, and brought back a snippet of overheard conversation—one of the Qesh invaders speaking with a human who obviously was some sort of leader in his community.

"It is important"—the artificial voice of the Qesh—*"to present the . . . how do you say . . . the people with an object lesson immediately, to prevent similar banditry in future."*

And the human leader replied, *"Of course, Lord."*

Perhaps the situation on Bloodworld wasn't as much about predarion invaders as it was about the human colonists and the struggle for power.

Think about it. Humans had been on Bloodworld for sixty-five years. There *might* yet be a few geriatrics still alive who'd come to Gliese 581 IV on board the *Outward Venture*, but the vast majority would be second, third, and even fourth-generation natives of the planet. Conceived, born,

and raised on Bloodworld, they would see that hell of storms
and tidal waves and volcanic eruptions as *home*. Dangerous,
perhaps, uncomfortable at times, but quite normal.

The first generation had come with the common goal of
escaping what they saw as a corrupt world, settling in hell
to save humanity—or at least that's what the rank-and-file
colonists had been told, what they believed. They must have
believed passionately, because nothing else would explain
their willingness to carve out a new life in that almost literal
hell. That kind of zeal and dedication, that closely bonding
enthusiasm of what amounted to a group mind, would have
kept the original colonists going—and perhaps their children as well.

But what about the children's children? And *their* children? None of them had ever seen Earth, save for through the
records the colony elders had brought with them. Earth and
its doomed, sinful billions meant nothing to them. Within
four or five decades, the colony must have begun losing its
focus, its *purpose*.

The colony's leaders might still believe the myth that had
landed the group on Bloodworld, but it was also possible
that a certain amount of cynicism had begun creeping into
their worldview. The original leaders would be dead, probably, given their mistrust of modern medical technology, so
the current rulers would be less interested in the colony's
"mission" to save Humankind than they would be in simply
maintaining control, in *staying in power*. In the early stages
of the colony's growth, simply struggling to survive in that
environment would have been challenge enough to keep the
colony united.

But humans are incredibly adaptable critters. Look at
us! Even with paleolithic technology—tools of wood, bone,
and stone—we worked our way into Earth's environmental
niches with astonishing adaptability, living, *thriving*, everywhere, from the edge of the polar icepack to the now-
vanished jungles of Amazonia; from the Sahara Desert,
before it was turned into a sea, to the Tibetan Plateau; from

the Ethiopian Rift Valley to the gaspingly thin air of the Andes—*before* we had respirocytes.

And once we developed some decent technology, *my gods*! From sea-floor habitats and ocean-surface megapoli to Geosynch, the Lunar caverns, Ice Station Pluto and the Oort Collectives, we built them all in the blink of an eye. The technology improved a bit more, and suddenly we were spilling out across interstellar space to Chiron, to Valhal, to Morrigen, to Nubes de Cielo, all environments as different from Earth—and each other—as Earth is from Bloodworld.

And back on Earth we were daring to battle the advance of the New Ice Age with microwaves beamed from orbit. Until we discovered the Arean permafrost biota, we'd seriously considered terraforming Mars. Now there are corporations back there planning the transformation of Luna from barren and airless waste to living world.

The Bloodworld's environment, to the third-generation colonists, would be as much *home* now as the icepack is to the Inuit, as the Alto Plano is to the Inca, or as the Kalahari is to the !Kung.

People being people, once they became adapted to life on Bloodworld, the colonists must have begun losing some of their tightly focused discipline, their sense of purpose, their willingness to endure hardship or privation for the sake of religious dogma. There would have been dissension, even rebellion. Within a religious context, there would have been new doctrines, new ideas, break-away sects. *Heresies.*

Acquiescenists and Militants.

As I thought about it, I decided that the colony's leadership must have seen the arrival of the Qesh as . . . dare I say it, even to myself? Heaven-sent.

Organized religion is *always* about control—the most serious form of control of all, the control of belief. If the rank-and-file Bloodworlders had been showing dissension—and Matthew and the Militants proved that they were—the Qesh-as-demons would have allowed the colony leaders to blame hardships on them, and to provide tangible proof that the myths that had brought humans to Gliese 581 IV were true.

That seemed a good fit for what we knew so far about the worldview of the Bloodworld humans. What about the Qesh? They would know—or care—little to nothing about human religious beliefs. What was their take on things?

I thought about those huge machines we'd seen digging out the pit beneath Salvation's walls. They were either some sort of heavy mining equipment using nano-D to eat through rock, or—more likely, given that they'd been devouring basalt, which isn't exactly hard to come by in the cosmos— they'd been engaged in terraforming.

No, not terraforming. *Qeshiforming*, perhaps, since we didn't know the name of their homeworld.

The Qesh felt they owned Bloodworld and its inhabitants.

Perhaps they'd been looking for a species whose members were willing to *allow* themselves to be owned.

They might have been doing so by seeing if some were willing to passively stand in front of a pit while nano-D dissolved their legs. Or perhaps that was simply a convenient means of getting rid of troublemakers, of leaving behind a population willing to do what they were told, or of conditioning *all* of the population to obey without question. *Acquiescenists.*

It didn't excuse what the Qesh had been doing to those people by any means, but given their likely Qesh-centric attitude—these creatures belong to *us*, to do with as we please—it made a horrible kind of sense. Humans are cantankerous, contrary creatures, but history is filled with populations that were conditioned to go along with the crowd, to obey orders, to snap to with a loud *"sieg, heil"* when called upon to do so. Such populations don't often last for long, but the Qesh wouldn't have known that about us. They'd been looking for obedience and, perhaps, a population that they could reshape for their own purposes in the same way that their Qeshifying machines had been reshaping the planet.

Reshaping.

That suggested something else. The Encylcopedia Galactica said that the Qesh came from a world circling a type F1 star. Their eyes, however, suggested adaptation to *both* a brilliant sun and to near darkness.

I'd been assuming ever since downloading the EG data on the Qesh that their homeworld might be like Bloodworld, tidally locked to its primary—either that, or the Qesh had evolved in caves or underwater, and needed two kinds of eyes to handle two kinds of light conditions. The trouble with that was that a planet close enough to be tidally locked with an F1 star would have surface temperatures of a thousand degrees or more, uninhabitable, at least by humans and by Qesh, who *were* somewhat similar in their basic environmental needs. I doubted that they'd started out underwater or in caves, either. Their physical anatomy showed no evidence of having been adapted to a marine environment at any time in the past 100 million years or so, and creatures that big would be severely restricted in cave systems.

But what if the Qesh had *changed* themselves, deliberately adapting their physiology through medical nanotechnics to a variety of environments?

It was possible. They had nanotechnology—likely had had it for a long time. I'd already noted that the break in their otherwise bilateral symmetry—their upper, seventh, arm—looked like it might be the fusion of two limbs into one. Possibly, that had been a deliberate self-modification, but it seemed more likely to be evidence that they'd evolved—not on the world of a relatively short-lived type F sun, but rather on the world of a much older star—type K, or type M, like Bloodstar. A world where a species might evolve across 100 million years rather than the half million or so for *Homo sapiens*.

A world of a dim, blood-red sun, like Bloodworld, where eyes might be large enough to capture low levels of long-wavelength light. The tiny eyes had been deliberately grown later, when they moved to a planet orbiting an F1 star.

Gods, the Qesh were *old*.

Chapter Twenty-Four

THE QESH-HUMAN CONFERENCE WAS BEING HELD ON BOARD THAT Jotun-class Qesh warship, a cigar-shaped asteroid 10 kilometers long and perhaps 3 wide at its middle. Going in, I noticed a hell of a chunk taken out of one end of the thing. It looked like one of our ships had caught it with a kinetic impactor powerful enough to give it a serious nudge. Seeing that gave me a serious jolt of pride; the Navy had hit the bastards, and hit them hard.

In the time between my release from Ward E on board the *Consolation* and my collection by Captain Reichert, the company CO, I was able to download an update on the naval engagement so far—the Second Battle of Bloodstar, as it was now being styled. First Bloodstar, of course, had been the diversionary attack launched by 3rd Fleet so that the recon Marines could get off the planet.

Admiral Talbot's strategy had taken the human fleet a long way, destroying seven of the enemy's forty-four ships, and seriously damaging nine more. That was a helluva showing, considering how badly their capital ships out-massed ours. But doing that much damage had cost the human fleet 132 ships and almost forty thousand naval and Marine personnel.

We'd been *losing*. The Marine division that landed on the surface had fought through and taken both Salvation and Redemption, but in space we were getting our asses kicked.

Once the Seabees and heavy engineer battalions had grown the planetary batteries out of solid bedrock on Bloodworld's surface, though, the Qesh had pulled back out of the batteries' range, had disengaged, in fact, and taken up a tight defensive position ten million kilometers out.

The logical countermove by the Qesh would have been to drop a high-kinetic planetary crustbuster on Bloodworld to eliminate the batteries. They still had troops and ships on planet, or they might have wanted to keep the world intact for themselves, but Talbot and his staff were bracing for the worst.

Instead, they'd received a message, in English, asking for the conference.

I wondered about Talbot and the Fleet Command Constellation accepting the invitation to board the monster enemy mothership. Yes, they were permitted to keep their sidearms, but those hardly posed any threat at all against the Jotun. And this would have been an opportunity for the Qesh to decapitate the human fleet's command structure with one blow.

But the message had certainly sounded like a sincere appeal for negotiations. And possibly Talbot didn't think we had any choice. We'd lost almost half of our fleet at that point, *and* no longer had the element of surprise. The engagement had deteriorated, I understood, into a static slugging match, and there was absolutely no way we could match the Qesh giants slug for slug.

Captain Reichert and three members of his staff escorted me to a ship's boat docked with the *Consolation*, and the AI took us from Bloodworld orbit out to the Jotun. The Qesh ship had been moved to a position about halfway between their fleet and ours. More evidence, perhaps, that they were trying to be honorable.

"So how's the leg, Carlyle?" Reichert asked. We were in zero-gravity at the moment, and adrift in the boat's small cabin. The seats had been reabsorbed into the deck, and one bulkhead had become a viewall, showing the feed from the boat's forward hull cameras. The Jotun-class vessel filled much of the screen, and was slowly expanding as we approached.

I looked down at the contraption growing from my left hip. They'd fitted me with a temporary prosthetic back on board the *Consolation*, a robotic leg that would do me until they could grow me a new organic leg from my own stem cells. It looked realistic enough inside the material of my dress uniform, and the neurolinkages grown into my spine while I was sleeping gave me both control and sensations of pressure.

"No problems, sir," I replied. "These things don't have much of a learning curve at all."

Walking in it hadn't posed a problem, though I felt slow and a bit clumsy. In zero-G, of course, there was no problem at all.

"Well, we're sorry to have rousted you out of your healtube," Lieutenant Kemmerer said. She was Reichert's exec, his company second in command, and also worked S-2, Intelligence. "Your doctors wanted to keep you out until they'd attached a new leg, but I'm afraid this wouldn't wait."

"They told me . . . the Qesh have asked for me?"

"They have," Reichert said. "Not by name, but they wanted to speak with "the human warrior who saved the Qesh warrior from the fire.""

"According to our records," Kemmerer added, "that was you."

"The one you saved," Reichert added, "evidently was clan-sibling to Thunder-in-the-Valley, who, we are told, is a high-ranking member of the Qesh warfleet. We're not sure yet *how* high, but he . . . or it . . . *damn* Qesh pronouns, anyway! Anyway, they're grateful."

"It's just possible, Carlyle," a senior chief named Alvarez said, "that you've managed to stop this war single-handed."

I honestly didn't know how to answer that. Forty thousand men and women had still died just in the one battle, which had been fought *after* I'd saved that alien's leatherskinned ass on Bloodworld.

But I was saved having to say anything when the cabin speakers announced that we would be under acceleration in sixty seconds, and that we should take our seats. Acceleration couches rose out of the deck, yawning open, and we allowed ourselves to be folded into their embraces. We felt the heavy drag of Gs as the ship's boat closed. On the viewall, a minute white speck just visible against a wall of dark gray and cratered rock and dust grew slowly larger and brighter, resolving a few moments later into a hangar bay with an entrance easily 100 meters wide. Still slowing, we entered the Qesh asteroid ship. The viewall had to stop down the brightness; this was definitely the harsh, white glare that might be expected on the world of an F1 sun.

We were met by an escort of seven Qesh in ornate honor, and led deeper into the cavernous depths of that ship.

Gravity. Funny, but I didn't notice at first. The EG says that the Qesh evolved on a world with a surface gravity of roughly two and half times Earth's.

"Sir," I said as we walked along inside the circle of Qesh septapods. "I thought the Qesh were from a high-G planet. This feels about right for Earth."

"It is. Nine point nine meters per second squared."

"And nothing rotating. It's not spin gravity."

"We've noticed that."

I'll bet they had. We come close to generating antigravity with our trick with quantum-spin flipping, like our stretchers and the quantum flitters, but that needs a surface—road, open ground, or water—to work against. True antigravity—taking gravity and making it do what you want it to do, including running backward—is something quite else. Some physicists will still tell you it's impossible. Others say there *might* be a way to do it, but you need to juggle a couple of artificial black holes to twist the fabric of space, and that's just too cumbersome for daily applications.

But here was proof positive that the Qesh could do it.

"Sir, they dialed down the ambient gravity for us?" I asked.

"That's right," Alvarez said. "We'd really like to know how they manage to do that, too."

Doorways large enough to admit a frigate dialed open for us, and we entered a hall large enough that it could have had its own weather systems. The air was moist, but . . . yeah. That was puzzling too. I didn't have a sampler, but it tasted *fresh*, like Earth after a rainstorm. The EG suggested that the Qesh breathe something that starts off like Earth's atmosphere, but there's other stuff like extra CO_2 and sulfur dioxide added.

Well, we knew already they could breathe Earth-standard atmosphere. We'd watched them doing so through our spycam in Salvation. But apparently they'd gone and special-created an atmosphere that we would find comfortable on board their ship, at least in this hall, and along the passageways through which we'd come.

Was the trick so inconsequential for them? Or were they telling us we were special?

There must have been around a thousand armored Qesh inside that hall, lining the walls, on the deck or standing on floating platforms. There were at least as many Qesh there as there'd been people at the Geosynch Military Assembly Hall when they gave me that medal, but Qesh are a lot bulkier than humans.

There were others there as well: beings like enormous caterpillars on eight legs, striped green, black, and yellow, two meters long and low to the ground. When I saw one rear up on its four hind legs, though, I realized that these were Qesh as well, but with *eight* limbs, not seven, and no massive head claw. They had the independently mobile, turreted eyes, but all four were the small variety, adapted for high levels of light.

Okay, that might give us a little more insight into their biology. We knew from the EG that the Qesh have three sexes, but had never seen anything indicating how sex worked for them. Apparently there were considerable differences between at least two of those sexes; I wondered what the third one looked like.

"You are Hos-pit-al-man Sec-ond Class El-li-ot Car-lyle," a deep-rumble of a voice boomed at me. The speaker, astride a long, narrow bench on a raised dais before us, was one of the familiar seven-limbed Qesh, wearing the ornately chased ceremonial armor I'd noticed on the one individual in Salvation. For all I knew, it was the same being.

I couldn't tell if it was inflected as a question or as a statement, but I decided not to take chances. "I am," I said.

"In the recent conflict on the surface of the planet you call Bloodworld," the voice went on, "during the blood-tide of hot battle, you came across *Veddah* Fall-of-Lightning in the wreckage of her warflier. Though engaged in a withdrawal, you stopped, pulled her clear of her burning craft, and gave her medical assistance."

Veddah, I assumed, was a rank or title, untranslatable by the software they were using. The *her* surprised me, though I suppose it shouldn't have. We've long been fuzzy about Qesh sexes and pronouns, and most people use both *he* and *it* more or less indiscriminately when they're talking about them.

Did the sexual differences extend to role differences in Jacker society? Were the females warriors? What were the human-sized eight-limbed individuals?

"*Veddah* Fall-of-Lightning," the speaker went on, "is my clan-sibling-daughter, and precious to me. I have asked that combat be honorably suspended, that I might reward your gallantry."

There was more. Lots more. Other warriors—again, females, I thought—took turns speaking, reciting lists of battles and of generations of warriors. Much was in the rumbling booms and rattles of the Qesh language—untranslatable, perhaps. Or maybe they were words too special to be put into another language.

The entire ceremony struck me as intensely religious, though not, perhaps, in a way the Salvationists would have understood. *Sacred*, perhaps, was a better word. For perhaps an hour, we listened to what I swear was Qesh *opera*, with six or eight Qesh bellowing and thundering at one another

on a low stage opposite Fall-of-Lightning's dais, accompanied by creaking, groaning, and rumbling noises that just
might have been an alien equivalent of music.

Captain Reichert, the others, and I stood through the
entire performance, and I was enormously glad that they'd
dialed the gravity down to levels comfortable for humans,
because if it had been up to 2.6 Gs we would not have been
able to remain standing. The Qesh rarely seemed to bother
with furniture; they didn't need to, with that arrangement of
massive legs, though the narrow benches did seem to serve
as functional acceleration couches.

At last, the painful sounds died away, and Fall-of-
Lightning was addressing me again.

"Hos-pit-al-man Sec-ond Class El-li-ot Car-lyle," she
said, "by your will, you chose to save the life of my sibling-
daughter. By your will, you have bound her and her clan to
you. Do you, in turn, accept the binding?"

"Say 'yes,'" Lieutenant Kemmerer whispered, her voice
close by my ear. "And make it flowery."

"Did she just ask me to marry her?" I whispered back.

"No, but damned close. She wants you, and your clan, to
be her clan siblings."

I didn't know what that meant, but had to assume that Intelligence had been studying Qesh and Qesh culture nonstop
since the fighting had begun, certainly since the beginning
of the truce.

"Thunder-in-the-Valley," I said, "I would be deeply hon-
ored to be your clan-sibling. I accept this binding, and thank
you for the honor."

I hoped I'd sorted it all out straight, and that this *was*
Thunder-in-the-Valley. Lieutenant Kemmerer had said I'd
saved Thunder-in-the-Valley's relative, and it all seemed to fit.

"And are these humans with you of your clan, Hos-pit-al-
man Sec-ond Class El-li-ot Car-lyle?"

"They are . . . as are *all* of the Marines of Deep Recon 7,
1st Battalion, 1st Marine Division."

There was a long pause, and I heard an undercurrent of

drumming. Maybe I shouldn't have thrown in that last, made the whole of Marine Force Recon my clan . . . but damn it, they *were*. My family, *more* than family.

"Hos-pit-al-man Sec-ond Class El-li-ot Car-lyle, we accept you and your clan as our siblings and daughters. Welcome to the Passage of Night!"

I felt Captain Reichert and the others sag with relief behind me, felt Reichert's hand pat my shoulder. "Well done."

Thunder-in-the-Valley came down off her throne and bumped my head with her massive claw. I had the feeling that, had I been a Qesh female, we would have exchanged clunks of our head ornamentation, the way humans might shake hands or give one another a high-five. Hell, she could have brained me with that double-claw horn, but her movement was astonishingly precise for so massive a being, the touch of her horn a delicate kiss.

I saw other Qesh in the room butt heads as well, and the clashes sounded like colliding e-cars.

Eventually, we were escorted back to the ship's boat, and we returned to the *Consolation*. I wanted to go back to the *Clymer*. I wanted to see Doob and the others. But I was told that I'd been transferred to the hospital ship for the duration.

Exactly what that duration might be, I had no idea.

SO, WAS I A ZOMBIE, OR WASN'T I? I STILL DIDN'T KNOW, NOT FOR sure. It all hinged, I thought, on whether or not there was such a thing as a soul.

I still remembered looking down on my own body, with Dubois lying beside me. The memory had lost some of its crisp, clean edge, so much so that I now wondered if I had, in fact, dreamed the whole thing. My brain had been starving for oxygen, my circulatory system was on the point of collapse. I could easily believe, now, that I'd hallucinated it.

I also remember the thunderclap when Doob triggered the CAPTR mechanism. *I'd gone back into my body.* I was certain of that. Surely, if that *had* been my soul floating out-

side my dead body, there wouldn't be that continuity of link-
age with my corpse.

And, so far as I was concerned *now*, here on board the
Consolation, it *didn't* matter, not a bit. My memories went
back in unbroken succession, from now, past the lost days
and nights of unconsciousness, and on back into my past.
Dad, telling me he was counting on me for General Nanodynamics' future success. Me, raising my hand and repeat-
ing the oath as I was inducted into the Navy. Paula Barton's
eyes sparkling in the Texan sun. And, yes, her eyes growing
glassy as our boat pitched and yawed in the glacier-stinging
winds.

The cold and barren surface of Niffelheim, the terror as
the Rocs passed overhead.

The landing on Bloodworld, the *first* one, with volcanoes
glowing sullen on the horizon. Faces and names. Doob.
Lewis. Michael. Joy. *Especially* Joy.

Howell. What had ever happened to him?

All there. It was me.

So even if my brain had died, me, the *essential* me, had
survived, had returned, was still here.

Lieutenant Baumgartner came over to the *Consolation* a
few days later. Chief Garner and Dr. Francis were with him.
I was in one of the hospital ship's open rec areas, up in the
spin section. The compartment was pulling about half a G.
I was up there as often as I could manage, breaking in the
new leg. The surgery had gone well, everything seemed to
be working well, but the leg was weak. Pale white and achingly weak. It would take a while to bring it up to match the
other one.

"How are you doing, Carlyle?" Baumgartner seemed af-
fable, even relaxed. "How's the leg?"

"Good, sir." I flexed it for him. "Almost good as new."

"We brought you a little present."

They attached it with its strip of nanoadhesive to my
utilities—a yellow-bordered purple ribbon with a heart-
shaped medal beneath, bearing the profile of George Wash-

ington. It was the Purple Heart, the medal awarded to service personnel who are wounded in the line of duty.

"Congratulations, son," Garner said.

"Thank you, Chief. Usually I'm the one writing up reports to give *other* guys this thing."

"We'd prefer you kept it that way, actually," Dr. Francis said.

"So would I."

"They've put you in for the Medal of Honor, too," Baumgartner said. "Don't know if that will fly yet. I suppose it depends on the success of the negotiations."

"Yes, sir? How is that going, anyway?"

"Surprisingly well, actually. Our xenosophontologists are telling us that the Qesh put enormous importance on family, on clan bonds. They don't think they're going to want to attack us again, not if it means attacking the Marines. You did good."

"What's more important," Dr. Francis said, "is that we may be able to open trade relations with them. They know a lot of things we'd like to know."

"Antigravity," I said. "I know."

The fiction downloads like to paint glamorous pictures of interstellar trade, of trading empires, of costly cargoes shipped between far-flung worlds. I don't know where they get that crap from. One solar system is much like another in terms of the distribution of elements. If tellurium is rare on Earth, it's rare on Alpha Centauri A II as well . . . and on Bloodworld, and on just about any other world you might be able to name. That's not an absolute, certainly. We haven't gone very far out into the Galaxy yet. But from what we've seen so far, rare minerals and treasures valuable enough to make finding them and shipping them across the light years worthwhile just don't exist. Same for alien life forms.

In fact, the one commodity worth shipping from one star to another is *knowledge*—and data can be transmitted quite cheaply indeed. Alien biosystems? Alien art or artifacts? If it can be encoded as data, it can be transmitted by interstellar laser. It might take one year per light year crossed, so you have to be patient, but it'll get there eventually. That's how the EG works, after all, a far-flung web of laser light carrying quadrillions upon quadrillions of bits of data, much of it information about worlds and species extinct for a billion years.

The entire point of establishing contact with alien species directly is to trade information.

New star drives. New and better power taps, drawing unlimited energy from the quantum sea. A means of controlling gravity, of bending it to our will. New ways of growing, programming, and disseminating nanobots. Methods for engaging in planetary engineering, reworking entire worlds to our will.

Or—think bigger still. There are species listed in the EG that are so far beyond our ken we may never understand them, or their technology, or their artifacts. There's someone in toward the core of our own Galaxy, reshaping suns, and drawing energy from the supermassive black hole at the galactic heart.

There's someone out there reshaping an entire *Galaxy*. We know it as NGC 4650A and it's 165 million light years away. For a long time we thought it was a pair of colliding galaxies. Only recently have we learned the truth from the EG—or a very small part of the truth, anyway. As much, perhaps, as we're currently able to understand.

Trouble is, we can learn only so much from the Encylopedia Galactica. We can learn much more when we actually meet these other starfaring species, learn to communicate with them, learn what they know.

And perhaps the biggest payoff of all is learning more about ourselves.

I must have looked worried. "Problem, Carlyle?" Baumgartner asked.

"Sir . . . you've seen my records, right? You know I was . . . captured."

He nodded.

"Am I going to be transferred to another unit?"

He looked surprised. "Depends. Do you want to be?"

"*No*, sir!" I was surprised by the strength of my own voice. "I'd like to stay with the Black Wizards, if I can."

Garner made a face. "You *do* know what they'll call you."

"I know." *Zombie.* "It's just a name."

"Marines can be damned superstitious, Carlyle," Baumgartner said. "Especially about anything connected with death and dying."

"Sure, but there are always at least two ways of seeing things. There are zombies. And there's *resurrection.*"

They laughed.

"Good attitude." Dr. Francis looked at Baumgartner. "*I* don't see a problem."

"Tell you what, Carlyle," Baumgartner said. "For the Hero of Second Bloodstar? Sure. You can stay aboard, at least for now. If you decide later that you want to put in for a transfer, see me."

"Yes, sir."

"I wouldn't like to lose you, Carlyle," Dr. Francis added. "It's a pain in the butt to train new Corpsmen."

"Thank you, sir."

I'd heard that zombies didn't *always* get transferred out to other units—that they generally had a choice or, at the least, could state their preference one way or another.

I wondered if Kilgore had been transferred, or if he was still on board the *Clymer*. If he was, I would have to look him up when I got back on board.

"Okay, Carlyle," Baumgartner said. "You've got more visitors out there, so we're going to head back to the ship. You take it easy, okay? Get better. That's an order."

"Aye, aye, sir!"

"Good man, Doc."

Dubois had been waiting in the compartment outside.

"How's my man?"

"Excellent," I told him. "Thanks to you."

"Aw, shucks and gee whiz." He weaved a careless hand. "Just doing my part to save the Galaxy."

"Well, you saved me. And I appreciate it."

His eyes narrowed. "You, ah . . . you do know . . . uh . . ."

"I know you ran a CAPTR on me, yeah." I grinned. "I watched you do it."

"How the hell did you do that?"

I told him about my hallucination, or whatever it was. "So I was watching over your shoulder the whole time."

"Huh. I've heard of weird shit like that. Never believed it, though."

"Well, if I'm a zombie, I don't think it shows."

"That's good. Because there's someone else out there who wants to see you. Although I don't really think she cares whether you're a zombie or not."

My heart quickened a bit. "You mean . . ."

"And, as an extra special one-time-only service, I bribed the ward Corpsman next door. He's promised to let me stand watch here. Cost me a bottle of my best, but I trust it'll be worth it."

"But—"

He pointed toward a pressure door in the bulkhead. "*That* is the duty room. Complete with rec unit, full sim connections, and a sleep tube. As long as you're out of there by 2200 so the guy on duty can rack out, you're golden."

I was no longer listening to him. Joy had just walked into the compartment, and I wasn't aware of much at all, save for her smile.

"Well, hey," Doob said. "Don't thank *me*. Just enjoy yourselves."

I took her hand.

"We intend to," I said.

The glaciers of Maine, at that point, were very, *very* far away—more than twenty light years.

They seemed a lot farther.

Epilogue

SIX WEEKS LATER I WAS ON THE SPACE ELEVATOR, HEADING DOWN-El to Earthport after the *Clymer* docked at Geosynch. The deck was configured as a viewall to show Earth, stretching almost bulkhead to bulkhead in ocean blues and white streaks and streamers of cloud and the dazzling glare of ice over Canada and the Northeast. Doob was with me, and Chief Garner, and a few others from *Clymer*'s med staff. My new leg felt fine, I'd been given two weeks' leave, and all was right with the worlds.

Well, mostly.

No, I never got the Medal of Honor and I didn't come back to Earth with the xenotechnological insights that would put General Nanodynamics on the map and make us all rich. The medal had been downgraded to a cluster on my Silver Star in lieu of a second award. Turns out Congress wanted to award Admiral Talbot the MOH for his role in the Second Battle of Bloodstar, and they certainly didn't want to detract from that by spreading the glory around to a bunch of mere mortals.

It happens.

As for General Nanodynamics, I think they're going to have all the shiny new xenotech data they can handle, beginning anytime now.

The question is whether we're going to have time to do anything with it before the next crisis.

You see, the Treaty of Bloodstar provides for an exchange—Qesh technological data for the right to exploit Gliese 581 IV. It seems my guess was right; the Salvationist leaders *want* the Qesh there.

That revelation alone beggars belief. The Jackers were *slaughtering* those rebel prisoners outside Salvation, slaughtering them in the most horrible fashion imaginable, and yet the Council of Elders has formally invited the Qesh in to "restore order." The gods preserve us from religious fanatics. The bastards were still sniping at our Marines on the planet before we finally withdrew.

The Qesh, if we can believe them, are busily Qeshiforming Bloodworld, and when they're done, they will leave a single clan behind to complete the domestication of their human property while the rest move on. Where will they go? They haven't told us. Not Sirius, probably; they've told us they already control another node of the EG out at Spica, a B-class double giant only about 120 light years from Gliese 581. In fact, they claimed they'd arrived at Gamma Ophiuchi from Spica, where they apparently had a major base of some sort, 130 light years from Gamma Oph.

But what if they decide to acquire more property rights in our interstellar backyard? What if they find Earth? We've checked. All references to Sol and to Sol's location have indeed been deleted from the Bloodworld networks, but there's still the possibility, even the likelihood, that their technology is good enough to tease the whispers of our civilization out of the hiss and crackle of background noise.

The Galaxy was already a dark and scary place; it's just become a bit darker, a bit scarier, and just a bit lonelier.

I'm sure General Nanodynamics and the other xenodata-miner corps will make good use of whatever information the Jackers care to share with us. Maybe we'll even use it to figure out how to manufacture true antigravity, or figure out how to switch off the new Ice Age and turn all of Earth into a semitropical paradise.

But I wonder if it will be worth it.

I and the whole of Marine Recon 7 are clan sib-daughters of the Qesh, now, yeah, but just how much will that buy us if they come knocking at Earth's doorstep, maybe with a near-c impactor?

Thanks to the Treaty of Bloodstar, our xenosophontology and x-bio people have a lot more to work with as well. I was wondering what the third Jacker sex looked like; turns out the big septopods are the females, the smaller octopods are "nurturers," a translation of the Qesh term for the nannies who take care of the babies after they're born, and the males are . . . well, I've seen one, now. They're glistening, wet, and black, about three centimeters long and look like a terrestrial leech with eight clawed appendages. They're *parasites* living inside the female's reproductive tract—completely mindless, almost completely brainless, and the babies eat them when they're expelled at parturition.

Charming. The xenosoph teams are going to be working on what that might mean for Qesh social structure and worldview for a long time to come.

"Huh? What?"

I realized Dubois had asked me a question. I'd been staring down at the slow-growing disk of Earth, lost in thought.

"I *said*, are you still putting in for the Black Wizards?"

"Oh . . . yeah." I shrugged. "It hasn't been too bad."

Some of the Marines had kidded me about my zombie status, and a few had seemed distant or scornful. Most of them, though, just called me Doc.

The thing is, when I'd talked to Lieutenant Baumgartner on board the *Consolation*, I'd forgotten that I was due for reassignment anyway. My deployment with 1st Battalion, 1st MarDiv had been temporary and provisional, pending my winning my upgrade to FMF. So I'd gone ahead and filled in my dream sheet, requesting assignment to the Black Wizards, Marine Deep Recon 7. I admit that a large part of that revolved around the fact that Joy was Marine 1/1, 1st

MarDiv—and right now I was *very* interested in keeping in touch with her.

Of course, *my* interests didn't count for a whole hell of a lot. Now it was up to the gods of Division Personnel and MarDeepSpaRecGru to grant or refuse my prayers.

"If I were you, Carlyle," Garner told me, "I'd be putting in for xeno-res. Maybe a contact-study team with the Hymies."

There'd been a lot of scuttlebutt lately about the Hymies, as they were commonly known—the enormous abyssal life forms eight kilometers and more across, living in the lightless depths of Niffelheim-e's world ocean. The evidence suggested that they were *intelligent*, though we still didn't understand the nature of that intelligence, the form it took, its worldview or cultural mapping. The xeno-research groups were excited about the new contact, though I suspected that the Commonwealth's *real* interest had more to do with establishing a base inside the Gliese system where they could keep an eye on our new neighbors. We have an embassy ship orbiting Bloodworld now, but if the Jackers decide to do something nasty to Earth, that'll be the first to go. Maybe they'll spot the preparations first out at Niffelheim, though, and send a courier with a warning.

It wouldn't be *much* warning, but even a little would be better than no warning at all.

"Maybe," I told Chief Garner. "But I was kind of hoping for something *warmer*."

"Well, you discovered the critters. I'm sure the research boys and girls would be glad to have you on the team." He shrugged. "Hell, after opening the door with the Qesh, you can probably write your own ticket, anywhere you want to go. Maybe even the Xenoscience Bureau at Bethesda!"

So . . . where *did* I want to go?

Not Earth. I was going to spend my leave there with relatives, but no. Not Earth.

I was Fleet Marine Force now.

My place was with the fleet—with the Marines.

STAR CORPSMAN TIMELINE

2069: Discovery of pseudobacterial mats beneath Martian permafrost.

2072: Collapse of the North Atlantic Conveyor. Beginning of the New Ice Age.

2095: Cayambe Space Elevator enters service.

2098: Terran Commonwealth established. Glaciers form across northern hemisphere.

2100: Neo-Luddite revolution against nanotech and genetic engineering.

2105: Alpha Centauri Expedition. Success of Plottel-Alcubierre Drive.

2109: Chiron [Alpha Centauri A IV] colony established.

2115: Terran Commonwealth takes over Cayambe Space Elevator.

2117: Sirius Expedition. Discovery of Encyclopedia Galactica.

2120: Jovian Expedition. Discovery of Europan Medusae.

2131: First AI transcriptions of Encyclopedia Galactica.

2140: White Seraphim Incident on Chiron.

2143: *Human Endeavor* expedition to Gliese 581.

2146: Establisment of base at Conomara Chaos, in Europa.

2149: Founding of General Nanodynamics.

2150: Contact with the Durga, at Delta Aquarii.

2181: Salvation Colony established on Bloodstar's World by CCS *Outward Venture*.

2186: First contact with Qesh by *Zeng He* at Gamma Ophiuchi, 84 light years from Earth.

2194: Contact Protocol—location of Earth kept secret.

2198: Establishment of Cernunnos, at Psi Serpentis IV.

2204: *Hippocrates* Expedition. Contact with X'ghr.

2212: Development of cybertelemeric engineering.

2241: Elliott Carlyle joins the Navy.

2245: Bloodstar Rebellion.

2246: Second Battle of Bloodstar. Treaty of Bloodstar.

Star Corpsman Glossary

apneustic center: portion of the brain, located in the pons, that stimulates breathing.

atrioventricular node: also AV node. Collection of cells at the upper end of the right ventricle of the heart, which can take over pacemaker duties from the SA node if it is suppressed.

atriums, left and right: the two smaller, upper chambers of the heart that receive blood from elsewhere—from the body for the right atrium, the lungs for the left. When they contract, they force the blood down into the heart's ventricles.

Bainbridge reflex: automatic response to a sudden drop in blood pressure within the atria, slowing the heart rate.

BP: blood pressure.

bradycardia: from Greek for "slow heart." A heartbeat considerably slower than normal.

BVE: blood Volume Expander. A fluid such as saline, Ringer's Lactate, or human blood plasma, used to prevent circulatory collapse in the event of severe blood loss.

C1 through C7: designations for the seven cervical vertebrae in the neck, located between the skull and the thoracic vertebrae.

carotid arteries: major arteries, one on either side of the neck, delivering blood to the head.

cc: cubic centimeter. A standard unit of volume used in medicine.

cingulate cortex: portion of the brain's limbic system that, among many other things, processes the neural input from the body we register as pain.

diastole: the second number of a blood pressure reading, measuring the lowest pressure against the arterial walls, in millimeters of mercury, between each contraction.

DRG: dorsal respiratory group. Column of nerve fibers within the medulla oblongata that initiate breathing.

fibula: long bone in the lower leg, more slender than and next to the tibia.

hippocampus: portion of the brain's limbic system that, among many other things, helps process acute pain.

humerus: long bone in the arm, between shoulder and elbow.

intercostal nerves: from Greek for "among the ribs." Nerves arising from the thoracic spinal nerves and running through the thoracic pleura and abdominal peritoneum.

medulla oblongata: in common usage, the medulla. Portion of the brain, the lower half of the brainstem, between the spinal cord and higher portions of the brain that controls, among other things, heart rate, blood pressure, breathing, and various involuntary or autonomic functions.

mesothelium: a thin membrane lining several body cavities, including the thoracic cavity.

micron: 1 millionth of 1 meter. A human red blood cell is about 5 microns across. A typical human hair is around 100 microns in thickness.

nananodyne: from "nano" and "anodyne." A nanobot, about 1 micron across, programmed to reduce or eliminate pain. Slang: *nanonarcs*.

nanobots: nanotechnic robots—tiny machines, first hypothesized in the late twentieth century, that operate inside the human body, either under autonomous programming, or through teleoperation by a human or artificial intelligence. Typically, they range in size from 1 to about

20 microns, are powered by the heat of the body within which they operate, and can communicate with one another and with an outside operator by radio.

neuroreceptor: a neurotransmitter receptor—a membrane protein allowing a cell, particularly a neuron or a glial cell, to communicate chemically with its surroundings.

neurotransmitter: any of a number of chemicals that transmit signals from a neuron across a synapse to another neuron or some other target cell.

NMDA: N-methyl d-aspartate. A type of neuroreceptor in the brain associated with consciousness. Certain anesthetics, such as Ketamine, block these receptors, inducing dissociative anesthesia.

nociceptor: pain receptors; sensory receptors that send nerve signals to the spinal cord and brain where they are interpreted as pain.

pericardium: from Greek for "around the heart." The thin, membranous layer of mesothelium surrounding the heart and the roots of the primary blood vessels.

periostoma: from Greek for "around the bone." Sheath of nerve- and blood-vessel-rich tissue surrounding each bone.

phrenic nerve: from Greek for "mind." Nerve that branches through the diaphragm, the mediastinal pleura, and the pericardium. It provides the only motor supply for the diaphragm.

pneumothorax: from Greek for "air in the chest." Caused by a penetrative wound piercing the pleura, allowing air to enter the chest cavity. Also referred to as a "sucking chest wound." It can lead to the collapse of one or both lungs.

RBCs: red blood cells. Natural, disk-shaped cells 5 microns across that transport oxygen and carbon dioxide through the circulatory system.

respirocyte, Freitas respirocyte: artificial blood cell, a spherical nanobot approximately 1 micron across and containing approximately 18 billion atoms, first proposed by Robert Freitas in the early 2000s. Respirocytes carry 236 times as much oxygen as human RBCs. If all of a human's RBCs were replaced by respirocytes, that person could hold his breath underwater for hours, or sprint at top speed for fifteen minutes without taking a breath.

sinoatrial node: also SA node, collection of cells on the surface of the heart's right atrium that serves as a pacemaker, causing all of the heart's muscles to contract together.

systole: the first number of a blood pressure reading, a measure of the highest pressure on the arterial walls, in millimeters of mercury, during the heart's contraction.

T1 through T12: designations for the twelve thoracic vertebrae in the spine, located between the cervical vertebrae (above) and the lumbar vertebrae (below).

thalamus: portion of the brain serving as a central switching station for incoming neural impulses.

thoracic cavity: space within the chest containing the heart, lungs, esophagus, and associated structures.

tibia: long bone in the lower leg that, together with the smaller fibula, runs between the knee and the ankle.

ventricles, left and right: the two larger, lower chambers of the heart, which receive blood from the atria. When they contract, they force blood out of the heart—into the lungs in the case of the right ventricle, and out into the body for the left.

VTA: ventral tegemental area. Portion of the midbrain responsible for triggering dopamine release during orgasm. Among other things, it is associated with motivation, addiction, and the emotions associated with love.

IAN DOUGLAS's
MONUMENTAL SAGA
OF INTERGALACTIC WAR
THE INHERITANCE TRILOGY

STAR STRIKE: BOOK ONE
978-0-06-123858-1

Planet by planet, galaxy by galaxy, the inhabited universe has fallen to the alien Xul. Now only one obstacle stands between them and total domination: the warriors of a resilient human race the world-devourers nearly annihilated centuries ago.

GALACTIC CORPS: BOOK TWO
978-0-06-123862-8

In the year 2886, intelligence has located the gargantuan hidden homeworld of humankind's dedicated foe, the brutal Xul. The time has come for the courageous men and women of the 1st Marine Interstellar Expeditionary Force to strike the killing blow.

SEMPER HUMAN: BOOK THREE
978-0-06-116090-5

True terror looms at the edges of known reality. Humankind's eternal enemy, the Xul, approach wielding a weapon monstrous beyond imagining. If the Star Marines fail to eliminate their relentless xenophobic foe once and for all, the Great Annihilator will obliterate every last trace of human existence.

THE BATTLE FOR
THE FUTURE BEGINS—IN
IAN DOUGLAS's
EXPLOSIVE
HERITAGE TRILOGY

SEMPER MARS
978-0-380-78828-6

LUNA MARINE
978-0-380-78829-3

EUROPA STRIKE
978-0-380-78830-9

AND DON'T MISS
THE LEGACY TRILOGY

STAR CORPS
978-0-380-81824-2

In the future, Earth's warriors have conquered the heavens.
But on a distant world, humanity is in chains . . .

BATTLESPACE
978-0-380-81825-9

Whatever waits on the other side of a wormhole must be
confronted with stealth, with force, and without fear.

STAR MARINES
978-0-380-81826-6

Planet Earth is lost . . .
but the marines have just begun to fight.